STORMBREAK

STORMBREAK

NATALIE C. PARKER

RAZORBILL

RAZORBILL

An imprint of Penguin Random House LLC, New York

alloyentertainment

Produced by Alloy Entertainment
30 Hudson Yards, 22nd floor
New York, NY 10001

First published in the United States of America by Razorbill,
an imprint of Penguin Random House LLC, 2021

Visit us online at penguinrandomhouse.com.

LIBRARY OF CONGRESS CATALOGING-IN-PUBLICATION DATA
Names: Parker, Natalie C., author.
Title: Stormbreak / Natalie C. Parker.
Description: New York : Razorbill, 2020. | Series: Seafire; [book 3] | Audience: Ages 12+. |
Summary: "In this epic conclusion to the Seafire trilogy, ... Caledonia Styx will risk
everything—her heart, her crew, and even her life to defeat Lir and take back the
Bullet Seas once and for all"—Provided by publisher.
Identifiers: LCCN 2020031152 | ISBN 9780451478863 (hardcover) |
ISBN 9780451478870 (ebook)
Subjects: CYAC: Ship captains—Fiction. | Sex role—Fiction. | Seafaring life—Fiction. |
Adventure and adventurers—Fiction. Classification: LCC PZ7.P2275 Sto 2020 |
DDC [Fic]—dc23 LC record available at https://lccn.loc.gov/2020031152

Printed in the United States of America

1   3   5   7   9   10   8   6   4   2

Interior design by Corina Lupp
Text set in Elysium

This one's for my dad,
always and forever my first captain.

BEFORE

The fire crawling through Lir's veins had started hours ago and was only getting worse.

In spite of the cool air piped throughout the ship, sweat itched along his brow and he barely resisted the urge to tap his feet as he joined the long line of Bullets heading into the galley. He'd never needed Silt this badly before. He'd never felt this insistent surging of his blood or this erratic knocking of his heart. But he'd missed his last two doses and the lag was beginning to take its toll.

Lir ground his teeth at the sudden lightness in his head and turned to survey the Bullets lining up behind him until his eyes found the one he searched for: Tassos. The boy was barely a turn older than Lir, but his body told another story. He was broad where Lir was narrow, his muscles stacked like bricks where Lir's were lean. Like Lir, he was pale as salt but for his dark eyes and twisted red hair, and he always seemed to be smiling at something. Right now, that something was Lir.

Tassos stood with his arms crossed over his chest, his eyes

loosely locked on Lir, and a disdainful curl to his lips. He was surrounded by a small swarm of sycophants, every one of them too afraid of his capricious moods to risk standing anywhere but by his side. It was Lir's recent refusal to similarly acquiesce that had landed him in the too-bright light of Tassos's attentions.

A sharp-jawed girl named Cepheus leaned up and, with her eyes on Lir, whispered something that made Tassos laugh. Lir glowered, turning away from the sight.

Two doses. Tassos had stolen the previous two doses from Lir by getting ahead of him in line and swiping it from his tray before Lir had even managed to find a seat. It was insulting. Maddening. But the only thing worse than not having his dose of Silt would be admitting to Ballistic Ennick that he'd lost it. Twice. Asking for assistance wasn't an option. This was a situation he'd have to deal with on his own.

An unfamiliar weakness needled in his muscles and bones, and strength leached from his skin like sweat. But he would not give Tassos the pleasure of seeing him squirm. The rivalry between them was new. Until two days ago, Tassos had never spared a second glance for him. Then Lir made the mistake of taking down Cross in hand-to-hand exercises and suddenly the once-middling Lir of sixteen turns wasn't so unobtrusive anymore. He was the one everyone wanted at their side.

And Tassos, it seemed, had decided Lir was the one to drive into the ground.

Clenching his fists against a sudden tremor, Lir steadied his breathing and tried to focus on the soothing simplicity of a gun. He ran through each piece, mentally dismantling his preferred sidearm before putting it back together again. At each step, he imagined the unmistakable slide of steel against steel, the sharp click as pins snapped home, the quiet groan as springs depressed. By the time he'd completed the process, the line had coiled into the galley and the smell of fresh bread made Lir's stomach clench with anticipation. Soon, there was a tray in his hand and his plate was filled with seed brick smothered in gravy, seaweed salad, and that delicious fresh bread.

His blood surged faster, and the fire burned in his veins as he followed the line to the end where Bullet Sanno handed out the evening ration of Silt. Sanno raised one thick eyebrow as Lir approached. It was warm in here, but not warm enough to warrant the beads of sweat sliding from Lir's temples.

"From Silt comes strength," Lir said, and it took some effort to keep his voice steady.

"The Father gives you Silt," Sanno answered, the suspicion in his voice clear, but he handed over a single ration without question.

Lir flicked his eyes quickly down the line as he turned away, spotting Tassos picking up his own tray at the end. Relief washed through Lir. The wait was nearly over. All he needed to do was stay calm, eat his meal, then take his Silt the same way every other Bullet did. After the meal.

His mistake was keeping his eyes on Tassos. He knew that as soon as his shoulder collided with something hard. His tray tipped, the contents spilling to the floor with a clatter.

Lir snapped to attention, instinctively raising his fists for a fight even as Cepheus backed away with an apologetic shrug. And a barely concealed mocking half grin.

"Clean it up, Bullet," the Galley Master called, voice rising above the sounds of snickering and chatter.

Cold stole over Lir as he stooped to collect his tray, plate, glass, and cutlery. There was the mess of his food at his feet and nothing else. His Silt was gone. Behind him, Tassos emerged from the line, a knowing grin on his smug face.

A small, distant part of Lir's mind told him to ignore this. He would find another way to get Silt even if it meant another night going without. He was strong enough to survive until morning rations and he would rise before anyone else, be first in line, and take his Silt before Tassos ever stepped foot in the galley.

Then Tassos smiled with his teeth and Lir's mind went very, very still.

Lir crossed the room in two swift strides, swinging his tray like a sword. Hot blood sprayed across one side of Lir's face as the tray gouged a thick trail through Tassos's cheek.

Before Tassos could retaliate, Lir brought his fist down like a hammer, punishing the same mangled cheek with a second strike. Tassos stumbled, then recoiled, readying for the next attack, but before either of them could move again, a triple horn beat punctuated the air.

The galley fell silent but for the rhythmic ticking of the old stove. In spite of the call to report topside, no one moved to respond.

Lir and Tassos stood three feet apart, eyes locked in a new kind of rivalry. Dark red blood dripped steadily from the trench in Tassos's cheek, staining the front of his shirt.

Then Lir stepped forward and stooped low, catching up a single packet of Silt in his fingers and tucking it into his pocket. He blinked once, letting his gaze drift across the galley, then he turned his back on Tassos and aimed unhurried steps topside.

Galley Master Harrow was reporting to Ballistic Ennick when Lir arrived on deck. The two men, both still in the full and bristling power of their youth, were cast in the orange glow of deck lights, the night sky flat black behind them. As Bullets filled the main deck in neat rows, those who hadn't been in the galley shot nervous glances toward the Ballistic. Those who had been watched Lir with a confident kind of curiosity. Whatever was about to happen, it wouldn't be happening to them.

Lir planted his feet wide and waited.

"Bullet Lir." Ballistic Ennick's voice was flat. "Step forward."

Lir had always viewed the man as a superior, someone so much closer to Aric's right hand than he'd ever be, but something had changed in the galley. Lir had changed, and in a strange moment of clarity, he saw Ennick for what he was: a Ballistic too afraid of his own power to ever really own it.

"You attacked a fellow Bullet in the galley," Ballistic Ennick said. "Do you deny the charge?"

Tassos stood in the corner of Lir's vision. The blood on his cheek flared bright red in the deck lights, a single flame licking up his skin. With dark satisfaction, Lir realized that flame would bloom into an orange scar as it healed. He barely kept a smile from his lips as he answered, "I embrace the charge, sir."

A quiet disturbance breezed through the rest of the clip. His peers surely thought he'd lost his sail. Maybe he had. He'd never felt so certain, so defiant. Even the Ballistic seemed taken aback. He hesitated before speaking again.

"You will soon embrace more than that." Ballistic Ennick moved down the line of Bullets. "There is no greater display of weakness than turning on your brothers and sisters, no greater shame than striking your own. And we do not bring shame to the Father. What do we bring him?"

"Glory or death!" the clip shouted in one voice.

"Bullet Lir, have you brought glory to the Father today?"

Lir swallowed a hard lump in his throat. "No."

"Would you bring him your death instead?"

Lir's conviction wavered under a knife of fear. They would not kill him for such a small infraction, but they would make him suffer for forgiveness. So that everyone knew exactly how little power he held. He had to make that power grow, or death *would* be his only option. Lir raised his chin. "I would not."

"We must have one or the other." Ballistic Ennick paused theatrically and raised a hand to the moonless sky. "But now is the time of the Nascent Moon. A time for new beginnings. Would you have a new beginning, Bullet Lir?"

"I would." He could taste the sour shape of those words.

"Then you will be cleansed by the sway of the pendulum."

Lir ground his teeth at the thought of being strung up by his ankles and dangled over the deck like a damn fish. It was a slow, painful way to die, but if he survived the night, he would be redeemed in the eyes of his Ballistic and his clip.

"Prepare the pendulum! He hangs at midnight!" Ballistic Ennick called. The order dismissed the clip and to Lir he said, "With me."

Ennick turned on his heel and led Lir to the aft deck. The ship was anchored just west of one of the two largest islands of the Bone Mouth.

"Go ashore," Ennick said, thrusting a canvas sack into Lir's bloodied hands. "We could use the fruit and you could use a minute to clear your salt-crusted head."

Below them, a small shore runner waited on the water. For a fleeting moment, Lir considered jumping ship and taking his chances away from the bountiful hands of the Father. Surely, Ballistic Ennick had to know he would be tempted.

"What makes you so sure I'll come back?" he asked.

"You're not the running type." One side of Ennick's mouth twitched in something more grim than a smile. "But don't come back without something good."

Anger bloomed in the back of Lir's throat. He was being manipulated, toyed with, and they both knew he had no choice but to obey. Planting one foot on the rail, he climbed down to the small boat below. He revved the engine and sped toward the pale strip of beach all while a furious storm blew through his mind.

They didn't need the food. That had been a lie. This errand was just a prelude to his punishment, forcing him to choose to return for it. It was a brutal kind of arrogance, so assured, so damned binding. Well, maybe Lir would surprise them all. Maybe he would walk to the end of this island and swim to the next, strike out on his own. What did he have to lose? His life? That was the only thing he possessed in the world and he would lose it eventually. At least if he left now, it would be on his own terms.

He dragged the boat ashore and impatiently scrubbed the blood from his hands in the shallows. He shouldn't have let his anger get the better of him. Self-control, strength, and discretion were how he'd made his way, and how he'd planned to survive. But he'd let Tassos get under his skin, let his desire to hurt him outweigh all his careful calculations. Lir wiped his palms down the front of his shirt, suddenly uncomfortable with how easily he'd been enticed to act recklessly. There was no undoing it, and no denying that from this moment on, he'd be a target.

With a growl of frustration, Lir sprinted down the beach. He ran as hard as his legs could manage, pushing past the burn in his thighs and calves until everything was numb. He didn't want to go back. The pendulum was a cruel punishment. Lir had seen it enacted twice in his sixteen turns and in both cases the offender hadn't made it to sunrise. Lir's death would be a win for that dead round, Tassos. His *brother*. But the word had never felt so hollow as it did now. Tassos was not his brother. He was his opponent.

Disdain and rage wrapped long fingers around Lir's throat and started to squeeze. Nothing belonged to him. He had no power. And what little he'd managed to scrape together had been sacrificed on the altar of bloodying Tassos's smug face.

And this report would go straight to Aric Athair himself.

The thought sent Lir crashing to his knees, his body suddenly filled only with dread and weakness, his blood itching hotly beneath his skin. He could leave right now, avoid all of that, but without Silt to strengthen his blood, abandoning his Bullet life might be simply choosing a slower death than the pendulum.

And if he survived it, he stood to gain so much more.

Gritting his teeth, he tugged his stolen ration of Silt from the zippered pocket on his thigh and ripped open the small packet. He dumped the contents into his mouth, letting the earthy sweet flavor coat his tongue. A moment later he felt that familiar wave of peace wash over him. His heart still raced, but now his mind felt cool and distant. He could *think* instead of react, be strategic instead of impulsive.

Tassos would recover. But he would never forget. No Bullet who'd witnessed that moment of violence would forget.

Lir just had to figure out how to make the memory work in his favor.

Tugging at his canvas sack, Lir turned his attention to the dark beach where the trees shed coconuts and jackfruit. Stooping to snatch up a coconut, he caught the barest hint of motion.

Behind him the leaves whispered long and low. Just beneath it, the sound of a foot pressing into sand. Lir dropped the fruit he held and raised his hands to his head, a splinter of fear sliding toward his heart. Had he underestimated Ennick's desire to be rid of him?

"Whoever you are, you have me," he said.

No response came. Ahead, the ocean was dark and deadly. The Nascent Moon offered no light as black waves sliced toward him, darkening the shore like blood. Instinct told him there was a finger on a trigger just behind him. A decision being made.

"Would it make a difference if I asked you not to shoot?" Lir asked, curious more than hopeful. "If I begged for mercy?"

"Killing you would be a mercy."

That voice. It was like the first burst of dawnlight against the horizon. Warm and bright and commanding.

Not a Bullet. A girl. She was young, he knew that without

looking. And if there was a young girl here on this island with him, then there was a ship nearby. Not just any ship, a rogue ship filled with people who had betrayed the Father simply by refusing to serve him.

Ballistic Ennick's words snapped through his mind: *"Don't come back without something good."* He didn't want to return with something good. He wanted to return with something unparalleled. Something Tassos could never deny. Something that would bring the Father perfect glory: a ship full of traitors.

"Maybe so." Lir let his voice bend low. Let it become a soft net awaiting its prey. "At least, if you're going to kill me, let me see your face?"

When she hesitated again, Lir took the opening. He spun on his knees, careful to keep his hands up. Nonthreatening. Compliant.

"Move again and I'll shoot!" The girl raised her aim from his chest to his head, but Lir wasn't looking at the gun.

He was looking at *her*. Vibrant red curls tumbled around her face like falling petals. Their color rejected the darkness around them as if they burned with their own secret fire. Her eyes were dark, perhaps brown or green, and so deeply rooted he thought he could follow them to the center of the earth. Her skin was unevenly tanned, light beige along the top of her nose, fading to the palest sand in the slope of her cheeks.

"At least if I'm to die, it'll be at the hands of someone lovely." The words were out of his mouth before he'd considered them.

Impulse instead of strategy, but he marked how her cheeks flushed and her lips fumbled to form her next question.

The more she spoke, the less he feared her. She demanded information about his clip, but her finger hesitated on the trigger. She was the perfect blend of cautious and sympathetic, of fear and hope.

"What's your name?" she asked, and that was the moment Lir knew he had her.

"What does it matter if you're going to kill me?"

"It doesn't," she responded quickly. Her finger curled around the trigger, but she did not shoot.

Lir offered a resigned smile. "Lir. I'm called Lir. And I expect you'll be the last to know it."

"I'm . . . I'm sorry," she said, again clearly trying to convince herself to shoot.

"Please." The spike of panic in Lir's voice was real even if the words were not. "Please, show me the mercy the Father never does. Take me with you. Whatever life you have, it's got to be better than the one he forces on us. Please, help me."

There it was. The pained tightening of her eyes, the tragic dip of her shoulders. She was how he would restore his status. She was how he would vault out of the lowly ranks of Aric's Bullets to something with real power. And when she ordered him to his feet, removed all of his weapons but two, and still did not kill him, he knew his plea for mercy had taken root.

"What's your name?" he asked.

The frown that bent her lips brought a smile to his. There was something magnetic about this girl. Something so vibrant he didn't want to look away. The dark night was powerless against the constant burning of that hair, and he thought touching it must feel like caressing the sun.

"How about I call you Bale Blossom, then? Seems fitting."

"Call me whatever you like," the girl answered, unable to muzzle the spark of a smile. "I still won't give you my name."

He didn't need her name. He needed her ship. But first, he needed something else.

"You don't trust me. There's no reason you should, but I'm going to show you why you can."

Carefully, he reached inside his vest and removed one of two slender push daggers, holding it out to her hilt first. She snatched it, horror widening her eyes as she quickly tucked it into her belt.

"How's that for trust, Bale Blossom?"

"No one trusts a Bullet." Her aim faltered as a crucial piece of her resolve was chipped away. "But maybe I can help."

"Are you going to take me to your crew?"

The hope that shot through him died just as quickly as she answered, "No, but I'm not going to shoot you."

He was so close. All he needed was for this girl to believe he wanted nothing from her. One small push.

"You should leave," he told her. "Go back to your ship. Get out of here. I'll hide or I'll die, but I'll do it under my own sail."

There. Her eyes shifted to a spot just southwest of where they stood now. Without meaning to, she'd revealed her ship.

"Do you know what we call this moon?" he asked as a dizzying wash of excitement settled over him.

"There is no moon tonight." Bale Blossom's answer was assured and defensive, as though some part of her recognized that she was about to surrender.

"It's the Nascent Moon. It's a time of potential and growth. A promise for things to come." He raised his hand to the pale moon of her cheek and slid his fingers into her hair, delighted at her gasp of surprise. "It's the moon of beginnings and endings."

They were two sides of the same coin, and this girl's end would bring about a new beginning for Lir. Understanding flashed in her eyes a second before Lir's second dagger bit into the soft skin of her belly. He almost regretted her pain.

As her body convulsed against him and Lir lowered her to the sand, he bent close to whisper, "Thank you for your mercy, Bale Blossom. And thank you for your ship."

He did not yet know all the glorious gifts her defeat would bestow upon him, nor of her survival. But in turns to come he would realize that he had placed the wound as he did intentionally. To ensure her survival.

To invite fate to bring her to him again.

CHAPTER ONE

Caledonia stood high above the bridge of the *Luminous Wake,* the sun-bright arrowhead driving her fleet forward. What once had been a single ship, a single brilliant crew, was now eight ships, with hundreds of crew members, all hers. She was still adjusting, but every time they sailed out together like this, they got better at it and so did she.

To either side of the *Luminous,* the *Blade* and *Piston* cut deep tracks into choppy waters. Farther behind, the five remaining ships of Red Fleet held back, ready for the order that would call them into battle. Sledge and Pine were in command of the *Blade* with a crew of their own. The *Piston* was under Mino's command and the entire crew was made up of Hesperus's people. Their cerulean capelets had been transformed into jackets more suited for seafaring, and they burned brightly against the muted blue of the ocean.

Down on the rounded nose of the *Luminous Wake,* Amina moved methodically along the rail, stepping around the newly installed catapults to check that everything was secure and in working order. Behind her, Hime carefully positioned carbon-shelled bombs in the cradle of each catapult before strapping them in place. Directly beneath Caledonia's feet, Nettle stood at the helm, driving them forward with a steady hand. On the main deck, the five Mary sisters moved as a flock, keeping the rest of the crew on their toes.

The sun was halfway up its morning climb, the sky clear and blue. A bit of cloud cover would have benefited their sightlines, but after enduring Cloudbreak's dreary weather for weeks on end, it was hard to wish blue skies away.

"Heading up!" a voice called from the level below. Pisces appeared a moment later, hauling herself onto the reclaimed ghost funnel that now served as Caledonia's lookout. The past six moons had given Pisces a resolve of stone and physical strength of the same. Her new confidence was matched only by her right hook.

"Closing in?" Caledonia asked, feet braced wide against the wind.

"Closing in," Pisces confirmed with a nod of her smooth shaved head. Sweat glistened against the dark tan of her cheeks. "We'll be on them in another mile."

Pisces wasn't the only one to change since the attack on Cloudbreak. Since Lir killed Aric and took command of the Bullet Fleet. Since Caledonia's brother, Donnally, had looked Caledonia in the eyes and chosen Lir instead. In that time, Caledonia and her command crew had gathered their own fleet and transformed Cloudbreak from a bustling market town into their base of operations, and Sly King Hesperus from a reluctant accomplice into their most trusted ally.

News of Caledonia's victory at Cloudbreak had spread quickly. Rogue ships looking to join the fight had arrived in a near constant stream, adding ships to her growing fleet and willing hands to its ranks. Even a few Bullets had defected, which presented a very specific set of problems, but Caledonia wasn't in the business of turning people away. Sledge and Ares had created a system for supporting Bullets as they slowly squeezed the Silt from their veins. It didn't always go smoothly; no matter how willing a Bullet seemed, or how well they came through their withdrawals, it was difficult to trust them enough to put a weapon back in their hands. For his part, Hesperus had a small, dedicated team working on soiltech, while his sister Kae partnered with Far to keep everyone fed, watered, and organized.

Oran, as always, was Caledonia's eyes and ears whenever she was away from the city. He was her proxy in spite of Hesperus's copious, unbridled objections.

Their efforts kept Caledonia free to do what she did best: hunt.

Caledonia narrowed her eyes against the wind and swept her gaze along the horizon. They'd been en route to the Braids to meet with the Hands of the River when her scouts unexpectedly spotted an AgriFleet barge just south of their location. They'd changed their plans, radioed to Cloudbreak for additional support, and held position until Silver Fleet arrived.

"Sledge was right," Pisces added. "Looks like Fiveson Decker's fleet is escorting them. Ships are all marked with green."

Caledonia smiled hungrily. She'd been waiting for an opportunity like this for moons. Aric's death had ripped through the Bullet Seas like an electric current, igniting small pockets of rebellion from the Colonies to Slipmark. In response, Lir had recalled nearly all his ships to the Holster, which he'd claimed as his seat of power like Aric before him. The infamous city was entrenched in the southern peninsula, protected by a devastating crown of gun towers. But well-fortified as he was, he still had to provide food and Silt for his Bullets, and that meant eventually the AgriFleet barges had to sail. Barges that Caledonia could steal or destroy.

"Silver Fleet is on standby?" Caledonia asked.

"Holding back and awaiting our signal," Pisces confirmed.

The first blush of orange blossoms appeared against the brilliant blue sky as the towering barge came into view. Caledonia felt an answering spike of adrenaline in her blood. The barge stretched a quarter mile in each direction, its long platform deck covered in baleflowers reaching for the morning sun with their mouths open wide like baby birds.

Caledonia turned to Pisces. "Looks like trouble," she said, invoking the words their fallen friend Redtooth had said so often.

"Trouble" was code for a fight, for an opportunity, for a chance to strike back instead of turn tail and run.

One side of Pisces's mouth tipped up at the memory of their friend. "There'll be more on the other side," she warned.

"I hope so," Caledonia said, offering her sister a mischievous smile before sliding down the ladder to the command deck. "Drive us in, Nettle!" Caledonia called, striding onto the bridge. "Harwell, alert the *Blade* and *Piston* that we're sailing for gold."

Harwell's voice rose softly from his station at the radio. It had taken some convincing for Caledonia to go along with using the thing, but it turned out coordinating with ships was a lot easier if you could just talk to them. The Blades had set up a system that allowed them to communicate on open frequencies without broadcasting their plans to their targets. "Gold" was code for driving in together and hitting the target like a spear.

"Amina's silencers are ready for a test run, Captain," Pisces reported from the hatchway. "As long as Nettle can get us close enough to launch them."

"I'll get you close enough to spit on that barge if you want," Nettle said, never shifting her eyes from the searoad ahead. She'd grown an entire foot and every part of her body had stretched thin but for her cheeks, which were as round as the scrolling scars upon them.

"Shouting distance will do," Pisces responded with a smile.

"Ready for gold, Captain," Harwell announced.

"Good. Engines to full!"

Caledonia's eyes landed on the furious orange of the baleflowers ahead. Above, two purple flares unfurled spidery petals, signaling to whoever was near that the barge was under attack. They would have a few precious moments to prepare before Caledonia and her flagships were within range. All she had to do was be faster than the rest of Decker's fleet.

Pisces leaned in close and whispered, "Lir won't like us taking down his brothers."

Anger pooled in Caledonia's gut, leaving her mind with a cool kind of clarity as the seas rushed by. "If Lir didn't want us coming after his brothers," she said, savoring the dark edge of her rage, "he should have left ours alone."

CHAPTER TWO

The sea curled away from the steel hull of the *Luminous* as the three flagships roared ahead. Beyond the barge, Caledonia spotted Decker's fleet now maneuvering to intercept her, their decks ringed in spikes, each studded with decaying bodies that shuddered in the stiff wind. Once, the sight of five Bullet ships would have sent a shock of panic down her spine. Now it felt like an invitation.

From the main deck, Amina barked orders. "Gunner teams Quick and Gale, I want you starboard; Knots, I want you port! Target inbound ships and fire at will!"

Soon, they were in range and gunfire cracked through the air. In another minute, they would be near enough to launch Amina's new weapon—bombs filled with modified skintech. Each sphere contained hundreds of little balls like stones that would soften when the bomb exploded, scattering like shrapnel and adhering to whatever surface they struck to deliver a nasty shock on impact.

After seeing the cruel reality of the star blossom bomb at the Battle of Cloudbreak, Caledonia had asked Amina for an alternative. A way to take out Bullets without mass casualties and without destroying ships. The silencer was her solution.

Pisces's team took position at each of the five catapults bolted against the forward deck. "Activate!" she called, and in response they flipped each switch. "Fire!" The arms snapped forward and five blinking bombs flew from *Luminous Wake*.

Matching volleys launched from the bows of the *Blade* and the *Piston*. Fifteen spheres arced high, moving so much slower than a bullet or missile. For a moment it seemed even the Bullets stopped to watch, curiosity temporarily winning out over caution.

As Caledonia tracked their progress across the sky, she recalled the weight of a star blossom bomb in her hands. The look of dreadful understanding she'd shared with Oran before heaving it onto the deck of the *Titan*. The cries of agony as those star-shaped blades slashed a hundred Bullets to their deaths in an instant. It had been the single most devastating weapon she'd ever used, and for just a second, she feared these would be no different.

The silencer bombs found their targets, landing on the decks of the two closest Bullet ships. A cry of warning cut off sharply as skintech shrapnel struck chests and arms and heads. There was no spark of electricity, just a sudden hushing of battle as dozens of Bullets jerked on their feet and fell unconscious. Exactly as planned.

Immediately Caledonia's crew began to reload their catapults to prepare for a second wave. The two ships they'd struck in the first round drifted idly by, while the remaining three rushed ahead. Behind those, the barge spread massive wings in either direction; on its surface figures hurried to carry whatever they could belowdecks.

"Harwell, tell the *Blade* to stay on that barge and set those baleflowers on fire. I want *Piston* on the incoming ships."

"Yes, Captain," Harwell confirmed before relaying her orders.

A second round of bombs vaulted from the catapults. This time, the Bullets were ready for them. They opened fire at the slow-moving targets, hitting two. But instead of harmlessly bursting in the air, skintech rained down on the Bullets below, delivering their shocks wherever they landed.

It wasn't enough to stop them, but it was enough to distract all three Bullet ships, giving Sledge and Pine the opening they needed. The *Blade* soared ahead and its crew launched a series of fire-bringer bombs at the barge. Where they landed a solid wall of fire stretched ten feet high before reaching outward to consume the waiting sea of baleflowers.

Ripping her eyes from the sight, Caledonia tracked the Bullet vessels. Two had gone east, one west. But it was the lead ship she was concerned with. An Assault Ship with five blades of grass painted on the hull: Decker.

"Harwell, send *Piston* west," she said. "Nettle, take us east."

In answer, Nettle issued her commands to the bridge crew. "Starboard thrusters to full; reverse port thrusters, on my mark. Mark!"

The ship spun east, then shot forward as Nettle reversed her orders at exactly the right moment. They'd run drill after drill in preparation, but nothing quite matched the energy of battle. Nothing came close to that feeling of a crew pulling together and acting as one.

"Gunners ready!" Amina's voice was a clarion from the main deck. "Team Gale, I want you on the bow. Target the lead ship and don't let up! Go!"

The *Luminous Wake* assumed a collision course with Decker's vessel. Gunfire shattered against their nose, but still they pushed forward, moving closer and closer until—"Port spin!" Caledonia cried.

The ship lurched and spun. In a single movement Nettle pulled their nose back, letting the hull bite deep into the ocean and revealing their broadside to Decker. It was a dangerous move, but it put their starboard launcher in position.

"Fire, fire, fire!" Amina's voice shouted from the main deck.

The pop of their hull puncher echoed in Caledonia's chest, followed by the deep grunt of metal piercing metal. They'd landed a direct hit to the vulnerable belly of Decker's ship.

"Give them some space!" Caledonia called.

The *Luminous* withdrew aggressively, wrenching the deadly

harpoon free of Decker's hull and leaving a gaping hole behind. Instantly, Decker's ship listed to one side, making a deep gulping sound as it began taking on water. The wound was low on the hull, perfectly placed to sink a ship. Decker had just been removed from the fight.

"Come around, Nettle." Caledonia eyed Decker's clip, now scrambling to stay afloat by whatever means necessary. Just beyond, the second Bullet ship charged. "I want us nose-to-nose with that second ship!"

As Nettle complied with her orders, Caledonia turned briefly westward where Mino and her crew had already dispatched their Bullet ship and the *Blade* continued to fire on the barge. Energy surged through her: They were going to win this fight. They'd taken down a Fiveson and now they were going to take down his entire fleet.

Almost as soon as she'd had the thought, a shout came from on high, "Tails! Five tails closing in fast!"

Caledonia spied them a second later: five new ships shooting out from behind the barge. Not counting the four ships they'd already disabled, that made six to her three. Good.

"Pull back!" Caledonia called. "Harwell, alert Silver Fleet and the rest of Red that we're preparing for blue hawk!"

The crew of the *Blade* launched a third set of fire-bringer bombs toward the barge. On the broad deck, Scythes ran for cover or leapt overboard to avoid the explosion of fire.

The bombs landed, sending flames scrawling across the barge. Then the *Blade* spun away to begin its retreat.

"Pi! Send another round to our friends out there!" Caledonia cried. "Harwell! It's time to retreat to blue hawk!"

Amina and her gunners immediately moved to Pisces and her team as they prepped the next set of silencers, and Harwell sent his message across the radio.

"Nettle, get ready to take us out of here!" Caledonia marked the pursuing Bullet ships as five silencers flew from the bow of the *Luminous Wake*. Three landed in the water, slipping quietly beneath the waves, but the other two struck the lead ship. Bullets dropped in droves, providing the distraction Caledonia needed.

"Now, Nettle!"

The *Luminous Wake* spun its nose away from the barge, swinging in behind the already retreating profiles of the *Blade* and *Piston*. Without missing a beat, the five Bullet ships still able to sail pursued, drawing together like an arrow chasing a target. One thing she had learned about Bullets was that they couldn't resist a chase. Every Bullet needed a target, and she was glad to give them one.

Caledonia watched them chew through the waves, thinking they had her on the run, while the plane of Decker's barge burned. This was her favorite moment of any battle. When the plan she'd drafted in her mind came together in perfect, bold strokes of fire against water.

They ran, and the Bullets chased. Right into the midst of

Silver Fleet and the additional five Red Fleet ships holding back for this very purpose. The Bullets were surrounded before they'd even spotted the trap.

For a moment, the battle seemed to pause as the Bullet clips realized their mistake. Then they moved again. Three chose to fight and were quickly subdued, while a fourth fled, and the fifth surrendered immediately.

Caledonia surveyed the scene with grim satisfaction. The battle was theirs, and if his ship was still afloat, so was Fiveson Decker.

CHAPTER THREE

Decker's ship listed hard in the water, its hull biting ever deeper as the ocean surged into its gut.

"We can't latch on without endangering the *Luminous*." Pisces considered Decker's ship with a studious frown as they lapped it once more, searching for signs of the Fiveson himself. "They'll be underwater before we could detatch. Hell, they'll be underwater before you can give another order."

"Cover!" Amina called, bringing everyone to their knees.

Caledonia ducked beneath the rail as a few Bullets opened fire from the sloped deck and Amina's Knots returned the gesture with far more efficiency. This was not the focused attack of a brutal Fiveson, but the last, desperate sounds of a dwindling clip unwilling to surrender.

"Clear," Amina called again. "Stay steely, Knots."

The lip of the deck was nearing the water now. Pisces was right. Decker's ship would soon be nothing more than a memory. But there was still no sign of him, nor of anyone trying to escape.

"Decker should be out here. Looking for a deal or looking death in the face. It's not like a Fiveson to hide." Caledonia watched as a fresh wave of struggling Bullets rushed topside to renew their attack.

"Cover!" Amina's command came again. This time, the gunfire from the Bullet ship was thin. The Knots returned fire and then all was quiet. No more Bullets appeared, and the ship began to sink more rapidly. In another few moments, it would be submerged entirely.

"He might have abandoned ship already. Unless he was never on board to begin with," Pisces suggested, tipping her eyes toward the barge. The entire western sweep of the vessel was engulfed in flame, the rest still smoking, every inch of the surface charred.

Decker would have wanted to be at the helm of battle, but maybe he'd been taken down by the Knots in the first wave of attack. Maybe he'd hidden belowdecks and drowned. Or maybe he'd been on the bale barge checking his crop when her fleet arrived, and he hadn't had time to return to the Assault Ship. If that was the case, Caledonia wanted confirmation.

"I'm leading a boarding party," she said, leaving Pisces to return to the bridge. "Harwell, tell *Piston* to send a team as well. We'll need as many hands as possible to search that barge. Nettle, get us as close as you can."

"Yes, Captain," Nettle answered, delivering orders to the bridge crew with her next breath.

The deck rumbled and soon the *Luminous Wake* skimmed alongside the towering barge. If the structure was imposing from a distance, it was more so up close. The barge itself had four hulls, which curved outward at the edges and supported a massive platform deck covered in destroyed crops. Within minutes, Caledonia's boarding party was scaling a tall hull and planting boots on a deck still steaming and sticky with wet ash. There wasn't a single speck of orange in sight; every blossom had been consumed by the fire. Even the sweet scent had been seared from the air, replaced by the acrid bite of smoke.

Between rows of blackened crops were the charred bodies of those unlucky enough to be tending the blossoms when the first fire-bringers fell. Caledonia swallowed hard at the sight. Across rows of scorched earth, a few figures directed hoses over the fields, spraying seawater into what flames remained.

But no one came to meet them. Nor did they attack at the sight of their invaders. They kept to their work, dousing flames. Unconcerned with Caledonia and her crew.

"Huh," Pisces said, perfectly echoing Caledonia's confusion.

"Spread out," Caledonia said when the *Piston*'s party arrived, letting Pisces make search teams of the forty crew members. "Bring survivors topside. I want Decker alive."

The inside of the barge was every bit as massive as the exterior. The lower decks were primarily reserved for storage. There were drying rooms filled with blossoms in various stages of dehydration; storage vaults with crates packed full of already dried flowers; rooms piled high with fresh soil and fertilizer. The air smelled sweet and dry and only faintly of smoke so far beneath the main deck.

"Nothing to eat," Pisces said mournfully. "We'll have to sink this entire thing just to make sure no one gets their hands on this stuff."

"We should keep the soil, at least," Amina added, peering into another chamber and scanning for survivors. "If we can move it."

"Silver Fleet has a hauler with them," Caledonia said. "Once they load up whatever soil they can take, we sink the rest."

"One hauler?" Amina's voice was tight. A single hauler would only take a fraction of the clean soil they'd found. They'd be sinking a treasure. One that could give them the capacity to grow more than the paltry crops they'd managed to establish on Cloudbreak.

But they were too far from home to defend the barge if Lir sent reinforcements. And hauling it would leave them too vulnerable.

"One," Caledonia answered, holding Amina's gaze.

Sacrifice was a familiar part of their world, but sometimes it was easier to sacrifice when you had less to lose.

"Captain." Folly jogged down the long corridor, her usually peach tones pinked with sun and exertion. She smiled less since her girlfriend Pippa's death, and for a while her fight had taken on the reckless edge of grief, but she was finding her balance again. "We've gathered the survivors topside. Eight in all."

"Amina, you take point on soil collection. I want it wrapped up before sundown," Caledonia said. "Pi, with me."

Back on the main deck, the survivors waited on their knees, hands bound in front. Caledonia scraped her gaze across the eight faces before her. Three had been dousing the lost crops when she arrived and five had come from down below. None of them looked remotely fierce enough to claim the title of Fiveson.

"Where is Decker?" Caledonia demanded.

"There's no Decker here, Caledonia Styx. Not anymore." The answer came from a woman with an irreverent smile. Her sun-tanned skin was smeared with ash, but her eyes were bright. She knelt in the midst of the survivors with an air of confidence that the others leaned toward: the leader.

Caledonia stepped closer, forcing the woman to tip her head back to look at her. "What's your name?"

"Remi," the woman answered. She stared at Caledonia with some kind of edgeless wonder, as if they hadn't just lost their entire crop of baleflowers and a small fleet of ships.

"And why won't I find him here, Remi?"

"Because he's dead."

"And who is your new Fiveson?" Caledonia asked, irritation inching toward anger. Lir's three remaining Fivesons—Venn, Decker, Tassos—each maintained control over some element of the Bullet Seas. Venn was in charge of recruitment, operating out of Slipmark, which had closed its iron jaws soon after Aric's death; Tassos controlled the Net; and Decker had protected the AgriFleet.

This time, Remi gave a low chuckle before she answered. "Didn't you hear? There are no more Fivesons. They're dead." She paused, and her smile turned knowing before she added, "By Lir's order. But not his hand. Do you want to know by whose?"

Caledonia felt a knot form in her stomach. She didn't want to hear the answer, but suspected she knew it already.

Remi's eyes brightened with a delight so cruel she might as well have a knife pressed to Caledonia's heart.

"Lir sent Donnally to kill them all."

CHAPTER FOUR

The scent of smoke clung to the back of Caledonia's throat.

Donnally. She hated the casual way Remi had said his name, as if she knew him. As if she knew him better than Caledonia did.

The twist of nausea in Caledonia's gut told her it was true: she didn't know her brother at all anymore. She hadn't known him in a long time, but in spite of everything, she didn't know how to conjure a Donnally in her mind who was capable of what Remi claimed. Yes, Bullets killed. But not their own.

Or, that was the way it used to be. Things would be different now that Aric was dead and Lir was in charge. If Caledonia let her thoughts detach from her heart, she could see the purpose behind the strategy. Without Aric to control the Fivesons, what was to stop them from challenging Lir's claim to the Bullet Seas? Perhaps they'd started to do just that, and he'd asserted his dominance and removed them from play.

She could picture him commanding Donnally to do it as a

twisted test of loyalty. Donnally had almost been a Fiveson himself. Had he killed the others to show he was no threat to Lir? To his *brother*?

Caledonia closed her eyes as the freezing waters of memory swept over her. The moment she'd seen Donnally on the deck of the *Titan* rushed through her mind; the strong surge of her relief breaking against the firm edge of his resistance; the fluttering panic as her brother looked into her eyes and said, "I can't abandon my brother." The slow pain that had seeped in after and never left.

Her brother. Was he even that anymore? It was the word he'd used for Lir, and if he had truly done what Remi claimed, then perhaps he was more Lir's than Caledonia had ever wanted to believe. Once, she'd had hope that she could win him back, but now, knowing this, that hope was all but gone. In its place, her anger burned like the sun.

A hand twisted softly in the back of her shirt, Pisces pulling Caledonia back to the task before her. "Your orders, Captain?" she prompted.

With a deep breath, Caledonia cleared the anger from her thoughts. Without Fivesons, there was no one to divide Lir's power. No one to challenge him. He was consolidating his forces. Making sure there was no one left to stand against him.

No one except Caledonia.

She'd been determined to take him down before, when he was

only responsible for the death of her family. Now that he was remaking himself in Aric's image, Caledonia had no choice but to destroy him. And the only way to do so was to take all his power away from him. Then with it, create a world that wasn't ruled by fear.

"You each have a choice." Caledonia's mind relaxed as she stepped into the increasingly familiar words. "You can come with us, or you can stay here. If you stay, we'll leave you the bow boats and you can go wherever you like. If you come with us, you'll have everything you need: food, shelter, a new life."

Remi's face twisted into a mask of disgust. "We know what you do to Bullets, Caledonia Styx. Give us an impossible choice, take our Silt and watch us die, or send us crawling back with noth-ing but failure to report. We see you exactly as you are: a killer in the guise of a savior."

Caledonia knew from experience that every Bullet before her believed the lie they'd been fed their entire lives: from Silt comes strength. There was nothing she could do or say in a few short minutes that would convince them otherwise, and Lir had done a brilliant job of disseminating fear of withdrawal. Every Bullet she encountered said the same thing: she was a killer in the guise of a savior.

"You're going to kill us one way or the other," another Bullet said, eyes dull and fearless, emboldened by the drug in his veins. "And there's no glory in a slow death."

The Bullet was on his feet before Caledonia registered move-ment, but not before Pisces did. She spun around Caledonia, strik-ing the man's throat before he'd gone two steps. He dropped to his knees with his hands on his neck, his mouth stretched wide as he attempted and failed to draw a breath. Pisces stood over him, ready to strike again, but as air slowly filled his lungs, he made no move to continue the fight.

"There is no glory in any death," Caledonia said. "It's true that if you choose to come with us, you may die. It is not easy to recover from Silt."

"Silt gives us strength," Remi countered.

The words were now as familiar to Caledonia as her response: "You were strong before Silt. You can be strong again, but it is your choice."

"Why should we choose you?" Remi asked, suspicion painted across her face. "When you want to take away the thing Lir gives freely?"

Every Bullet she encountered used the same language: glory, strength, family, service. They believed their lives were caught up in the web of lies started by Aric and continued by Lir. It was never enough to tell them they were wrong. All she could do was be honest. Show them that her words meant something different. Even if that meant sending Bullets back to Lir's ranks.

"Lir murdered his brothers. That's what you're choosing

if you choose him. But I don't want you to choose me instead," Caledonia answered, voice calm and level. "I want you to choose you."

With that, Caledonia and Pisces left the survivors to make their decisions while the crew salvaged what they could from the barge and set charges to send the rest to the deep. Caledonia watched from her tall perch on the *Luminous Wake* as evidence of the battle and Fiveson Decker were slowly pulled apart or sank beneath the murky blue chop of the ocean.

"Nearly done, Cala." Pisces pulled herself up the ladder and joined Caledonia on the platform where they'd started the morning. "Most of the fleet has moved out. Just a few more and then we can get underway."

"Reports?" Caledonia asked.

"*Piston* took a direct hit and we lost six souls in all, no ships."

The two of them had grown so used to this conversation that they no longer struggled to have it, but it landed just as heavily on their shoulders. Just because they had grown used to discussing their people in numbers didn't mean they had to think of them that way. She'd have the names later for the Parting Ceremony, which happened all too frequently now.

Nodding, Caledonia asked, "And recruits?"

"Remi chose to stay."

Caledonia's jaw nearly dropped at the news. "Suspicious."

"To say the least," Pisces agreed. "All but one other from the barge chose to go and seventeen from the surrendering vessel chose to stay as well."

"More than usual," Caledonia said. "How many are we releasing?"

Bullet recruits were never easy news. Their surrender was suspect, their recovery brutal, and after all of that their loyalty was never certain. Bringing them back to Cloudbreak was like returning with a basket of poisonous snakes, all poised to strike. Sending them back to Lir was almost as bad. But the war was bigger than an individual battle, and they wouldn't win this fight with guns alone.

Pisces hesitated before saying, "One hundred and thirteen."

"So many." The number was always discomfiting, but this was more than usual.

"The silencers worked exactly as we'd hoped. Nearly everyone struck by them survived. And nearly all of them are going back. That's a . . . good thing." Pisces sounded like she was trying to convince herself more than Caledonia. When they'd first discussed using a weapon that didn't kill Bullets but only incapacitated them, Pisces had been skeptical. She'd argued that sparing them now only meant killing them later.

But Caledonia had responded, "We can't save the world by killing it first," and Pisces had reluctantly ceded the point.

"It *is* a good thing. Our goal right now is to diminish Lir's fleet, not decimate his army. They have to know that we aren't just like him." Caledonia reached for her sister's hand and squeezed. "How many ships did we get?"

"Eight, bringing the standing fleet to fifty-four."

Caledonia frowned. It wasn't enough. Lir had nearly two hundred, and if they were going to sail against a fleet of that size, they needed to be gathering more than a handful of battle-ready ships every other moon. At this rate, all she'd ever manage to do was hold her perimeter.

"Hey, these are the bright bits," Pisces admonished even as she smiled.

"You're right." Caledonia shrugged the glower from her face and returned the smile. "Every ship we gain is a victory."

"I know you want to be ready now. But we'll get there. We *are* getting there. And we're a hell of a lot closer than we've ever been." Pisces looked at the place where the massive barge had been this morning. A single spearing tower was all that remained of the ship and even that was slowly sinking beneath the waves. "And if Lir is taking down his own Fivesons, then he's worried. About something."

Caledonia doubted that Lir would ever admit to being worried about anything. Lir's view of the world and his place in it didn't leave room for doubt. His was a narrative of self-assurance, one that constantly repositioned him as a destined, all-powerful leader. Lir did everything out of ambition, not worry. He'd killed his brothers not out of fear, but for power.

"Maybe," Caledonia said, always uncomfortable with how naturally she imagined Lir's mind. "We're going to need more of Amina's silencers. Tell Nettle to resume course to the Braids."

As Pisces left for the bridge, an even darker thought ghosted through Caledonia's mind. If it was so easy for Lir to kill those he called brother, how long would it be before Donnally shared the fate of the Fivesons?

CHAPTER FIVE

As they turned northward, the sky settled into a clouded steely gray and a cold breeze tipped the waves frothy white. The last time Caledonia sailed these waters it had been under the guise of a Bullet ship headed to Slipmark. This time, however, she didn't need to hide. Though they were close to Slipmark, the northern seas belonged to her. Any Bullet would think twice before sailing this far.

Before the Battle of Cloudbreak, contacting the Hands of the River had not been possible. Not only because of their reclusive lifestyle, but because their overlapping river system was notoriously laced with traps. Ships that braved those guarded waterways were rarely seen again. Under Aric's regime, the Hands had maintained their independence by staying deftly hidden. But the seas were changing, and Caledonia needed their help.

Amina had used all the skintech she and Hesperus could get their hands on to make the silencers they'd just exhausted taking out that barge. It had been a gamble from the start—even Amina couldn't say if they'd perform as intended. But they'd worked. They'd worked perfectly. Taking out entire crews for the duration of a battle without killing them. If Caledonia and her crew could keep making them, they could change the face of the Bullet Seas forever. Skintech was going to change this war. By saving ships and lives, it was going to *win* this war. Caledonia could feel the truth of that thought buzzing beneath her skin.

But only if they could make more.

A light rain had started to fall, and it smothered the wide window of the bridge in droplets on the brink of freezing. Beyond, the sea was folding over itself in long layers of blue and gray.

"Here." Amina spoke quietly, brown eyes trained on the misted world beyond the glass. She was wrapped in a gray slicker, her braids falling down her back to brush at her waist.

"All stop," Caledonia said.

Amina moved to Harwell's station and, taking the radio from his hand, brought the receiver to her mouth. She pursed her lips, hesitating before finding her resolve and drawing a deep breath. "This is Amina of Maryam Water. I bring with me friends of my life and heart. If you would hear us, we would speak."

Replacing the receiver, Amina crossed the bridge once more.

"We won't wait for a response?" Caledonia asked.

"If they're going to respond," Amina began, flipping her hood up over her head, "it'll be out there."

With a nod, Caledonia turned to her bridge crew. "Weigh the

anchor and alert the crew to ready the ship for weather. Nettle, you're with me. Harwell, you have the bridge."

"I have the bridge," Harwell repeated, shifting to take Caledonia's usual spot in the center of the small space.

Ducking her head against the cold rain, Caledonia followed in Amina's footsteps. Within minutes, the rain had grown from a drizzle to fat drops that stung her cheeks with cold, and she heard Nettle give a disgruntled growl. When they arrived at the rail, Pisces was there with a stack of slicker jackets in hand.

"Amina and Hime are already in the boat," Pisces said, tipping her head toward the shape of the bow boat waiting below. Just beyond, the *Blade* and *Piston* held their position a half mile away.

"Let's join them," Caledonia said, swinging her legs over the slippery rail.

Nettle took the wheel with a delighted grin, revving the engine once before letting the boat dart forward. Caledonia knew just how Nettle felt. The shift from the sturdy deck of the *Luminous Wake* to the thin shell of the bow boat's hull was exhilarating. As the small vessel bounced across the waves, Caledonia felt the ocean beneath her feet, catching them in its deep embrace before flinging them back up again.

The rain fell harder, streaking from the sky in heavy sheets that reduced their visibility to twenty feet or less. Amina and Hime sat pressed together, hunched behind the shallow lip of the vessel, their eyes narrowed against the slashing rain. When

Caledonia had raised the possibility of coming here for skintech, Amina had resisted.

"They do not welcome outsiders," she'd said. "They are my family, and when I left, I knew what that meant. I am in their hearts, but I have no claim to their aid. I can't promise they'll speak with us. I can't even promise they'll speak with *me*."

There had been two kinds of fear in her resistance. She'd been afraid that she wouldn't be able to give Caledonia what she needed, and she'd been afraid of rejection.

"I can make the approach on my own," Caledonia had said. "You don't have to come with me."

Caledonia knew what she was asking of her friend. When Amina left the Braids with a small group of her extended family to fight against Aric's oppressive regime, it had been with the knowledge that they would never return. The Hands did not fight. And any who chose that way of life acknowledged that the cost was exile. To return was to disrespect their entire people.

But Amina knew what was at stake here. And she had answered Caledonia in a firm tone: "I won't let you go without me, Captain."

Now Amina raised a hand and gestured straight ahead. When they had traveled for a mile or more, they cut their engine and let the vessel drift. Cold seeped into Caledonia's skin, making her fingers ache and the tip of her nose go numb.

Fog made it impossible to know how far they'd come or

whether or not they'd reached the rivers. Behind them, rain swallowed the silhouettes of their ships and ahead the world was nothing but gray water. All she could hear was the urgent scatter of rain against the ocean, all she could smell was cold and salt. They were completely, uncomfortably alone out here. It was as if they'd sailed into the sea and the sea had decided to keep them.

Then the rain thinned, and the clouds began to sift up from where they'd come to rest against the water, and suddenly Caledonia and her crew were no longer alone.

A cluster of slender-nosed boats appeared in the mist. Seated in each was a single figure, their legs cradled inside the vessel as though it were an extension of their bodies. Their skin was as dark as Amina's, all shades of brown earth and the night sky, and they wore their hair in braids that gave an impression of movement and power. Their fingers were wrapped with rings of silver and polished granite, and their clothing was woven in snaking patterns of blue and gray and silver.

The old world had ended in an explosion—of weapons and technology and maybe even people. Very few cultures had managed to survive intact, but the Hands of the River were an exception. They'd held on to each other and never let go.

Amina stood up and raised both hands, palms out to show she was unarmed.

For a moment, no one spoke, then a man raised his hands,

mirroring Amina's gesture. He did not smile, but he nodded.

A small sigh of relief fell from Amina's lips.

"I am Amina of Maryam Water and I have come to seek aid in the fight against Aric's Bullets," Amina called.

The man did not move his gaze from Amina as the sea shifted beneath him, shuffling him up and down. Around him, the others waited calmly, adjusting their boats with a single oar dipped low in the water.

"Amina of Maryam Water, I am Osias of Kyrasi Water. What sort of aid do you seek?"

It was only a question, but it filled Caledonia with hope. Perhaps they could be convinced. Perhaps they'd only been waiting for the right moment.

"This is Caledonia Styx," Amina said, sweeping one arm toward her captain. Caledonia stood, bracing her feet against the curved hull of the bow boat. For the first time, Osias looked away from Amina. His gaze landed heavily upon Caledonia.

Amina continued, "She is our captain and led the fight against Aric Athair. He no longer threatens these seas because of her actions. But another has assumed his power and his Bullets. We need your help to defeat him."

The rain continued to push north, dragging the low-lying clouds away from the water to reveal thin fingers of grassland on either side. Amina had led them directly to the mouth of the river.

"What aid do you seek, Caledonia Styx?" Osias asked.

"Skintech," Caledonia called. "Amina has designed a skintech weapon that allows us to stop Bullets without unnecessary death. We can take their ships and not their lives. We can do so much with so little, but we need your help."

"You want our tech to create weapons?" Osias asked. "You will implicate us in a fight we have no claim to."

The others made disapproving clicks behind their teeth. One shook her head, accusing eyes traveling to Amina.

Still, Caledonia pressed on.

"The Bullets are vulnerable right now. They have tormented the people of these seas for long enough. I intend to change that. I *will* change that. But I need your help. We all do." Caledonia paused, then, sensing their reluctance, she added, "Now is the time to fight this fight. We can make this world better than it is. We can work together and change things."

"How? You defeated Aric, but another has risen in his place. There will always be another Bullet." Osias shook his head. "We have nothing to gain from joining your war."

Frustration surged in Caledonia's lungs. She quickly pushed it down again. "You may be able to avoid the fight, but it has imprisoned you just the same."

"Our river is not a prison." It seemed the ocean was already pulling Osias away, ending the discussion on his behalf.

"What about your soils?" Caledonia asked, feeling desperation make her voice sharper. For all that the Hands had plenty of tech in their possession, soiltech eluded them.

"What are you doing?" Pisces muttered.

Caledonia ignored her. Now was not the time for caution. She had to do *something*. "We have Bullet soiltech and we are close to re-creating it, and when we do, we'll share it with you. We'll give you the tech and the plans for reproduction."

This time Osias seemed to consider her proposition. He paused, listening as the others slipped alongside him and whispered their own thoughts. Caledonia held her breath, not daring to make another sound in case she upset whatever might be working in her favor.

But her hopes plummeted when the discussion stopped and Osias bent his mouth in a frown.

"No," he said. Then he turned to Amina and added, "Do not bring strangers to our river again, Amina of Maryam Water."

Without another word, they turned their slender vessels, and vanished into the rivers.

CHAPTER SIX

The white cliffs of Cloudbreak sifted through the fog, darkening against the sky in a slow smile.

Though Hesperus had revealed to Caledonia that there were more ways in and out of the city itself than the lifts, they were still the fastest. And they'd gotten faster. Over the past six moons, Old Man Clagg had managed to cut nearly a minute from the time it took to travel up the harrowing cliffside. With Oran's help, he'd shaved off an additional thirty seconds. Now, as the command crew stepped onto the pallet and they pulled away from the ground, Caledonia felt every second of that speed.

Pisces planted herself in the center of the lift, where she rode the whole way seated with legs crossed and eyes closed. Hime sat with her, taking one of Pisces's tightly balled fists between her own hands. Amina stood at Hime's back, while Nettle swung from one of the stationary ropes with one hand. Pine hovered nearby. He might not be willing to admit it, but he was always close enough to reach out and catch the girl should she lose her grip. Sledge stood apart from everyone, arms crossed against his chest, eyes pressed serenely shut, as though the sensation of being whisked up a mountainside were commonplace.

Caledonia stood alone at the edge of their pallet. Cold wind ripped through her hair, and the force of the lift's speed pushed against her entire body, reminding her that if she stepped from the lift, she would sink like a stone in water, plummeting back toward the rocky shore.

As they approached the top of the cliffs, which curled protectively around the city within, their pallet slowed, then deposited them on a platform where five anxious figures waited. Hesperus was at the front, mouth pinched in a frustrated twist and brow creased. While the city was technically still his, it had transformed since the battle, and every time Caledonia returned from sea, he had something new to complain about. Today was clearly no exception.

Just behind Hesperus stood Ares. Unlike the Sly King, Ares did not look like he was chewing on something unpleasant, but his relief was visible when his eyes landed first on Sledge and then on his sister. Next to Ares was Kae, who was probably waiting for her own sister Mino to appear, and just behind her was Ennick. The man was several turns Caledonia's senior with skin as salt-pale as her own and dusty brown hair. A former Ballistic turned rogue captain, he and his crew had joined with Caledonia's during the Battle of Cloudbreak, and

Ennick had been the rallying point for rogue ships ever since.

And there, standing at the rear of the entire group, was the one person she most wanted to see: Oran. He leaned against the low wall on the other side of the dock. His strong brown hands were braced on either side of his narrow hips and he watched Caledonia step off the lift with a private smile. Recently, Caledonia had come to know how often Oran's expressions looked like one thing but meant something else. He laughed when he was worried, a frown that lit his eyes meant he was amused. But this slight narrowing of his warm brown eyes, the tightening of his lips, the tuck of his chin; these were things he only did when he wanted to kiss her.

The second Caledonia stepped off the lift, the five of them swept around her like a cloak. The entire group of twelve moved as one, a swarm of bees skimming through an orchard. As they traveled down a walled channel toward the stronghold, they gathered guards who moved ahead and behind until Caledonia was thoroughly and safely locked away in the center of the mass.

"You can't keep bringing people into my city like this, Captain." Hesperus dove right in.

Caledonia almost laughed.

"Our resources are strained as is. We don't have the capacity to keep feeding these Bullets. Especially if all they're going to do is sit there and sweat and eat my food!"

"They chose to be here," Caledonia reminded him, patient but firm. "And it's better than the alternative."

"We can stretch our stores, Hesperus." Kae spoke with the tone of someone tired of repeating themselves.

"But we can't stretch our beds and I'm running out of room. I'm certainly running out of goodwill." Hesperus spoke loudly now.

"There wasn't much of that to begin with." It wasn't in Ares's nature to seek out conflict, but when it came to what they did with defecting Bullets, he found all his sharp edges.

Hesperus's expression darkened. Without breaking his stride, he said, "Show me their worth and maybe I'll find a little to spare."

"Can we build?" Amina spoke up from the rear. "There's plenty of wood to be had in the forest. And there are plenty of hands to do the work."

"There's room to expand the current barracks," Kae supplied, her eyes darting once to Hesperus. "And we can spare the supplies."

"The Blades volunteer to provide labor," Sledge added, his long brown braid swaying behind him.

"First they come for my city, now they come for my forest," Hesperus muttered. "Yes, fine. If there's space in the Orange Quarter to expand the barracks, then you have my blessings, but that sector stays firmly secured or I'll burn it to the ground myself."

"Make it fast," Caledonia ordered. "Kae, you and Sledge coordinate crews and materials. Let's get it done before housing becomes a problem."

That was how problems went these days. While she was away,

command decisions fell to Oran, but the second Caledonia returned she was bombarded with every issue that hadn't been resolved in her absence. In this case, the problem of the former Bullets she'd sent back a mere day ahead of her own return. Relations between Oran and Hesperus remainded tense, but once a decision had been made, they moved on.

Up ahead, the stronghold of Cloudbreak ribboned out of the mountainside in layered concentric circles. From inside Cloud-break, it was a fortress sitting high above the city. But from outside, the fortress melted into the stony face of the mountain. The only exception was the topmost tier, where Hesperus's observatory capped the structure with a doomed roof.

"Captain," Ennick's voice darted in. "We've had three more ships come to join. Small vessels, I'm afraid, but each with willing crews. Eighteen in all."

Every time Ennick brought a report, Caledonia's heart leapt before she could stop it. Rogue ships were almost always small vessels. Too small to make much of a difference in a battle, but they were incredibly useful for noncombat missions—scouting, forag-ing, or quick transport. They were the ancillary fleet, filling the gaps that the primary fleet couldn't.

"That's good news, Ennick," Caledonia said. "Ares?"

"Other than needing more space, detox is going well. The new recruits are more resistant than usual, but nothing we can't handle."

"There's always the other option." Hesperus tossed the comment over his shoulder.

Before Ares could respond, Caledonia asked, "What do you mean, more resistant?"

Ares took a second to consider before answering. "Seems like most of them are already in the early stages of detox, so they're coming down faster and with fewer casualties, but fighting us a little harder."

Caledonia stopped in her tracks. The rest of the group stopped around her, some more gracefully than others. She turned and found Ares directly at her back. "Already in detox?"

She looked for Oran and found him moving to her side, responding to her on instinct. "We think their rations might have been reduced before they defected. Maybe well before."

"Reduced." She repeated the word, more to herself than anyone else. "Pine!"

"Captain," Pine answered, immediately stepping out from behind Ares.

"How much Silt was taken from the Bullets before we released them?"

"Two doses each," Pine said, his smoky brown skin in perfect contrast to the dark stubble along his jaw. "Though many were down to one."

Each time they apprehended a clip of Bullets, they inventoried the Silt before destroying it; no Silt was allowed to leave a battle site or to pass into the city. Bullets always carried a few doses with them, but it was unusual to find them down to a single packet.

"You think their supply is running low?" Caledonia directed her question back to Ares.

It was exactly why they'd been eager to target the AgriFleet in the first place, to put a considerable dent in Lir's Silt supply, but if the Bullets were carrying less than usual, perhaps the supply was already strained.

A thoughtful frown appeared on Ares's mouth as he considered. "It's possible. I doubt we'll get any straight answers from them now, but maybe when they've come through the worst."

Recruited Bullets weren't capable of anything once they'd reached the first sharp peak of their withdrawal. Their blood burned, their guts cramped, and they struggled to stay hydrated. The whole terrible process could last anywhere from three days to a solid week depending on the Bullet. During that time, they could barely speak, let alone be a reliable source of information. Interrogation had to wait.

"If their supply wasn't strained before, it will be soon, and things will get worse for Lir." Caledonia spun on her heel and started walking once more. "Where are we on soiltech?"

"Nowhere, I'm afraid," Kae answered solemnly. "But now that Nettle's back, perhaps we'll get a bit further."

Nettle skipped, her rainbow-colored ribbons flouncing in answer to her aunt. Now that Caledonia knew Hesperus, Mino, Kae, and Nettle were all related, she could see the resemblance. Though the prominent cheekbones that gave Mino and Kae a statuesque kind of beauty were wider on Nettle's face and Nettle's skin was more amber than earthen, all four of them had the same eyes that winged up in the corners and noses that stretched wide over full lips. Though Caledonia didn't know what had happened to Nettle's birth parents, her aunts and uncle each watched over her in different ways.

"Oran?" Caledonia said, slowing her steps to let him draw even with her. "Your report?"

"We've evaluated our recent arrivals and accounted for their resources," Oran began, bringing her up to speed on the changes in their standing fleet and its readiness. "All new ships have been assigned to existing fleets and we've started incorporating them into our drills. They're ready for your direction as soon as you're ready to give it."

"Anything else?" Caledonia asked as the walled path opened around the wide plane of the eastern promenade. When no one spoke, she gave a nod. "Good, then let's get to work solving our problems."

The group dispersed and Caledonia stepped inside the fortress, already feeling the pull to return to the water. Two guards followed close behind. No matter where she went in Cloudbreak, they were her constant shadows. They'd been Hesperus's idea and

Pisces had quickly agreed. When Caledonia protested that she didn't need protection, especially not in Cloudbreak, Hesperus had said, "They're as much for your image as they are your protection." And Pisces had added, "It's either them or me and Pine. You pick."

While she'd prefer to have her friends watching her every move, she also needed them getting their own tasks done. They couldn't do that if they were glued to her side day and night.

The inside of the fortress was always darker than Caledonia expected. The hallways were long and narrow, and here, near the outer edge, natural light filtered through intermittent windows built into thick walls. The air was cool and damp and always suffused with smoke from the night before.

Hesperus had given Caledonia a small office on the second level and as she headed there, she heard the whisper of a fourth set of footsteps behind them. She moved faster, her heartbeat speeding up to match.

She pushed straight through her office door leaving it wide open in her wake. As her guards took their position just outside, she turned. And there, trailing her down the dim corridor, was Oran.

He locked his eyes on hers and walked determinedly forward, passing her guards without a glance. He stepped inside the office and shut the door firmly behind him.

Caledonia's heart skipped into her throat. She could feel her pulse thrumming in her neck, her fingertips, zinging hot down to her belly and between her legs. She took one shallow breath and then his arms were around her waist, pulling her against him.

Their mouths were fast and hungry, their hands just as eager. When their kisses became tugging at hair and clothes, and gasps became little groans, Caledonia pulled away.

"Not here," she said, passing a thumb over Oran's crushed red lips. "Not yet."

Oran's eyes narrowed suspiciously. "You want my real report."

"I want your real report," Caledonia admitted, though her body certainly didn't agree. She wanted his hands on her skin, his mouth on her mouth, she wanted nothing between them but darkness.

With a sigh, Oran stepped away. Cold air rushed between them and Caledonia instantly regretted her request.

Oran nodded, and in an instant he transformed from the young man who saved smiles just for her to the Fiveson who smiled for no one.

"It's done." His voice dipped low, grim and hard, and Caledonia's heart dipped with it.

She hated asking him to work in secret like this, but she could see no other way. They'd come too far, lost so much to win so little. Everyone was looking to her to change the world. They had hope, confidence, so much faith that Caledonia Styx would be the one to free the Bullet Seas from the deadly hooks of Aric's legacy. She'd thought she had a partial solution in Amina's silencers, but without the ability to create more, she needed another option.

One no one knew about except for her and Oran.

"I was able to build four. Any more right now and I think Kae will notice supplies going missing. I can get these to the *Luminous Wake* as soon as she's docked in the canals. As long as you're still sure?"

Caledonia nodded as she blew out an uncomfortable breath. "I'm sure."

"The Hands of the River?"

The crushing sensation of rejection fell heavily on Caledonia's shoulders. "They're not an option."

Oran's lips tightened. He had been skeptical of their aid from the start, but if he felt any satisfaction in being right, he didn't show it. Instead, he seemed truly disappointed.

"You don't have to use these, Cala."

A thin, tragic laugh escaped Caledonia's lips. The memory of Aric using his Bullets as a living shield as she threw a star blossom bomb into their midst planted itself in her mind. She would never forget the chorus of their screams or the wet sound of their dying cries. She would never forget the burnt smell of the air even as it tasted of copper and pain. She would never forget that she had had a choice and, in an instant, killed a hundred Bullets in the worst possible way.

Had there been another option? If she'd given herself another moment, would she have found a solution that didn't leave the deck of the *Titan* washed crimson and black?

She still didn't know. But she did know that once a bomb was built, the question wasn't *if* it would be used, it was when.

"I wouldn't have asked you to build them if I wasn't prepared to use them," she said. The anger that threaded her chest as she spoke was partly for Aric, who had created a world in which star blossoms were ever a necessity, and partly for herself, for answering that need. She was supposed to be working toward a world without this kind of fear.

"I won't ever judge you for it." Oran spoke softly, his eyes holding on to her and keeping her afloat. "And I will make you as many as I'm able. Just say the word."

Using star blossoms was a terrible option. The worst she'd ever entertained. She couldn't really imagine what Pisces or Sledge would say if they knew she was building her own. It was better that they didn't know. Better that the decision wouldn't rest on their shoulders.

"Not yet," Caledonia said, and Oran released a tight breath of relief.

Then she reached out, twisted her fingers in his shirt, and pulled him back to her. She whispered, "For a minute, I actually thought skintech could be the answer. But Lir still outnumbers us and I can't build our fleet fast enough. He's brutal. I have to be prepared to end this one way or another."

They stayed that way for a long time. Her head against his chest, his fingers threaded through her hair. She quietly told him about Decker being dead, about Donnally, about the murdered Five-sons who used to be Oran's brothers, too. There was nothing she could say that he would hate or reject, because for all her growing familiarity with darkness, Oran had already been there.

CHAPTER SEVEN

Dawn was always dark in Cloudbreak. Mornings arrived muffled behind curtains of mist and fog or smothered beneath layers of clouds. It was a constant source of frustration for Caledonia. In her time here, she'd seen the sun rise gloriously exactly once. Every other morning, the light diffused slowly through dense white fog until the sun finally burned its way through. By the time it appeared, it was more than halfway across the sky, and dusk was ready to stake its claim.

Today had been such a dismal day. All filter, no brilliance. As the sun vanished on their second night since returning to Cloudbreak, Caledonia flung a shawl around her shoulders and climbed into the wide-open window of the observatory. A brisk ocean breeze greeted her, sliding cool kisses along her cheeks and down her neck. The stars were just beginning to spear the darkening sky and the moon was low against the horizon.

Below her the ships of her fleet were outlined in rings of glowing blue sun pips. There hadn't been room in the original harbor to accommodate a fleet of this number, so they'd built a new one, transforming the existing chain of breaker isles into two continuous jetties with a gate at the center. Just outside the gate, the eight newly recovered Bullet ships sat at anchor, awaiting inspection and repair.

Her eyes pushed at the eastern horizon, searching for what she knew was there but could not see. The Holster was three days' sail from here in good weather, which meant it was possible that right now, miles and miles from here, Lir was learning of his loss. She wished she could see it.

She wished she knew what to do next.

>><<

"Evening, Captain."

Caledonia turned at the sound of Amina's voice. She entered, carrying a tray with six steaming mugs. Hime walked beside her, a pile of blankets draped across her arms. Behind her came Pisces, a knit cap pulled over her bare head, with Nettle and Tin at her heels.

"Did I call a meeting?" Caledonia accepted the steaming mug, which turned out to be mulled cherry wine.

"Not out loud." Long braids spilled over Amina's shoulder as she tipped her head and considered her captain. "But it was time."

Overdue, Hime added firmly, throwing the blankets down in

a pile and turning her attention swiftly to the glowing embers in the fire pit.

Soon, a small fire was burning in the center of the room and Caledonia had climbed down from her perch in the window to join her sisters around it.

"Does Hesperus know you got into his stash?" Caledonia asked, eyes traveling to Nettle as she took a sip of her wine, savoring the bright blend of sweet and tart flavors.

"Why do you assume it was me?" Nettle smiled her devious smile. "I will admit, usually it's me, but this time . . ."

"I took it," Pisces announced. "And I'm not sorry."

"Unrepentant! Ha!" Nettle cried, hopping in her seat and spinning to Amina with a triumphant grin on her face.

"That's a word you should have known already, Nettle. Shameless as you are," Tin said, rolling her eyes fondly.

"Are you *still* teaching her new words?" Pisces teased. "That will only lead to trouble. The last thing we need is for Nettle to talk more."

They laughed, raising their glasses together and drinking the rest of their wine before it cooled. Amina gave Nettle a new list of vocabulary words while Hime rested against Amina's chest and Tin poked at the fire. It was an unexpected moment of relief, and Caledonia felt her smiles coming a little easier. She was glad to know she could still breathe and laugh and just exist in a ring of firelight with her sisters for a moment.

"Thank you," Caledonia said when their laughter had faded into the crackle and hiss of the fire. "For knowing me better than I know myself sometimes."

Pisces reached over and took Caledonia's hand in her own, braiding their fingers loosely together. "It's our job to know you best, Cala."

"It's our job to keep you closer than you want to let us," Amina added.

And it's our job to help you when you need it most, Hime signed.

"So, what help do you need right now?" Tin asked.

A breath caught in Caledonia's chest as though the air were made of the most delicate gauze and her lungs filled with thorns to snag in the material. They always knew when she was struggling, and even though they weren't on the brink of battle, war was waiting for them.

"I thought we had our way forward," Caledonia admitted. "Amina, your silencers were beautiful. With more, we could disable enough of Lir's fleet to turn the tide in our favor. I know we could, but without them . . . we need a new plan."

"But the silencers were only one piece of our plan," Pisces protested. "We're still building a fleet and giving Bullets an alternative while we work on soiltech."

"And as soon as I crack that, we'll be able to change everything," Nettle rushed in. "If people have the ability to clean the soil and grow their own food, the only thing Lir will be able to use to control anyone will be Silt."

"Which works just fine on its own," Tin said.

This had been the plan for six moons: to hold their own and build their fleet while they figured out how to replicate soiltech. It was a plan that took time, and Caledonia could not shake the feeling that their time was quickly running out.

"What has changed, Captain?" Amina asked, re-centering the conversation on Caledonia.

"Lir did." Caledonia chased the thought that had been bothering her since learning of Decker's death. "He tightened the reins on his own people, and I don't think it's because he feared the other Fivesons. It has to be more dangerous than that."

"So, he's shortening the chain of command?" Pisces asked thoughtfully.

"Exactly." Caledonia stood to pace the short length of the room. "And if he's shortening the chain of command, then he's consolidating power. Getting rid of anything that threatens that power."

"Like us," Tin said, anger already tinging her words.

"Maybe." Caledonia shook her head. "Probably."

We can close the harbor, Hime signed with a furrowed brow. *We can't beat him ship to ship, but if we cut off access to Cloudbreak, we can defend it.*

"Not indefinitely. Not without access to outside resources. So, let's call that a last resort." Caledonia didn't relish the thought of letting Lir barricade her on top of this mountain, but Hime wasn't wrong. They could survive up here for a while, but with nothing to threaten him on the seas, all Lir would have to do was wait her out.

"If our main problem is the size of his fleet, then why don't we just, ya know, sink a bunch of his ships?" Nettle asked.

Pisces narrowed her eyes. "You mean . . . the way we've been trying to sink a bunch of his ships?"

"No, I mean, not in battle, but get a bunch of tows and blue lungs and also bombs and slip into his harbor like a bunch of sneaky fish. We could plant the bombs and get gone before anyone knew anything, then boom! Half his fleet in a heartbeat." She bounced, hair ribbons and all. "There won't even be full clips on board every ship if we do it right. Lets us sink ships *and* save lives."

"We'd have to put our people in the water more than two miles out," Caledonia countered. "That's too much distance for them to cover with only a blue lung and a tow, especially if they're hauling enough explosive to sink a ship."

Nettle deflated a little as she considered the problem. After a quiet moment, she added, "What if it's the tows themselves, then?"

"What do you mean?" Pisces asked, leaning in.

"What if we fill the tows with explosives and our people only have to get close enough to set the course and let them go? Maybe it doesn't take down as many ships, but it'll take some, and they'll never see it coming."

For a moment everyone was quiet. Every few weeks they reconsidered what it would take to attack the Holster, but the numbers were always stacked against them. The place was protected by five gun towers perched high on a hill that could fire on incoming ships long before it would be possible for them to return the favor. It would take a fleet of hundreds and losses would be significant. With their small fleet, a direct attack wasn't an option.

Even if a direct assault were an option, the harbor itself was lined with concrete breakers designed to stem the flow of traffic in and out. A series of tows on autopilot would have to be extremely lucky to make it through them into the harbor itself.

But they also knew that Lir's fleet was too large for his harbor. At least half of his ships were outside the breakers, protected only by the firing range of the five gun towers. Perfectly positioned for a flock of armed tows.

The simplicity of the plan unfurled between them.

"We could send the tows in as a first wave," Pisces said, tracking Caledonia's thoughts.

"And be ready to drive in after the initial explosion," Amina added. "Taking advantage of the confusion."

"With their ranks reduced, we might stand a chance against the rest of the fleet," Tin said.

And as soon as we're inside the harbor, those gun towers will have trouble targeting us without destroying their own ships, Hime finished.

Caledonia let it all play out in her mind. They wouldn't be able to control the path of the tows once they released them, so there was still an element of luck at play, but with enough tows, they could take down a third of Lir's fleet without putting a single ship at risk. He'd still have her outnumbered three to one, but those were odds she could work with.

"I think we have a plan," Caledonia said at last. "We're going to attack the Holster."

"Yes!" Nettle was bouncing again, likely already plotting how she would build the bombs.

"Not you, Nettle," Caledonia said, breaking the girl's enthusiasm in half. "I need you on soiltech. Amina, I want you on this."

"There's a man named Tipper in town who came in on a rogue ship not long ago," Pisces added. "He has experience with bombs. If you can track him down, I'll bet he can help with production. We're talking about a lot more than fifteen silencers."

"I will definitely need the help." Amina absently ran a hand down Hime's arm.

"I can track him," Tin said. "I've got the manifest."

"Great." Caledonia couldn't help but let the energy of the moment infect her. "We have a plan. Let's get some sleep and then get to work."

One minute, Hime signed, standing and tugging Amina up after her. Nettle and Tin followed suit, and Pisces stepped in, all of them circling around Caledonia as they had so often done on the deck of their ship.

Caledonia's stones. She'd lost some—Lace, her sunny citrine, and Redtooth, her stoic, soft-hearted marble—and gained some—

Nettle, her crystal, reflecting rainbow color with the smallest hint of light, and Tin, her cool, sharp basalt—but they were always the solid foundation on which she stood. Amina, her strong, unflinching granite; Hime, elegantly layered agate; Pisces, her flint, every break making her stronger and sharper.

They looked at her with turns of trust and frustration and the kind of love that was so strong it split her heart in two. One half wanted to tell them about the star blossom bombs. The other, to protect them from that knowledge. If she ever had to use the bombs, it should be her decision alone. But maybe, with her sisters' help, she would never have to make that choice.

Her throat was tight when she whispered, "We fight together."

And tears burned in her eyes when they answered, "Or not at all."

CHAPTER EIGHT

For all that life in Cloudbreak felt slower than life at sea, Caledonia never seemed to stop moving.

Every morning began with a spar followed by reports that could either last a few minutes or several hours, and after that there were strategies to consider, rounds to conduct, and readiness drills to run. Today, Caledonia had been surveying yet another improvement to the lifts when the horn sounded in the triple beat pattern that signaled a drill and not a live attack. In this specific scenario, the idea was that Bullet ships had been spotted ten miles out and Cloudbreak's citizens had a matter of minutes to get their fleet on the water and ready to engage.

Tin had arrived at Caledonia's side a moment after the horns and together they'd raced into the western mountains, through the cherry orchard and work camp to the caves where the *Luminous Wake* was docked. They ran every drill as though it were real, so after racing to the ship, they took her out, sailing through the narrow canals at top speeds. If Caledonia ignored the towering walls and treacherously shallow passages, it was almost like being at sea. The drills were always over too soon, and as she disembarked Tin was already at her elbow, repeating Caledonia's schedule for the rest of the day.

Oran joined a step behind Tin, his skin slicked with sweat even as circles deepened beneath his eyes. If she wanted Hesperus and the rest of Cloudbreak to trust Oran, she had to be seen trusting him. Acting as Caledonia's proxy in her absence meant acting as her second in her presence. His days were filled with as many administrative tasks as hers, and his nights with all the work no one knew about except her. The long hours were beginning to take their toll.

Caledonia could hear Pisces, still on deck, shouting at the crew. "Folly, Shale, you were faster than last time, but still too slow. Far, I don't care if you're already on board, the minute we hit the deck, I want you reporting to Tin. We need to know who's accounted for and who isn't. Remember, this is a battle scenario! I know it's a two-mile run between here and town, and that's why I want you running the trails every morning and twice more right now, let's go!"

She was going hard on them, but the truth was, they'd done well. They were the only crew with so far to travel. Keeping the *Luminous Wake* in the interior docks ensured it was protected, and put them in position to flank any attacking ships by exiting the canals far south of the harbor. It also meant speed was essential. But every time they did this, they got a little bit faster.

"Tin, we'll check in on the barracks later," Caledonia said, choosing the cramped stairwell over the lift.

"Captain?" Tin asked, jogging at her heels.

"If the crew is running the trails, so are we."

"Yes, Captain."

Caledonia paused, turning to Oran and stepping closer so that her words were only for him. "You should head back to town. You could use the rest."

He responded with a one-sided smile. "If you're running, I'm running."

"Oran," she breathed, guilt gnawing at her lungs. "Don't make me order you."

"Don't make me refuse an order," he responded, still smiling as he moved around her and jogged ahead.

They were already panting by the time they reached the top of the stairwell. The rest of the crew followed just behind, racing up to the top of the stairs, where they gathered in a group, stretching out muscles in preparation for the run. Pulling up the rear were Pisces and Far, Far's array of black curls pulled away from her face in a wide ponytail. The woman rarely joined them for this kind of exertion. Judging by the look of resignation on her face, Caledonia suspected Pisces hadn't given her a choice.

"Mary sisters, take the lead!" Pisces called.

The air was cold up here and the rocky ground dry and steep.

The Mary sisters led them down through the work camp, picking a trail that darted briefly through towering pines and then along the edge of the cherry orchard before diving upward once more and curling around the northern edge of town. They moved all together, a stream of dusty footsteps and encouraging whispers.

Caledonia started at the rear of the group, jogged steadily at Pisces's side. Then she shifted, moving from one person to the next and saying their names as she went: Pax, Vera, Hildegard, and Deri. Oran stayed in the corner of her sight, jogging always a few paces away. Soon she'd reached the Mary sisters, still driving along like the tip of a needle. At the very front was Lurin, the second eldest of the five sisters. Her sandy pale cheeks were pink with effort, but her eyes were brimming with energy.

"Keeping us steady, Lurin," Caledonia called. "I'm surprised I don't see you lapping the ship more often."

Lurin laughed along with her sisters.

"That's only because we threaten to tie her to her rack," Abrasin teased. "She would run a rut right into the deck if you let her."

"Don't hurt my ship, Lurin," Caledonia warned.

"Noted, Captain," Lurin responded quickly, her smile growing.

They looped around, retracing their steps and then turning down the trail back to town. By the time they arrived at the stronghold, they were covered in sweat and dust and the sun was dipping low in the western sky.

"Showers!" Pisces called. "And I want to see every one of you on that trail at sunrise or it'll be twice again!"

"You, too, Tin," Caledonia said, dismissing the girl. "Everything else can wait."

Tin nodded, all too happy to take the opportunity for a quick shower, and Caledonia turned her steps toward the upper levels where Hesperus kept his office. Her muscles ached as she entered the spiraling stairwells and stepped into a slow jog. The stairwell was crowded with people heading to or from evening meals, shifts, or their quarters, but as she passed the fifth level, the traffic thinned until it was just her. The only people still on level six were the two guards standing outside Hesperus's office door, and they let Caledonia pass without challenge.

Inside the wide chamber, Hesperus stood with his back to the door, hands braced low against his hips as he studied the harbor below.

"You smell like the mountain," he said without turning.

"I'm certain I smell worse," Caledonia conceded. "How did we do?"

"Better." Hesperus jumped right into his reports. "Silver Fleet was all accounted for and on the water in seventeen minutes. A new record."

"A new goal," Caledonia murmured, glancing at the papers Hesperus slid across the desk toward her. "They beat their previous time by two minutes. What changed?"

Hesperus only shook his head. "Nothing but practice as far as I know. Amber and Cobalt Fleets came in at twenty-two minutes, just like last time, and Viridian at twenty-seven. You had the *Luminous* in play at thirty-one minutes, a new record for you, and the remainder of Red Fleet was ready in just thirty. They still have some trouble getting through the northern canals. Still, in this scenario, our first line of defense is on the water in plenty of time to meet inbound ships. I'm sure Sledge will give you a full report."

Caledonia imagined the drill as she never could when she was on her own ship, separated from the bigger picture by all but a radio. That was the most challenging part of commanding a fleet: letting the action unfurl as it was planned to instead of under her direct control. They were getting better, faster. If Lir moved on her before she could move on him, they'd be ready.

"And before you ask, no, I didn't sail with Viridian Fleet."

She'd known this was coming, but she'd hoped her suspicions were wrong. "Hesperus, I need you to run the drill at least once. I know you know what to do, but there's a difference between knowing and doing."

Hesperus was already shaking his head, an argument ready in his deep ocean eyes. "It's a moot point. I'm not running the drill because my place will always be on Cloudbreak. Nothing will ever convince me to leave. It's that simple."

"Yes, your place is here, and the likelihood of that changing is extremely small, but I would appreciate if you would run a damn drill at least once. Any of them. Pick one!" Heat colored Caledonia's words and some distant part of her marveled at her ability to speak to the Sly King of Cloudbreak as his superior. "Please, Hesperus."

A narrowing of the eyes was his only answer. Caledonia waited him out, expression unforgiving. For a moment, the silent battle raged between them, neither willing to move from their position. Then, finally, Hesperus sighed. He pulled out his chair and sat heavily, gesturing for her to take the seat opposite him. Caledonia relented, warily lowering herself into the old wooden chair.

"I have something for you." Hesperus's voice was tired, his eyes heavy as he reached into his desk drawer and produced a small pouch. He held it out for her. "A small token, but one I've been meaning to give you for a while."

Curious, Caledonia tipped the contents into her palm, catching a small, black stone just large enough to sit comfortably in her hand. She turned it over, noting the way a resilient reddish hue revealed itself almost resentfully, as if unable to resist the light in spite of itself.

"It's a garnet. Unpolished," Hesperus explained. "I found that one on my first day in Cloudbreak and have carried it with me ever since. It's always reminded me of how much more there is to this place than I'll ever be able to discover, how much there is to protect for myself and others."

It was a talisman. Several of her girls carried small symbols of the past that helped them look into an otherwise dim future. Even she carried one, though the knife sheathed at her waist was less hopeful than most.

"Hesperus, I—"

He held up a hand, brushing away the protest in her voice. "In a way, it's always reminded me of you." He lifted his broad shoulders in a shrug. "Though I am not enough of a poet to say why."

There was a smooth spot on the top of the stone where Hesperus must have worried his thumb thousands of times. The rest was shrouded in a rough exterior, as though the only way to uncover the truths hidden inside was through the constant pressure of a friendly touch.

Caledonia could think of no better comparison for herself, though she was certain Hesperus didn't recognize the perfection of his gift. He could not know that she had always imagined her girls as stones.

"Thank you, Hesperus. This is poetry enough for me." She closed her fist around the gift and added, "Next time we run the drill, I want you with Viridian Fleet."

CHAPTER NINE

Two weeks after their return to Cloudbreak Caledonia was itching to return to the sea, but every day conspired to keep her bound to land.

Rogue ships continued to arrive, Amina successfully modified a tow with enough explosive to sink a ship, and with Nettle's clever assistance, Kae was certain they were mere moments away from cracking soiltech. It all pointed to one thing: staying put.

Her days were endless rounds of finding problems and solving them while trusting that time would give them the tows and soiltech they needed to move forward with their plan. All she had to do was keep everyone prepared for the moment it came together.

Still, in the back of her mind, she could not quell the haunting voice that whispered a name over and over again like a slithering ocean breeze: Donnally. She could not subdue the ever-present fear that her brother had become the monster she was destined to kill. Her thoughts dragged her back to that moment on the *Titan* when he'd refused to go with her, and her dreams cut darker trails through her mind, conjuring memories she could not claim of the violent murders of Fivesons Decker, Venn, and Tassos.

This, at least, she could do something about.

"I'm going to talk to her," Caledonia told Oran as she slipped a jacket over her arms.

Oran stood with his back to the window of her office. Outside, storm clouds rolled slowly across the western sky, giving the room a liminal quality.

"Remi," Oran said, disapproving.

"Yes, Remi." Caledonia let defiance slip into her tone.

They'd had this conversation twice already. Each time, Oran had urged her to forget Remi's words. Even if they were true and Donnally had killed the other Fivesons, Oran argued there was nothing new that Caledonia could learn from Remi. Better to verify the information on her own and leave Remi to her recovery.

Caledonia was in the process of doing exactly that. She'd sent Gloriana and her crew out days ago to confirm the deaths of Fivesons Venn and Tassos, but now that Remi was recovered, it was harder to ignore that she was a potential source of information.

"I'm not saying you shouldn't see her. Only to be cautious. Don't let her inside your head." Oran spoke carefully, watching her as she twisted her hair into a thick braid. "I'm afraid she's already there."

"That's why I have to go," she said. "To get her out of my head."

Oran was quiet for a moment before he spoke again. "At least take the mountain with you."

As Caledonia exited the fortress, the sky above rumbled and the western distance flashed with lightning, brilliant blue against the black coil of a storm. Undeterred, Caledonia struck out for town, Sledge and Pine following close behind. Though Sledge followed like a dark cloud, Pine was the one who matched his stride to hers.

"There's only one way to get good info from a Bullet," Pine said, the opening bars to what had become a very familiar song. "Pain."

"We aren't torturing her," Sledge growled.

The dawn air should have chilled her, but adrenaline fueled her steps and even though her breath came in small white puffs, she broke into a light sweat.

"Pine," Caledonia warned.

"What choice do we have?" Pine protested. "You can't unmake a Bullet in two weeks. The only language she understands is pain and pleasure."

"We aren't torturing her," Sledge repeated, voice growing more dangerous.

"*You* don't have to." Pine tossed the answer out casually. Even now, it was easy to forget how swiftly Pine shifted between the Blade he was and the Bullet he'd been. Caledonia was suddenly reminded of the night he'd killed that Bullet in Slipmark, how he'd moved to intercept before she'd fully registered the threat.

Pine knew Bullets better than Caledonia could, but that didn't exactly recommend his methods.

"Withdrawal is torture enough. This is just a discussion," Caledonia said, putting the matter to bed as they journeyed through the heart of Cloudbreak.

Once, these meandering alleys had been indecipherable to Caledonia; they'd morphed as she passed, vendors claiming and relinquishing patches of rock almost as soon as she'd seen them. Now Caledonia traversed the streets with ease, weaving her way through the Body Quarter, then cutting between the chaotic press of hastily erected cabins that housed the crews of rogue ships until she came to the barracks that scooped across the far northern edge of town.

In the wake of the battle, Cloudbreak had gone from scheming black market town to burgeoning military operation. There were still vendors hawking their contraband wares, but they were fewer and farther between. In their place were people: families, crews, recovering Bullets, all waiting for Caledonia's team to bring them into the fight.

Thunder boomed, closer now, and lightning splintered across the clouds, briefly illuminating pale layers of mountain ridges to the west. The wind was picking up, bringing with it the promise of colder weather on the other side of that storm. They ducked inside the barracks a second before the clouds shuddered and unleashed a sudden, torrential rain.

"Cala!" Ares stood abruptly, his voice soft with surprise as he rose from behind a desk covered in stacks of yellowed paper. "I'm sorry, I wasn't expecting you."

Ares had come a long way since they'd found him on *Electra*, since he'd drifted through the hallways of the *Luminous Wake* like a shadow. He'd struggled with dreams and nightmares, fear more than anger. It wasn't what Caledonia would have expected of the boy she'd known as a child. Ares had been the sunniest of them. He'd been daring and bold and looked for any excuse to have fun. He'd also had a temper that flared hot and fast. Caledonia had assumed that would make him a better Bullet, or a tougher one. But she'd been wrong.

Being a Bullet had stolen all the joy from Ares's eyes; it had smothered the fire behind his temper and left him with nothing but coals.

"This is an unplanned visit," Caledonia admitted. "I'm here to speak with Remi."

"Ah, I don't think you're going to get what you want from her," Ares said, folding his arms protectively against his chest. "We lost two of the other Bullets last week. They, um, we couldn't get them through their sweats."

Regret was tight across Ares's features and exhaustion tugged at the corners of his eyes. He'd been up all night. Possibly longer.

"I'm sorry, Ares."

He shrugged his shoulders, then leaned heavily against

the wall. It happened at least once in each new group. Bullets started receiving doses of Silt around twelve or thirteen turns. After that, they got it every day with few exceptions. Caledonia had learned that withholding the drug was sometimes used as a punishment, a reminder that Bullets needed Aric and should do exactly as he asked. But some had received it so regularly for so long that their bodies simply didn't know how to function without it.

"More made it through than didn't," Ares continued. "But that doesn't make it any easier. For them."

Caledonia understood what he wasn't saying. Whether or not they'd chosen this was irrelevant. They'd lost some of their own and they were bound to resent Caledonia for that.

"Take me to Remi."

They followed Ares down the dimly lit corridor past rows of doors that looked exactly the same. Each was locked from the outside and made of a single piece of hard wood with a small window the size of a fist punched through at eye level. Given more time, they might have installed self-healing glass over the windows, but that was a luxury, not a necessity.

Ares stopped, then pulled the keys from his pocket and unlocked the door. "Incoming, Remi. Captain's here to talk."

The door opened on a figure that was not quite what Caledonia remembered. She seemed smaller now, huddled at the edge of her cot with her back in the corner and knees pulled up in front. Her auburn hair was cut short and it curled tightly toward her scalp. When she smiled, her mouth was wide and sharp.

"Morning, Captain." Her voice was raw but determined. "Come to count the bodies?"

"Good morning, Remi. I was very sorry to hear about your people." Caledonia ignored the sneer that curled Remi's upper lip. Sledge had told her once that this stage of withdrawal was sometimes worse than the pain of detox. Aric's emotional claws bit much deeper than his physiological ones.

"Just the ones you let die here? Or all of them?" Remi asked, a dangerous challenge in her eye. "Seems to me you only have room for sorrow when there's no glory to be had."

"There is no glory in this fight," Caledonia countered. "There's surviving and there's dying, but I've never seen glory on the Bullet Seas."

"I have." Remi's voice softened and her eyes unfocused as she let a memory pull her away. "I will again."

Glory. Always glory. Aric had used that word so effectively it had galvanized his entire army. The deadly combination of glorious rhetoric and Silt had given his Bullets the justification they needed to take children from their parents and turn them into soldiers. Aric's glory was a promise. One as violent as the guns he put in their hands.

"Glory shouldn't have to come at the expense of so many others," Caledonia said.

"That is the only way." Remi laughed. "Sacrifice is the truest kind of glory. To give yourself, your life in the service of someone so much greater than you, is glorious."

The thought sent a chill down Caledonia's spine. How had Aric—and now Lir—convinced so many people that killing and dying for them was the truest form of anything? But she knew the answer. Silt, food, power. Aric had figured out what people needed and then he learned how to control it. Lir had learned from him and decided he could do it better.

Somehow, some part of Remi had resisted that power. Enough to choose to follow Caledonia to Cloudbreak where she knew this would be her future. The question now was whether or not she would keep making that choice now that she'd experienced the reality. In some ways it would be easier to do as Pine suggested and keep every Bullet they collected under lock and key until the fight was over. But as dangerous as it was to extend trust to a former Bullet, it was the only way to truly win in the end.

"I won't let you die for him, Remi," Caledonia said. "I want you to stay here. I want you to get strong again and make your own choices. As soon as you're healthy, you can do just that: choose."

Remi's eyes watered as she watched Caledonia with a kind of agony. Her brow creased and her lips quivered as if something she needed were just out of reach. She drew a shuddering breath and said, "I don't want your mercy, Caledonia Styx."

"You have it, regardless."

This time Remi's laughter was disbelieving. "Why?"

Caledonia's answer came without a breath of hesitation. "Because mercy is what is left when glory fails us."

For a second, Remi only watched Caledonia with her mouth partly open, as if she couldn't make those words make sense in her own mind. Then she began to laugh. It started in her throat and bubbled up until there were tears streaming out of her bleary eyes.

"Mercy." She pushed the word out between spurts of laughter. "Mercy, mercy, mercy. You want to fight this fight with *mercy*? Caledonia, I think I overestimated you. Maybe Lir has, too."

On the other side of the door, Sledge made a low sound in his throat. The conversation Caledonia had intended to have with Remi was no longer the one she needed to have. Dismissing everything else she'd come to say, she settled on a new approach.

"I have one question for you, Remi."

"Only one? But I have so many answers to give. Don't you want to know what I know about Lir? Where he is and what he's doing now? Or Donnally? Wouldn't you like to know what kind of face he made as he murdered Fiveson Decker?"

Caledonia stepped forward, ignoring everything except the information she wanted in this moment. "Why did you come with us?"

Remi blinked, unable to mask her immediate surprise before her mouth returned to its sneer and she exhaled slowly. "Maybe I just wanted to see it all for myself."

"The inside of a barrack? Cloudbreak? Me?"

"How it all ends." This time Remi's smile spread slowly, exquisitely across her wide mouth into the kind of expression that suggested Remi's mind might never recover from decades of Silt.

"How what ends?" Caledonia regretted the question immediately.

Remi tipped her head back, sighing sweetly as she said, "You, of course. And him. And the two of you and the whole salt-sick world."

There was nothing more Caledonia could learn from this woman.

Yet, as Caledonia left the room, she felt a pinch of remorse for Remi. And foreboding for herself, too. Though on opposite sides, whatever end was coming for them all, it would be neither pleasant nor glorious.

CHAPTER TEN

Caledonia's chambers were one level below the observatory, a suite with one window in a curved wall overlooking the cliffs. The bedroom itself was larger than anything she'd ever had on a ship, with space for a mattress of dense foam that resisted the chill of the stone beneath.

Tossing her jacket on the foot of the bed, she lit the trio of candles on her low end table and went to scrub her face of the day's grime in her private bathing chamber.

A knock sounded at her door. Three firm raps of a knuckle told her who was behind it.

"Come in," she called, dragging a towel over her cheeks.

Oran stepped inside, pushing the door closed behind him. He was freshly washed, and water clung to the ends of his black hair, making them shine in the dim light. A simple long-sleeved shirt stretched comfortably across his chest and shoulders in a warm shade of brown just darker than his skin. The ends of the shirt were untucked, draping low over pants that hugged his thighs.

Without a word, Oran took three slow steps in her direction. His eyes locked on hers and didn't let go. Caledonia felt a knot in her stomach relax just as the beat of her heart sped up.

When he was only a few inches away, he paused.

Caledonia leaned forward and pressed her lips to his. Oran's hands slid along her waist, thumbs efficiently freeing her shirt from her pants. The chill in her skin zipped over every part of her as he pulled her body against his, flattening warm palms against her bare back.

She kissed him slowly as he walked her backward toward the bed. She pulled his bottom lip between her teeth as he lowered her to the slim mattress and gasped as his fingers slid along her ribs.

These were the only moments when Caledonia's mind released her problems and uncertainties. Cloudbreak demanded more of her than her crew ever had, but when Oran slipped into her chambers at night, she could put it all aside for a short time. These were moments when she made demands for herself, when Oran was the only person she allowed to take up space in her mind.

Later, when they were both flushed and out of breath, Caledonia slipped out of bed to prepare the bitter tea that would prevent her from conceiving a child. The drink warmed her insides even as her skin cooled. When she'd drained her cup, she slid beneath the blanket once more and pillowed her cheek against Oran's shoulder, enjoying the feeling of his arms wrapped around her and his fingers toying with her hair until they stilled suddenly.

"What's wrong?" he asked.

"Nothing." Her answer was too immediate. She knew it as soon as she'd said it, but it was too late to take it back.

"All right, nothing's wrong." He caught her hand in his, holding it against his scarred chest. "Then tell me what you're thinking about."

"Everything," she admitted with a long sigh. "I keep coming back to the Fivesons. Lir took out his competition, but he also thinned his own ranks, risking gaps in loyalty at best and sowing dissention at worst. Why take that risk? Is the power play, the symbolism, really worth it?"

Oran was quiet while she spoke, letting his fingers drift lazily up and down her forearm. The tickling sensation made it difficult to think clearly.

"They—we—were dangerous to him," Oran said at last. "Aric may have called us sons, and we may have called each other brother, but we were the furthest thing from it. Maybe Venn and Decker would have been loyal for a while, but Tassos? He hated Lir more than anyone."

"More than me?" The words were out of Caledonia's mouth before she could stop them.

Oran's fingers stilled in their path along her skin, then he pulled her closer. "Differently."

Caledonia hated to ask him these questions. Whenever she did, she watched him drift into the past, where he was forced to confront the terrible deeds that had made him a Fiveson. It left him dimmed for hours, sometimes days, after.

"How many different ways are there to hate Lir?" she asked with a teasing smile, but Oran's expression only darkened.

"Tassos was a threat for more than one reason, though," Oran continued. "And I suspect Lir killed the others because he needed Tassos out of the picture. Easier to take out all three at once rather than kill one and let Decker and Venn grow resentful or paranoid."

"What do you mean?" Caledonia asked, pressing two fingers against Oran's jaw to tip his face toward her. "Why was Tassos more of a threat than the others?"

"Because Tassos controlled the Net, and the Net isn't only there to prevent people from fleeing the Bullet Seas. It's there to protect what's behind it."

Caledonia was instantly alert. She'd heard stories of what was on the other side of the Net, but growing up, they'd all been about escaping the Bullet Seas. Nearly every tale she'd heard told of boundless seas and arable lands, but every so often there was talk of something else, too. Something Aric protected at all costs because without it, there was no Silt.

"There's a rig in the South Seas, a massive structure drilled directly into the seabed that Lir has to control if he wants to keep the loyalty of his Bullets," Oran added.

"What so special about it?" Even as she asked, Caledonia felt that she knew. That the stories she'd heard whispered as a child had contained more truth than she'd realized.

Oran's lips bowed into a small frown. "The first thing Aric did when he learned how to produce the drug was to compartmentalize its production. The rig is where all harvested baleflowers are sent to be ground into Silt and pressed into pills. With Tassos in control of the Net, he stood between Lir and Silt. Even if Lir had the blossoms, it would take more time than he had to build his own factory and produce his own Silt." Oran drew in a deep breath as he considered all the possibilities. "If we're right and he had started thinning Silt rations already, he had to kill Tassos."

There was a chilling sort of finality to the way Oran said those words. He understood Lir's motivation entirely. And the frightening thing was, Caledonia did, too. This made perfect sense to her. So much that she could almost imagine coming to a similar conclusion.

Caledonia shook the dark thoughts from her mind. She pressed her face against Oran's chest and gave a small growl of disgust.

"I want to sail *now*. Attack the Holster, take Lir out, and end this for good."

Oran sat up, resting his back against the cold stone and fixing stern eyes on her. "This fight is bigger than Lir, Caledonia, you know that. You're the one who showed us."

"My fight is with Lir." Anger bubbled through her veins. Everything inside her cried out for Lir's blood. She wanted him dead. For her parents. For Pi's parents. For Redtooth and Lace and Triple. And for Donnally, who he'd stolen from her. Twice.

"We both know that isn't true," Oran said with a humorless smile. "I think you have a habit of convincing yourself your goals are smaller than they are. This fight didn't end with Aric and it certainly won't end with Lir. Not if your goal isn't the person but the system they've created."

That was nearly impossible to believe. There might be other threats, but no one would ever supplant Lir in Caledonia's mind. Not even Aric had loomed as large. Lir would always be the burning core of her anger. "No one matters as much as Lir."

At this, Oran shook his head lightly. "Maybe that's what it feels like. Anger can do that. Rage can do that. Make you feel small when you are anything but. You, Caledonia, are bigger than your anger."

She wasn't sure that she was. For five turns, she'd kept her anger close and bright. It was like smoldering embers, a constant, quiet pain buried deep in her heart. Most of the time, she kept it under control, but sometimes it burned too hot and all she could think about was Lir.

"I don't know how long that's going to last," she said sadly.

Oran leaned in to cup her face between his palms, bending close to whisper, "I know you. And you will make it last long enough to get this done. Just—just make sure there's something left for after."

Her cheeks warmed and she felt the constant pressure of her worries becoming less under his touch. "You mean something left for you?"

"Yes." He tipped forward and caught her bottom lip between his teeth, lightly kissing before pulling away. He kissed her again and Caledonia let him lure her from the swift current of her anger.

"How do you know you'll still want whatever that is?" she asked with a teasing smile.

"Because I love you."

The words seemed to surprise them both. Caledonia pulled away sharply.

Oran watched her with a steady, unflinching gaze. Expectant and somehow also resigned to whatever she said next. As if now that he'd said the words, he knew their truth and was ready to accept whatever she said in return.

"Oran," she said and then there were no more words. Her heart beat a hasty, incomprehensible rhythm in her chest and her mind refused to settle on any single thought. Did she love him? How did he love her? Why had he chosen *this* moment to say it? When she was unprepared. Had considered no course, no strategy, no possible means of response.

"Oran," she repeated in a desperate attempt to trick her mind into finding an answer when all she wanted to do was ask her command crew for options.

The skin around his eyes tightened and he opened his mouth to speak when there was a pounding at the door.

"Captain!" Pine's voice filled the silence behind the pounding. "We've got news."

CHAPTER ELEVEN

By the time Caledonia and Oran arrived in the observatory, the rest of the command crew and Hesperus were already gathered.

It was late. The curtains were pulled against the chilly night air and a fire had been set in the low-lying fire pit. Kae pressed a cup of hot teaco into Caledonia's hand as she entered. Around the room her crew bore signs of having been roused from sleep. All except for Amina and Hime, who were bundled as though they'd just returned from town. And Nettle, who bounced on her toes and looked like she was physically restraining herself from speaking.

"Captain's on deck," Pine announced, fixing Oran with a dead-eyed stare.

The room snapped to attention, heads swiveling toward the sight of their leader. Caledonia took one of the seats near the fire, directly across from Amina and Hime.

"Captain," Amina said with a sharp nod. "We have a problem."

Behind Amina, Hesperus glowered at everyone. His jaw was

clenched and he bristled with energy, suggesting that the problem was something more of an imminent threat.

"I'm listening," Caledonia said, setting her teaco aside.

"A rogue ship came in after sundown," Amina began. "They went through all the usual channels: the ship was searched before moving into port, the crew questioned, everything seemed in order. Hime and I were doing rounds on the dock when they were assigned a berth and began to unload their cargo." Here she leaned forward, elbows pressed to knees, expression stony. "Their cargo included everything they needed to build a pulse bomb."

Pulse bombs weren't explosive in the way of mag bombs, missiles, or even star blossoms. They weren't incendiary, they were acoustic, made for shaking apart the foundations of buildings or shearing off the side of a cliff.

"Why wasn't it caught immediately?" Pisces demanded. "Everyone assigned to intake is supposed to know what they're looking for."

"They do," Tin said, rushing to defend the teams she worked so hard to organize. "They all do."

"But pulse bombs haven't been used in ages," Oran supplied. "Their pieces look practically harmless in isolation and Aric stopped their production because they're useless at sea."

"Not so useless if your target is basically a mountain," Pine shot back.

"Cloudbreak," Hesperus growled. "My city is their target."

"Yes," Amina confirmed without turning to look at the man towering behind her. "But there's more. A single pulse bomb is bad in isolation, but not enough to do more than a little damage. With two or more, they work in conjunction. They amplify each other."

"What happens then?" Pisces asked.

Hime raised her eyes and signed, *They blow a hole in the foundation of Cloudbreak. The entire city could crumble in an instant.*

"How many were they planning on building?" Caledonia asked. "How many would it take to destroy the city?"

"They only had enough to build a single bomb." Amina's answer lacked the reassurance Caledonia was hoping for. "I'm not sure how many it would take. Five? Six? And depending on where they're placed, it may take less. These things have a way of setting off chain reactions within structures . . . or mountains."

"That's it?" Pisces's expression went slack.

"That's good though, right?" Nettle was huddled close to the fire, knees drawn to her chin, all her earlier eagerness sapped by the news. "There was only one and we got it."

No one could return Nettle's hope, because they were all thinking the same thing: if they almost missed this one, how many others had they already missed?

"Where's the crew?" Caledonia stood, straightening her shirt and twisting her hair back into a braid.

"Just outside." Hesperus clenched his fists at his sides. "It was a small boat, so there are only two of them."

"Bring them in."

The room wasn't set up for interrogation, but Caledonia stepped away from the chairs ringed around the fire to stand with her back to the observatory windows. Pine and Sledge returned with the two men and pushed them to their knees on the hard stone, taking positions behind them.

The men were wide-eyed and strained to keep their balance with hands bound behind their backs. One of them was sandy-skinned with a short beard that wrapped his face in ruddy bristles. The other had skin the pale brown of seashells with hair shaved clean on one side.

"Are you both Bullets?" Caledonia asked. "Or only one of you?"

Neither spoke, but the sandy-skinned man seemed to relax ever so slightly. As though now that he'd been caught, he didn't have to hide anymore.

Caledonia nodded and Pine stepped forward, quickly divesting the man of his jacket to reveal the skin of his bare arms. There, along his left, were four orange scars.

"And you?" Caledonia asked the other man, whose mouth had gone slack with true horror.

"I didn't know," he muttered, shaking his head once. "I—I didn't know what he was doing."

Sledge had him on his feet in an instant, hauling him away and leaving the Bullet behind.

"How many pulse bombs are already in my city?" Caledonia

asked, crouching to study the man's face. Wrinkles creased the skin around dark ringed eyes, and gray scattered through his russet brown hair. This close, Caledonia could see just how hard he worked to keep his gaze level and alert, obscuring the effects of the Silt that doubtless coursed through his blood.

"I only brought the one," he said with an awkward shrug of his bound arms.

"What were you planning to do with that one?" Caledonia tilted her face closer to his, letting him feel the threat of her presence.

"I—" He paused, as if unable to find the lie he needed.

"Who were you supposed to meet with?" she pressed. "And when?"

This time he didn't even try to find a lie. He smiled, shrugged, and tilted his head to one side. "Doesn't matter now, does it?"

Before Caledonia could respond, Oran cast an urgent look in her direction.

"Take him away," she said to Pine, and then to Oran, "What is it?"

"Captain, if he's already missed his check-in, or if there are others in town, it won't be long before they know he's been caught. And if that happens—"

"Oh, hell." Was it already too late? Caledonia dismissed the question. If she wanted to save Cloudbreak, there was only one way to do it. "We need a full sweep of the town. Pi, Hime, wake the crew. Only people we know we can trust. Amina, I need you to make sure they know what they're looking for; Tin, organize the teams; Hesperus, create a city-wide search pattern."

They were gone as soon as the orders were given. In their wake, Caledonia's mind reeled with the possibilities. How many bombs had they missed? She had to assume there were others. Should she order an evacuation just in case? They'd always predicted Lir would attempt to infiltrate the city. Every layer of security they'd added was in preparation for that inevitability.

But no plan was ever perfect.

"Oran, I need to get on the ground, I need to—"

Before she could finish her thought, a thunderous bomb shook the ground beneath her feet.

CHAPTER TWELVE

Dust rained down from the ceiling and cracks appeared in the columns supporting the domed roof above. The rumble that shook the ground settled, then the entire structure began to quake. Outside, the horn released a constant stream of staccato beats signaling one thing: evacuation.

"We need to move, now!" Caledonia looked from Oran to Nettle. Everyone else was gone.

They dove down the stairwell, dodging increasingly large chunks of stone shaken free by the vibrations pulsing through the massive building. Nettle took the lead and Oran pulled up the rear, keeping Caledonia between them as they joined the rush of people now trying to flee the crumbling stronghold.

"Make a hole!" Oran roared over Caledonia's shoulder, attempting to clear her path, but it was no use. Everyone in the stronghold was trying to leave at once and there was nowhere for them to go but down.

"This way!" Nettle cried, darting out of the main stairwell and into a treacherously narrow corridor.

Caledonia ducked into the dim space, holding her breath as they rushed along. The ground continued to tremble, and she was sure that at any moment the small tunnel might come crashing down around them.

They emerged on the western edge of the stronghold, where a steep stairwell cut directly down the mountainside. Ahead, the town was unrecognizable. Lights flared at odd angles, fires burned throughout, dust and smoke created a dense haze, and gunfire popped continuously.

But who was firing? As soon as she'd thought the question, Caledonia knew the answer: whoever had planted those bombs had had more than enough time to plan a raid on Hesperus's armory. The Bullets were using Cloudbreak's own weapons against them.

Fury made Caledonia careless and she stumbled down the last of the stairs twisting her ankle sharply beneath her. Oran's hand was on her elbow a second later, hauling her back to her feet. Pain speared up her leg at the movement, but she pushed through it and ran.

Their path took them into town, where they turned at the first road that cut west. The ground shook and trembled and fire coursed through the streets, jumping from tent to tent, chewing up homes and supplies. The air was laced with screams, punctuated by gunfire, and beneath it all the mountain itself groaned as the cliffs fractured and sent large boulders crashing down on the fleet below.

Suddenly, the sound of gunfire was very near. Caledonia

reached for her weapon, pulling it from its holster as a familiar face raced into the path ahead of them. Remi's expression was full of glee, her eyes wild with joy as she spotted Caledonia and raised her gun.

A shot snapped through the air. Remi's smile froze on her face and she slumped to the ground.

Pine appeared a moment later, his gun clutched in one hand. "We need to move," he urged, lowering the pistol to his side. He turned shrewd eyes on the layers of tent and flame behind them. "There's more of them and they're sweeping the city."

"Have you seen any of the others?" Caledonia asked, her eyes on Remi's fallen body as they hurried past.

Pine shook his head. "I was barely out of the stronghold when it hit. I didn't see anything but dust."

"You're supposed to be heading for Red Fleet," she reminded him.

"I was cut off," he answered. "They'll go without me."

Caledonia nodded even as she imagined the spike of pain Sledge would feel when Pine didn't show up. But if all went well, it would be temporary.

They moved cautiously, eyes alert and guns ready. Every so often, another Bullet appeared in their path, or surprised them from behind. The four of them fired without mercy, dispatching every Bullet who moved to stop them.

Once they were on the western outskirts of town, no Bullets

pursued. Apart from crew members of the *Luminous Wake*, they saw no one else. Everyone was following their evacuation orders. Or attempting to. Without the lifts, getting down to the docks was infinitely more difficult, and even if they managed it, Caledonia wasn't sure how many ships would be left to carry her crews to safety.

As the trail inclined toward the mountains, Pine set their pace at a brisk jog. Caledonia's ankle ached more and more until it became clear that she was slowing them down.

"Pine, Nettle, go ahead. Tell them we're on our way."

Though a protest landed immediately in Pine's expression, he swallowed it and turned to chase Nettle up the mountainside. Caledonia and Oran continued more slowly, each step sending fresh pain shooting through her ankle. By the time they reached the cherry orchard, the town below was fully aflame. High on the southern wall, the stronghold was slumped and misshapen, its walls carved out or missing altogether, while smoke poured from every opening. On the very top, the observatory was cracked down the middle and Caledonia found herself thinking of those dense, blue curtains that shrouded the room from cold winds and rain. The crown of Hesperus's reign had been split in half and now lay in ruins.

As she watched, what remained of the stronghold gave a deep rumble and began to collapse in on itself. The sound reached them a second before the earth beneath their feet shivered with the force of a massive underground explosion.

The ground trembled harder and the remains of the stronghold vanished inside a destructive cloud, and Caledonia thought of Hesperus's words: "Nothing will ever convince me to leave Cloudbreak. It's that simple."

"Hesperus," she said. Caledonia knew without knowing that the Sly King had not responded to the call for evacuation. He had remained in his stronghold until the very end; perhaps he'd even added to that final explosion. It wouldn't surprise her at all to learn he'd made sure that no one could ever take his fortress.

"Let's move," Oran said, gesturing for them to stay low as they moved through the orchard of cherry trees.

Here, the grass had grown tall in the late summer warmth and it hissed against their legs as they ran. Ahead, they could see shadowy figures darting into the ribbon of pine trees that led to the work camp, all heading for the *Luminous Wake*. Compared to the roar of the town, the gentle quiet beyond the trees was unsettling. It was just another normal night up here.

"Lift's busted," Folly said as they climbed to the entrance. "Stairs aren't much better, but passable."

"Thank you, Folly." Caledonia smothered a wince at the sharp twinge in her ankle.

Oran moved ahead of her down the stairs, offering his hand whenever stones obscured the way. After running several miles on a twisted ankle, this was somehow worse, and every step sent fresh shivers of pain up Caledonia's leg.

Finally, they spilled into the hidden harbor, eyes landing on the shape of the *Luminous Wake*, sun pips glowing pale blue against the cavern's black walls. The sounds of her crew preparing the ship ready to sail echoed softly over the water. Here, tucked away from the flames and the gunfire, it was almost peaceful. The walls bore no trace of the ruin they'd just left, the air no hint of smoke. But there was a quiet anger in the scattered voices of the crew.

Oran stayed by Caledonia's side, and together they boarded the small tender and paddled out to the *Luminous Wake*. The second she was aboard, a familiar voice called out, "Captain on deck!"

Pisces. Relief stole her breath so suddenly, she nearly gasped recovering it.

All eyes turned to her. Their faces were dusted in faint blue light and their eyes carried the same anger she'd heard in their voices. She looked from one to the next, naming them in her head, composing a list of those who had made it. She spotted Tin standing near the bridge, one side of her face covered in soot, a small notebook clutched in her hands.

"Do you have a report for me?" Caledonia asked. As she drew closer to Tin, she saw that the smear she'd taken for ash from afar was a rich, glistening red. "Tin, are you hurt?" Caledonia raised a hand to the young woman's cheek, tentatively searching for a wound and finding none.

"It's not my blood," Tin said, her voice so soft it barely landed.

She didn't provide any additional information and Caledonia

didn't ask. Now was not the time to feel the full brunt of their losses.

"Are you with me?" Caledonia asked, voice hard. In another handful of minutes, they'd be underway. No matter who was on board and who wasn't. There was no telling what awaited them outside of this sheltered cove, and Caledonia needed everyone sharp.

Tin offered only a tight nod, turning her eyes to her notebook. "We're missing a dozen, including Amina."

"Amina was headed to the armory." Pisces stepped forward even as she turned to peer in the direction of the stairwell. "She might have run into trouble."

The armory. The Bullets had headed straight for it, Caledonia was certain. Amina was clever and quick, but none of them had expected this.

"Who else?" Caledonia waited as Tin gave her full report. Most of the crew was aboard, and they were fully stocked and armed.

"Ready to sail at your word, Captain," Tin finished, snapping her notebook shut.

"We cannot wait much longer," Pine said into Caledonia's ear. His own expression was unreadable, though Caledonia knew him well enough to see the barely there signs of distress.

"We can give them a little more time." They had lost enough tonight. Caledonia didn't intend to lose anyone else. Not if there was a chance that a few more minutes would save lives.

The crew continued in their quiet work until there was nothing left to be done. They stood ready to cast off the lines, to weigh the anchor, and to bid farewell to yet another home. And all the while, nothing moved within the stairwell.

Hime had come to stand at the rail. She'd bound her hair back in a single blue ribbon, exposing the old scar along her jaw, and she stood with her eyes pinned to the dark. She hadn't signed a word to Caledonia, but they'd sailed together long enough to know what was at stake here.

"Captain." Pisces's voice was a reluctant note. The time had come. Amina had not.

Caledonia nodded and raised her voice past a pain she feared had become a permanent fixture in her chest. "Let's go!"

As the ship rumbled to life and shoved off, Caledonia kept her eyes on her friend. She would never forget the way Hime watched the stairwell until the very last second, the way her hands clutched the rail as though hope had turned her fingers to stone. And she would certainly never forget the expression of exquisite bravery as Hime finally turned away, her chin held high and her black eyes shining in the pale blue light.

CHAPTER THIRTEEN

They sailed smoothly between the high walls of the canals. Once, these waters had seemed as chaotic and impenetrable as Cloudbreak's twisting pathways. Now they were as familiar as the workings of this ship.

Joining Nettle on the bridge, Caledonia trained her eyes on the channels that opened and closed before them. The *Luminous Wake* was broad where their first ship, the *Mors Navis*, had been sleek, which limited the paths they could take, but not so much that Caledonia had considered adopting another ship. They could have chosen from the many that had arrived in the hands of Bullets or those few sent from Hime's people in the Drowning Lands, one more similar in heft and speed to the *Mors Navis*, but after having sailed into battle aboard this old sweeper, Caledonia wasn't ready to trust another.

"Slow and steady," she reminded Nettle. Needlessly. The girl was as skilled at the helm as Caledonia had been at her age. Possibly better. But in the dark, it was difficult to tell stone from water. If they weren't careful, they'd gouge their belly or crush their nose.

"Captain." Oran appeared in the doorway, one hand pressed to the frame. "I think we have a problem." He turned to look over his shoulder, the strong line of his neck glistening with sweat.

"You think?" she asked. "Or you know?"

He turned his eyes back to her, a quiet frown pulling his brows together. "I don't think we're alone out here."

No friendly ships would be sailing these canals; it was against protocol. A few yards ahead, the channel forked in two directions. The left offered them the shortest route to the western seas. But as it was the fastest way out, it was also the fastest way in.

"Nettle, change course. Go north at the fork, not west."

"Yes, Captain."

As they neared the fork, a growling sound joined the low rumble of their own thrusters. Nettle cursed and Oran raced onto the forward deck. The northern channel was longer, less accessible from the outside, but that didn't mean a ship couldn't worm its way through.

The sound could be coming from either, and Caledonia couldn't tell the difference.

"Which one, Oran?" Caledonia called.

Nettle pulled the ship out of speed. The approaching engines grew louder, echoing off the tall walls.

Oran shook his head in frustration. "I can't tell!"

Caledonia left the bridge and raced along the nose to study the eddies in the water. An approaching ship would stir the current. Maybe not much, but enough for Caledonia to decipher which side of the fork they were coming down and choose the other path.

"Pine!" she called over her shoulder. "I need gunners on the forward deck!"

The orders echoed behind her and still she studied the dark waters where they rushed out of the two channels, neither of which looked any different from the other.

"Both!" Oran shouted, coming instantly to her side. "Captain, they're coming down both channels."

For a swift and terrible second, the meaning of that sentence left Caledonia speechless. There was more than one ship. Her only way forward was blocked by incoming vessels and the *Luminous Wake* was far too large to turn around.

Caledonia could call the ship to a halt and they could brace for impact, but even if she succeeded in subduing the incoming ships, she would still be trapped in these canals. And that, she realized, was exactly the point. To rush her into picking one direction where she would be forced to fight head on while the other ship swept around to flank them. Neither channel was an option.

Knowing that what she was about to do was either going to get them killed or get them free, Caledonia returned to the bridge with hurried steps.

"Nettle, I need you to maintain the helm and I need you to trust me."

"I trust you," Nettle responded instantly.

"I am going to be your eyes. I need you to be my hands." Satisfied by the spark of recognition that flared in the hazel rings of Nettle's eyes, she turned to the rest of the bridge crew. "Reverse thrusters, engines to half speed."

Alarm marked each of their faces as they understood her intentions.

"Now," she said, voice even and deadly calm.

"Incoming!" Pine shouted seconds before the first hail of bullets sang against the hull.

"Reversing thrusters!" shouted one voice.

"Engines to half speed!" shouted another.

"I am your hands, Captain," Nettle said, standing close enough that Caledonia could hear the tremor on her breath.

Two Bullet ships roared out of the channels, guns firing and lights flaring now that they'd spotted their prey. They were smaller, faster, lighter, and as the *Luminous Wake* reversed and gained speed, the Bullets gave chase with vicious glee.

Caledonia turned her eyes away and studied the channel now rushing up behind them. She stood with her shoulder to Nettle's, ready to direct her hands.

"Steady," she said to Nettle. "Now two degrees port."

Nettle responded by turning the ship exactly as Caledonia

requested. The *Luminous Wake* soared down the center of the canal, and a fresh round of bullets pierced her nose.

"Engines to three-quarter speed," Caledonia ordered. "Nettle, one degree port. Good. Now . . . two starboard."

The walls of the canal blurred in Caledonia's peripheral vision. Nettle stared straight ahead, her grip tight against the wheel, her lips set in a steely line as she reacted to Caledonia's commands as seamlessly as if they were her own. But when a bullet shattered against the self-healing glass inches from her face, her fingers jerked and so did the ship. The movement sent them sharply to port, the hull scraping along the wall of the channel with a scream of metal against stone.

Half of the bridge crew hit the ground. Caledonia was thrown against the wall, her head smacking against the steel barrier. Pain burst behind her eyes, her vision flashing white as she regained her feet.

"Three degrees starboard, Nettle, NOW!"

Nettle did as she commanded, pulling the ship off the wall and back into the center of the canal.

"Cover!" Oran shouted on the forward deck just before a missile exploded against the hull.

Caledonia felt the sudden flush of warmth at her back and knew without looking that the missile had struck their nose. Judging by the stuttering vibration in the deck, it had struck them hard.

This wasn't sustainable. But it didn't have to be. It just had to last a little longer.

"We're closing in," she told Nettle, keeping her voice steady. "Just hold on."

"Three hundred yards, Captain," Harwell said, having rightly guessed her mind. He stood by the map table tucked in the back corner of the small room, one hand braced against the bulkhead for stability.

She nodded, her mind on the task of getting them safely through those three hundred yards. Though her crew had spent plenty of time training in the canals, including reversal maneuvers, they'd never trained at these speeds. It was hard enough to thread these narrow channels when you were pointed in the right direction.

But she had the finest crew on the seas.

"Engines to full," she ordered.

There was collective shift in the room, a ratcheting of tension visible only in the sudden press of lips or narrowing of eyes. All except for Nettle. If anything, the order seemed to relax her, as though the final piece of this outrageous plan had fallen into place and there was nothing left to surprise her. In that way, she and Caledonia were exactly alike; they didn't crack under pressure, they settled beneath it.

Blood slipped down from Caledonia's temple, but the pain was gone, replaced by the rush of battle. All the uncertainty and sorrow she'd felt as they fled Cloudbreak was muted beneath the demands of the moment. Here, in the midst of battle, her mind was clear and her heart calm.

Another missile exploded against the hull, this time with enough force to send the ship skimming against the wall. Rocks rained down from high above as Caledonia issued instructions to Nettle.

"Two hundred yards, Captain!" Harwell called in a voice pulled taut.

"Be prepared for a full reverse on my mark! We need to be fast, our redirect as tight as we've ever done." Caledonia looked over the familiar faces of her bridge crew, knowing they understood her intentions.

They'd made these canals their own in the past six moons. The Bullets pursuing them had the immediate advantage, but Caledonia had laid a trap for them long ago. Of course, when she'd set the charges that would bring down a small section of the walls, she hadn't imagined approaching the site in reverse. And she hadn't imagined needing to change directions.

"One hundred yards!" Harwell's warning came amid a fresh hail of bullets.

"Pi," Caledonia said without taking her eyes off the dark waters ahead.

"On it." Pisces was already shouting for Pine as she left the bridge, readying the gunners to provide cover when the *Luminous Wake* made her move.

"Fifty!" Harwell called

"On my mark, Nettle," Caledonia said quietly. At her side, Nettle was breathing evenly, her expression steely as she steered by Caledonia's command. "Engines to half power!"

The ship slowed beneath their feet, giving the Bullets room to assault their nose with a fury of explosives. Caledonia ignored it all. Whatever damage they took, they would deal with it. Her only concern at the moment was making sure she had a crew left to do the dealing.

"Twenty-five!"

"Kill the engines! Ready on thrusters!"

Caledonia searched the dark strip of sky soaring above the channel walls. Behind her, the Bullets roared, and she heard the heavy plunk of hull puncher harpoons hitting her nose. She ground her teeth at the sound.

"Fifteen!"

The cliff wall to their right was nearly at an end. If she gave the order too soon, they'd destroy themselves. If she gave it too late, this wouldn't work at all. She needed to give the order at precisely the right second and then trust her crew to change directions on the head of a pin, leaving no room for the Bullet ships to get in front of them.

Caledonia took a deep breath. *Blood. Gunpowder. Salt.*

The ship slowed beneath her feet, its nose sliding past the end of that cliff wall. "Now!" she called.

The ship growled as thrusters stopped them in their tracks and pushed their nose sharply to starboard. The maneuver exposed their port side to the Bullet ships, who wasted no time in renewing their attack.

Pine's gunners returned fire, doing their best to provide cover as the *Luminous Wake* swung in a steady arc.

Then, finally, a new channel opened before them, empty and waiting.

"Engines to full!" Caledonia called.

They soared forward, leaving the two Bullet ships scrambling for speed in their wake.

Just as the two ships made to round the bend, Caledonia turned to Harwell, who stood ready with the remote in his hands. "Hit the button, Harwell."

"Aye, Captain," he said.

Behind them, the top of the canal walls exploded outward. Boulders crashed down on the two Bullet ships, driving their noses into the water and punching massive holes in their decks.

They vanished inside dust and rock and did not reappear.

CHAPTER FOURTEEN

"Engines to half speed. Harwell, plot a new course out of here. Nettle, release the helm for a minute and follow me."

Nettle hesitated so briefly Caledonia almost missed it, but she stepped aside, giving the helm over and following Caledonia outside. Quiet echoes of the eruption rumbled along the canal walls, sending smaller stones skittering onto the deck of the *Luminous Wake*. The crew hurried to assess the damage, every one of them aware that the danger might not be over just yet.

Caledonia directed Nettle to the rail. "Three deep breaths," she said.

A frown appeared on Nettle's slender lips, but she complied. Closing her eyes, she filled her lungs three times, releasing each breath in a slow, steady stream. When she opened her eyes again, a thin wall of resistance had crumbled. Her shoulders deflated and the tension she'd clung to while driving the ship backward at high speeds without being able to see where she was going lifted, leaving her shuddering in the rush of wind.

Caledonia let her feel it all, and then she pulled the girl against her own chest, wrapping her arms firmly around Nettle's slender shoulders.

"Good work," Caledonia said, brushing a hand down the back of Nettle's hair.

"I don't know why I'm shaking."

"If you weren't, I'd be concerned," Caledonia soothed.

"You never shake." Nettle sounded disappointed in herself, and for that Caledonia felt a stab of guilt.

"You just never see it," she admitted. "I trembled for hours after we sailed through that whirl. I just have more practice hiding it."

Nettle was quiet for a minute, shoulders shivering against Caledonia's touch. It was easy to forget how young she was. She'd joined this crew with such insistent bravado and proven herself both brave and skilled. Giving her control of the helm had been one of the most natural decisions Caledonia had ever made. Nettle demanded responsibility in a way that placed her on equal footing with everyone else in Caledonia's mind, but she was barely fourteen turns. And here she was, having just carried them through an impossible situation in the wake of a tremendous loss, trying desperately to hold on to her stony exterior.

Caledonia struggled to mark the moments when her crew was more in need of a kind word than a stern one, but she could see this clearly. Cloudbreak had been Nettle's home before it had been any of theirs. Hesperus, Mino, and Kae were her family, and for all they knew, all three of them were gone.

"You shouldn't hide that sort of thing," Nettle admonished her captain. "Hiding it from us doesn't make us stronger, you know. We know you're not made of steel."

"I wish I were."

Laughing lightly, Nettle leaned back. Her round cheeks were flushed around the delicate scrolls of her scars. "That's not a real wish, Caledonia."

Caledonia smiled. "I'm allowed a ridiculous wish now and again."

"If you say so," Nettle said with a suspicious twist of her mouth. Then, with another deep breath, she pulled away from Caledonia's embrace. "Do you want some good news, Captain?"

"Now is the perfect time for good news," Caledonia answered, unsure what to expect.

"We did it," Nettle started, her eyes glossy with tears. "Kae and I. Earlier tonight, just before everything happened. We cracked soiltech."

"You—" It was so far from what she'd been expecting to hear that for a second, she didn't believe it. "Soiltech." She repeated the word.

Nettle laughed again, this time with real joy. "Yes. We were still working on it when we were called to the meeting, and I grabbed it. I thought I'd be able to show you then. But, well, the point is I know how to make it work."

"Nettle, that is great news," Caledonia answered, voice strained.

"With the right supplies, we can make more," Nettle promised, popping up on her toes.

It was the smallest bit of light in an otherwise dark night. The smallest of victories.

"I will do everything I can to get you those supplies," Caledonia said with a smile. "For now, keep it safe."

"Yes, Captain."

Caledonia studied her for a long minute before letting go. One day, Nettle would command her own ship. She would be smart and skilled and good, and Caledonia would do everything in her power to ensure that the challenges facing them today would not be the ones facing Nettle as she matured into a brilliant captain.

The thought swept the wind from Caledonia's lungs and she placed a hand on the rail to steady herself. One day. It was a powerful thing to hope for, and she realized with a sudden crushing sadness that the only future she'd ever imagined for herself was the one in which she slid a knife into Lir's belly.

For Nettle, she could hope for better things.

"Captain." Tin approached from the main deck. She looked ghostly in the dim light, as though the fight had leached her capacity for anything but grim sorrow.

"Who did you lose, Tin?" Caledonia asked, her gut crimping.

The girl's mouth pinched and twisted. Her eyes were suddenly wet and full of moonlight. "Lurin," she said, a gasping, painful word.

Lurin Mary. A memory bloomed in Caledonia's mind. Of the day they'd run the trails together, when Lurin had led the entire crew at a steady pace. When she'd endured the teasing of her sisters and her captain with a cheerful smile and a ready laugh.

"She fought well," Caledonia said, letting grief soften her words.

Tin's eyes brimmed with tears. She ground her teeth against them and swallowed hard, clearing her throat to speak in a voice that was all fire and stone. "I have a damage report."

Bitterly, Caledonia realized that their world had been reduced to a single ship. The damage report Tin would offer would not include all of Cloudbreak, nor would it account for all the lives that had been ruthlessly ripped away in an instant.

"Continue," she said.

"Our injuries are more structural than mechanical. We can sail as long as we're careful about it, but there are two sections of the forward hull that we'll need to patch sooner rather than later."

"Can we get free of the canals?" Caledonia asked, and when Tin nodded, she added, "Good, tell Harwell to plot the course out of here and get us moving."

"Yes, Captain."

"Pine!" Caledonia spotted him along the port rail, reloading and replacing the guns snapped beneath. He turned at the sound of her voice. "Keep our gunners ready. There may be more surprises waiting for us before we're free."

Pine gave a smart nod and returned to his task as the ship nosed through the narrow canals. The night air was cool and brisk, the canals close and dark and quiet, wrapping them into a false sense of security. Caledonia walked the deck, murmuring words of encouragement to her crew as she passed. These were dangerous moments: when the raging storm of battle broke and bodies yearned for rest. Only when the far western walls of the canals appeared before them did Caledonia call for an all stop, giving the repair teams one hour to accomplish their work.

Early ribbons of sunlight pushed across the domed sky, sweeping darkness along until the canals were filled with a hazy, ethereal kind of light. It wasn't much, but it was enough, and the repair teams rappelled down the hull of the ship with metaltech plates and welding masks.

Now you, Hime signed, her fingers pointing firmly at Caledonia in a way that brooked no argument from her captain. *You've been limping since you came aboard and you've bled all over the ship. If you don't care about your wounds, care about the mess.*

With light fingers, Hime investigated the gash on Caledonia's temple, then cleaned it and applied a small patch of skintech. It warmed immediately, its nanotech knitting her skin back together with brutal precision. Caledonia winced, but did not complain.

"Didn't think we had any of that stuff left," she said, distracting herself from the strange sensation.

Only small stuff, Hime answered. *Amina—*

She stopped abruptly and Caledonia felt a shock of panic, pain, sorrow shoot through her lungs at the reminder of their missing friend.

"Not up to the task of the silencers," she finished, steering them out of those sticky waters.

Are you dizzy? Hime asked, blinking rapidly. *How many fingers do you see?*

"Three," Caledonia answered dutifully. "And I'm not dizzy, just nauseated."

The sun rose a little more, the light shifting from blue to silver. Hime studied Caledonia without expression, yet her eyes revealed a bone-deep exhaustion. They were all pushing through, trying to hold their hearts and hopes together in spite of what had happened. None of them wanted to admit that the people who hadn't made it aboard this ship might have been abandoned back in Cloudbreak.

After a long minute, Hime nodded. *Drink some water. Get off that ankle as soon as possible. Let me know if anything changes.*

Caledonia wanted to tell her that Amina was a survivor. Just because she hadn't made it to the *Luminous Wake* didn't mean she hadn't escaped some other way. But the truth was there was every chance she hadn't. Every chance that she'd been shot trying to protect them all.

And Caledonia didn't have it in her to make empty promises.

"I will," she said instead, smothering her distress beneath the weight of all she still had to accomplish.

As the air filled with the clanking of hammers and the throaty hiss of welding guns, Caledonia and Pisces retreated to the chamber beneath the bridge.

Pisces leaned her back to the door and released a heavy sigh as Caledonia slumped into a chair. For the first time in hours, the pain in her ankle surged and now throbbed in rhythm with her pulse.

"How did we miss this, Pi?" Caledonia asked.

"I've been wondering the same thing. I think there are only two possibilities."

Caledonia had been thinking the same thing, though she was loath to admit one was just as likely as the other. "Either the bomb parts were not as conspicuous as Amina says . . ."

"Or someone made sure they got through inspection." Pisces folded her arms across her stomach as though the thought made her ill.

"Who was in charge of crew intake?" Caledonia knew she should have the answer, but her mind was exhausted.

"Ennick." There was a note of reluctant suspicion in Pisces's tone.

"Ennick," Caledonia repeated, picturing the old man with his salted hair and weathered orange scars. The man had been a Ballistic, but he'd never tried to hide that fact, and he'd fought at their side through the Battle of Cloudbreak; he'd had so many previous opportunities to betray them before now. "If it was him, he went far out of his way to establish his cover."

Caledonia searched her mind for any clues she might have missed, any sign that he'd been working against her the entire time. But she could find none.

"Doesn't seem likely," Pisces admitted. "But it *is* possible."

"Just as possible as the individual pieces making their way past inspection."

"He knows about the rendezvous." Pisces was already thinking ahead.

Only the captains of each ship had the rendezvous coordinates. As the captain of his ship, Ennick was one of the trusted few. If he was responsible for the attack on Cloudbreak, then the rendezvous was in trouble as well.

For a second, a taunting chorus sang in Caledonia's mind: *This is what comes of trusting Bullets.* Rage simmered beneath her ribs, hot and eager for release. But this wasn't an answer, she reminded herself firmly, only speculation.

"We'll know more when we get there," Caledonia stood, wincing at the pain in her ankle. "We'll make our approach with caution, as planned. Otherwise, this stays between us. I don't want the crew looking for traitors in their midst, especially when there may be none to find."

"Agreed," Pisces said with a nod.

As they left the small chamber and returned to the stream of activity on deck, another thought slithered through Caledonia's mind, sinking down through her spine to anchor itself in the nauseated bowl of her belly: the only person responsible for this disaster was herself.

CHAPTER FIFTEEN

They sailed again inside the hour. The sea fanned open before them in endless bands of blue, crashing into the horizon, where the sky was trapped beneath a thick layer of clouds. The wind blew from the south, carrying an edge of warmth. Caledonia welcomed the kiss of salt against her lips, the cloak of fine sea mist, the sensation of the world rushing beneath her feet. It was a single good feeling in a crush of sorrow and loss.

The rendezvous was still more than a day's sail from their current position, and Caledonia scanned the horizon for signs of pursuit. Finding none, she ordered Tin to walk her through each repair, the list of each wounded crew member, and the status of their supplies. When that was done, the only thing left was to stay alert and sail hard.

They weren't out of danger yet. As a crew, they would need to mark the loss of their siblings, warriors, and friends. They'd need to mourn the loss of their home. And Caledonia would need a chance to regain her footing. There wasn't time for all that now, but if she didn't give herself a moment to breathe, she was going to suffocate.

"Pi!" she called across the deck. "You're in command."

Her sister gave her a nod before repeating the order for all to hear. "I have command."

Belowdecks, the air was cool and smelled faintly of smoke and gunpowder, reminders that though they'd repaired the worst of it, their ship was just as compromised as its crew. Caledonia had chosen speed over repairs: one more decision that could get them all killed. If they had to fight before they reached the rendezvous, their recent wounds could become a liability. Before the attack, Caledonia would have made the call with confidence. Now uncertainty crouched on her shoulder, whispering urgent questions into her ear: Had she made the right call? Had she missed something vital? Had she lost her edge and put everyone at risk again?

Caledonia rushed inside her chambers and pressed her back against the cold steel of the hatch, taking a deep breath and letting it out slowly. When she'd managed three in a row, just as she'd instructed Nettle, she moved to the sink and splashed cool water over her face, dragging wet hands through her hair. Her fingers trembled as she cupped them beneath the spigot to bring water to her mouth, and she had to pause to grip the sides of the sink; her hands couldn't shake when she flexed her muscles. But she knew the only way to stop this unsolicited reaction was to let it work its way through her body, so she released her grip and curled up on her bed.

As a shiver traveled from her hands to her shoulders to her torso, all she could think was that Nettle would be so disappointed that her captain was hiding again. Imagining the girl's frown helped her breathe a little easier. They had lost so much. *She* had cost them so much. So much that she couldn't even bring herself to quantify it in any way. She couldn't even if she'd wanted to. Radio silence was her order. No one except a Bullet would be listening for her call.

When they arrived at the rendezvous, though, she wouldn't have any choice but to quantify those losses in numbers—how many missing; how many dead; how many of them left to take up the fight or abandon it altogether?

And how had they missed it?

Three knocks sounded against the hatch. Without waiting for an answer, Oran pushed through, his face fixed in an expression of grim determination. Two long strides brought him to her side, where he kneeled to take her hands. His were rough and warm and when he wrapped them around hers, the trembling stopped.

"Did I do this?" she asked in a voiced thinned by exhaustion.

Oran's sharp brows crashed together. "Caledonia."

"I know you'll say it was Lir, but if it weren't for me, would he do any of this?" She sat up, and her head spun just a little.

"Caledonia."

"If I hadn't tried to build an army, this wouldn't have happened. I don't even know how many people died back there, Oran. How many people did I get killed because I thought I could stand up to him? Because I thought I knew how to fight him?"

"Caledonia, stop."

"I can't. Oran, do you understand that hundreds of people just died and I'm the one who got them killed?!" She stopped. Her mouth falling open in horror, her own words echoing in her head: *hundreds of people.*

"Caledonia." Oran's voice was softer now. He rose from his knees, taking her face in his hands and leaning in to press his lips lightly to hers. When she didn't immediately pull away, he deepened the kiss until her moment of panic subsided. "I want you to listen to me," he said, smoothing his hands from her chin to her shoulders. "Nothing I'm about to say is going to make any of this go away. It won't even make it better. I honestly don't know that anything can."

"Then what?" Caledonia had never felt the spiraling sensation in her chest, this feeling that she was falling, sinking, plummeting beneath the surface.

"I can give you something to hold on to," he said, sitting back on his heels. There was no sympathy in Oran's eyes. Only understanding. Whatever she was going through, he'd been there before, and he was offering her a way through. Not out.

"Tell me," she said, missing the warmth of his touch on her shoulders.

"The decisions you make now will never be over," he began, careful not to touch her while he spoke, aware that even if he understood what she was going through, he couldn't inhabit it with her. She was on her own, but that didn't mean she had to be alone. "The consequences are too big, too important to end in a moment. You will carry them with you until the day you die, and others will carry them longer than that. Because that's what it means to change the world. It means making the kinds of choices that people remember."

"The ones who survive."

"Yes, the ones who survive. They aren't the only ones who matter, but even if they don't like how you fought, they will always know that you fought for *them*."

There was something almost calming in that statement. It felt inevitable and perhaps even simple in the way the Bullet Seas had always seemed simple. You were either a Bullet or you weren't. Fighting or dead.

Except that wasn't exactly true. Caledonia knew that. It was why she fought the way she did. Why she released Bullets after battle instead of killing them outright. Maybe if she'd been more ruthless Lir wouldn't have been able to infiltrate her city, but she was trying to change the Bullet Seas without decimating them. But what would it matter if merciful tactics got everyone dead?

"How can I ask anyone to keep fighting for me after this?

How can I ask them to keep trusting me when I hardly trust myself? What kind of leader does that make me?"

"It makes you exactly what we need." His answer came quickly, without a breath of hesitation. "We missed this, and our losses are terrible, but you didn't do anything wrong. It's—war doesn't work like that. Winning doesn't mean you were right and losing doesn't mean you were wrong. All it means is that Lir hit us harder this time."

"Every time I think I'm capable of beating him, he crushes me instead, crushes my people, my home, and all I can think about is hurting him. I used to want to hurt him for all the ways he'd hurt me, but I don't think that's possible anymore. I—I'm afraid of what it will take to stop him." She paused, realizing she'd pulled his hands into hers and now squeezed them to her chest, realizing also that this was the first time they'd spoken since Oran had confessed that he loved her. "I'm afraid of what I'll do to stop him. I'm afraid of who I'll be afterward."

This time, Oran's answer came more slowly. He pursed his lips, and his brow furrowed before he spoke again. "When you're in command, you have the power to create change in the world around you. That's what power is: potential for change. But you can't create change without also changing yourself. And you can't change *this* world without making decisions that will haunt you forever."

Caledonia realized he was talking as much about himself as

he was about her. All the decisions he'd made as a Fiveson were still with him. He'd done things she never wanted to imagine, and they would stay with him for the rest of his life. It mattered that he had changed course and now fought against the structure he once upheld. And it also didn't matter at all. There was too much blood on his hands to ever be rid of it.

There was blood on her hands, too. Not because she'd done the killing but because she'd been in charge. She bore the weight of responsibility.

"The truly terrible thing, Cala, is that you are probably more prepared to be the one to lead us than ever. Because you know what it feels like to lose like this and it hasn't broken you yet. Half of war is just enduring hell."

It felt true. Every time Caledonia thought a moment would send her to her knees, she found a reason to stand up again. She'd been enduring hell since the night she met Lir. Surely, she could endure it a little longer. Besides, if she stepped down now, someone else would stand up in her place. Someone like Pisces or Sledge would have to shoulder this burden.

"No good options," Caledonia said softly.

"No good options," Oran repeated, watching her with a mournful expression. "And there will be even fewer tomorrow."

Caledonia gave a grim nod. It would take them more than a day to reach the rendezvous coordinates, but the point remained: the number of ships that joined them now would determine her next move. Yesterday, she'd been hurtling toward the moment of sailing to the Holster and attacking Lir. Tomorrow, she might have only a handful of ships.

"But bad options have never slowed you down for long."

Two sharp bangs on the hatch had both of them on their feet before the door swung open. It was Pisces. The news was on her face before she spoke, and Caledonia was reaching for her discarded gun belt when Pisces said a single word: "Bullets."

CHAPTER SIXTEEN

The ship was a black point near the horizon on a course to intercept the *Luminous Wake*.

"Ready missiles, Captain?" Pine stood with one foot hoisted on the rail, a hand braced against his knee. He'd been on deck since the escape and though the rasp in his voice was evidence of the long night, his eyes were as sharp as ever.

The repairs to the *Luminous Wake* had been hurried. They'd sealed two weakened points in the forward hull and patched a long gouge on the starboard side, but every repair left them vulnerable.

Caledonia nodded and Pine shoved off to ready their weapons, leaving her with Pisces and Oran.

"Think it's a trap?" Pisces asked, eyes narrowing on the approaching vessel.

Caledonia studied the ship. When Bullets sailed alone, it was almost always a trap. A single ship was a lure, meant to draw you close before its friends circled in for the kill. It was how Pisces had been captured in Caledonia's absence. And how they'd lost the *Mors Navis*.

"Could be." The location was not ideal for such a maneuver, but that didn't mean it wasn't still the case.

"Could be a scout," Oran suggested.

The ship was moving in fast, quickly closing the distance between them. Though slower than an Assault Ship, the vessel was ringed in those gruesome spikes, each studded with dead bodies. Caledonia's instincts said it wasn't a trap and the sooner she gave the order to engage the better, but how could she be sure? Maybe this was a moment to run, not fight.

She didn't know what to trust.

"Cala?" Pisces faced her sister with a knowing expression. "What do you see?"

Caledonia looked from Pisces to the approaching vessel. The problem was she didn't see anything. Just like she hadn't seen anything before the attack on Cloudbreak. There was no clear path, no obvious right answer. Fear clutched at Caledonia's throat. Her next decision could get more people killed, and she didn't trust herself to know which was the right one.

Pisces moved in closer, her hand twisting in the fabric of Caledonia's shirt. Such a small yet familiar gesture, one that calmed Caledonia just enough. If she couldn't trust herself, she could at least trust that her crew was up to one more fight.

Spinning on her uninjured heel, Caledonia called, "Maintain course and speed!"

The bridge crew answered with a confident chorus of "Yes, Captain!" and she turned her attention to Pine and his gunners, now ready on deck with an impressive array of missile launchers.

"The second they're in range, I want you firing. Understood?"

"Yes, Captain!"

Caledonia returned to her position on the nose of the ship, doing her best not to limp. Behind her, the rest of the crew was coiled and ready, eyes trained on the approaching vessel, fingers resting firmly on triggers.

The wind ripped strands of red hair from Caledonia's braid, lashing them against her cheeks and eyes, the very tips still bleached a brassy blonde from her short disguise as a Bullet. As it grew out, it looked less like her mother's vibrant curls and more like hungry flames burning in her peripheral vision.

The ship was closer now. Barreling forward at high speeds. Either they planned to swing around and flank her immediately or they had no intention of stopping. A direct hit of any sort could be devastating for the *Luminous Wake*, but as this ship grew nearer, she knew without a doubt that a hit from its broad nose would be catastrophic.

She would have to strike first.

"Ready!" Caledonia called, pacing the ship's approach. "Fire!"

Three missiles flew overhead, screaming against the sky. In response, the Bullet ship attempted to adjust its course while gunners on deck sniped at the incoming artillery. In seconds, they'd destroyed one of the missiles. Two remained.

Caledonia shouted for her gunners to ready themselves as the Bullet ship veered hard to starboard, narrowly avoiding a second missile. The third found its home on their aft deck, exploding with a pop of orange flame.

The ship soared closer still, hemorrhaging smoke into the blue sky. Pine roared for his gunners to raise their shields and open fire.

Now that they were near, Caledonia could see the Bullet crew scrambling to put out the fire. What they weren't doing, she realized, was taking aim against the *Luminous Wake*. Not a single gun was pointed at her crew.

"What are they doing?" Pisces asked, dread making her confusion sharp. "Why aren't they firing?"

That's when Caledonia saw her.

Standing tall on the forward deck of the Bullet ship was a woman with round hips and dark hair pulled into a severe braid. In her hand, she held a gun, arm resting at her side. Over the narrowing slice of water between them, she found Caledonia's eyes. Then she raised her gun and fired a single shot into the ocean.

Recognition washed over Caledonia. This was no Bullet, but her friend and ally Gloriana.

After Slipmark, where Gloriana had helped Caledonia to free the captured crew of the *Mors Navis*, the woman had vanished into the night, only to turn up after the Battle of Cloudbreak with a different ship and a small crew of defected Bullets. They'd become a crucial part of Caledonia's information network, constantly sailing out and back with news of the Bullet Fleet. Caledoina had dispatched them to verify the Fivesons' deaths a week ago.

On a different ship.

Before she'd completed the thought, her gunners fired. Gloriana's crew hit the deck, while she stood tall and unflinching, the gun hanging nonthreateningly in her hand.

"Cease fire!" Caledonia shouted. "They're friendly! Cease fire!"

The guns stopped, the air cleared, and each crew eyed the other warily. Soon, the two ships were port to port with a bridge laid between them.

"Captain," Gloriana said, crossing the bridge to the deck of the *Luminous Wake* with a wide smile. "We thought this looked like the *Luminous*. Didn't mean to startle you."

"Sorry for the less-than-warm welcome," Caledonia said with a glance toward the still-smoking patch on Gloriana's aft deck.

"Warm enough," Gloriana answered with a shrug. "No one was hurt, and we found the crew we were searching for. Seems like a good day. Or, good enough. We saw what happened to Cloudbreak."

"I'm glad to see you safe." Reluctantly, Caledonia started a new fleet tally in her mind. She'd had fifty-four, but as of right now, she had two. "Did you find any others?"

Gloriana gave a regretful shake of her head. "Just us, I'm afraid. We were on our way back in to report when we came upon twenty of Lir's fleet holding position south of Cloudbreak. We had to sail east to avoid them, and by the time we were making our approach, well, we could see the smoke from miles away."

Twenty ships.

"They were waiting to pick off the survivors." The bombs had only been part of the plan.

"How'd you find us?" Pine loomed close, stance rigid. "How'd you get past Lir's fleet if you were out east?"

Gloriana shifted her eyes to Pine. "That's the interesting part— we didn't have to avoid them. Almost as soon as we'd spotted them, they sailed south, straight out of our path. All we had to do was wait them out. Probably helped that we looked like one of them."

That was enough to rekindle a small flame of hope in Caledonia. If the larger Bullet fleet had moved off so soon, maybe more of her people had made it out of Cloudbreak; maybe they'd survived. And if they'd survived, they would find their way to the rendezvous.

"What happened to the *Arrow Sweet*?" Caledonia asked.

"We ran into trouble in the southern seas," Gloriana said with a shrug. "Had to make do with what we could hunt."

"But why pull his ships away?" Pisces asked, still chewing on Gloriana's report. "He had us. Why sail before finishing the job?"

"To respond to a bigger threat?" Caledonia said, though she couldn't fathom what that might be.

"It's what we were returning to report when we encountered the fleet." Gloriana gave a tight smile, then tipped her head forward. "Fivesons Venn and Decker are dead as rumored, but turns out Tassos is alive and well, and he still controls the Net."

CHAPTER SEVENTEEN

For the remainder of the short trip to the Bone Mouth, Caledonia settled into a strange kind of peace. Knowing that Tassos had survived Lir's assassination attempt meant little to her on the surface. She didn't know Tassos, but she did know that in failing to kill him, Lir had created another enemy. One who was situated between Lir and Caledonia.

It was a strange kind of comfort, but for the moment, it was all she had.

The Bone Mouth came into view at dusk. The archipelago didn't surge out of the water so much as it appeared to be slowly melting into it. The islands crumbled toward the horizon, making smaller and smaller splotches against the dimming sky, and to Caledonia and Pisces, they looked a little like home.

The two girls stood together, their arms linked and their eyes reaching for the islands that had sheltered and fed them while they rebuilt the *Mors Navis* five turns ago. It had been more than a ten-moon since they'd sailed into these warm waters. The last time they'd been close, it was to say farewell to Lace and leave Oran in the shallows, where the sea would decide his fate. Instead, Oran had recognized the family sigil tattooed against Caledonia's temple, a blunted arrowhead half-filled with black ink, and set them on a course that carried them far from these cradling islands and into cold northern waters in pursuit of Donnally and Ares. They hadn't set foot on the Gem since.

When they'd settled on this place as their meeting point, neither of them had expected to need it. At least, not so soon. And not like this. On the run because they'd been stymied before they'd ever really begun.

With Gloriana sailing just a few lengths behind, the *Luminous Wake* slowed to quarter speed and approached the islands on a course that would mark them as friendly to any members of the fleet that had beat them here. This had been Oran's suggestion, and was perhaps the only time Pine had agreed with him without fighting about it first.

The course took them through a treacherous channel between two islands. Steep walls gave the appearance of deep waters when that was only partly true. Rocks tall enough to gouge the hull of a ship littered the sea floor, while swift waters made them difficult to avoid. Of all the possible ways to approach the Gem, this one came with the fewest number of obstacles. She'd selected it because it was the easiest one to explain and map. Anyone with her instructions should be able to navigate the route without any trouble.

The familiar scent of fragrant scrub plants on the air reminded Caledonia of nights when she would lie on her belly along the nose of the *Ghost*, listening to the water singing against the hull as her mother called quiet commands to her father. From Rhona, Caledonia had learned to read the water and commit its secrets to memory. Later, when she and Pisces were on their own, she'd learned to thread their ship through the deceptively simple channels with greater and greater speed until she had surpassed even her mother's skill. Now she needed these same waters to protect her again, and it seemed strangely fitting that she should return to them in the wake of another terrible loss.

"Didn't think I'd ever see this place again." Ares joined them at the rail, eyes tracing the once familiar outline of the islands. "Brings back memories I'd rather forget."

Pisces pressed a hand to his arm and his lips tipped into a sad smile. "There were good ones, too. Remember those shells Donnally used to collect?"

"The purple ones," Ares answered with a laugh. "They were always in his pockets."

Caledonia hadn't thought of Donnally's purple shells in turns, but suddenly, she remembered them vividly. He kept so many that their dad threatened to get rid of them, so Donnally started hiding them anywhere he could. Even inside his pillowcase. "He was going to make a mask with them. A crab mask."

"Why purple, then?" Pisces asked.

"Because of the sky." Ares tipped his head back to study the darkening dome above. "He was always talking about constellations and stars and making stories out of nothing. He wanted his mask to be like the crab constellation. And the purple shells were as close as he could get to the blue he wanted."

"I still don't know why he was so obsessed with crabs." Pisces murmured.

Caledonia rarely ventured into her memories of her family, not until they surged out of her mind like a ship in the night and gave her no choice. When she thought of her mother or her father, or Donnally, she pictured them doing whatever they'd loved most, but as the three of them conjured her little brother, she remembered so much more. Early mornings on the bow practicing their knots while her father demonstrated and corrected their loops; stormy nights spent belowdecks with the entire crew bundled together around rousing card games; afternoons working in the box gardens while Pisces and Ares's mom played her breathy pipes.

"Our dad," Caledonia explained. "Donnally used to have nightmares. He'd wake up crying and afraid because he was too little to fight. Dad told him that sometimes being small was its own kind of protection. Like crabs. They're very small and even though they have mighty claws, their first instinct is to burrow into the sand and wait until the danger passes. They don't have to fight to survive."

"Sometimes it's hard to remember him that way." Ares's voice dipped low, heavy with memories of a different Donnally.

Caledonia had a few memories of that Donnally, too. She pinched her eyes shut, doing all she could to hold on to the Donnally of the past, but he slipped away. All that was left was her brother's stark expression as he said, "I can't abandon my brother."

"Gunners ready!" Pine's voice jolted them from their reverie as they neared the meeting place. "Stay alert!"

Nettle steered the *Luminous Wake* using only the thrusters for power. Gloriana followed close behind, sure to tack and adjust precisely as Nettle did. They emerged as the sun slashed the Gem's white sands and dense green forests in bands of gold and fiery orange. For a moment, it shone like its namesake, glittering against the gloaming like a jewel. Fanned out a short distance from its shore was a sight that brought Caledonia's heart to her throat.

Thirteen ships.

Her ships.

Her crew cheered and lowered their weapons, their relief at discovering they were not alone too enormous to contain. Pisces hugged Caledonia's arm to her body.

"This is good," Pisces whispered, pressing a kiss on her sister's cheek. "Let yourself know this is good."

"I do," Caledonia promised. This was so much more than she'd dared to hope for. She turned to look over her shoulder to where Hime had appeared, her dark eyes hard and her elegant chin raised. "But I hope it's more than good."

Hime had kept herself busy, constantly running her rounds and tending to the wounded, making sure everyone else had what they needed when the one thing, the one person, she needed most was missing. Caledonia had tried to speak with her once more, but at the mention of Amina's name, Hime walled her off, unwilling to entertain possibilities and uncertainties until there was a reason to.

That reason had just appeared before them. Hime looked from the island to Caledonia and Pisces, one side of her face gilded in golden light, and for a haunting second, her desperate need to know pulled her expression into one of extreme agony. It was there and gone in a flash. She pushed her chin a little higher and stood her ground, waiting in place when what she so clearly wanted to do was throw herself overboard and swim to each of the ships anchored nearby, searching for her love.

Caledonia wished she could make any of this easier or at least faster for Hime. And a little for herself, too. She wanted Amina to be alive, and even if the feeling twisted differently through her chest than it did through Hime's, she knew it was just as strong.

If she focused on it, it might consume her. It was easier to feel it through the filter of her concerns for Hime. Easier to defray some of her cold panic over having lost another of her command crew by worrying about the woman Amina loved.

I won't believe she's gone until I have to, was all Hime would say.

They would know one way or another. Anyone who had survived Cloudbreak would make their way here eventually.

The cheers of her crew were met by cheers from the nearby vessels. As the sun plunged beneath the horizon, the air warmed with their cries. Along the beach, tents had been pitched and fires skipped down the shoreline. As Caledonia surveyed the sight before her, she felt her own hopes rising.

"We've got incoming!" Pine called from the bow, voice uncharacteristically light.

A ship peeled away from the cluster and sliced through the water toward the *Luminous Wake*. On its bow stood a figure as tall as he was broad. Caledonia and Pisces rushed to join Pine on the forward deck, each of them too afraid to vocalize their hopes. But as the ship grew nearer, they didn't have to wonder anymore. There was no mistaking that mountain of a boy. Or the ship that carried him.

The *Blade* slowed as it nosed right up to the *Luminous Wake*. Pine didn't even wait for it to stop before he raced toward the edge, using a cleat to boost himself up and over the rail and ocean, landing squarely on the deck of the *Blade*.

Sledge gave a disbelieving shake of his head, but he smiled and let Pine pull him into an uncompromising embrace. They stood like that for a long minute, arms locked around each other and completely still but for the subtle movement of a jaw as each whispered to the other.

When the *Blade* came to an actual stop, the crew lowered a gangway between the two and Pine pulled Sledge across to the *Luminous Wake*. Sledge had a gash on his forehead, crusted with blood but healing, and a bruise had purpled on his cheek, but he appeared otherwise uninjured.

Caledonia stepped forward and before she could decide whether or not Sledge would endure a hug from her, he scooped her up in his tree-trunk arms and pulled her close.

"It is very, *very* good to see you, Captain," Sledge said into her hair.

Caledonia smiled, or, she tried to. It was hard to tell exactly what her lips did smooshed against the side of a mountain. She answered by squeezing his neck as tightly as she could, then tapped his shin with the tips of her toes to indicate she was ready to be placed on her feet once more.

With a sheepish laugh, Sledge obliged, setting her down on the deck before turning to Pisces and hugging her with a little more care.

For a moment, Caledonia convinced herself that everything was going to be as fine as it could possibly be. They'd suffered an incredible blow, but they would survive it. Together.

Then Sledge's eyes settled on a point over her shoulder and his joy dimmed.

Hime stood just behind the group. Her hands were twisted in the apron tied around her waist and her bottom lip was trapped between her teeth. Her tortured expression was all Sledge needed to understand who she'd lost, whose name she was desperate for him to speak.

One look at Sledge's face told them all what they didn't want to know.

"I'm sorry, Princelet," Sledge said. "Amina's not here."

CHAPTER EIGHTEEN

Reports arrived long into the night. In the galley of the *Luminous Wake*, Caledonia and Pisces received representatives from the thirteen crews who'd made it safely to the Bone Mouth. While Far served fresh teaco to every new visitor, the rest of the crew had been tasked with getting some rest before their work began anew in the morning.

With each new report, Caledonia's understanding of the evacuation gained detail, and the tally of individual survivors grew to four hundred and nine. Last to arrive was Ennick. He strode into the room with a grim nod of thanks to Far for the teaco. Pisces shifted in her seat, catching Caledonia's eye with a wary expression.

"It's good to see you, Captain." There was no hesitation to his words, no suggestion of guilt or wrongdoing. He met Caledonia's gaze straight on. "We are all relieved to have you back with us."

"It's a relief to see so many survivors," Caledonia answered, searching his expression for some sign of deceit. Had he betrayed them and let the bombs into Cloudbreak? Not long ago, she'd have believed it instantly. Now, though, her reactions were tempered, cautious, even trusting. "How did you escape?"

Ennick set his teaco aside and folded his hands together, bracing his forearms against his knees as he began to tell his story. "Most of my crew was asleep when the bombs went off, but several made it to the lifts before they went down. We thought we were preparing for a seaborne attack." He paused to shake his head, eyes focusing on the recent past. "By the time I was on deck, the boulders were falling. We got out with a handful of others and sailed directly here."

It was one of two stories they'd been hearing all night. One set of ships made it out just before the boulders fell, the others were all Red Fleet and had been docked in the northern canals. If anyone made it out after the stronghold crumbled, they weren't here yet.

"And before that," Pisces began, taking the lead on the interrogation so Caledonia didn't have to. "Were you at the intake station when Amina and Hime took a crew into custody?"

"I was." Ennick's eyes darted swiftly from Caledonia to Pisces. "Were those two involved?"

"There were others as well." The note of accusation in Pisces's voice was unmistakable.

"Already inside the city?" Ennick's eyebrows arched in alarm, then crashed again almost as quickly. "And you want to know if I was responsible for letting them in."

"We do," Pisces confirmed, and for the first time her discomfort left her steely demeanor frayed around the edges.

The man nodded as though the question were unsurprising even if it was disappointing. He studied the floor as he collected his thoughts, then drew himself up as though resolved to something unpleasant and spoke again. "Intake was my team, and if that's how the bombs got in, then it was my fault."

"Do you know what a pulse bomb is?" Pisces asked.

"Pulse bombs? I—" Ennick's expression grew slack as he reconciled what he'd seen with what he knew of the bombs that destroyed Cloudbreak. The evidence was there on his face: he knew what pulse bombs were, and now he knew that he'd let their components pass through unhindered. "Hell. It *was* my fault," he said, defeated.

"You did see them?" Caledonia asked.

"I know what those parts look like. I should have recognized them, but I didn't," he said, voice heavy with regret. He raised his head and cast a slow gaze from Pisces to Caledonia. "I left that life behind long ago, but if my ignorance led us here, then I will accept your punishment."

He made no attempt to defend himself, but his response also revealed a ready well of remorse. And remorse suggested loyalty. In the deepest pockets of Caledonia's mind, her mistrust of Bullets argued that this was all a ploy to win her trust and convince her to keep the traitor in her midst. It would be so easy to let that voice win, especially right now when they'd been defeated so painfully.

But the world she was fighting for was a world in which there always had to be room for trust. Mercy instead of glory.

"I don't want to punish you." Caledonia stood and took two steps toward the man, her ankle protesting the sudden motion. "You've been with us for many moons, and you have fought hard and well. We only need to know how this happened, so that we can prevent it in the future."

"Yes, Captain." Ennick's answer was barely a whisper.

"Ennick," Caledonia called as the man stood to leave. "This wasn't your fault," she offered, knowing it was weak comfort in the face of so much loss.

"Thank you, Captain." His smile was wan as he left the galley.

"Do you really believe him?" Pisces asked Caledonia as they returned their empty mugs to the kitchen and called goodnight to Far before heading topside.

"I do," Caledonia answered. "As much as I can."

They climbed the stairwell to the main deck, where the night air was warm and smelled faintly of salt and dry earth. It was the middle of the night, and most of the fleet was dark but for a few spots of light here and there as various crews attended to repairs.

"I do, too," Pisces admitted. "But if we're wrong . . ."

"Then Lir already has our location, and the only thing standing between us and him is Tassos," Caledonia finished as they took a turn around the deck. "We can't stay here long."

"Well, at least that's a familiar position for us." Pisces's voice was grim, but she was right. They'd spent so much of their lives running, the prospect of having to do it now was almost a comfort. Here, there was no city to consider, no separation between crew and ship. They would live in a state of readiness that hadn't been possible in Cloudbreak.

They climbed up to the bridge, nodding to Folly, who was on dead watch, then continued toward the nose. There, perched on the eastward-facing rail, was a small figure. She was wrapped in a thin blanket, but the simple blue ribbon tied at the end of her long black braid gave her away.

"Hime?" Caledonia straddled the rail on one side of the girl, while Pisces did the same on the other.

In the dim light of the sun pips ringed around the deck of the *Luminous*, tear tracks gleamed against her moon-pale cheeks. Her eyes were pinned to a spot in the east through which friendly ships would know to sail.

"How long have you been here?" Pisces asked.

Hime shrugged her response.

"I'm sorry, Hime." Caledonia felt her own heart twisting around Amina's absence. "If there was something we could do, we would."

There is. Hime's answer was immediate. She turned to face

Caledonia, her eyes shining with unshed tears, her expression a little wild. *We can go back to Cloudbreak. We can search for her. Find her. Bring her back with us.*

"Hime," Pisces said in a mournful voice.

Don't tell me we can't. She could be hurt, trapped, dying. *I can't sit here and do nothing. Give me a ship. I'll go back on my own and find her. She would do the same for me. Please, give me a ship.*

Anger, terror, grief, it was all wrapped up in Hime's words, and it took every bit of Caledonia's strength to look her in the eye and say, "No."

A quick gasp shot from Hime's lips and her face twisted into a mask of furious sorrow. *Please,* she signed. *I love her. Do you understand that I love her? What am I even fighting for if I don't fight for her?*

Caledonia marveled at how easily Hime said those words: I love her. It was as easy for her as it had been for Oran, and Caledonia couldn't even start to think about saying them out loud. It left her breathless. Tears warmed her eyes and she looked to Pisces for help.

"You fight for Amina every day," Pisces soothed. "Right now, the best thing you can do is stay right where she expects to find you."

Hime wilted a little, the fight she'd aimed at Caledonia receding like the tide. She nodded, solemn and small once more, fresh tears slipping down her cheeks.

Caledonia felt all the fear and grief she saw in Hime's face and wished there was a better answer than the one a captain would give. Wished she could do something other than stand in her way and tell her "no." She wanted to apologize. She wanted to tell Hime that they would sail to Cloudbreak at first light, that they would rescue Amina and make their small family whole again. She wanted it so badly that for a moment her lungs flattened and refused to fill again.

"You should get some rest." Caledonia's voice was soft. "If she can get to us, she will."

At this, Hime shook her head sharply once. *I'm not leaving. Not yet.*

"Then we'll stay with you," Pisces said, determined.

Caledonia nodded, a small spot of relief opening in her lungs. This, at least, she could do.

Hime's lips trembled as her sisters wrapped her in their arms and turned their eyes to the same dark point on the horizon.

CHAPTER NINETEEN

Sand slid beneath the balls of Caledonia's feet as she and Pisces walked along a narrow strip of beach the next day. Her ankle ached a little less with each step, but it was still slow going. Waves rushed toward their toes, seeping into the sand where small crabs burrowed, and little birds skittered back and forth at the edge of the water.

After holding vigil all night with Hime, waiting and hoping and fearing the worst, the day had dawned on the sight of five new ships. Hime rose immediately, ready to receive every ship on her own, to mark every member of their crew with her own eyes. She was a spear of determination in the face of looming sadness. But where she cleaved stubbornly to hope, Caledonia felt her own heart begin to grieve the loss of her friend.

Amina had not been aboard any of the new ships, and Hime had reluctantly returned to her cabin alone. Exhausted, Caledonia had done the same, finding Oran still asleep in her bed. She'd crawled in next to him, grateful when he'd merely tucked an arm around her instead of asking where she'd been or whether or not anything was wrong. For a few hours, she'd fallen into sleep as a stone through water and only awoke when Tin roused her, regretfully bringing a stack of requests that only the captain of the fleet could answer.

The day had passed in an unending series of decisions, and now Caledonia was ready to apply her mind to what came next. For that, she needed space and the ocean over which she could cast her thoughts and reel them back in one at a time.

Pisces walked quietly at her side, unwilling to let Caledonia out of her sight.

"Pi," Caledonia called, reaching for her hand.

Pisces threaded their fingers together and gave Caledonia's hand a firm squeeze. "What are we going to do, Cala?"

Long ago, they'd sat on this very beach pondering that same question. Caledonia felt just as lost now as she had then. Just like then, she was licking her wounds, counting the dead, and trying to decide what was possible with what was left. Just like then, her thoughts were consumed by a sharp jaw, an explosion of sun-bleached hair, and cutting blue eyes. How could so much have changed and also so little?

"I'm thinking that Gloriana's report means we have more than one enemy out there." In the little time Caledonia had had to herself, she'd worried this issue back and forth in her mind, always with the same frustrating lack of results.

"You think they'll work together? Even after an assassination attempt?" Pisces asked.

"Oran says there is no love lost between Lir and Tassos," Caledonia said. "I doubt they'll unite. That's good for us because it means Tassos is a buffer between us and Lir. However temporary. But that doesn't mean Tassos won't decide to attack us himself."

"Two enemies, then," Pisces said, voice grim.

"We don't have the power to move against Lir, much less Lir *and* Tassos," Caledonia said. "And I don't know how to fight either of them in a way that doesn't trap us. We move against Lir and he smothers us. We move against Tassos and Lir waits to see who survives. We don't move at all and when those two are done with each other, the victor will come for us."

"We need a bigger army." Pisces stabbed a toe into the sand. "Or maybe we just try and punch the Net. If we wait until Lir draws Tassos out or at least thins his forces, our chances will almost be good."

Not long ago, punching the Net had been the dream. The line of ships stretched from the Holster to the tip of this very archipelago a mere ten miles southeast of their current position. Aric had put it in place so long ago, Caledonia didn't know a world without it. There were stories, of course, of the few daring ships that made it through and found better lives on the other side, but they were only stories. Told by people who needed to believe there was something more to this world than Bullets and Scythes, Ballistics and Fivesons.

But Caledonia had never spoken to anyone who'd seen the other side. Not even Oran knew. The stories were nothing more than dreams repeated so frequently that someone somewhere along the way took them as truth.

Without Aric in the picture, the Net was as much a question as it was a promise. Maybe they could make it through or maybe Tassos was every bit as terrible as Lir himself. None of that changed the fact that no one knew what the world was like on the other side.

And Caledonia had decided to fight for this one.

"I'm sorry, Cala. I know Donnally is here and I—I didn't mean to suggest that we leave him. I was just looking for solutions," Pisces said, mistaking Caledonia's silence for reluctance.

"It's not that," Caledonia admitted, though part of her thought it should have been. "It's that punching the Net feels like giving up. It feels like breaking the promise I've made to everyone who's still with us. They're ready to fight and push ahead. I just want to make sure I'm giving them the right fight. A smart one. With a group this size, we can only hide for so long."

The light turned gray and blue as the sun stitched itself down into the horizon. Above, the stars were just starting to push pinpricks of light through the darkening sky and the wind carried a chilly edge.

"We need a bigger army," Pisces repeated.

She was right. To pursue any of the paths Caledonia could see before them, they needed more people, more ships. But now that they'd been pushed into hiding, no one else would be able to find them, and it didn't matter anyway because their defeat at Cloudbreak would likely dissuade any Slaggers or colonists or rogue ships from joining her, or any more Bullets from defecting. At least not to her. Maybe they would leave Lir for Tassos. He was the only one who might have the power to stand against Lir.

Frustration built quickly in Caledonia's chest. "Pi, I just can't see what to do next. Every possible way forward looks choppy and impassable."

Pisces gave a humorless laugh. "When have choppy waters held you back?"

Caledonia growled and turned her eyes once more to the ocean, where her fleet sat at anchor. Her too-small fleet. Her fleet that was tired of running from enemies.

"Tassos." In an instant, her vision cleared, and all the pieces started to draw together.

"What about him?" Pisces asked. "You've already said we can't fight him."

Caledonia shook her head as the thought spun into a vivid possibility. "I don't want to fight him. Not yet."

A frown crushed Pisces's face. "Then what do you want to do?"

It was a wild idea. And new. It had landed suddenly and just as suddenly taken shape.

Caledonia's head spun as she said the words: "I want to join forces with him."

CHAPTER TWENTY

"Just so I'm clear: you want to join forces with Tassos. A former Fiveson and current commander of the Net." Sledge's voice filled the small space made even smaller by his mountainous presence.

The command crew was crammed into the private chamber beneath the bridge of the *Luminous Wake*; Sledge had his back pressed into a corner, his head nearly brushing the pipes along the ceiling. The rest of the group was clustered awkwardly around him. They barely fit, but this was the only location that gave them the opportunity to speak discreetly.

Caledonia and Pisces had hurriedly returned to the ship before lifting the order for radio silence and sending Gloriana and her crew to get eyes on the Net ten miles away. Then Caledonia had summoned her command crew and brought them up to speed.

Holding Sledge's gaze, Caledonia made sure she looked as certain as she felt when she gave her answer: "Yes."

"Oh, hell," Pine grumbled, turning his eyes toward the ceiling in disbelief.

This brought a small smile to Caledonia's lips. "Maybe Tassos can hold Lir off on his own, but if he wants to beat him, then he needs us."

"Cala." Oran pressed his eyes shut, giving himself a moment to collect his thoughts. Caledonia braced for impact. "We can't. You can't make alliances with him, he's not capable of it. He's a—"

"Fiveson?" Caledonia asked pointedly.

It was Oran's turn to growl. "Yes, but he is—" This time he stopped himself, unable to find the right words.

But Caledonia had a few to offer. "The worst of you? More vicious than I can imagine? Untrustworthy?" Oran's lips crashed together as she continued. "You know what else he is? An enemy of Lir."

"Yes, all of those things," Oran countered. He spoke with a rare kind of authority, one that left no doubt in anyone's mind about the sincerity of his words. "He is all of those things. Even if we help him now, there's no guarantee he won't just turn around and attack us."

"I really hate to agree with him," Pine spoke from the other side of the room. "But if anyone knows how a sick fish Fiveson operates, well, it takes one to know one."

Caledonia had been prepared for resistance. It didn't surprise her that it was coming from Oran and Pine, but that didn't make it any less frustrating.

"I assume he'll turn on us eventually." Caledonia refused to back down. "But I'm not proposing a lasting alliance, only a temporary one. We work together long enough to take down Lir, then we go our separate ways."

"We'll be putting ourselves in a very vulnerable position." Oran's eyes were cutting.

"In this case, I think it's worth the risk."

The silence that bloomed between Oran and Caledonia was thick. There were things he wanted to say and would not here in front of her crew. Things he would only say to her.

Pine looked shrewdly from Caledonia to Oran, then stepped forward, crowding Oran in the already cramped space. "Care to share with the group?"

Without backing down, Oran responded with a measured blink of his eyes. "If I had something to say, I'd say it."

The two young men were inches apart. Pine was broad, and his hands curled into heavy fists at his sides, but there was something dangerous in the loose coil of Oran's body.

"But can we actually *trust* a Fiveson?" Pisces asked, spearing the tension.

Everyone turned to her in surprise. For a second, silence hung in the air, then Caledonia began to laugh. It started as a small throaty sound, but quickly pushed slightly hysterical tears into her eyes.

"Pi," she said. "You are the one who told me to trust—"

"Oran!" Pisces shouted. "I told you to trust Oran! Not the entire league of Fivesons! And I didn't know he was a Fiveson at the time or I'd have been much more specific!"

Caledonia's smile faded. "I don't trust Tassos and I'm not suggesting that we should, but I do have confidence that he will act in his own best interest." Caledonia shifted her gaze back to Oran, who watched her with a shuttered expression. "I think he'll see the benefit of a temporary alliance with one of Lir's other enemies."

Oran didn't speak right away. He had that faraway look he got when he was revisiting his past. After a long minute, he drew in a breath and fixed Caledonia with narrowed eyes. "There's no one he hates more than Lir."

That was exactly what Caledonia wanted to hear. "Then we have something in common."

If we leave this place, how will other survivors find us? Hime asked, stepping away from the wall where she'd been listening with one hand pressed against her mouth.

"We'll leave a small team behind to point new arrivals in the right direction," Caledonia answered swiftly, all too aware that time was a crucial piece of this plan. "They'll find us."

"He outnumbers us." Pisces wasn't yet convinced. "If he turns on us immediately, we won't have any option but to run."

"Then we'll run. He's bound to the Net and we know these waters better than anyone."

Pisces braced her hands on her hips as she considered everything she'd heard. Then, after a long moment, she gave a reluctant nod. "It's a terrible plan, but I don't see that we have any better options. The rest of the fleet will need convincing."

"Bad options seem to be our captain's specialty," Pine added with a note of begrudging admiration.

"We do this and we reveal our numbers and location to Lir." Sledge's voice carried a warning.

"And if Tassos doesn't go for it, then we could be walking into the middle of a massacre," Oran added. "He's not likely to just let us sail away, you understand."

Caledonia nodded, nerves thrumming. It was all true. A move like this would expose them and there was absolutely nothing they could do about that, but if Tassos took them at their word, they stood to gain so much more.

"Then we'll have to be compelling," she said.

Let's do it, Hime signed. *Using them against one another is what they deserve.*

Amina's absence was suddenly very loud. If she were here, this was when she'd offer some brilliant tactic or issue some note of caution or the encouragement of her spirits.

"So." Sledge's voice rumbled in the enclosed space. "How do we do this?"

Caledonia looked across the faces of her command crew.

She'd given them a terrible plan and they'd accepted it. They would follow her orders and stand by her side and do everything in their power to make this plan work.

With a decisive nod, she said, "Let's go make a deal with a Fiveson."

CHAPTER
TWENTY-ONE

In the bay of the Bone Mouth, just off the curved shoreline of the Gem, eighteen ships closed around the *Luminous Wake* like the petals of a flower. Their bows were crowded with all who had survived the attack. People clung to the rails or climbed atop the bridges or lined the companionways, all pushing in as close as they could get to lay their eyes on the *Luminous*, where Caledonia stood atop the bridge surrounded by her command crew.

Her hair was loose and tumbled around her shoulders in tired waves, and she was dressed for battle. Her steel-plated jacket was cinched tight against her torso and her short blade was belted at her side. The ships had collected quickly, giving her very little time to dwell on the fact that she was about to ask the same people she'd failed in Cloudbreak to join ranks with a Fiveson.

As she looked over the gathered crowd, she was once again in awe of how many people had chosen to follow her. Fifty-four ships had been reduced to twenty, nearly a thousand people to four hundred and nine. But for Gloriana's ship, they were all here, watching her with strong, resilient faces.

"We have lost a great deal," Caledonia began, taking the receiver from Harwell and turning in a slow circle. She fought the urge to apologize, to lay bare every ounce of pitiful remorse she felt. Instead, she focused on their immediate needs. She could blame herself in private, but an army needed to know their leader trusted herself. "We were prepared, and we were taken by surprise, but we are still here."

There was no immediate cry of approval, no roar of ready rage from the crowd. This was not the pre-battle moment of near-visible energy and anticipation, when the possibility of victory was as real as that of defeat. This was a trembling moment on the other side of defeat.

It was Caledonia's job now to lift them up, to invite them to feel this loss and return to the fight.

"We have all lost people we love. That has been the way of the world, the way of Aric's world and now Lir's. Fighting against that has always been hard. Once, it was impossible, but *you* made it a reality. And as long as you choose to stay, I promise to lead. To choose our battles well." She paused, sensing unease worming its way through the crowd. "Our next fight is far from here, and it's one we cannot undertake alone. Aric's Fivesons have long been our enemies. Lir most of all. But Lir has turned against Fiveson Tassos and they are brothers no more. This gives us an opportunity: if we ally with Tassos, join our forces with his, we stand a chance at stopping Lir once and for all!"

A quiet murmur threaded through the air. In the faces before her, Caledonia spied uncertainty, mistrust, and deep hurt. It was impossible not to feel responsible for all of that. And wasn't she?

"You want us to join a Fiveson?!" a voice shouted.

The crowd shifted and another voice called, "We've been fighting to get away from them!"

"I want you to win this war with me! And to do that, we have to keep driving into it. Not away," Caledonia continued, forcing them to bend their attention back to her voice.

"Why should we trust you?!" a voice called from one of the ships.

At her back, Sledge growled deep in his chest. She could sense Pisces shifting, too, and Oran glaring through the crowd. Hime tipped her head to one side in a deceptively soft challenge, Nettle balled her fists, Pine thumbed the grip of his gun. But none of them could help her with this.

This was her role. And part of being the leader meant accepting responsibility for things she could not always control.

"I have been asking myself that same thing." Caledonia swept her gaze across the whole crowd. Answering as though the question had come from all of them. "I will not always be right." She gave the statement room to travel, to be heard before she continued. "I cannot promise you that we will win. I can't promise you we won't lose again. I can't promise we will survive this fight." She paused again, taking a deep breath. "The only thing I can promise is that I will never stop fighting to stop Lir, to change this world and give those who survive us something better than what we have!"

Caledonia's voice was a roar and her command crew took up the cry, raising their voices and slamming their feet against the deck.

"We can do this, but we have to act now!" she shouted. "Are you with me?"

All at once, the rest of the crowd took up the call, raising their voices and stomping their feet. It was so much more than the urgent song of war that vibrated in the air on the dawn of battle; this was the steady pulse of the ocean current, the constant coiling and uncoiling of the wind; this was the cut of a blade, the sting of sweat, the grinding pain of a throat screamed raw.

It was a song of survival.

"Prepare your ships!" Caledonia cried.

In moments the fleet was mobilized, their noses aimed for the Net with the *Luminous Wake* running out in front like a banner. At her starboard side was the *Blade*, Sledge and Pine in command.

"Captain," Harwell called as Caledonia entered the bridge. "Gloriana reports that there are signs of a recent battle, but as far as she can see, the only ships still at the Net belong to Tassos. She's holding position until we arrive."

"I guess we know where Lir sailed after Cloudbreak," Pisces muttered.

"He doesn't like to fail," Caledonia confirmed, following Pisces's line of thought. "But seems like Tassos outsmarted him."

"Not something anyone saw coming, I promise you," Oran added.

Leaving Nettle at the helm, Caledonia moved onto the command deck, where she could keep the horizon in view while the wind whipped at her cheeks. Her ankle ached only dimly now and she walked without any sign of a limp. Behind the *Luminous Wake* the fleet spread out like the wings of great bird. Even leaving one crew stationed at the Gem to wait for more survivors, they were eighteen ships strong. Eight ships flanked either side of the *Luminous* and the *Blade*, each one with Caledonia's sigil emblazoned on its hull in stark white paint. Together, they churned up the sea, boldly leaving a slashing trail in the surface of the ocean as they passed between the smaller islands of the Bone Mouth.

A whistle from on high signaled the first sighting of the Net. In the seconds that followed, Caledonia saw them: a line of small shapes pressed against the horizon like smudges of paint.

The ships grew larger as they drew closer, their hulls sheering out of the ocean. Before them, the water was littered with evidence of a recent battle, jagged leaves of metal clawing out of the sea with edges still smoking.

An involuntary shiver rushed down her spine at the sight.

These ships had haunted her thoughts all her life and now she was approaching them, not under cover of night, but in the full light of day. Not with the intent to slip past them, but to engage them. Even now, it went against every instinct she'd ever honed, and her mother's voice whispered in the back of her mind, *Run*.

"I can't tell if I'm nervous," Pisces said quietly at Caledonia's side, "or if I only *think* I should be nervous."

"They're just ships," Caledonia answered, doing everything she could to sound sure of herself, but she knew exactly what Pisces meant. They'd spent their lives equating these ships with captivity, with Aric's biting grip. Coming here intentionally was like sailing into a nightmare.

"If you believed that, we'd have come here long ago." Pisces's voice turned wry as she called her sister's bluff.

Inside the bridge, the crew had grown steely and quiet. Every terrible story they'd ever heard about failed attempts to breach the Net present in their minds as they drew approached.

Caledonia took a minute to study the impassive structure, calming her own mind with a practical task. The ships were uniformly large, their forward-facing hulls reinforced with long spikes ready to skewer approaching ships, their decks lined with automated cannons. She could only imagine there were more surprises waiting in the water between them.

"Slow us down, Nettle," she called. "Keep us out of range of those cannons."

"Yes, Captain," the girl answered as the ship slowed.

Caledonia searched up and down the row, looking for any indication of movement. They were close enough now that they'd surely been spotted, but still, there was no sign from the Net. Caledonia had intended to rush in and stop her ships just out of range, but with every minute that passed she grew less and less certain of that plan.

"Why . . ." Pisces whispered, echoing Caledonia's concerns.

Caledonia only shook her head. She had no answer. And that was never a good sign.

She was on the brink of calling her fleet to a stop when a second whistle sliced the air, this one a pattern of four sharp sounds.

"They're on the move!" one of Amina's Knots called. "Ten tails on course to intercept."

Relief twined with a new kind of tension in Caledonia's gut as ten ships peeled away from the Net and headed directly toward them.

"Send Silver ahead." Caledonia kept her eyes on the ten approaching ships as the *Luminous Wake* slowed even more. Seconds later, Silver Fleet took the lead with Gloriana joining in at the fore. Much as Caledonia wanted to be the one out in front, she'd come to accept that part of commanding a fleet was staying where she could see the field. "Harwell, tell the others to follow our lead. Nettle, keep a half mile between our noses and Silver Fleet's tails."

"Aye, Captain," Nettle called from her post at the wheel.

Silver Fleet glided forward at half speed like an arrowhead. Caledonia led the rest of the fleet a short distance behind while ahead the ten Bullet ships moved faster, their thrusters frothing at their sides.

All Caledonia needed was to get close enough to be in contact. To show that they hadn't come for a fight, but to talk. Of course, that was easier said than done. No one ever encountered a Bullet ship without intending to do one of two things: run or fight. Caledonia only hoped that her refusal to do either would keep them from an all-out battle.

"Harwell, remind everyone to hold their fire."

The distance between Silver Fleet and the Bullet ships constricted until they were within firing range. Caledonia held her breath, waiting for that first missile to streak through the air, but none came.

"So far, so good." Oran was braced against the hatch, eyes narrowed and cast out to sea.

Then the Bullet ships cut their engines. They glided forward on inertia and nothing more. Not even their thrusters churned. It was a cautious way of sailing and one Caledonia wasn't used to seeing from Bullets.

"That's encouraging." Pisces had a scope pressed to her eye. "Never seen a Bullet ship take a hint before."

All at once, Caledonia knew it wasn't a hint at all. It was a trap.

"All stop!" Caledonia cried. "Radio Silver Fleet to cut their engines!"

But before the command was out of her mouth, the waves slapping at the sleek hulls of Silver Fleet sparked with blue-white electricity.

Nine ships flashed against the deep blue of the water.

Lightning cracked across steel plates. It leapt from the tips of waves, striking out with deadly kisses. The air snapped and even though the *Luminous Wake* was some distance away, they heard the screams of their crewmates as they tore through the sky.

CHAPTER TWENTY-TWO

I t was over in the space of a breath.

"Harwell," Caledonia said, voice as flat and cool as ice. "Radio Silver Fleet."

"Yes, Captain." Harwell's hushed voice filled the small cabin as he repeated the words, "Silver Fleet, come in," three times with no response.

The only other time they'd seen this kind of tech had been in the electrified hull of *Electra*. Not even Amina's small nets had had the power to turn an entire ship into a live wire. Caledonia tried not to imagine how terrible that shock must have been as fear slowly expanded in her throat.

They could be alive.

They could be dead.

And there were still ten Bullet ships she needed to consider. They held their position on the opposite side of Silver Fleet. Ten noses aimed straight ahead. Threatening her without moving.

Behind them, the cannons atop the tall ships of the Net seemed to watch them through hollow unblinking eyes.

Harwell repeated his message to Silver Fleet once more. Then, in the long stretch of static that scratched at their ears, came a pattern of clicks.

"I think it's them, Captain," Harwell said, unsure but hopeful. "Maybe . . . maybe the electricity knocked out their receiver."

The clicks continued, randomly to Caledonia's ears, but it was enough to give her a sliver of hope.

"We've got eyes on!" Tin called from the command deck, a scope pressed to one eye as she pointed toward the stern of Silver Fleet's flagship. "They're alive!"

Relief swelled through the bridge. Nettle gave a whoop and Harwell lowered his forehead to the comm station. Pisces reached for Caledonia's hand and squeezed.

Oran came up behind her. "We're not in the clear yet."

All of Silver Fleet was dead in the water. The ten Bullet ships revved their engines once more, daring Caledonia to send more of her fleet into whatever web lay just beneath the waves waiting to stun their systems. If this were any other kind of fight, they might drive around the blockade of stilled ships and engage the Bullets. But they needed more from this encounter than a fight.

"Drive us in closer, Nettle. Just a bit," Caledonia commanded. "Harwell, tell the others to hang back."

The water sped by, peeling away from the hull like wings.

The closer they came, the more the Bullet ships seemed to shift, as though itching to drive out and meet them. But they held position.

"Why aren't they moving?" Pisces asked.

"They're up to something," Caledonia answered. But what, exactly, was a mystery. One that left an uneasy storm turning in her gut.

When they'd nearly reached Silver Fleet, Caledonia called an all stop. Almost as soon as she had, a voice came over the radio.

"Uh, Captain." Harwell looked up from his station, face paler than usual. "They want us to surrender."

Nettle scoffed, bouncing on her toes like she might take a swing if anyone got too close. "Surrender?! This isn't our surrender face, you brine-blooded bloat fish!"

"Quiet." Oran's command was both soft and unyielding.

Caledonia took the receiver. "This is Captain Caledonia Styx. I've come to speak with Fiveson Tassos."

"The commander has no interest in anything other than your surrender, girl." The voice that spoke was gnarled.

Pisces made a noise that landed somewhere between a growl and a grunt.

"Oran," Caledonia said, bringing him near with the implied command. There was no time to waste on pride. The faster she got Tassos in front of her, the better.

Oran took the receiver, his fingers curling briefly against her palm. Wetting his lips, Oran turned his eyes on Caledonia and pressed the button. "Tell Tassos that Fiveson Oran wants to talk."

The title sent a chill around the room, and Caledonia saw the way speaking it aloud changed Oran himself. It was a subtle shift, so small that she might have been the only one to see it. The cord of tension that pulled taut across his shoulders, the slight squaring of his jaw, the way his breath turned intentionally deep and slow. These were all marks of the Fiveson, every terrible decision and act he'd ever perpetrated etched so thoroughly into his bones that he would never be just Oran.

Once more, Caledonia was asking him to resurrect the past. Forcing him to inhabit the person he was trying so diligently to escape. And every time she did, guilt left another slice in her heart.

She wished there was any other way. But more and more, the truth of the matter was becoming clear: if they wanted to change the world, they'd have to embrace the changes the world had forced upon them.

Silence stretched through the cabin. The radio was dead in Oran's hands, and the ships before them kept their guns trained on Caledonia's fleet. Then the radio clicked and the room snapped together around the sounds of a voice as rough as a stone shearing into gravel.

"Steelhand."

A faraway pain flashed through the tree-ring layers of Oran's brown eyes. Caledonia wanted to reach across the small distance between them, to soothe him and encourage him, but she needed his heart jagged like the serrated edge of a knife.

"Tassos." Oran's voice was flat.

"Have you come here to fight, *brother*? Or surrender?" There was something both buoyant and cruel about the way Tassos spoke, as though either option would bring him joy.

"We've come to talk."

"Ah, yes, the girl." Caledonia had never seen Tassos, but she could hear the grin in his words now.

"The captain," Oran corrected him.

"The obsession," Tassos retorted. "It is interesting, and I suppose not all that surprising, that the two of you are so fixated on the same girl. I have to admit, I'm curious to meet her. But the longer she stays in my waters the more likely it is Lir will return. I should sink you here and now. Take something precious from him. And you."

"You won't find us so easy to sink, Tassos." Oran didn't blink as he delivered the threat.

Tassos laughed. "My Bullets have rigged your friends with enough mag bombs to crumble an island. Send any of your ships forward and they blow. Do anything but leave here and they blow."

"That rot fish!" Nettle punctuated her declaration with a sudden slap against the wheel.

Caledonia clenched her teeth. The Bullets had disabled Silver Fleet, and while they sat helplessly, seeded the water around them with mag bombs. In the space of a breath, Tassos could take half her fleet from her. She was ready to snatch the radio and tell Tassos exactly what she intended to do when Oran spoke once more. This time, his voice was smooth and cool, the whisper of silk across skin.

"Keep them," he said. "Hold them hostage while we talk. If you don't like what she has to say, you can pull the trigger."

At this, Tassos hesitated, and when he answered there was an unmistakable hint of interest in his tone. "I want you there, Steelhand."

Oran's expression was an impenetrable mask. Whatever existed between them still, it was dangerous. Caledonia had the sudden overwhelming urge to protect Oran from it. And the terrifying knowledge that she wouldn't be able to.

"I'll be there."

This elicited a long pause. "One ship each to the center," Tassos said at last. "You have five minutes and then we open fire."

CHAPTER
TWENTY-THREE

"He will try to intimidate you." Oran checked the clip of his sidearm before returning it to its holster. "And he's always been a little . . . unpredictable."

"He's not my first Fiveson." Caledonia checked each of her weapons. Oran was hiding something, she just wasn't sure what.

"I know, I just—" Oran stopped himself, looking up at Caledonia with a grim determination. "He's . . . not Lir."

Caledonia narrowed her eyes, trying to decipher what Oran wasn't telling her. As she gave him a tentative nod, a call went up on deck.

"Bow boat on approach!" Folly shouted. "Ready lines!"

The small vessel cut its engines and came alongside where Caledonia's crew was ready with hook and lash. Soon, the boat was lifted from the water and Sledge and Pine vaulted over the rail.

"Welcome aboard," Caledonia said, the smallest bit of relief bringing a smile to her face at the sight of them.

"Ready when you are, Captain," Sledge said in his solemn way.

Pine only nodded once in agreement, but his expression was locked down as tight as Oran's. Tassos made all three of them nervous in a way Caledonia had never seen before, and it was starting to make her anxious.

"Let's move!" she called to her crew.

The *Luminous Wake* sailed forward alone. No one made a sound as the protection of their fleet slipped into their wake, but their eyes widened as they moved within reach of Fiveson Tassos.

Caledonia spied Gloriana on the forward deck of the *Firebird*, arms crossed and stance wide. As they passed, Caledonia gave her people a stern nod, projecting steely confidence she only barely felt.

Directly ahead, the towering ships of the Net obliterated the horizon. They were Assault Ships, but each was larger than those Caledonia was used to confronting. They rose out of the water like hulking beasts, each tethered to the next by sturdy planks, turning them from a series of individual ships into a massive road. Where other Bullet ships ringed their decks in deadly spikes, these ships wore similar spikes pointed toward the water, ready to puncture the hull of any ship attempting to sail past. Between them, rows of razor wire and sharpened hooks hung low. It was exactly as terrible as Caledonia had always expected it to be. And so much worse.

She had only a second to take them in, then there was nothing between the *Luminous Wake* and the ten waiting Bullet ships. One sailed out to meet them.

"Prepare for port-to-port!" Pisces's call rang out.

The Bullet ship nosed alongside them, the spiked crown ringing its deck only inches away. Though each pike was clear of bodies, brown blood dripped down the hull as though the metal were stained with it.

As both ships engaged their thrusters and closed the distance, the Bullets let their griphooks fall into place with a vicious squeal and an angry slap. Pisces shouted an order and the *Luminous Wake* dropped her own griphooks to latch the railing of the Bullet ship. With six hooks between them, the two ships were securely locked together.

Two crews stood on opposite decks, their bodies rigid and ready. The desire and instinct to fight a nearly audible hum. But neither side moved. Guns remained in holsters, knives in sheaths, and shouts in throats.

Directly across from Caledonia stood a young man made of wrath. He was tall, his shoulders blocky and broad, his skin fractured a thousand times by thin orange scars, including a jagged gash that split the skin from his left eye to his jaw. A long tail of hair the dark, blackened red of burning coals swung past his waist, and as he stepped forward, he skewered Caledonia with a disdainful glare. He had handguns fastened to each thigh, and over his shoulder rose the long hilt of a sword heavier than anything Caledonia could fight with.

She didn't need Oran to tell her that this was Tassos.

A woman followed close behind, her own frame densely muscled. Her creamy skin was clouded by patches of deep tan and deeper burns laced with ribbons of orange scarring. Tight braids coiled into a bun at the crown of her head, and her only visible weapon was a whip holstered against one thigh.

As Caledonia strode forward to meet them, she imagined what they saw: a girl shorter than either of them, her hair burning under the bright sun, her features chiseled and fierce. A girl who had rallied a rebellion and found herself stymied by Lir. And at her side, Fiveson Oran, fallen from the glory of the Father. Disgraced and still reviled.

There was no wind to cool their skin as they climbed onto the narrow bridge of the griphooks. Moving to the center, they braced their feet against the smooth metal planks as the two ships rocked, their opposing rhythms a constant challenge.

When they were face-to-face and only an arm's length apart, Tassos transferred his gaze from Caledonia to Oran as though now that he'd seen her, she was of little consequence.

"Oran." Tassos spoke the name without any intonation, yet it left a chill on Caledonia's skin just the same.

"Tassos," Oran said, and then. "Cepheus."

The woman's eyes flicked to Oran and away. The tightening of her fists betrayed the cool brush of her disdain.

"I've come to make an offer of alliance," Caledonia said, determined to take control of the moment.

Tassos grinned, eyes holding tight to Oran. "We have business first," he said.

"Any business you have with Oran is business you have with me."

"Is it?" Tassos stepped forward, moving so quickly Caledonia barely had time to reach for her gun before his hand was on hers. "I don't think you want to make that kind of offer."

Oran inched closer as Tassos leaned in, smiling as his hand tightened around hers, pressing her fingers painfully against the grip of her gun. She braced herself, fighting to keep her expression steely, but she was at his mercy.

And he knew it.

Caledonia heard her crew shifting at her back, sensed Oran reaching for his weapon as Cepheus reached for her own.

"Oran is my crew," she ground out through gritted teeth.

"Oran," Tassos repeated, his voice softening, a clear prelude to an attack, like a snake coiling before a strike. "Lir. Don't you know they're the same?"

Oran made no move to speak or defend himself. He stood at Caledonia's side, his eyes locked on Tassos.

"Were," Caledonia said, stepping forward and forcing Tassos

to release his painful grip on her hand. "They were the same. But he's no longer a Fiveson."

Tassos stepped back with a predatory smile. "There are no Fivesons any longer," he said, directing his words to Oran. "But we both know you'll always be the Steelhand."

"He's my Steelhand now." Caledonia spoke loudly. "And you can bring your business to me."

The smile fell from Tassos's face. In an instant he'd gone from reckless brute to something much colder. His eyes were a dark, muddy brown and they landed on Caledonia like a punch to the chest. He regarded her, tilting his head slightly as if deciding whether or not she was worth even this much of his time. Then the corner of his lips hinted at a smile and he nodded at Cepheus.

Cepheus handed him something that looked like a glove, or, rather, that looked like two gloves missing the thumbs and joined at the fingertips. It glinted in the sunlight, articulated joints clinking softly together as Tassos draped it across his palm. He returned his gaze to Oran and this time his lips slashed across his face in a cutting half grin.

The muscles in Oran's jaw tightened and his brows crashed together. He knew what this device was, and he wasn't happy to see it.

"This is the price of my goodwill," Tassos said, voice hooked and cruel.

"And how do we benefit from your goodwill?" Oran asked.

Tassos shrugged. "A conversation. Isn't that what you've come for?"

"What is that?" Caledonia asked.

Cepheus laughed, the sound lonely and rancorous.

"The steel hand," Oran said after a moment. It took Caledonia a second to understand that he wasn't referring to himself but the device. "One of my first designs. Once you put it on, there are only two ways to remove it."

"The right way and the wrong way," Cepheus said with another laugh.

Oran's only response was the flexing of muscles in his jaw.

"Oran," Caledonia said, waiting for an explanation and doing her best not to fear it at the same time.

"You either let it cinch all the way, breaking one or more of your bones before it releases, or you pull and the blades inside strip the skin from your fingers." Oran spoke in a dull voice.

Caledonia rounded on Tassos, anger making her brazen. "No. I won't allow it. You talk to me or you don't, but torturing Oran isn't part of the deal."

"Torture?" Tassos asked. "I think you misunderstand the purpose of the steel hand. It's a means of proving loyalty. Commitment. Fortitude. I require Oran to prove himself." He smiled again, savoring each word. "And it's the only way I'll entertain your proposal. Or I can sink your ships. I'll be satisfied either way."

Caledonia didn't move. Her blood sang in her ears and she

struggled against the urge to lash out at Tassos, to strike him or kill him. Either option would end in a losing battle. But everything about this moment felt like losing. Whatever was happening right now, it was deeply personal. There was nothing Caledonia could say to convince Tassos to forgo his vengeance.

"Do you give us your word that you'll hear her out?" Oran asked.

"I give my word," Tassos said lightly.

Caledonia caught Oran's eyes. Though she didn't trust anything Tassos said, it seemed that Oran did. She knew she should tell him that he didn't have to do this, that they would find another way, one that didn't involve this gruesome kind of payment. But she couldn't. The truth was, there was no other way. She'd considered all their options, and this was the only viable one. The truth was, she was willing to trade his pain for the chance keep her fleet alive.

And so was he.

He nodded, the movement far too gentle for what he was consenting to. Caledonia returned the gesture. It was an agreement between the two of them. Both of them understanding that their actions, their choices had led to this place.

But nothing had ever felt as horrible as the moment she denied Oran all mercy and allowed him to slip his right hand into the glove. Nothing had ever darkened her heart as when she didn't stop him before the steel glove engulfed the fingers of his left hand. And no sound had ever speared her as thoroughly as when the steel bands of the glove slowly crushed his fingers.

Caledonia kept her eyes on Oran's as he struggled under the pain. She did not flinch when the first bone popped. The sound was almost gentle, the swift snapping of a branch.

Somewhere behind, she heard Pisces exhale sharply.

A second snap.

Oran's breath crashed like waves against Caledonia's heart.

A third crack.

This time a small, strangled sound emerged from Oran's throat in spite of his efforts to contain it. Behind them, an uneasy whisper ghosted through the crew, and Caledonia felt her stomach twist viciously. Yet through it all, Oran kept his eyes on her, and Caledonia was surprised to see that there was no anger in them. Whatever this was to Oran, some part of him felt he deserved it. With horror, she realized that this was what he'd been expecting. He'd known this was going to happen and he hadn't warned her. He hadn't asked for help or to stay behind. He'd come anyway.

The metal made a final, vicious shriek and Oran winced in pain.

Caledonia did not look away. Nor did she move to help. She stood under the burning sun as Oran dropped to one knee and Tassos smiled triumphantly.

"Now we are even," Tassos said.

It was then that Caledonia realized why he'd chosen the steel hand to exact his price. Whatever had happened in their past, Tassos had endured this same punishment, and Oran had either commanded it or delivered the device. Tassos hadn't agreed to meet them simply because Fiveson Oran stood with her, but because he'd waited a long time to see Oran suffer as he had.

Oran climbed to his feet, chest heaving, sweat beaded across his forehead and the bridge of his nose, eyes bright with pain. He let the steel hand fall from his broken fingers, flinching only slightly. It landed with a loud clatter against the metal planks. Then, with his eyes on Tassos, he kicked it off the edge. The ocean received it soundlessly, tucking it away where it would never taste flesh or blood again.

CHAPTER
TWENTY-FOUR

"Shall we talk?" The smile on Tassos's face was both empty and cruel.

A hard lump sat in the back of Caledonia's throat as she returned her attention to Tassos. Clenching her teeth against a sudden desire to vomit, she raised her chin.

"I'm here to offer an alliance against Lir." Caledonia let cold anger clip her words into daggers.

Behind Tassos, Cepheus smiled, her lips curling in a practiced sneer. It was then, when her lips pulled tight, that Caledonia saw they, too, were laced with delicate orange scars, as though sliced with something as thin as a butterfly's wings.

"Ah," Tassos said, as if this were news. "I'm not interested."

One turn ago, that answer would have brought Caledonia to her rage. She'd have countered hotly without a care for what happened next, because what happened next would have affected her and her crew alone. Not a fleet.

Not the entire Bullet Seas.

She let the sea air fill her lungs, let it cool her from the inside. Tassos didn't think he had anything to gain from an alliance with her, and she was going to prove him wrong.

"I think you are," she said.

"Do you? What do you have to recommend you?" Tassos folded his arms across his chest. The move was calculated to make him bigger and more imposing. "You stood against Aric, but it wasn't you who defeated him, was it? Not really. Lir did that for you."

"We both benefited from what Lir did," she answered. "You got the Net, after all."

"And you got—or I should say *had*—Cloudbreak. Lir tried to come for me and he failed. He'll try again, but I suspect you'll take priority now that you've emerged from hiding. So, tell me again, what do I possibly have to gain from allying with Lir's next target?"

As he spoke, Caledonia could feel Oran bristling at her side. Behind her, her crew watched with a kind of intensity that pressed against her back like many hands holding her up. Tassos wanted her to feel small, but Caledonia wouldn't do what any Fiveson wanted.

Taking a measured step forward, Caledonia dropped her voice, forcing Tassos to pay attention and cutting their crews out of the conversation. "I know what you need most in the world right now."

Tassos narrowed his eyes. "And what is that?"

Caledonia leaned in, the first taste of blood on the tip of her tongue as she said a single word: "Silt."

Doubt sliced Tassos's eyes while want curled his fingers into fists. He wanted what she offered to be real, she could see that plainly. But more than that, he needed it to be.

"You have Silt?" His eyes tripped from her to the deck of her ship, skating over her crew as if one of them would reveal the truth. "You don't have Silt."

"No, I don't have Silt," she admitted. "But I can help you get it."

"I don't need your help." Tassos pulled back. "We can fight this war without you, and when we're done, I'll crush your fleet without a second thought."

There was no denying that Tassos outnumbered and out-gunned her, but he was still here, standing suspended over the ocean between their ships. And that meant he thought there was something she could give him.

"You're running out of your drug. Lir is, too. Two weeks ago, I destroyed a massive crop of baleflowers—from what was one Five-son Decker's AgriFleet. The Bullets in that fleet were already on reduced rations and I'm willing to bet the AgriFleet doesn't have many barges of that size left. If any. That means one of you is going to break very soon." She looked into the eastern horizon, toward the Holster. "If Lir has more than you, all he has to do is wait you out and attack when your fleet is in withdrawal. Do you think that's a fight you can win? Maybe I should do the same. Wait and see which of you emerges as an actual threat. Which of you shrivels into something too weak to hold a gun."

The ensuing silence stretched thin. Tassos studied her intently, searching for the lie that was not there.

"Can you say for certain it will be you?" Caledonia allowed herself a second to appreciate the way the muscles flashed in the Fiveson's jaw. "I can tell you why it won't be. You might be secure for the moment, but the only thing you really control is the factory on the other side of the Net. You have neither the existing blossoms nor the seeds to grow them, and you'll need both very soon. Maybe you already do."

When Tassos didn't immediately refute her claims, she continued, emboldened.

"Lir has blossoms and seeds. All he needs to do is figure out how to produce those pills you rely on and he'll have you. Your Bullets will figure that out sooner than you think." She paused, noting the new flush in his cheeks. "Or, we can work together, and both get what we want."

"How?" Suspicion clouded his voice. Suspicion and just a sliver of desperation.

Now Caledonia let a humorless smile bend her lips. "We combine our fleets and take the Holster. We win and whatever seeds and bale barges we find are yours."

"And what do you get?" he asked.

"I keep the Holster," she answered. "And Lir is mine."

Tassos's gaze grew distant as he considered the strategy, playing it through to ensure he could get what he wanted from the deal.

"Why do I need you to take the Holster?" he asked at last. "You and your . . . nineteen ships, is it? Not much of a fleet."

"You need me because all you've ever done is protect that Net." Caledonia had been prepared for this argument. Here, she was on solid footing. "You may be good with defense, but if you want to hit Lir where he lives, then you need an offensive strategy. And you won't find better than me."

Tassos almost smiled, considering her as though seeing her for the first time. Finally, he shook his head. "Even with the seeds, we still need the means to grow them. We need soil, and that's kept in Slipmark. You can't get me what I need. No deal."

The wind gusted between them and the ships rocked steeply together as if even the ocean wanted them to join hands. Frustration gnawed at Caledonia's throat, but she swallowed it down. She had one final card to play and no one was going to like it. No one except Tassos.

"Soiltech," she said. "I have it and if you agree to fight, if you help me take the Holster, it's yours. I'll let you walk away with the means to produce your own Silt."

Oran went rigid at her side. Tassos had also tensed, though for different reasons. Silt was at the root of every piece of this fight, the toxic center from which everything else bloomed. It was so powerful it controlled everyone it touched. Perhaps especially Lir and Tassos. They both held such power, but they were also terrified that without that poisoned powder, they'd have none.

"Show me." Tassos was ready to call her bluff and walk away, but she could see he wanted her to be telling the truth almost as much as he wanted to deliver her fleet to the bottom of the ocean.

Caledonia turned to her waiting crew. They were stone-faced and tense, their hands resting near holstered weapons.

She nodded at Pisces. "Bring me the soiltech."

The hesitation in Pisces's expression was there and gone almost as quickly as the young woman herself. She returned in a minute, their only functioning soiltech device clutched in one hand and a canvas sack of bleached soil in the other as Nettle watched with a pinched expression.

"Show him."

Pisces activated the device with the press of a button. It flared with pale green light as she emptied the contents of her sack over it. White soil filtered through the sieve and when it emerged on the other side, it was a dark, healthy brown scattering in the wind.

Not even Tassos could hide his pleasure, his mouth parted in delighted surprise. Cepheus went still, her eyes tracking Pisces. Oran made no sound, but Caledonia could feel his frustration.

"Do we have a deal?" Caledonia asked.

Tassos stuck out his hand. "We have a deal. We'll work to-gether to take the Holster and in return, you deliver your soiltech and a blueprint for replication."

Caledonia thrust her hand into his, feeling new bruises where he'd gripped her just moments ago. They pinched less painfully than the guilt she felt when she said, "Deal."

With a quick jerk of his hand, Tassos tugged her close, putting his face so near to hers she could smell the too-sweet notes of Silt on his skin. "And after that," he said. "I'll gun you down if you so much as blink in my direction."

CHAPTER TWENTY-FIVE

"**S**oiltech?" Pisces snapped as Hime ushered Oran to an exam bed. "What were you thinking? We're meant to get that tech into the hands of the colonists, not Bullet warlords in the making. That wasn't part of the plan, Cala."

Pine, Sledge, and Pisces stepped inside the med bay, sealing the hatch behind them. Caledonia remained halfway between Oran and the door. She watched as Hime carefully manipulated his fingers, as Oran breathed intentionally through his nose. Pain etched itself into the shadows of his jaw, the lines around his eyes, and Caledonia stood rooted in place, guilt stacked on her shoulders like massive boulders. She hadn't done this to him, but she'd let it happen. She'd *needed* it to happen.

She felt sick.

"Or maybe it was." Pine kept his voice light as he crossed the room and stretched out on an empty exam bed. "And she didn't tell us because she knew we wouldn't agree."

Pisces rounded on Caledonia. "Is that true?"

"It's true." Caledonia had never been good at lying, and especially not to Pisces.

"Do you know what you've done?!" Sledge burst forward, striding across the room in three terrifying steps. "Do you have *any* idea?! You're making the next Aric Athair."

She recognized the fear in his eyes, but she didn't share it. "Only if he gets everything he wants."

"If?" Pine asked, crossing his legs at the ankle and tucking his arms behind his head.

"If," she repeated. "I didn't promise him baleflowers or seeds. Only that they would be his for the taking."

"You want us to find them first?" Pisces asked, incredulous. "Get rid of them before they claim them? That's a hell of a gamble."

"Everything we do is a gamble," Caledonia countered. "We can't contain soiltech. In fact, our goal is *not* to contain it, which means at some point, it will end up in the hands of Tassos or someone just as terrible. The point is, we can make more. We can make sure it gets into the hands of colonists, Slaggers, and whoever else needs it. That's how we keep him from becoming Aric. By making sure the only thing he controls is Silt. Not food."

The room was quiet but for the humming of machines and Oran's harsh breath. Everyone knew there was truth in Caledonia's argument, but it wasn't the clean kind of truth they wanted. It settled between them awkwardly, a bomb waiting to go off.

I'm going to set his bones now. Hime's signs were decisive.

Oran sat completely still, eyes locked on the small girl in front of him as she reached for one of his fingers and pulled. The tip of Oran's left trigger finger was drawn outward, the skin stretching like fabric before Hime guided the bone back into place. Oran exhaled sharply and fresh beads of sweat appeared on his brow.

No one spoke as one by one Hime repeated the same motions on the other two fingers. Oran breathed deeply through it all, never complaining, never asking Hime to pause. And though his muscles seemed to quiver as Hime tugged on the third finger, he never gave in.

If he only would have let himself pass out, he'd have woken to bound fingers never knowing the pain his body endured in his absence. But Oran clung stubbornly to consciousness as though part of him felt that he deserved to feel every bit of this agony.

Caledonia couldn't help but think that maybe he did. And she couldn't help but feel that she did, too.

When Hime was done, she wrapped Oran's fingers in gauze, then produced two gloves. They were made of black clothtech, supple and gleaming in the blue light. She set them on the table between his hands.

"Gloves," Oran said, a laugh threatening behind the word. "Are you telling me that you want me to put on gloves, Princelet?"

Hime's cheeks blushed a pale pink at the name Redtooth had given her so long ago. She nodded, signing to explain, *The fabric will compress to keep the swelling down. Splints will go on over them.*

"You want me to put on gloves that compress?" This time, Oran's laugh was loud and quickly followed by a wince. "I appreciate your sense of irony."

Healing isn't ironic, Hime answered, reaching for one of his hands. As gently as she could, she began the process of sliding the glove into place.

"I'm fine," he said when she paused at the knuckle of one shattered finger. "None of this pain belongs to you."

"Oran." Sympathy flooded Pisces's voice, spilling over into Caledonia and renewing her sharp guilt.

"It had to happen." Oran grimaced as the glove applied a steady pressure around each of his fingers. Without a word of protest, he offered his other hand to Hime.

"Did it?" This time Pisces spared an accusation for Caledonia.

"It did," Oran said. "Tassos has been waiting a long time to visit some of my own designs on me. If it buys us what we need to tip the scales in our favor, then it's worth it."

"You'll be useless in a fight for a while," Pine said. "Well. More useless."

Oran frowned, eyes darting briefly to Hime as if hoping she would tell him that it wasn't true. In response, she reached for three slender splints and began to bind them to his fingers.

Only three of the fingers are broken. The others are bruised deeply, maybe fractured. The gloves will speed the healing, she signed when she'd finished her work. *Three weeks if you're lucky and not stupid.*

"Define stupid," Pisces said.

Letting Tassos put you in the steel hand! Hime's expression jumped from placid to outraged in a heartbeat. She turned to Caledonia and added, *Letting it happen! Would you have let the same happen to one of us?*

"That's not fair, Hime," Pisces soothed.

Isn't it? Hime asked. *I don't recognize her choices anymore. We didn't go back for Amina, now this, and I've seen what's in the weapons locker. Did you think no one would notice?*

"What do you mean?" Pisces asked. "What's in the weapons locker?"

A sharp breeze of panic swept through Caledonia, too sudden for her to mask her reaction. Oran shifted on the exam bed, ready to take the blame, but Caledonia shook her head.

"Star blossom bombs," she admitted. "Four of them."

Pine sat up straight, dark eyes sharpening on Caledonia while Sledge turned and slowly paced across the room.

"I thought we'd agreed that was a one-time thing," Pisces said, trying not to sound hurt, but failing. "After the Battle of Cloudbreak."

"'An act of desperation' were your exact words," Sledge nearly growled. "One we would never repeat."

No one had blamed Caledonia for using the star blossom at the time. The results had been viscerally terrible, and no one knew that better than Caledonia, but they'd all agreed that Aric's methods should never be repeated. If they wanted to change the world, they had to start with themselves and the very tools they used to change it.

Having the star blossoms was a betrayal of everything they'd agreed to.

Where did you even get them? Hime asked.

"That seems fairly obvious to me." Pine shot Oran a contemptuous look.

"I asked Oran to build them." Caledonia made her voice uncompromising. "Just in case."

The room settled into an awkward silence. Sledge scowled while Pine shook his head and Hime's mouth bent in a steep frown. Pisces stood apart from all of them with her arms wrapped tightly around her middle. She was trying to look stoic, impartial, but she couldn't hide her hurt from Caledonia.

"And you're right, Hime, I let this happen," Caledonia said. There was no point pulling her punches now.

"This was between Tassos and me," Oran added hurriedly. "Caledonia couldn't have done anything to change that."

"I could have," Caledonia admitted. "I could have refused to let it happen, but I didn't. Because I want what Tassos has to give us. I don't think we'll survive much longer without it. If you want to be mad about it, be mad. But don't let it get in our way."

What she didn't say was that this was one more decision none of them had to make. This was one more wound they did not have to carry. Every one of them had their demons. Every one of them would be haunted by the things they'd done for the rest of their lives, but when it was all over, they would have to move forward without letting those things control them. They needed someone who could shield them from the worst decisions.

And, Caledonia realized as her friends and her crew watched her with increasingly shuttered expressions, that person was always going to be her.

"Steely?" she asked.

She could sense the strain in the room as they answered with varying degrees of conviction. Their trust had stretched thin, and while it was still there, she could feel the way it was unravelling at the edges. The threads that wove them together might be strong, but they were not invincible. They would all need time to recover from this.

But time wasn't something she could give them.

"Good," she said, knowing that what came next wasn't going to sit well with any of them. "Then we need to discuss who will join me on Tassos's ship."

"For a meeting?" The skepticism in Sledge's tone suggested he knew the answer and didn't like it.

Caledonia shook her head once. "Tassos has agreed to a brief alliance, but while we work on exactly how to go after Lir, he wants me on his ship as a gesture of goodwill and assurance. No one from either side will fire on a ship if we're both on board."

"Maybe not, but they can still slit your throat in your sleep," Pine retorted.

"Which is exactly why I'm not going alone." Caledonia took a breath before offering the rest of her plan. "Hime, I'm leaving you in charge of the *Luminous Wake*; Pine, you have the *Blade*. The two of you are in command of the fleet. I want Pisces, Sledge, Oran, and Nettle with me."

"Nettle?" Sledge asked, appalled. "You can't be serious. She's just a girl." Somehow, he was still unable to reconcile Nettle's actions with her appearance. Even after so many moons.

"A girl who navigated Slipmark better than any of us," Pine reminded him.

"Which is exactly why I need her," Caledonia said. "She can get in and out of places we won't be able to. Any other objections?"

The rest shook their heads, still in various stages of shock, both at what was happening and what they'd learned. Caledonia wished there was time to sort through everything, but there was barely time to pack a bag.

"All right, then make your preparations."

》《

One hour later, they gathered again on the main deck. The Net loomed large against the sky, stretching into the east as far as the eye could see. Between each of the towering Assault Ships, smaller ships roamed like sentries. If the Net could be dismantled, there were enough ships here to make taking the Holster more than possible. Enough to do more than simply resist Lir.

As quickly as the thought occurred to her, another followed. Tassos may not have overstated the security of the Net, but he had undersold his need for Silt. There had to be hundreds of Bullets aboard these ships, each with a craving for the drug that they could not create themselves. The minute they ran out, things were going to get ugly.

"Captain." The word landed at her feet like a stone. Pisces appeared at her side, face fixed in a scowl.

"What is it, Pi?" she asked.

For a second, it seemed Pisces had determined not to speak. Her mouth pinched into a thin line, and her eyes darted from Caledonia to the crew standing near enough to overhear if she weren't careful. "Star blossoms!" Pisces hissed, stepping in close enough to keep her accusation between the two of them. "Cala, what are you thinking?!" Caledonia opened her mouth but before she could say anything, Pisces rushed on. "And why wouldn't you discuss that with me?"

"I'm not proud of it. I didn't want to discuss it with anyone." Caledonia reached for her sister's fingers.

"You discussed it with him!" Pisces snapped her hand back, gesturing to Oran, who stood a short distance away, his eyes on them as Hime tucked additional medtech into his bag. "Him and not me. And I know I'm the one who urged you to trust him, but not over me. Not *instead* of me."

The hurt that trembled in the bend of Pisces's mouth was worse than anything else. Caledonia hated that she was the cause, even if she couldn't apologize for the reason.

"This isn't about trust."

"Isn't it?" Pisces shook her head. "I know what kind of fight this is, Cala. I know there are hard decisions ahead of us."

"There are some decisions you shouldn't have to make, Pi," Caledonia said, wishing instead she could just apologize.

"We can fight them as long as we don't become them. That's still true, isn't it?" Pisces peered into Caledonia's eyes, a demanding, haunting look in her own.

"It's true," Caledonia answered. For everyone but herself.

Pisces sighed, her skeptical gaze traveling to the deck of the Bullet ship waiting to receive them. "I hope so," she said, shouldering her bag and stepping away to meet Nettle.

»«

The sun was quickly abandoning the western skies, and Tassos waited at the other end of the griphook bridge with a greedy smile. It seemed to Caledonia that the ship itself was waiting to consume them.

When they were finally ready, Caledonia turned to Hime and Pine. "If this goes bad, you know what to do."

"Blow a hole in the Net the size of Cloudbreak and get you out?" Pine planted his hands on his hips as though restraining himself from reaching for her. "All of you." His eyes traveled to Sledge, standing a few feet away with hooded eyes.

We'll get the fleet out, Hime signed with a darting glace for Pine.

Joining Tassos aboard his ship was necessary. Joining her fleet with his was necessary. But neither of those things meant she had to trust him. In fact, it was prudent that she cling to her mistrust as tightly as she did her desire to make this work.

"I'm giving you both command because I know you can make that choice." Caledonia looked between the two of them. "Steely?"

Hime nodded and Pine blew out a hard breath. "Steely," he said, then he crossed the distance between himself and Sledge. Sliding his hands along the mountain's shoulders, Pine pulled him close for a deep kiss.

The open display made Caledonia smile. The intimacy between the two of them wasn't a secret, but it was usually private. Hime watched with a pained expression, her eyes as sad as they were happy. If Amina were here, she'd be staying behind, commanding the *Luminous* at Hime's side.

"It's time," Caledonia said.

Her crew shuffled around her, uncomfortable and agi-tated, scattered across the deck as though still expecting this moment to turn into a fight. Caledonia faced her many sisters and in a quiet voice, she asked, "On the back of the sea, who do you trust?"

The response came in whispers lined with steel: "Our sisters."

They would not be with her, but they would stay alert and ready, they would endure whatever came next, and they would keep fighting. With a nod, Caledonia turned toward the bridge and left the *Luminous Wake* behind.

CHAPTER TWENTY-SIX

Voluntarily stepping aboard a Bullet ship felt like stepping in front of a loaded gun.

Tassos greeted them with a snarl and a smirk. As soon as Caledonia's foot touched the deck, he swooped in like a massive hawk, hooking one brawny arm around her neck and tucking her against the solid wall of his chest.

"Welcome aboard the *Deep Cut*, Captain," he growled, the sound of his voice equal parts vibration and amusement.

Caledonia's pulse pounded three staccato beats high in her throat, panic momentarily overwhelming her thoughts. His arm was a vise around her neck, her chest wedged against his stomach. She could feel the metal plates shifting inside his doublet.

She quashed her flashing panic, and instead of struggling against the entire bulk of Tassos as he certainly wanted her to do, she unsheathed the knife at her waist, sliding the tip into the narrow gap between the bottom edge of his doublet and the top of his pants.

Tassos stiffened as the blade bit lightly into his abdomen.

"Unless you greet everyone this way, I recommend you keep your hands to yourself."

Caledonia added enough pressure that she felt the skin break beneath the point of her knife. Tassos, however, only grinned harder, bending his face uncomfortably close to hers.

"Give it a little push, dear," he said, goading her. "And all my Bullets will be yours."

"Your Bullets and your problems," Caledonia answered. "It's too soon to kill you now, but I will if you don't withdraw your arm."

Tassos laughed, a great bellowing sound that echoed across the deck in the mouths of his Bullets. But he released her and stepped away without any indication that her knife had cut as deeply as she knew it must.

"I can see why my brothers like you." The words were offered in the vein of a compliment, but they sounded more like an insult.

"I can see why they don't like you," she countered, and this time, his bullish smile turned sour on his face.

"Cepheus, let's move!" Tassos barked.

Caledonia turned to confirm the rest of her team was aboard the *Deep Cut*. Pisces stood nearest. She bore an expression of cold malice, one hand resting on the grip of her gun. On top of that hand was Oran's, fingers glinting with silver splints as he prevented her from shooting the Fiveson. Just behind them,

Sledge and Nettle stood side by side, their expressions equally stormy.

"Make ready," Cepheus called.

Across the water, Tin echoed the order and the griphooks of both ships rose and snapped loudly into place, leaving the *Deep Cut* and *Luminous Wake* free to sail.

"Join me on the bridge, Captain," Tassos commanded as the ship surged forward.

"Let's go," Caledonia said in a low voice, giving each of her team a pointed look.

When Tassos strode across his deck the entire ship responded as though he himself was a ship in the ocean pushing waves in all directions. His crew made way or marked him warily, orbiting around him like insects circling a carcass. They eyed Caledonia and her command crew with a mix of keen disinterest and hunger. Caledonia noted the ones who seemed unable to look away from Oran. For now, they were under the protection of Tassos, but what would happen when he looked away?

The ship was similar in design to the *Luminous Wake*, except instead of climbing up to the bridge, they skirted around it to where the deck swept low toward the racing water. Tassos took the lead as the ship darted ahead of the fleet.

The Net was suddenly very close and now Caledonia could see exactly how it had earned its name. The ships weren't just evenly spaced but woven together like a flexible, yet treacherous scarf.

What she'd taken for long ropes of razored wire and hooks was, in truth, a vast array of webbing. The webs draped between the stationary ships like canopies, but Caledonia felt certain that any rogue vessel attempting to slip through the Net would trigger the trap. Those webs would drop, ensnaring an entire ship to prevent its escape. And if previous experience was any indicator, they were likely electrified, too.

"Cala," Pisces said, her eyes locked not on the Net itself but the water. "Fins."

Caledonia followed her sister's gaze to the sight of six fins. They slashed through the water in lazy rocking motions, deep gray sails above shadowed bodies. These weren't the blunt dorsals of dolphins but the black-tipped flags of sharks. As she searched the bright blue water, she found more of the creatures swimming far beneath the surface and clustering close to the hulls of other ships down the line. There were dozens of them.

"Keep your crews on their ships," Tassos said.

"Is that what they're here for," Caledonia answered, ignoring the threat. "To keep *your* crews in line?"

This won another laugh "I don't need sharks to keep my clip in line."

"But you do need something."

At this, Tassos abandoned his jovial tone, his voice dipping low when he answered, "We all need something, Bale Blossom."

The closer they drew to the Net, the more Caledonia marveled at the intricacies of its design. Here at the end, there was a ship unlike the others. It was long and flat, its base marked by what appeared to be two narrow tunnels leading straight through to the other side of the Net. The deck seemed to rise and fall chaotically, without a thought for function, and the whole of it crawled right up to the shore of the Bone Mouth's nearest island. Beyond this point, the the islands themselves became the barricade.

Caledonia tried to peer between the ships to catch even a glimpse of the Silt Rig, but with only seconds to scour the sea, she had no luck. The ship approached swiftly until all she could see was the Net itself. Every piece of it fed so seamlessly into another, she realized she had no idea where they were going to dock. Just as soon as she'd had the thought, the ship cut its speed, then rotated and began to slide backward toward a narrow space in the matrix. Docking orders were shouted up and down the main deck and the *Deep Cut* inched backward.

The air here was stale with salt and sulpher. Sharks cut close in the waters below, as much at home here as the ships themselves. Massive griphooks came down on either side, snapping the *Deep Cut* in place, one more link in the chain.

"Follow me," Tassos said, rounding on Caledonia and directing his steps back toward the main deck. "We have a lot to discuss."

》《

Leaving the *Deep Cut*, they immediately found themselves on the deck of the strange, flat ship that extended outward from its anchored point on the Bone Mouth. But as they walked, Caledonia realized this wasn't a single ship at all, but several. She was crossing from the deck of one ship to another, each connected to the next by a combination of griphooks and broad sheets of metal welded in place. Unlike the Assault Ships that composed the rest of the Net, this was more of a building stitched together entirely of ships. The whole thing must have covered a square mile of shallow waters.

Tassos led them inside the megaship, its mazelike corridors rivaling the chaotic weaving paths of Cloudbreak. Stairwells led to hallways and more stairwells, taking them up and down and up again as they moved deeper inside the mysterious structure. Caledonia did her best to ignore the small alarm singing in the back of her mind as she admitted she would not be able to retrace their steps to the surface. Tassos could be taking them anywhere. Straight to the hold or worse.

Finally, he led them down a narrow corridor and into an isolated room at the end. Cepheus was already inside, along with two men. One was old and grizzled, bearing a shock of pure white hair pulled into a bun at the back of his head and tanned skin so long tortured by the sun that it had turned leathery, wrinkles digging into his face and arms like deep crevices. The other was younger with shoulders and fists that matched those of Sledge.

"This is Tug," Tassos said, gesturing to the bludgeon-fisted man standing beside a long table cutting the room in half. "And that's Heron. You've met Cepheus already." He paused and said, "This is Caledonia Styx."

"The infamous Bale Blossom. Well, isn't that a hell of a thing." The white-haired man had taken a seat across the room, back pushed against the wall, and showed no interest in standing to greet their semi-hostages.

"This is Pisces," Caledonia began, eager to get these strange pleasantries over with. "Sledge, Oran, and Nettle."

"Oran." Tug's voice was an ominous rumble. "Fiveson."

The word was more than a title. Caledonia had heard it used in many different ways in the time she'd known Oran. It had been a curse and a threat. Spoken by Tug, it was both.

"Is it too much to assume you already have a plan?" Tassos asked, bracing his hands against the table.

"I'll have one soon," Caledonia countered, moving to stand across from him. "But first I need everything you have on the Holster: the harbor, the city, everything."

Tassos sucked on his teeth as he considered his response, clearly weighing the benefits of withholding his intel against making actual progress. Finally, he gestured to Heron, who produced a map so expertly rendered, Caledonia could perfectly imagine the gasp that would have dropped from Lace's lips. Her wide, blue eyes would have consumed the unmarred paper, the careful markings of latitude and longitude. Before Nettle, Lace had steered their crew through rough and clear waters alike, and she would have exclaimed over the degree of detail inscribed in every inch of this map. Even Caledonia recognized it for the prize it was, though she did her best to hide that from her current company.

"The Holster," Heron said with a small flourish.

The map zoomed in tight on the western side of a peninsula where the shoreline scooped gently inward, creating a protected valley for the city of the Holster. In the center was the harbor, and the cartographer had taken great care to illustrate the series of breakers that limited ingress and egress. Beyond that, the western seas extended to the edge of the page. A small arrow in the upper left corner indicated how many miles to Cloudbreak, and a similar arrow in the bottom left did the same for the Bone Mouth.

Plucking a pouch from a nearby chest, Heron began dropping small metal ships into the harbor. "The harbor itself holds a full cohort of ships. Probably seventy-five at any given time. The rest"—he paused to place several metal blocks in a row— "are outside of these breakers."

The breakers were evenly spaced, meaning only a few ships could pass into the harbor at once. Not unlike the metal islands in the waters of Cloudbreak. A barrier, but not a complete barricade. This was information they'd had, but seeing it mapped out like this brought new clarity.

"Can we bomb them?" Pisces asked.

"Sure." Heron bobbed his head. "But they run deep. No guarantee you won't gouge your hull trying to pass over one. Might be better to just leave them where you can see them."

Caledonia nodded. "What else?"

"The gun towers." As Heron spoke, he marked the towers with a jab of his finger. "All five are on high ground, outside of town, and impossible to target without putting your ships within range of their damned powerful guns."

"One for every son," Oran added, settling in at Caledonia's shoulder. "Aric built them as we were named."

"We protect him as we protect each other." Tassos gave the response as though reading a script, and for a fleeting second Oran and Tassos shared a look thick with history.

"We won't get anywhere near the Holster without taking them out first." Tassos looked back to Caledonia, expectant in a way that bristled beneath her skin.

"How long does it take to sail to the Holster from here?" Caledonia asked.

"Only a day," Cepheus answered. "Less at full throttle."

"Good. Then we have some time to prepare," Caledonia said, eyes tracing the distance from the breakers to the gun towers and all the way to the tip of the southern peninsula.

"How much time do we need for that?" Cepheus stood at

Tassos's elbow, arms crossed and hip cocked to one side.

Caledonia shrugged. "A few days. Maybe more."

"Is that a problem?" Pisces asked.

"It's not a problem." Tassos nearly growled his response.

But Caledonia knew it was.

"How much Silt do you actually have?" she asked.

The look Tassos gave her might have gutted a lesser person. As it was, Caledonia let it wash over her to reveal what truly lay beneath it: fear.

"Enough," he ground out. "Now, do you have a plan or not?"

"That depends on how many ships we have to work with. How many can you spare from the Net?"

"The Net isn't something you just take apart, Bale Blossom." Heron leaned back in his chair, dragging a finger along the lower portion of the map where the Net butted up against the southern tip of the peninsula. "Wasn't designed that way."

"But you just sailed the *Deep Cut* in and out," Pisces protested.

"Wouldn't be much of a Net if it was easy to dismantle," Tug answered.

"Aric couldn't have a single Fiveson in command of more ships than him," Oran added.

"What does that mean?" Caledonia asked.

"The stationary ships have no engines," Cepheus offered. "No engines and about five anchors each. We can pull the planks and trawling nets in for a storm, but the ships themselves don't move."

"So." Caledonia drew a careful breath as she prepared her next question. "How many sailing ships do you have at your disposal?"

"You've seen it for yourself." Tassos threw a hand in the air.

It took Caledonia a second to understand his meaning, and when she did, she felt her chin drop. "You're telling me that the ships I saw today are your entire fleet?"

"Forty-three in all. I had a few more before Lir came at me, but then, so did he."

Caledonia tried not to focus on the numbers. She'd expected Tassos to have more; she'd expected the Net to be more of a resource. But she needed to consider what she did have: sixty-two ships, hundreds of soldiers, and not much time before Tassos's diminishing supply of Silt made both irrelevant. Silt aside, she had as many ships as she'd had in Cloudbreak, and she'd been ready to attack then. She could do it again now.

"How many ships does Lir have?" Caledonia asked. "Last count we had was near two hundred."

"He did have that many and he brought them all to my doorstep!" Tassos shouted, a wild glint in his eyes.

"You held off two hundred ships?" Caledonia asked, disbelieving.

"Didn't have to. Not for long." Tassos smirked. Cocky and

amused. "Because I have something he wants almost as much as he wants me dead."

"The rig?" Caledonia asked.

"No." Tassos rose to his full height, looming over her with an excited smile. "His brother Donnally."

CHAPTER
TWENTY-SEVEN

The storm that rose in Caledonia's ears was like no other.

She felt her body turning to vapor, her mind to wind, her blood to rushing rain. There was nothing connecting her to the world except the song of Donnally's name tossed on the turbulent waves of her mind.

Then she felt Pisces tapping a foot against hers. Heard Oran saying something in unforgiving tones. Saw the satisfied twist of Tassos's lips.

"I want to see him." Her voice vibrated in her chest though it sounded muffled to her ears.

Everyone looked to Tassos. He grinned, happy to cause pain simply because he could.

"I want to see him, now," she repeated. "Or we take our ships and inform Lir that you're at the end of your Silt and let him return with his entire fleet."

Tassos didn't laugh, but his smile suggested that he believed her about as much as respected her. Still, he shrugged. "Cepheus."

The woman moved immediately toward the hatch, and whether or not Caledonia was supposed to follow, that's exactly what she did. Behind her, she heard shuffling and the hatch closing again, then fingers caught hers and gave a light squeeze. Pisces.

She pinched the skin on the inside of Caledonia's wrist, forcing Caledonia to focus on her for a split second. "I'm coming with you."

Caledonia nodded. Her heart was a hammer inside her chest, her lungs were tight, her skin prickled with sweat, but soon, she would see Donnally.

Cepheus led them through corridors lined with dull-eyed Bullets and then into a sparsely populated section of the megaship where the air was cool and carried a metallic taste that was almost electric. Caledonia could barely focus on the ship as they passed through it, could barely mark where they turned or how many hatches they passed through. Finally, they came to the hold. The large room contained rows and rows of barred cells, many of which were occupied. Though she barely spared the prisoners a glance as she passed, she could hear them; shouting or moaning or begging for something to drink.

Caledonia tried to tune them out, but with each cry, she imagined her brother—injured, abused, alone—and her lungs constricted a little more.

At the end of the row were four doors, two on either side. Cepheus stopped in front of one, then pulled a key from the ring at her waist that Caledonia hadn't noticed and unlocked the hatch before spinning it and pulling it open.

"He's all yours," she said. "What's left of him."

Beyond the door, Caledonia could see nothing. She hesitated, suddenly unsure what she would say, unsure what she would find. Their last encounter had torn a hole in her heart. She didn't know if she could survive another.

Then Pisces's hand was in hers. Their fingers wove together, and the warmth of Pisces's skin was soothing. "I'll wait out here."

Caledonia drew a deep breath and stepped inside the room. The door shut behind her.

The smell hit her first. Sweat and vomit and blood. All of it stale. The room itself was larger than she'd expected. On one side there was a crude toilet bolted to the floor and a chair stuck in one corner. On the other was a cot upon which a body rested with his back turned on her.

Though he looked small with his knees tucked to his stomach, his figure was thin and muscled. His dark curls flopped over the pillow and his shirt was stained unevenly in splotches of dark brown. Beneath his bed, his boots were lined up, side by side as if creating a sense of order was important even under the worst conditions.

Caledonia tried to recall if he'd always been that way. She remembered his insistence that his overlarge jacket fit, and the way their father had threatened him with a comb every so often. She even remembered sharing a bunk with him until he kicked so much that she'd been given her own. But she couldn't remember if he'd been tidy or a disaster. It shouldn't have mattered so much, but staring at those perfectly aligned boots was like a straight punch to the gut. Was this her Donnally? Was it possible any part of him had survived and was trapped?

She didn't know. But she did have to find out.

"Donnally."

At the sound of her voice, he stiffened. From where she stood, she could see the surprised flutter of lashes as he opened his eyes.

Caledonia's heart skipped to a run. Even now, there was a part of her desperate for him to turn around and dive into her arms.

"Donnally." She took a small step forward and barely restrained herself from reaching out to touch his shoulder.

Slowly, carefully, Donnally pushed himself up and twisted around to face her. An assortment of bruises was splashed across his forehead, the bridge of his nose, and his jaw, each in a different stage of healing. His lips were dry and deep shadows rested in the hollows beneath his eyes, but when he looked at her, there was no drug haze layered over his bright brown eyes. Of course not. If Tassos was running through his own supply, why would he continue to give it to his prisoners?

"What are you doing here?" Donnally's voice was thin from disuse, his body weak from coming off Silt, but he looked alert and sharp and so much like their father from the long slope of his nose to the squared corners of his chin. Caledonia had a sudden flash of their mother running one finger down the bridge of that nose and tapping once on the tip, saying, "Tall as a mast." For a second, it was all Caledonia could do to draw a single breath.

"I came to ask you that same question," she said, regretting instantly that she'd moved into the position of interrogator. "But we don't have to start there. If you don't want to."

"Where else would we start?" Donnally's eyes darted between her and the door. "I guess you're not a prisoner. Tassos wouldn't let you near me if that was the case." A sudden look of understanding landed on his features and a disbelieving laugh fell from his lips. "An alliance. Well, I have to hand it to you, Caledonia, you have always made bold moves."

"There is no other way to resist Lir," Caledonia answered defensively.

The nod of Donnally's head was measured. The movement dislodged his curls just enough to reveal the bottom edge of his family sigil, the matching arrowhead to her own. "You can't trust Tassos, you know."

Caledonia ground her teeth together. She wanted to demand he tell her why he'd chosen Lir over her. She wanted to know why, after all this time, he wasn't overjoyed to see her again. How was it so easy for him to look at her and not want to stay with her?

"And you won't want to be here when Lir comes back," Donnally said.

"Are you so sure he will?"

"For Silt. For me."

"Donnally!" Caledonia couldn't stand it anymore and dove forward, landing on her knees to pull his hands into her own. "Stop protecting him or working for him or whatever it is you're doing. I'm here! *I came back for you.* You never have to go back, and no matter what Tassos says, I will get you out of this cell. You don't have to be a Bullet anymore!"

Donnally gazed down on his sister with a kind of maddening sympathy. "Caledonia." He said her name and stopped, biting down on whatever he'd meant to say next.

She held firm to his hands and forced herself to be calm when she spoke again. "I lost you once long ago and once again in Cloudbreak. I don't want to lose you again. Do you remember how Mom taught us to find lost things? To retrace our steps until something reminded us where we'd lost it, or we just got lucky. You were better at it than me. You always remembered and I only ever got lucky. I just promised never to lose anything I'd need to find again. I didn't realize I'd lost you at first and I'm so sorry it took me this long to figure it out."

The knot of his throat plunged as he swallowed some strong emotion. His eyes lost the lines of tension around the corners and he seemed to remember the children they'd been. At least, that's what she wanted to believe. "I thought you were dead."

"I know." A sudden pang of loss crashed over her, along with the sharpest edge of memory, of waking up the morning after she'd spotted his gray coat flapping at the top of a Bullet pike, unable to decide if the wound in her gut was worse than the one in her heart. She knew the pain he'd felt, but she also knew the joy of discovering her brother was alive. "But I wasn't. I'm not. I'm here. Go with me."

"Lir—" He squeezed his eyes shut, as if he could not bear to see her face when he said, "He's my brother."

Those words. They fell around Caledonia's wrists like manacles, making her as much a prisoner as he was. It was what he'd said in Cloudbreak and what he said so often in her dreams. Always in them, he was just out of reach or moving away, his sorrow at leaving her never enough.

She felt the tears on her cheeks before she could do anything to stop them. "No," she said. "He's not, but I am still your sister and I know that has to mean something to you."

"Caledonia." He exhaled slowly. "Lir saved me. He plucked me out of all the other children coming into the family and gave me the strength I needed to survive. I wouldn't be here if not for him."

"That—that—" Caledonia sputtered, launching to her feet in a rage. "That is true, Donnally, but not in the way you mean it! He is the reason they found our ship that night! I believed he wanted our help, and he took that—he used that stupid moment of mercy against me and he murdered our families! We would not have been found if not for that. You never would have been taken into their ranks and you never would have needed someone like him to make you strong."

She was breathing hard now. Her skin tingled and her head felt light, but she felt fully rooted in her mind.

"Would you leave Pisces if someone asked you to?" he countered. "Would you throw away everything that you've done together if I were the one asking you to abandon your cause?!"

"Pisces didn't kill our parents."

"Neither did Lir."

"*Hoist your eyes*, Donnally!"

Donnally reeled back as though she'd slapped him. He blinked rapidly, then stood and strode angrily across the small room. He stopped at the other side, keeping his back to her. A fresh tension was visible in the line of his shoulders and the slight tuck of his chin.

Caledonia held her tongue and waited. This gesture was so familiar that she did it on instinct. When they'd fought as kids, Donnally always reached a point where he turned his back and shut everything out. It had taken Caledonia far too long to learn that the best way to lose the fight was to intrude on those quiet moments.

As she watched, Donnally's breathing slowed, the tension dropped from his shoulders, and he opened his eyes. He nodded, agreeing silently with himself, and Caledonia recognized the way one corner of his mouth twitched as if the desire to smile, to concede, to consent was whisper thin, but present.

Caledonia stood on the brink of relief, but when Donnally turned around, he spoke a single, devastating word, "Leave."

CHAPTER
TWENTY-EIGHT

Tassos was waiting for her when she left the cell.

He leaned against the opposite wall, speaking quietly with Cepheus. The two of them looked up when she dragged the hatch closed behind her and spun the lock herself. Pisces started forward, doing her best to mask her concerns, but Caledonia could see the question in the smallest pinch of her sister's eyes: *Steely?*

Caledonia felt as though she'd been driven beneath stormy seas, sucked down a whirl she had no hope of fighting until she could do nothing but inhale all the salt of the sea. Her insides screamed for relief, but on the surface, she was a stone.

"Do you know what I like?" Tassos asked. When he grinned, the scar on his left cheek pinched together, distorting the corner of his mouth and the shape of his eye.

"I'm certain I don't care what you like, Tassos." Caledonia's voice was flat.

"I like when things come together as though I planned them," Tassos continued with no regard for her response. "And I like when seemingly useless things turn out to have value. Or, in this case, *more* value. Donnally? I thought he was only important to Lir, but it turns out"—here he paused to drive a finger toward the shape of her family sigil high on her temple, half-hidden by her hair—"he's the honest-to-salt brother of the Bale Blossom. And he's mine."

The spike of panic Caledonia expected to feel was dulled by a sudden rush of anger. In a rush, she closed the distance between them until it was no more than a sliver of stale air.

"Donnally made his choice," she snapped, letting anger and disappointment and panic weave into uncompromising confidence. "If you think you're going to control me through a brother I barely remember, then you're as dumb as you look. And if you only have forty-three ships to offer me, Tassos, then you are less valuable than I'd hoped." The look of shock on his face was pleasing on some distant level, but Caledonia didn't take time to enjoy it. "But we can fix that."

"What do you mean?" Tassos asked through grinding teeth.

"Take me to your comm center," she said, all authority. "We have an announcement to make."

"Listen to me, Caledonia Styx." Tassos pushed off the wall and drove her back with two menacing steps. "Working together doesn't mean I'm working *for* you. And it certainly doesn't mean I'm taking orders from you."

Caledonia took a calming breath and reminded herself that she had nothing to gain by angering him. "It won't be long before

Lir knows that we've allied against him. It does us no good to keep that fact quiet, and we need as many ships as we can muster. We're going to broadcast on an open frequency and let everyone know that if they want to join the fight, now's the time."

"You want to tell Lir that we're planning an attack?" Cepheus didn't bother to hide her skepticism.

"I do," Caledonia answered with a ready nod. "I want his eyes on the sea."

"And . . . isn't that where we'll be?" Tassos asked.

Now Caledonia smiled. "Not all of us."

Tassos considered her thoughtfully, eyes narrowing before he nodded to Cepheus.

"Follow me," she said.

≫≪

Cepheus led the way to a windowed chamber atop the megaship with clear views in all directions. What she saw from that perch made Caledonia's breath catch in her lungs. There was her fleet, dotting the water before her, nineteen beautiful ships. To the west, the sun was dipping low, throwing the shuffling islands of the Bone Mouth into extreme divisions of light and shadow. They bowed out in two directions, little islands reaching toward each other like the disjointed bones of a hand. In the center, the water was clear and inviting, a mouth opened wide.

In the opposite direction, sunset ignited the Net in flashes of punishing yellow and orange. It was like a strip of fire pointing due east, running all the way to the peninsula that housed the Holster.

Caledonia turned her eyes south to a point a few miles away that could only be the Silt Rig. It glimmered like a beacon against the darkening sea, roughly the size of an Assault Ship, a perfectly attainable target. If she could get any part of her fleet past the Net, she could destroy it. Of course, getting past the Net was always the problem.

Tassos moved in front of her, blotting out her view of the rig with his chest. "Comm's this way."

"Something out there you don't want me to see?" Caledonia feigned innocence.

Tassos paused, a small smirk punching in one side of this face. "You mean the rig? You can look as long as you like." He stepped aside, hooking one arm around her neck as he was too fond of doing. "I'm certain you're making a plan to destroy it. Or, trying to. Go ahead!"

He released her just as suddenly as he'd grabbed her. Caledonia only shrugged, resisting the urge to back away.

"There will be time for that," she promised.

"Oh, I'm certain there will," Tassos responded, that wild grin returning to his face. "But trust me, anyone who wants to take that rig from me will die trying."

He said it with such certainty that Caledonia understood it to be true. He wasn't as clever as Lir, but he was every bit as stubborn, every bit as ambitious. Something more than the Net was protecting that rig. She just couldn't see whatever it was.

Tassos swept forward again, scooping up the receiver and fiddling with the dials on the panel before handing it to Caledonia. "Let's get on with our business and one day—soon—you and I will dance."

Just over Tassos's shoulder, Caledonia caught the way Cepheus tried and failed to cover a disapproving frown with a quick duck of her head. But whether it had been for her or for Tassos, Caledonia wasn't sure.

"Open frequency. And recording," the Bullet stationed at the comm announced.

Caledonia raised the receiver. Her mouth went dry and she swallowed hard, suddenly unsure. Would anyone be listening? Would anyone respond? Instinctively, she slipped a hand inside her pocket, finding the garnet Hesperus had given her. She pressed her thumb to the smooth spot where he'd worried his own thumb. Knowing that even the Sly King of Cloudbreak had needed reassurance from time to time bolstered her and she licked her lips.

"This is Caledonia Styx, commander of the Cloudbreak Fleet. Many of you have heard of the recent attack on our city. We were forced to flee, but many survived, and we are still fighting against the legacy of the Father, against Fiveson Lir and all he represents. We have joined with Fiveson Tassos at the Net, and I am asking that any ready and willing crew join us here." As she spoke, she imagined how that news would land. She imagined fear and mistrust and hope colliding like an explosive star. "You have no reason to trust Tassos, but I am asking you to trust me. Sail to the eastern edge of the Bone Mouth and my people will be there to meet you."

She released the receiver and turned to Tassos. "How often can you loop that message?"

"As often as you want," he answered, nodding to the Bullet stationed by the comm, who held a small speaker up to one ear and set to work.

"How far can the signal travel?" Pisces asked. Their own ship-board radios were limited to a range of ten miles, but Hesperus's comm had been much more powerful. "Can it reach Cloudbreak?"

Caledonia caught the slender flame of hope in Pisces's eyes and felt it kindle quietly in her own chest. A single name whis-pered there: Amina.

"On a clear day," Cepheus answered, stepping closer to Pisces.

Pisces nodded, hiding her emotion by clearing her throat.

"Good?" Tassos was growing irritated. "Now, what in the deepest hell is the rest of your plan?"

Caledonia gestured for them to follow her back into the bowels of the megaship. She said, "We cannot defeat Lir ship to ship, so we'll have to go about this another way."

"What way is that?" Tassos asked, falling into step at her side.

"We're going to take control of those gun towers."

"But how will we get to them?" Cepheus asked, keeping pace at their heels with Pisces at her side. "You've already said we can't go ship to ship, and the only way to reach them is through the harbor."

"That isn't exactly true." Caledonia turned down a broad hallway, hoping she was leading them in the right direction. "There's more than one way inside the Holster."

"You want to flank them? Over land?" Tassos asked, incredulous, as they reached the chamber where the others waited.

Tug and Heron were seated on the opposite side of the room, the former looking more relaxed than the latter, while Oran, Sledge, and Nettle were almost exactly where they'd been before. The only difference was that Sledge had a hand on Nettle's shoulder, though whether he was holding her back or she him, Caledonia couldn't tell. Oran was across from them, shoulders squared, chin tucked, using every bit of patience he had to stay put. At the sight of her, he exhaled so subtly only she saw it.

"I don't see how moving over land helps us," Tassos continued. "That approach is twenty miles. They'll spot our troops long before we can get close enough to engage. And those gun towers fire in all directions."

Caledonia bent over the map and pointed to the eastern border of the Holster, where the five gun towers stood at equal intervals. "I don't want to send in troops, just a small team. Maybe twenty-five, five per tower, who can move over land and hijack those towers."

"That's why you sent out the call." Tassos bobbed his head in understanding. "To make sure Lir is preparing for a seaborne attack."

"We'll have an entire fleet to distract him from what's happening in his own backyard," Caledonia confirmed.

"If we control the towers, we control the town, the harbor, everything in range of their fire," Tug said, studying the map as if it would reveal a solution. "If we got them, we could just destroy the entire town. Boom! No more Holster."

"Sure, kill everyone," Nettle muttered. "Good plan."

"The Holster isn't just a base of operations," Oran said, shifting his attention to Caledonia. "It's a city. There are children, elderly. Firing on the city is firing on them."

"What difference does that make?" Tassos asked.

"We want to take the Holster, not kill it," Caledonia answered swiftly. "Once we have the gun towers, we aim for the fleet, not the town."

"I don't know how you like to fight, but I'll aim for anyone that aims at me," Tug said with a condescending smirk.

"I fight to win." Caledonia pressed her hands flat on the map. "And if we want to win this battle, the fleet is our priority."

"We won't have contact with the team that infiltrates. They'll have to go in dark, and we'd have no way of knowing if they were successful or not." Cepheus leaned a hip against the table as she spoke, thoughtful and not yet convinced.

"So we send our best," Pisces said, turning to Cepheus. "And then we trust them."

"It's a day's sail to the peninsula, then another on foot to reach the outer perimeter of the Holster. They'll need a third to prepare, but any longer and they'll risk detection. That means we attack at dawn of the fourth day. The question is . . ." Caledonia paused, turning to face Tassos. "Will your Silt last long enough to get this done?"

Tassos looked from the map to Caledonia, mouth set in a stern line as he considered the question. Finally, he nodded confidently. "It's a good plan. We'll make it last."

》《

They spent the better part of an hour discussing who to send to infiltrate the Holster. Tassos appointed Tug as his proxy; Caledonia chose Pine. Glimmer would temporarily command the *Blade*, and the infiltration team would leave at first light. When that happened, their plans would be irrevocably set in motion.

It was night by the time Cepheus led Caledonia's team to their quarters: a single room shared by the five of them. Cepheus shoved the door open to let them into the tight chamber, handing out orange armbands as they passed.

"Keep these on you," she said. "They'll mark you as under the protection of Tassos. No one will bother you as long as you wear them."

She left and it wasn't long before the five of them collapsed for the night.

Tassos might have meant the sleeping arrangements as an insult, but all things considered, Caledonia preferred it while they were his reluctant guests. She didn't even mind that her bed for the next three days was a hammock. What she did mind was the snoring. Sledge she'd expected. Nettle was a complete surprise, as always.

When sleep eluded her for more than half the night, Caledonia rolled out of her hammock and padded quietly across the floor. Nettle and Pisces had taken the upper hammocks, their bodies cocooned at the level of Caledonia's head, while Sledge and Oran's beds hung low like hers. Other than the hammocks, the room contained very little. Not even a window. Oran was in the very center of the room, his eyes pinched shut, his brown skin reflecting the dim orange lights that glowed along the ceiling. He looked peaceful. Caledonia almost didn't want to wake him.

Careful to avoid his gloved fingers, she squeezed his arm and shook. He blinked. "Trouble?" he whispered.

Caledonia shook her head. "Walk with me."

The megaship was designed to be confusing, but Nettle had discovered a trick: if you followed the very thin strip of orange painted so low along the wall it almost disappeared into the floor, you'd find yourself on the main deck.

Though the ship was quiet at this time of night, it was hardly asleep. Everywhere they turned, Bullets patrolled the deck and the halls. They cast wary glances toward the two unusual figures, but one look at the bright orange armbands and they left them alone.

"Have you ever seen it?" Caledonia peered into the darkness where the sky and sea smeared together. "The rig?"

Oran shook his head. "Aric kept us compartmentalized."

Like the rest of the Net, the megaship was not a sailing ship, and from what Caledonia had seen, she suspected most of it was rooted into the same bedrock that connected all the islands of the Bone Mouth. Here the Net met with those perilously shallow waters her mother had loved so well. It was amazing to think she and her own crew had sailed this close to the rig for so long.

"It's the key to all of this," Caledonia said, lowering her voice as a sentry passed near. "The thing both Lir and Tassos need if they want to keep their power."

Oran nodded thoughtfully. "You want to destroy it."

"I want to destroy it," she repeated. "But Tassos has safeguards in place and I need to know what those are."

The same sentry looped back on his path, passing closer to them than he had the first time.

"C'mon." Caledonia found a southward-facing section of the deck and settled into the shelter of a curved bulkhead. Here at least, they would have the illusion of privacy. "I don't know that I'll sleep at all while we're on this ship."

"Is this really so different from what you did in Slipmark?" Oran asked as he lowered himself next to her, splints clinking together softly like wind chimes. "At least here there's no chance you'll be discovered as an imposter."

Until this moment, sneaking an entire crew into Slipmark disguised as Bullets had been the most terrifying thing Caledonia had ever done. But in Slipmark she'd had a very specific goal and a very specific plan. At least then, she wasn't trying to pretend she was surrounded by anything but a city full of enemies. Being on board this ship, literally locked into the Net itself, felt like stripping herself to the skin and leaping into shark-infested waters.

"In Slipmark, I was working against an enemy, not *with* one."

Oran laughed once, a mirthless sound. "That is very true."

Moonlight glinted on his splints and Caledonia felt an answering glimmer of guilt. Tassos had only agreed to meet with her because Oran stood by her side, but he should be somewhere else. He should be with Hime, letting his fingers heal so that when it came time to fight once more, he'd be able to defend himself. Instead, he was in an unbearably vulnerable position: surrounded by Bullets who had more than one reason to hate him and unable to pull the trigger of a gun. He would argue it was the right choice. But she should have protected him better.

All at once, she was overcome with a feeling like exquisite

sadness. It expanded inside her like wings, filling her up and pushing into every dark corner of her mind. "Oran," she said, suddenly breathless. She leaned in, pressed her lips against his, and took a kiss so sweet it felt like a cleansing wash of tears.

When she pulled away, his eyes were soft and content. "I love you, Cala," he whispered.

She drew a sharp breath, all the warmth of the previous moment chased away by a sudden wintery chill in her bones. "Oran," she said again, accusing and confused.

"Cala," he repeated, mouth tightening in amusement.

"Why do you— Why do you *say* that?" she asked.

"Why shouldn't I? It's the truth and there's no point in not telling you." He shook his head once, unapologetic. "And I don't say it so that you'll say it back to me. I say it so you'll know." When all she did was stare disbelievingly, he continued. "I have to be so many different versions of myself in this fight. One moment, I'm the Fiveson defector; the next, the Steelhand. Every terrible thing I've done is always with me."

A flush rose in Caledonia's cheeks. Every day, without saying a word, she was asking him to hold the worst parts of himself close enough that she might use them if, no, *when*, she needed them.

"I'm sorry." She dropped her chin in guilt, but Oran reached out and ran a thumb along her jaw. "If there was another way—"

"I would be those things with or without you, Cala. My past is not your burden to carry." He tried to cup her cheek, but thwarted by his splints, he settled instead for hooking an ankle around hers, locking their legs together. "Sometimes, for a brief second, I'm just Oran. I didn't think that was even possible. But it is with you. And you should know that."

"But how do you know that's love?" Caledonia shook her head, realizing that wasn't the question she meant to ask. "Why is it so easy for you to say it?"

Oran stilled. Moonlight pooled in the rings of his brown eyes, making them sad and deep. "Because the only thing I know for sure is that I am alive right now. Tomorrow might change that. And even if I somehow manage to survive this whole fight, I don't see how I fit in the world after it changes. So, I have to say it. Because being in love with you is the best thing I've done with my life."

Caledonia nearly stopped breathing. It was impossible to parse all he'd just shared, but her mind hung on one word: *after*.

When she imagined the future, she imagined a world where her crew and everyone who had ever felt the pressure of Aric's thumb might live without fear or constant coercion. She imagined cities that weren't founded on violence and the ruined lands to the north covered in verdant crops. She imagined Nettle in command of her own brilliant crew; Hime working to ensure soiltech and medtech traveled far and wide; Sledge finding ways to help Bullets transform their lives.

She imagined herself . . . not at all. She imagined the end, the moment her fight would be finished, but there was never anything after except a feeling of relief. A kind of absence of feeling, as though she had been so focused on this fight for so long that without it she might cease to exist.

"How can I possibly love?" she asked, horrified. "I keep asking you to do terrible things, to endure terrible things and—" She nearly gasped. Tears threatened in the back of her throat, but they weren't for him. "I will probably ask you to do something just as terrible again."

"And I'll do it willing—"

"No." She stood abruptly. "No. I'm sorry. I can't love you, Oran. Not until this ends."

She turned, biting down on an incomprehensible maelstrom of emotion, and walked away.

CHAPTER
TWENTY-NINE

Pine, Gloriana, Tin, Ares, Folly, and eight others of Caledonia's crew gathered on the low docking level of the megaship the next morning. Early dawn washed their figures in shades of purple and gray as they met with Tug and the additional twelve Bullets appointed by Tassos. Twenty-six in all. The team was to sail behind the Net all the way to the southernmost tip of the peninsula, where twenty-five would disembark and the remaining Bullet would return with the boat.

The docking level was a dank, foul-smelling chamber that ran the entire length of the megaship. These were the tunnels Caledonia had spotted on their approach, which were the only way from one side of the Net to the other not threaded with traps. A broad dock extended down the center of two channels, allowing space for cargo to be onloaded and offloaded. The channels were too narrow for anything other than small vessels or barges. Perfect for transporting bale blossoms from the Bullet Seas to the rig, Silt from the rig to the Bullet Seas.

"Don't take your eyes off them," Caledonia said, tracking Tug as he threw a pack of seed brick into the forward compartment of the boat and barked an order at the deck crew.

Pine and Gloriana made expressions of such similar displeasure, they could have been related.

"The thing about being raised as Bullets?" Gloriana asked.

"We know better than to trust Bullets," Pine finished, voice deep and quiet.

Tin and Folly were already in the boat, working with a Bullet named Sharp to store the supplies Tug was tossing their way. Sledge looked on from the dock, Nettle standing at his side as they called farewells to Pine. Pisces stood with Ares a few paces away from the group, their hands clasped tightly between them as he spoke to her in an urgent whisper.

When it was time to go, the whole crew loaded up and shoved off, traveling through the tunnel to the other side of the Net. In their wake, shark fins slashed at the dark water, searching for the chum Bullets so often tossed over.

Once they'd gone, the day was packed with preparations for the battle ahead. There were soldiers to transport from the stationary ships of the Net to the mobile fleet, systems to check, and weapons to ready. All of it required Caledonia and Tassos to be in constant contact with one another. It was not unlike being shackled at the wrist to a Fiveson. At least Caledonia could appreciate the irony in that.

The day had given her the opportunity to study the rig from a distance and consider the myriad protections Tassos had in place. She judged the distance between the megaship and the rig to be no more than a mile, and it stood on legs that must have been drilled down into the same bedrock as that of the Bone Mouth. She'd seen no traffic moving to or from it, which could only mean Tassos was truly out of the baleflowers he so desperately needed to make Silt.

Their last stop of the day was in the windowed overlook chamber, where they could see the entire fleet spread out before them. Though there were sixty-one ships in all, Tassos was loath to take all of his into battle and leave the Net vulnerable. They'd settled on leaving five behind to serve the Net, which gave Caledonia fifty-six. So far, her radio message had resulted in no new arrivals, but there was still time and Caledonia still had hope that more survivors would hear her call and respond.

"Are you afraid that whoever you leave behind will take the Net from you?" she asked. "The rig?"

Tassos offered her a lazy smile in return. "No."

It was unlike him to respond with so little. "Wouldn't you?" she asked.

"Are you trying to convince me to stay behind?" he teased, still with that lazy smile. "To keep me from my prize?"

"No, but I'd like to know what makes you so confident," she said. "I need to know that when we're fighting out there, you won't be worried about what's happening back here."

"You *do* want to know my secrets," he said, letting his eyes travel the full length of her body. "I wouldn't mind learning a few of yours."

Strangely, the comment wasn't a threat, but that didn't make it any more welcome. "I'll share all my sharpest secrets with you, Tassos," she promised.

Laughter spilled from his lips, that scar digging more deeply into his cheek. "I see why my brothers are so smitten with you." He paused, gaze drifting out to the rig before returning to Caledonia. "You want to know why I'm so confident? It's because of this."

He tugged a remote from his belt, holding it just out of her reach. It was a small black box with a six-digit keypad concealed beneath a door that snapped open at the press of a button.

"No one will try to take that rig from me." He said the words with a dark kind of satisfaction. "Because if they do, I'll enter the code and the rig will blow."

With a wave of barely contained shock, Caledonia realized that Tassos would rather destroy the rig than see it in the hands of someone else. It was a choice she couldn't imagine Lir making and so she hadn't expected it of Tassos. Lir would always assume he could recover. He wouldn't destroy something that might be useful to him in the future. But Tassos would rather lose everything than give Lir an ounce of satisfaction. It was a reminder that while Lir and Tassos might both be Fivesons, she couldn't think of them as the same.

»«

On the second morning, Caledonia awoke with a plan of action. Before the ship stirred, she rolled out of her hammock and shook each of her companions awake. In the dim orange light of their cabin, she told them everything she'd learned from Tassos the evening before.

"He's willing to destroy the rig rather than give up control of it?" Pisces asked, eyebrows climbing high.

"I don't think he expects to survive a struggle like that," Caledonia explained.

"That's one way to keep his Bullets in line," Sledge said, fingers quickly working a braid into his long hair. "No one wants to kill the man who can kill Silt."

"We need that code," Oran said from somewhere behind Caledonia, the space between them chilly and distant.

"What are the chances he keeps it written down?" Pisces asked.

"Better than good," Caledonia answered. "I spent all day with the man, and he may know how to manipulate people, but he keeps notes on everything. His people, his ships, his rations. There's no way he doesn't have the code somewhere. The trick will be finding it."

All eyes turned to the same spot in the room. Nettle, who

had been quietly listening until now, smiled. "Sounds like my kind of trick."

"That's what I was hoping you'd say," Caledonia answered. "Now we just need to create a distraction."

Moments later, they were waiting on the recreation deck when the first Bullets emerged from their racks. Caledonia waited as more arrived, allowing time for the crowd to grow. When it was large enough, she moved to the center of the deck.

"You sure you can't think of anything better?" Pisces asked.

"Nothing faster than this," Caledonia answered.

There were more Bullets now. They moved uneasily around her, haphazardly beginning their own morning routines. When the deck was nearly full, Caledonia stomped her foot to command their attention.

"You've all had plenty of time to size me up!" she shouted. "Now, who wants to see if they can hold their own against Caledonia Styx?"

There was an answering rumble of laughter from the Bullets, a pitched glower from Sledge, and a grin of sheer delight from Nettle. Sunlight warmed Caledonia's skin and she let it fill her with energy like she was a solar scale, soaking up the power of the sun.

"I'll take that challenge." The voice was familiar, but Caledonia was still surprised to see Heron push through the crowd. He was on the shorter side when he wasn't sitting, which put him almost perfectly eye-to-eye with Caledonia, but he was blocky, every joint squared off as though they'd been flattened by many rounds in the ring. "Might be best for you if we end this quick."

Caledonia answered, grinning, "All my Bullet encounters end quick, Heron. You'd do better to hope for something a little less permanent."

The crowd was growing as more Bullets emerged expecting to join their morning regimen. Tassos, however, remained absent.

"Well, you've got their attention," Pisces muttered, pulling Caledonia's hands out and beginning to wrap her knuckles in lengths of fabric.

"Be ready, Pi." Caledonia squeezed her hands into fists as Pisces tied off the wraps. "Round two will fall to you and Sledge. Nettle!"

"Yes, Captain." The girl hurried over, always closer than Caledonia expected her to be.

"As soon as this starts, you're up."

"Consider it done," Nettle chirped, popping up on her toes.

"Shouldn't I take the first fight?" Sledge asked, eyes on the ever-increasing circle of Bullets.

Caledonia tracked Heron as he moved into the center of the deck. He was older than her by decades. He would inevitably be slower, but there was a reason he stood at Tassos's side and she was sure that reason would soon become clear.

"I'm in the mood for a little blood," she said, still watching Heron.

"Moon and tides, Cala." Sledge said it like a prayer and a curse.

Caledonia only shrugged her shoulders, letting the motion turn into a small stretch. Behind her, Oran watched the whole thing with arms folded over his chest. He hadn't said a word through all of this, but now he stepped forward until he was so close to her back she could feel the heat of him through the thin fabric of her shirt.

"He's an old salt," he said. "He'll go for force, but he's faster than you think. Don't let him pin you."

They'd barely been alone together in the past day, and the hurt she'd caused him was very near the surface.

"You changing your mind?" Heron called.

"You aren't so lucky!" Caledonia shouted back, flexing her fists and striding into the ring.

She saw the flash of Nettle's rainbow-colored hair ties slipping around the ring of Bullets, and then she was gone. All Caledonia had to do now was take her time.

The second she was within range, Heron initiated his attack, charging forward like a beast. Though his fists were raised, he saved his strike for the moment she attempted to spin away. She saw it coming and had just enough time to absorb the blow with her forearms instead of her face. The impact stung against her bones, sending quakes of pain to her elbows and wrists.

It was as bracing as a cold wind and Caledonia relished it.

"Feel like starting for real now?" Heron asked, and though his expression was focused, Caledonia had the impression he was teasing her.

"Do you?" she challenged.

Heron responded with his fist. He struck sparingly, but every time he did, his aim was brutal. It was like being attacked by very precise hammers. Every time he dropped his fists it was to strike, which made finding room to retaliate nearly impossible.

But only nearly.

Blood rushed in Caledonia's veins and her body moved on instinct. She gave herself to this fight, letting all her other senses collect around a single point of focus. She was never so clear-headed as in moments like these, and as she dodged another of Heron's punishing blows and spun perfectly to deliver a swift knee to his kidney, she found that she'd missed the simplicity of fighting with her own fists instead of a fleet.

It wasn't until Caledonia's fist glanced off Heron's chin that the gathered Bullets crowed their approval.

"Slowing down, old man!" a voice cried.

"Lucky shot, Bale Blossom!" another shouted.

Heron landed a sharp blow to her jaw and Caledonia tasted blood. The bright flavor sent a fresh wave of energy through her, and she grinned viciously, knowing blood coated her teeth and lips.

Laughing, Heron blew her a kiss.

Before Caledonia could retaliate, a sudden commotion spilled onto the deck. Both Caledonia and Heron turned toward the clump forming up by the railing and rushed to find the cause.

Sledge appeared at her side, shoving through the crowd and making room for her to reach the center. What she saw made her cold.

Nettle was on her knees. A Bullet stood behind her, hand fisted in her hair and holding her head firmly back. Blood streamed from her nose and a bruise was already darkening beneath one eye.

"I caught this one prowling around the Fiveson's quarters!" the Bullet announced. He threw a bag on the ground, spilling ammunition and a slender bottle of amber-colored liquor. "Stealing!"

Caledonia understood that once Nettle knew she'd been discovered she had grabbed the first things of value she could find. Anything to make them think she was stealing and not spying for her captain.

The knowledge twisted in Caledonia's heart.

"See that orange band? Hands off the girl, Fray." This came from Cepheus. She and Pisces appeared on the opposite side of the circle, positioning themselves on the rail so they stood above everyone.

"Tassos brings them in and they steal from us?" Fray made

his voice loud. "They want Bullet help they should abide by Bullet rules. And punishments."

He punctuated this last with a tug of Nettle's hair that made her cry out.

Sledge was there in a flash. His fist driving into Fray's chest with so much force the Bullet was thrown back in the air. Caledonia saw Sledge pull Nettle into his arms just as a fight broke out in earnest.

From the rail, Cepheus and Pisces waved their arms and shouted for everyone to stop. But it was no good. The fight had an energy of its own as several Bullets turned on Sledge, and Heron did his best to pull his Bullets away. In an instant, it was a chaotic swirl of fists, elbows, and knees and no one seemed to care who they struck or why.

Caledonia reached for her gun, ready to fire a shot in the air. Before she could, the fight surged suddenly, pushing into the railing as though the megaship itself had lurched to starboard. Pisces was knocked off balance. She tipped back, frantically wheeling her arms to keep herself upright. But it wasn't working. Caledonia sucked in a sharp breath as Pisces leaned backward perilously far only to regain her footing at the last minute. Slowly, she pulled herself upright once more. Safe.

But before Caledonia could exhale in relief, she spotted Cepheus whirling to reach for Pisces. As she spun, her foot slipped from the rail and she disappeared over the edge. Plummeting into the shark-infested waters.

There was a gasp of silence.

Then Pisces dove into the water after her.

CHAPTER THIRTY

"Oh, hell," Heron growled, darting forward, bellowing at the crowd the whole time. "Make a hole! Gunners to the rail! Ladders over, now!"

The fighting stopped.

Caledonia reached the railing in time to see Pisces pulling a bloody-nosed Cepheus to her side. Twenty-feet away, five fins appeared in the water, cutting a swift path toward the two young women.

The air fractured around the *pop-pop-pop* of rifles as gunners aimed to keep the sharks away from Pisces and Cepheus.

"Where's that damn ladder?" Heron shouted.

The gunners fired again. This time, their bullets struck home. Blood clouded the water, brilliant, wispy red against crisp turquoise blue. The sharks broke away, snapping their heads around as though they'd been slapped, but it was a temporary reprieve. Caledonia watched in horror as they whipped back around, aiming once again for the two women.

Finally, a ladder appeared. It rolled down the side of the hull, its tail landing a few feet from Pisces's reach.

"Hurry!" Caledonia shouted as Pisces shoved Cepheus ahead of her. The woman grabbed the ropes and began to hoist herself onto the rungs while Pisces treaded water behind her with swift strokes of her arms.

The gunners fired again, their shots peppering the water far too close to Pisces. The girl never flinched. "Now, Pi! Climb!" Caledonia shouted.

Pisces was on the ladder in an instant, her body flying up the ropes as sharks pressed in below. Caledonia didn't move from the rail until both women had reached the top, their feet firmly planted.

The deck was silent. Bullets looked from Cepheus to Pisces to Heron. No one seemed to know what to do.

Then Cepheus wiped water from her face, smearing blood from her nose and bottom lip to her chin, and held her hand out to Pisces. Tentatively, Pisces took it.

Cepheus turned and, pointing at Nettle, shouted, "The little girl is the responsibility of Captain Styx! She will mete out whatever punishment she determines is fair. Anyone else who touches one of her people without permission will answer to me!"

Caledonia's heart was still beating rapidly in her throat, but the crowd listened to their second-in-command even if they didn't like what she had to say.

"Back to work!" Heron moved across the deck with angry steps, directing traffic with the firm set of his brow.

With a nod for Caledonia and a separate one for Pisces, Cepheus followed, leaving only Caledonia and her crew still clustered near the rail. Sledge had his arm around Nettle's small shoulders, and it seemed like he might never let her go again.

And in spite of the blood now clotting in her nose and the bruise clouding her eye, Nettle had a look of satisfaction about her.

"Nettle?" Caledonia asked.

"Captain," the girl said, sure to keep her voice low. "I got it."

≫≪

After the fight, Caledonia expected Tassos to pounce on her at any second, but he remained conspicuously absent until midday, when she spotted him crossing onto the megaship from the bridge of the adjacent ship.

In the full sun, sweat gleamed on his broad shoulders. His brow was furrowed, his fists clenched, and there was a splatter of fresh blood across the front of his shirt. He glared as Caledonia stopped in front of him. She dropped her eyes to the blood, and just below to where that remote trigger was always clipped next to the hilt of a knife.

"Do we have a problem?" she asked.

"Not anymore," he said. Anger simmered beneath every word.

"We sail at first light, Tassos. If we have a problem, I need to know. Now."

Tassos bared his teeth and flared his nostrils. "Follow me."

Tassos strode into the megaship, charting a swift course to his quarters. After a brief moment to acknowledge that following this man into a small room was surprisingly not the worst idea she'd ever had, Caledonia trailed him inside and shut the door.

When Tassos spoke next, his voice was thick with distaste. "Sedition." The word was as much a mark against him as it was those who'd committed the act. "I've had to make a few changes to our Silt rations to stretch our supply and keep as many of my Bullets in fighting form as possible. Some get their usual dose; others get less. When Bullets don't get their Silt from me, they start looking elsewhere. Five Bullets were caught attempting to defect. And when a limb is sliced and there is blood in the water there is only one way to save the body."

Caledonia frowned, unsure that she liked where this particular metaphor was leading.

Tassos leaned in again, his hands thumping against the blood darkening his chest. "Take the limb."

Bullets had died today. There was no doubt about that, but Caledonia suspected more than those five had suffered from this mood of Fiveson Tassos.

"You said you had enough Silt to make this work," Caledonia said. "Was that a lie?"

Tassos snarled, stepping close enough for her to see the thin coat of sweat painting his forehead. "I said I'll make it work and I will."

"You need your dose," Caledonia said, marking the pallor of his lips.

"Mind yourself, girl."

"Until we take the Holster, your business is my business. Do you have control of your fleet or not?"

The muscles in his jaw flashed and Caledonia had the impression that if he'd been at full strength, he might have done more than glare at her. "I have control," he growled.

"One more thing," Caledonia said when he'd swallowed. "I'm calling the shots out there."

Now Tassos moved. He stepped forward, reminding her that he was the punishing wave and she the tumbling stone. "No one commands my fleet."

"In this fight, it's my fleet."

"And why shouldn't it be mine?"

Caledonia raised her eyes, holding her ground. Tassos liked to try to obscure the truth with his size or his might, but Caledonia had had several days to study him, to peel back the layers and find what lay just beneath his mask. He wasn't as cunning as Lir, but he didn't like to lose. And he would do whatever it took not to lose to Lir. Even if that meant giving ground to Caledonia.

"Because you can't do what I can." She pushed her chin forward and Tassos moved back so slightly she almost missed it. "You may know how to defend your Net, but you don't know how to fight at sea. This is my plan, my strategy. You have your hands full minding your own clip, so I'm calling the shots. Agreed?"

Tassos narrowed his eyes. "I look forward to the moment our alliance ends, Caledonia."

Caledonia heard the threat in his words. Lir would have been more explicit, but then, Lir had been dreaming of her death for a lot longer than Tassos.

"Ready your ships, Fiveson."

CHAPTER
THIRTY-ONE

They sailed out in double-arrow formation, like two giant birds skimming low across the waves. In their wake, the stationary ships of the Net stood like silent sentinels. Each bore a cohort of ten Bullets. More than enough to keep watch and hold the line if necessary.

No additional ships had responded to Caledonia's call. She couldn't blame them, but the absence of any additional aid hung heavy in her heart. The thirty-seven ships of Fiveson Tassos, each marked with deep purple starbursts, brought their total fleet to fifty-six. Their scouts, who could only surveil the Holster from a distance, estimated Lir's fleet to be at least three times that number.

That wouldn't matter as long as their teams got control of those gun towers. But they wouldn't know if those teams had been successful until the battle begun.

Getting into position took the better part of the day, and they settled over anxious waves to wait out the night. It had been three days since the infiltration team departed. They had until tomorrow morning to be ready. At the first blush of dawn on the fourth day, Caledonia's fleet hovered like a cloud a half mile from shore, where the Holster was a dark spot nestled against hills edged in faintest bronze.

In all the stories she'd heard of this place, the town was like a cage. Caledonia had expected it to be like Slipmark, with intimidating gates outside the harbor and a knifelike boundary to its buildings. But as sunrise drew the Holster against gentle hills, Caledonia realized she couldn't have been further from the truth. There were no gates outside the harbor, and the edges of the city were smudged and indecipherable. This place was sprawling, like a spill of blood in water, spidery fingers stretching in seemingly random directions, all stemming from a dense center.

Caledonia stood on the bow of her ship as the wind drove into her eyes, determined not to move until she had placed every landmark she'd studied on the map. Five towers of black stone stood at intervals around the city, each bearing heavy guns capable of firing over miles. Between them and the harbor, the city crouched low, buildings capped in reflective solar plating that would blind anyone in the harbor as soon as the sun sliced west. The breakers Heron had marked on the map crouched low in the water, marking the edge of the harbor. Just outside of those breakers, a hundred ships sat ready to receive her.

Somewhere inside that city, Lir was watching as dawn slowly

withdrew the cover of night to reveal her fleet. The thought left her flushed with satisfaction.

"Hime," she called. "Launch the flare!"

"Gunners ready." Pisces shouted to be heard across the deck.

Above, the sky burst with a single red flare. Bloody against the purpling sky. A battle cry.

For a single moment they sailed as if suspended in time.

The Holster was a quietly glimmering jewel in a rough cut of stone, and they were the rumbling storm rushing forward. Then an alarm rose over the town. In response, the harbor, and all those hundred ships outside the breakers, came to life.

Pisces and Hime gathered at Caledonia's sides. Behind them, the rest of the crew stood with hands twisted together and mouths bent into stern lines, their hearts steely, their eyes pinned to the towers on the hill.

"Think they made it?" Pisces asked.

They made it, Hime answered.

Caledonia only nodded as she pictured Pine and Gloriana, Folly and Tin, Ares, and the rest of her brave crew who'd accepted the mission without protest. Nothing would stop them from completing their task. She knew that the way she knew to trust the ocean beneath her hull.

They saw the orange flash of a muzzle before they heard the crack of the gun. It was followed by four others as one by one each of the gun towers fired.

On them.

Wherever the infiltration team was, they didn't have control of those towers.

"Incoming!" The shout echoed across the deck as the crew scrambled, half to take aim at the incoming artillery, half to train their guns on the ships now roaring toward them.

Lir's fleet was on the move. The towers were still in his control.

Caledonia had a choice to make: stay and fight knowing she was at a steep disadvantage, or run.

"Your orders, Captain?" Pisces asked. Her eyes were bright with alarm and furious determination.

Turning to Hime, Caledonia saw that same determination flashing in her dark eyes. *Your crew is brave, Captain*, she signed.

That was all Caledonia needed. She spun on her heel and hurried back to the bridge, calling, "Engines to full! Take us in, Nettle, and keep us in range of those guns."

"Yes, Captain!"

The *Luminous Wake* surged forward, driving toward the incoming ships as up on the hill the gun towers fired again.

"We knew this was a possibility," she said to her bridge crew. "Our job now is to trust our team. We need to give them time to seize the towers. In the meantime, I want us on Lir's ships. Make it as difficult as possible for those gun towers to get a clean shot."

With a single voice, the bridge crew responded, "Yes, Captain!"

The gun towers fired again, and Caledonia caught a round of

vibrant explosions in her peripheral vision as the missiles landed among her fleet.

"Harwell," she said, locking her eyes on the incoming ships. "Radio the *Deep Cut* and tell them to follow our lead."

Together, the fifty-six ships of their combined fleet soared forward, guns blazing. The *Luminous Wake* bucked as a missile struck its nose, yet Caledonia held tight to her resolve. All around her fleet was suffering under the onslaught of a hundred ships and the constant battery from those towers.

"*Deep Cut* reports they're down five ships!" Harwell shouted. An explosion shook the cabin and he paused to maintain his grip on his station. "We've lost three of ours!"

Eight ships down still left forty-eight. Forty-eight to Lir's one hundred and seventy. In an instant, the air had filled with the bite of smoke. It clung to the back of Caledonia's throat as her ships struggled to hold its own.

They wouldn't be able to resist much longer. Everything hinged on those towers. Without them, she was marching her entire fleet into a massacre, and if the infiltration team had been discovered, then that was exactly what she was doing. But backing down too soon would be just as bad as staying too long. For a brief second, fear gripped Caledonia's lungs and squeezed. She heard the screams of her people, tasted the hint of copper on the air, and felt the flush of explosive heat rising around her.

The wrong decision now would be catastrophic.

As the gun towers fired again, striking a ship on their starboard side, Caledonia steeled herself. Time. She needed to give the infiltration team just a little more time.

But as an arm of Lir's fleet split west, aiming for her flank in an effort to surround her entire fleet, she knew time was the one thing she no longer had.

"Hold this course, Nettle." Caledonia left the bridge at a jog, then slid down the companionway ladder to the main deck.

She spotted Oran, hunched beneath a rail, reloading weapons he could not fire with his fingers still wrapped in braces, but one look from her and he was on his feet. Without a word, they hurried belowdecks, racing to the weapons locker on level two.

"You're sure?" he asked as they reached their destination.

"I'm sure. We don't have any other options, and we are so close, Oran." She hesitated, feeling the full weight of what they were about to do land on her shoulders. "We can end this here. Now. We just have to hold on."

There were no more questions. Oran unlocked the storage container, revealing a wall of star blossom bombs. Four black orbs rested in stabilizing racks, but at the pull of a lever, their restraints came loose. Oran pulled a cloth hammock from the floor of the locker, stretching it between them so they could carry all four bombs.

The ship lurched to port, nearly knocking them off their feet as they raced topside once more. The sky was clouded with smoke and streams of fire. Round after round fired from the gun towers, exploding against Caledonia's fleet. Smoke clouded her vision, stinging her eyes and making them water as screams threaded the air. It was all they could do to face off with the ships between them and the breakers, while still others were close to flanking them. Caledonia could see Lir's fist quickly closing around them, getting ready to squeeze the life from her entire fleet, and her stomach twisted painfully.

"Hurry!" she shouted, beginning to climb to the forward deck.

They rushed to four of the catapults bolted against the nose and as quickly as they could loaded a star blossom bomb into each.

"Captain!" The call came from the lookout atop the bridge, where one of Amina's Knots pointed toward the city.

She turned in time to see the southernmost gun tower explode. Spires of flame shot into the sky as black stone crumbled down. For a moment, the crew paused in horror, and Caledonia knew they were all wondering the same thing she was: who had been inside when it exploded? If they'd been unable to wrest control from the Bullets, destroying the tower was likely the best option the team had had, but which team had it been?

"Ready," Oran said, racing back to her side.

Caledonia ripped her gaze from the fire. The tower was out of play, which meant their team was still fighting. Maybe if she could give the remaining members a little more time . . .

"On my mark," she said. She left Oran by the catapults as she rushed back to the bridge. "Nettle, bring us around. I want us nose-to-nose with those ships coming around our flank."

In a moment, Nettle had the ship facing west, their nose driving hard toward a cluster of Bullet ships swooping around behind her.

As soon as they were close enough, Caledonia nodded to Oran.

One by one, he fired the star blossoms. They flew high, black orbs against a dawn sky blossoming with pink and purple and the sharpest blue. It had hardly been any time at all since the attack began.

As the bombs fell on four Bullet ships, the screams that rose pierced the percussive song of battle. The pain of that sound settled into Caledonia's blood like thorns of ice.

The flanking fleet stopped advancing, their thrusters churning fearfully against their own momentum as the four ships she'd struck coasted ahead. Their guns were quiet, while their engines revved with no one left to guide them.

The star blossom bombs had done their work and cut through hundreds of Bullets without an ounce of mercy.

CHAPTER THIRTY-TWO

"Caledonia!"

Her name, but also an accusation. Pisces stood just inside the bridge. Her mouth gaped and her eyes were wide and unbelieving. But there was no time for discussion. A new volley of fire loosed from one of the four remaining gun towers. It flew high and Caledonia held her breath as she tracked its progress.

One of Lir's ships stuttered, its nose shoved into the water by a sudden explosion.

Caledonia's crew roared in triumph.

"That's one!" Caledonia grinned. "Bring us back around, Nettle! Harwell, tell the fleet to keep driving in. Our team just needs a little more time to get the rest of those towers!"

Ahead, Lir's ships were stacked three deep in front of the breakers, blocking all access to the harbor. Caledonia's fleet, though much smaller, was driving in as hard as it could, nosing into the blockade where the gun towers would be unable to target them without also hitting their own. Caledonia cut a glance at Pisces.

The look she wore wasn't one Caledonia could easily decipher. This wasn't the practiced mid-battle grimace she was used to, but something bristling with frisson.

Caledonia opened her mouth to say—what? She didn't know and now wasn't the time. She snapped her mouth shut again. For a second, they watched each other, then, with a tight nod, Pisces departed the bridge.

"Brace for impact!" Nettle shouted a second before a Bullet ship rammed them.

The *Luminous Wake* listed sharply to starboard. The Bullet ship latched on, throwing griphooks over the rail and pulling the hulls together. Caledonia's crew surged across the deck, raising shields and firing on the Bullet clip attempting to board them.

Though she wanted to join the fray, Caledonia stayed put, kept her eyes on the battle surging around her.

For a moment, it was difficult to tell who was firing on whom. Her own ships were hopelessly mixed with Lir's, and three of the four remaining gun towers fired haphazardly on both fleets erratically, as though inside each tower, the infiltration teams struggled for dominance. Beyond the breakers, a fresh contingent of Bullet ships waited in the harbor, their guns ready to snipe at any of her fleet lucky enough to break through. Caledonia was certain Lir was among them. Watching and waiting for the moment she was at her weakest.

Then, just as she was beginning to entertain the idea of retreat, a second gun tower turned its aim from her fleet to Lir's. In the next moment, a third did the same.

"That's three!" Nettle cheered.

Immediately, the battle shifted. With three gun towers firing on Lir's fleet and the fourth oddly silent, it didn't matter that Caledonia's fleet was smaller. They finally had room to maneuver.

One of the towers targeted the ship latched on to the *Luminous Wake* and took it out with a single well-placed shot.

"Remind me to thank Pine later," Caledonia said with a smile as sweat slipped from her temples to her neck.

"How do you know that was him?" Nettle asked.

But as soon as she'd asked the question, the fourth and final gun tower fired. The missile landed squarely on their bow, rocking the ship. Caledonia dove for Nettle as fire crashed against the pane of their self-healing windshield, shattering it beyond repair. She felt the painful flush of heat scrawling into her back as they crashed against the floor.

It was over in a second. She blinked. Smoke crowded her vision. Nettle's multicolored ribbons tickled her cheek. All she could smell was the tang of burning metal, of ignited gunpowder, of singed flesh. Her ears rang, but beyond that piercing sound, she could hear her crew shouting, recovering, getting back to their feet. Somewhere in the distance, there was pain.

Nettle squirmed beneath her, urging Caledonia to her feet.

Smoke coiled from a crater in the bow. Already, the crew was directing hoses into the wound, smothering the fires with seawater. High on the hill, one gun tower swiveled its eye, taking aim at the tower that had just fired on the *Luminous Wake*. They fired, a single perfect shot, and demolished the tower.

"That's definitely Pine," Caledonia said, offering a grim smile to Nettle. "Are you well?"

"Well enough, Captain," Nettle confirmed as she reached for the wheel.

Now all three remaining gun towers belonged to Caledonia, and the battle was swinging swiftly in her favor. She left the bridge, surveying the damage on her bow and starboard side. The crew was in no better shape than the ship. Hime crouched next to a prone figure on the deck, her hands flashing red in the sunlight as she worked to save a life. Everywhere Caledonia looked her crew was bloodied, but still fighting.

Pisces hauled herself up the companionway ladder. Her sunny brown skin was streaked with ash and blood. "Flanking ships are breaking off, Captain," she reported.

Caledonia turned her gaze to the west, where Lir's ships did exactly as Pisces said: they were leaving, retreating, *running*.

"Then I think it's time we find the sick fish himself."

Pisces followed Caledonia back to the bridge, where Harwell opened a channel and released his station to his captain. With only a second to fully appreciate what she was about to do, Caledonia brought the receiver to her mouth and pressed the button.

"This is Caledonia Styx of the *Luminous Wake*." She paused, knowing just that would be enough to pique his interest.

As the first of Caledonia's ships sailed into the harbor, her gun towers fired ruthlessly. They concentrated on the harbor, forcing Bullet ships to flee toward the breakers.

Caledonia watched as Lir's fleet lost all semblance of cohesion, as they transitioned from order to chaos, with many retreating, and she felt the first stirrings of victory within her reach.

And then the radio crackled to life.

"Caledonia." Lir's voice slid across her skin like ice.

She wanted to tell him not to say her name. She hated the way he softened the sound of the "c" in the back of his throat, how he lingered through the length of it as though tasting each subsequent letter. He said it fondly, she thought, like a lover might.

"Lir," she said, resisting the urge to give him anything more than her voice. "I'm offering you a chance to surrender."

"Surrender?" True surprise brightened his response. "Oh, I don't think now is the time for something as final as that."

"I have your gun towers, Lir. Your fleet has lost confidence in you. In another minute I will have the harbor and the town. The Holster will be mine and you will be dead. Unless you surrender now."

"Will you destroy my entire fleet?" he asked. "Will you gun down every last Bullet you see here? Kill us all?"

Caledonia hesitated. *No unnecessary deaths.* That was how they'd started this. But was it possible to finish that way? She'd already used the star blossoms. What ground could she stand on after that?

"I don't think you have it in you," Lir continued in his self-satisfied way. "And until you do, I will always win."

Before she could respond, the Bullet ships still in the harbor turned their guns on their own town and opened fire on the Holster.

CHAPTER THIRTY-THREE

Explosions bloomed over the city.

"He's firing on the Holster! Wait. Why is he firing on the Holster?" Harwell asked.

Caledonia had no answer for him.

Flames rose from inside the city. Alarms sounded, and even from this distance the chaos within those streets was palpable. Caledonia recalled what Oran had said about the inhabitants; there were children and elderly inside that city. And now they were dying.

The only thing she could do for them was drive Lir's forces from the harbor.

"Send word through the fleet. I want as many of my ships charging the breakers as possible."

"Yes, Captain," Harwell chirped, taking the receiver from her hand.

"Captain!" Oran stepped onto the bridge. Fresh blood smeared his right hand. "There's something you need to see."

Caledonia followed him to the port side, Pisces at her heels.

They skirted the gaping hole in the center of the bow, careful to avoid touching the jagged leaves of still-steaming metal. They crouched behind a team of gunners, letting their shields protect them from enemy fire.

"Lir's ships are forming up." Oran pointed beyond the breakers to the north side of the harbor. "Looks like a barricade."

Even as he spoke, more of Lir's fleet turned from the fight. They created a solid line of ships that stretched from one side of the concrete breakers to the other.

"For what?" Pisces asked. "There's nothing on the north side except land."

"He's staging an exit, moving ships out." Caledonia traced the hint of movement just behind the barricade.

"Are those barges?" Pisces narrowed her eyes.

There, in the space between ships, Caledonia saw them, too. Barges gliding across the water toward the open ocean, each one covered in barely budding baleflowers.

"He won't be far behind them. We can't let him get away!"

All of this—the battle, the alliance with Tassos, their losses at Cloudbreak—would be for nothing if she didn't capture Lir. If she didn't find a way to stop this cycle of running and fighting and dying.

"Target that barricade!" Caledonia called out to her crew. "Keep your eyes peeled for the *Bale Blossom*! When it lands in our sights, fire everything you have!"

"Yes, Captain!" the crew shouted.

"Approaching the breakers," Nettle announced when Caledonia stepped onto the bridge once more.

Moments ago, the breakers had been clogged with Lir's fleet. Now they were nearly clear. The *Luminous Wake* shot between them, her deck rumbling with a sudden surge of power. On either side, the rest of her fleet did the same, shooting into the harbor and turning hard to north. They aimed their guns at the barricade, firing relentlessly. Above, the gun towers provided cover, taking out barricade ships one by one.

Caledonia's focus narrowed. Every minute of the past turn had brought her to this point. She and her crew had grown strong together, they had lost together, they had survived and decided to keep fighting together. And now they were here, on the very brink of the victory they had yearned for and bled for and endured for.

They were nearly upon the barricade when a gun tower missile demolished the ship directly ahead. Smoke clouded the sea, dense and billowing, but as it thinned in the breeze, the silhouette of a familiar ship appeared inside.

Caledonia and her entire crew stopped in their tracks.

The elegant sweep of the hull, the line of four mast blocks studding the centerline, the way it seemed to glide atop the water as though nothing could hold it back. They would know that ship anywhere.

"The *Mors Navis*." Caledonia almost couldn't breathe as she said the words.

And then she knew, without a doubt, that Lir was sailing her ship. Lir was sailing the *Mors Navis*.

Before any of her crew could gather their wits again, the ship was gone, vanished beyond the barricade and heading out to sea.

Caledonia heard a faint ringing in her ears as she searched in vain for another glimpse of that familiar vessel. But it was gone. The barricade was failing. More of Lir's fleet was peeling off, racing away from the harbor and the onslaught of the gun towers. The day was hers.

But Lir was getting away.

"We have to pursue," she said.

A hand caught hers as she spun toward the bridge. Pisces pulled her to a stop, forcing their foreheads together as the cacophony of gunfire faded from a constant, overlapping barrage into occasional bursts.

"Cala." She breathed her sister's name. "We cannot pursue. Not like this. We have to take the win. And let him go."

Caledonia ground her forehead into Pisces's. "We can still get him," she protested. "We can still end this."

But Pisces shook her head. "Listen to me, Cala: you won. The Holster is ours. This was a good fight."

"We won," Caledonia said.

Pisces nodded, repeated, "We won."

Caledonia raised her head to find her crew gathered near, their eyes trained on their captain and her second-in-command. Dozens of Lir's ships were dead in the water, their crews destroyed or fleeing in whatever vessels they had left. The Holster, though injured, was theirs. And beyond the breakers, Lir's fleet was running.

Lir was running from her.

Caledonia let a ferocious smile split across her face as she cried, "For Cloudbreak!"

And her crew answered viciously, "For Cloudbreak!"

CHAPTER
THIRTY-FOUR

Victory rushed through Caledonia's veins.

A warm wind seeded with the scents of burning metal and salt drove them farther into the harbor. The Holster was inked into the sprawling hillside, its rooftops beginning to shimmer with the afternoon sun, its glittering eyes like a spider's. Deep in the city, fires burned, painting the sky with coils of black smoke.

Their losses had been heavy. Only thirty-eight ships remained in Caledonia's fleet—twenty-two belonging to Tassos. The rest were too damaged to sail or destroyed altogether. Repairs would be their top priority after securing the town. In the meantime, Caledonia sent two ships under Ennick's command to track Lir's retreat. He'd fled north, toward Slipmark, where he would doubtless replenish all his resources. She had to assume he'd be back, but maybe not immediately. Still, she positioned ten ships within the harbor and five beyond the breakers to keep watch.

Sledge and Heron took the remaining crews ashore to secure the town, coordinating teams to put the fires out and then sweep the city for survivors. Caledonia and Tassos would follow shortly. Together.

Settling into the chamber beneath the bridge, Caledonia and Pisces took stock of their new situation while Hime saw to the worst of their wounds. Now that the rush of battle was fading, Caledonia felt every single cut, bruise, and burn. Her back ached whenever she moved, though she did her best not to show it.

Hime's fingers were stained red and black, and the lower half of her long, black braid was missing. Caledonia reached for it automatically, feeling the rough ends where something hot had seared straight through.

Could have been my head, Hime signed swiftly, offering a tired smile. *I prefer this option.*

"So do I." Caledonia winced as the girl applied a cold nanogel to her burns. The glossy substance warmed immediately and soon her skin was blissfully numb.

Not a cure. Hime gave her a knowing look. *Don't get rough with it.*

"I'll do my best," she promised.

"Tassos is docking," Oran said, swinging around the hatchway.

"Hell." Pisces was on her feet in an instant. "I'll ready the landing party."

Hime hurried to apply a final bandage as Caledonia stood to follow Oran. Pisces's orders could be heard throughout the ship and almost before they'd arrived on the main deck, the crew had the aft starboard bow boat ready to go.

"Ready to drop!" Pisces shouted the instant Caledonia hoisted herself over the rail and into the small vessel.

Oran landed beside her. Caledonia spared a moment to give him a disapproving look. "Has Hime seen your hand?"

"She will," he promised. "After."

Caledonia frowned, but the boat was already descending, rushing toward the water below, where it landed with a jarring slap. Oran winced as he reflexively braced a hand against the lip of the boat, and Caledonia's frown turned into a glare. The engine roared and they rushed ahead, aiming for a dock where a similar bow boat paused to let Tassos and Cepheus disembark.

Apart from Lir firing directly on the Holster, the town had been largely untouched by the battle. The harbor was lined with buildings that looked remarkably similar, each one built of concrete walls with tall doors that rolled up like mouths. Three main thoroughfares led up the hill to town, each dug deep into the ground with high, narrow sidewalks on either side. Here, the streets were empty. Every available Bullet had joined the battle, and the rest of the Holster's residents were farther inland.

Tassos chewed up the road with his steps. His shoulders were hunched, and his dark red braid swung behind him. Cepheus had to jog to keep pace with the man, her whip bouncing at her thigh. By the time Caledonia, Pisces, and Oran had boots on the ground, Tassos and Cepheus had followed three Bullets to the southernmost road and were two blocks ahead.

"Tassos!" Caledonia called when they had closed half the distance between them.

Tassos paid no attention, but continued to climb with angry, hurried steps.

"I could shoot him," Pisces offered, pausing as Caledonia came to a stop. "That would stop him."

"Redtooth would be proud of that suggestion," Caledonia answered.

"But she would have been serious about it," Oran added.

"Who says I'm not?" Pisces raised an eyebrow.

"Tassos, if you don't stop right now, I'll blow your ship out of the water!" Caledonia shouted.

At this, Tassos stopped, then spun around on his heel and moved just as quickly toward Caledonia. His eyes were narrowed and dark, and at his sides his fists swung like anvils.

The soft pop of Pisces pulling her gun from its holster sounded just behind Caledonia. On her other side, metal whispered against metal as Oran instinctively tried to make fists.

"Where are you going?" Caledonia demanded. "We agreed to enter the city together. After the initial sweep."

"Lir destroyed the baleseeds!" Tassos shouted, driving his face toward hers. "That's what he was firing on. The bale stores! And if I don't get what I came for, then I'll consider our alliance through."

Caledonia lifted her chin and held her ground. "Should I do

the same? I came for Lir and I don't have him, but if our alliance is over, then I'll invite you to leave my city."

She shouldn't be so reckless with him. She knew it, but her patience was spent.

Tassos loomed over her, chest heaving. "I'm going to search every inch of this city for Silt, and you're going to let me," he said, voice menacing and strained. "Or you're going to have an even bigger problem on your hands than my anger."

The threat was clear enough: Tassos was out of Silt and so were all of his Bullets. If they didn't find something to satisfy their craving, they would spin out of his control. They would feel no pain and their violence would be aimless and hungry. With so many of their people already ashore, the situation could turn rapidly against her.

She might even lose control of the Holster.

Caledonia stepped forward, no longer as certain as she needed to appear in this moment. "If you're about to lose control of your Bullets, then you have two choices: either you get everyone on board whatever seaworthy ships you have and leave my city, or you stay in my prison hold while you get clean."

His hand snaked out, crushing her wrist in a powerful grip.

Behind her, Pisces started forward, but one of the three Bullets was there first, stopping Pisces with the barrel of a loaded gun.

"Release my hand," Caledonia said, voice steely and low. "And we'll discuss this."

Tassos's lip curled and sweat stood out along his forehead in spite of the cooling afternoon. Caledonia saw the answer in the twist of his shoulders but had no time to prepare before his fist crashed against her cheek and drove her into the ground.

Blood coated Caledonia's tongue. Her vision flashed white and pain speared her from cheek to cheek. She rolled, dodging a second strike and finding her feet in one smooth motion. Then she stood, throwing a hand in the air to stop Pisces and Oran from rushing to her defense.

"I consent to your challenge, Fiveson Tassos," she said, wiping the blood from her chin.

The street was abandoned but for the eight of them. Caledonia would have preferred more of a Bullet audience for this fight, but the four here would have to do.

"Caledonia, this wasn't the plan," Pisces said, coming near.

"It is now," she answered, spitting blood from her mouth. Tassos had no more room for reason. He was furious and half out of his mind for want of Silt, and for fear of what his Bullets would do when he couldn't provide it. The only language he would understand right now was violence. "A clean fight between the two of us is the only way we avoid a Bullet uprising."

"Let me take the fight." Oran moved in close, his face mere inches from hers, his eyes burning with a cold, distant fire. "Let me do this for you."

"No," she said with a shake of her head. "Even if your hands were completely healed, you couldn't do this for me, Oran. You know that."

Frustration showed in the flare of his nostrils, and for the first time in her memory, she knew what Oran looked like when he was worried. His eyes darted down, and his shoulders shifted forward and back before he looked at her again. "Please, Cala. You don't need to be the one to do this."

"But I do."

Pisces looked uncomfortable. "What do you want us to do?" she asked.

"Don't take your eyes off them," Caledonia answered smoothly, eyes still locked with Oran's.

"Understood," Pisces answered.

"Cala—" Oran started and stopped. "Stay steely."

"You too."

With a grim nod, he stepped back. He and Pisces planted themselves near enough that if something went wrong, they'd be ready.

"You have made your last mistake," Tassos said, raising his fists.

"Every time I think that's true, I surprise myself," Caledonia answered, waiting for his shoulders to tell her where he meant to move. He might be as broad as the ocean, but she'd learned to read the ocean a long time ago; reading his shoulders was no different.

He attacked like a snake, coiling back and darting out in a single, brutal strike meant to lay her low. She dodged, twisting around him to deliver two tight blows to his side. She landed them with firm fists and heard the involuntary grunts he made before laughter spilled from his lips.

"Not much without your guns," he taunted.

Caledonia let the irritation show on her face. Let him think he could read her the way she read him.

He dove in again, twice more in rapid succession. Caledonia dodged the first attack, but the second blow caught her shoulder, shoving her back with such force her teeth clattered painfully together. On his third attack, she bent low, landing a kick in the side of his knee.

Tassos grunted as his knee slammed against the street, and the surprise on his face morphed into anger. He rounded on her, darting forward, forcing Caledonia to retreat faster than she was ready to move.

His fist crashed into her chest. The force of it sent her flying through the air. She landed flat on her back. Pain shot through her body as the muscles in her stomach clenched hard and her lungs pinched tight. She couldn't draw a breath, but she opened her eyes in time to see Tassos draw back his leg and drive the toe of his boot into her chest.

She felt this pain as if it were a tight embrace, squeezing against her muscles and bones. Her vision narrowed and Tassos kicked again, snapping her head sharply back.

"Caledonia!" Pisces's voice splintered through the haze.

"Caledonia!" Pisces shouted again.

"Cala!" Oran cried.

Suddenly, she was aware that both Oran and Pisces were fighting. The Bullets had surged forward, and they attacked now with glee.

Caledonia grit her teeth and rolled, catching the wind of Tassos's next kick against her cheek. Her vision blurred, but as she crouched on her feet, she felt her lungs loosen. She sipped at the air and spread her fingers against the ground.

"You might be a hell of a girl, Caledonia Styx," Tassos was saying as he stalked toward her again. "But you're still just a girl."

Caledonia grimaced. Blood coated her teeth, filling her mouth with its coppery flavor. She licked her lips and heard the meaning behind his words. She was just a girl. And he was just a man.

He was part of Aric's legacy. He'd been raised violently and groomed to seek power over others. As long as he lived, he would find ways to continue the merciless story of the Bullet Seas.

And he was going to kill her.

The crack of a whip sounded in the air and Pisces roared. Somewhere, Oran was struggling to defend against two attacking Bullets, his hands all but useless in their metal splints. Caledonia could sense the two of them more than see them. Neither could help her.

Tassos moved in again. This time when Caledonia dodged his fist, she crouched, lashing out with a swift kick to sweep his legs out from under him. He went down hard, shoulders slamming against the stone. He groaned, rolling to his side and climbing to his feet.

But Caledonia was there. She drilled an elbow into his neck. Tassos fell again to his knees, and as he gasped for breath, Caledonia circled to stand behind him.

Without pausing to think, or give Tassos time to recover, Caledonia planted her feet wide. Then, pulling the push dagger from her waistband, she yanked his head back and slid the blade into his throat.

All sound vanished as Tassos's body fell to the ground at Caledonia's feet.

CHAPTER THIRTY-FIVE

Caledonia's chest heaved painfully, and nausea threatened to reject the meager contents of her stomach, but she remained where she stood. Little by little, her fractured vision righted itself until she could see Pisces and Oran. And oddly enough, Cepheus standing at their side, as though she'd joined them against the other three Bullets.

She focused on Cepheus and the Bullets, all of them having stopped their own fight the instant Tassos hit the ground. As Lir had demonstrated by killing Aric and taking command, violence was how leadership passed between Bullets. If another Bullet had killed Tassos, they would assume his authority, but Caledonia wasn't a Bullet.

"If any of you wishes to challenge me, now is the time." Thumbing the blood from her chin, Caledonia curled her fingers into fists to mask the tremble of her hands. She would fight if she had to, but she wasn't sure how much more her body could take.

Cepheus was the first to take the invitation. She stalked across the short distance, her chin tucked and her fists knotted at her sides. Sunlight flashed off the orange scars that laced her lips and jaw, and her mouth pulled into a stark line. Nausea twisted again in Caledonia's belly and hot saliva flooded her mouth. A fresh surge of adrenaline pushed at her heart as her body prepared to fight. To kill.

Then Cepheus stooped to roll Tassos onto his back. His eyes stared at the sky and his head lolled to one side, blood painting his throat scarlet. With a surprisingly gentle hand, Cepheus drew his eyes shut, then reached for the gun still holstered at his side.

The instant she drew the weapon, Oran and Pisces drew theirs. But Cepheus ejected the clip, then cleared the round from the chamber and laid the empty weapon against Tassos's chest. When she was done, she offered the clip to Caledonia.

"Tassos has been defeated in a challenge of his making," she said, and the words had the ring of ritual. "His clip is yours to take, his bullets yours to spend."

Caledonia searched Cepheus's face for any sign of resistance or calculation. The woman met her gaze openly, a tiny smile perched in the corner of her mouth. If it was a ploy, Caledonia could see no trace of it. The other Bullets shifted but made no move to resist.

Reaching out, Caledonia took the offered clip in her own hand, suddenly unsure of her role in this ritual. But it didn't matter. She was not a Bullet. She would never be a Bullet, and if she wanted to make room for others to choose *not* to be Bullets, then she had to start somewhere. This, as Sledge was so fond of saying, was the real fight.

"I do not spend bullets lightly," she said. "And I do not take anyone who does not consent to fight for me. But before you can consent, you must purge the Silt from your blood."

Even as she spoke, she could see the first signs of withdrawal in Cepheus. Her skin blanched white around her lips and eyes and sweat beaded along her brow and temples. Soon, she would succumb to the full effects of Silt withdrawal and she would need care. They all would.

"No." Cepheus shook her head sharply, a threat building in her eyes. She stepped forward, closing the three Bullets out of their conversation. "From Silt comes strength. Tassos was right: if we don't find whatever Silt is left in this town, then it won't matter that you killed Tassos. His Bullets will defect to Lir. We need Silt."

Caledonia nodded, thinking of all the times she'd sent Bullets back to Lir rather than force them through their sweats. Then, it had been a question of resources. Cloudbreak simply couldn't support the process of weaning several hundred Bullets from Silt, and she couldn't assume the risks that followed. She could do the same thing now. Send these Silt-deprived Bullets to join Lir's ranks and drain his resources. But this wasn't Cloudbreak, and she was tired of releasing Bullets just to fight them again another day.

"This is not a negotiation. Every Bullet in this city will be relocated to the prison hold. They will be fed and cared for while they recover, and after that, they can make their own choices."

"That's not a choice," Cepheus said through bared teeth. "That's coercion."

"Cepheus, please," Pisces urged, stepping forward. "Let us help you."

Cepheus seemed to soften under Pisces's concern, and she bit down on whatever it was she'd been prepared to say.

"I won't make you fight," Caledonia continued. "But that drug doesn't make you strong. It makes you weak. It makes you dependent on whoever controls it."

"You'd rather we were dependent on *you*."

Caledonia leaned in. Cepheus was imposing, but Caledonia was no longer the same girl she'd been a turn ago, and as she closed the distance between them, she caught a quiver of uncertainty on the woman's lips.

"I don't want anything from you. You are all but useless to me," Caledonia said, not unkindly. Where once this conversation would have frustrated Caledonia, now she understood it. To Cepheus, there had never been life without Silt. She didn't yet trust that its absence was anything more than a punishment.

"If we're so useless, why should we let you imprison us?" Cepheus asked.

Stepping around her, Caledonia returned to Tassos's body. For a moment she could only stare at the blood pooling beneath his head, recalling its slick heat as it had coated her right hand. Then she reached out and, swallowing hard, tugged the black box from his belt.

"Because if you stay here, you'll get clean and, after that, have a future." Caledonia turned the box over in her hand as she stood once more. With a twist of the lid, it popped open to reveal a keypad. She returned her gaze to Cepheus. "But if you leave and follow Lir, you'll lose your drug anyway, and then you'll see what happens when Lir doesn't get what he wants from you."

CHAPTER THIRTY-SIX

There was still so much Caledonia didn't know. Who had survived the attack at the gun towers? How many civilians remained in the city? Had Lir taken Slipmark as his own? Was he rallying the troops there for a fresh attack? And now what was happening to the Bullets left behind at the Net? Were they as close to withdrawal as the Bullets here? Or were they already in their sweats?

She'd had a plan for discovering the answer to each one, but that plan was gone now. If Cepheus was starting to show signs of withdrawal, the same was true for every other Bullet in the Holster. Caledonia's claim to leadership was valid but it was also tenuous. There was no time to lose.

"Pi," she said, letting her focus settle on the most immediate threat. "Go back to the *Luminous* and put the crew on alert. I need you to direct Tassos's Bullets to the prison without raising suspicion." With a sharp nod, Pisces was gone, and Caledonia turned to Oran. "I need you to find Sledge and ready the prison. It's . . . north from here?" she asked, picturing Heron's map of the city.

Oran nodded, his eyes marking every one of her cuts and bruises. "Straight north from here," he confirmed.

"Meet us there," she said, ignoring the concern in his eyes as she turned to the three Bullets, who appeared to be awaiting orders. From her. "Pick him up."

As the Bullets raised Tassos's body between them, Oran moved off at a brisk jog and Cepheus walked at Caledonia's side. Together, they turned north, following an unbending road. Cepheus glanced over her shoulder once, gaze lingering on Tassos, but she made no sound of remorse. Her eyes remained dry as they passed through the unfamiliar streets.

In the time it took to cross the city, Caledonia had considered half a dozen new problems. From making repairs without leaving her defenses weak to rebuilding the gun towers and guarding a landward flank; from managing the civilians still inside the city to treating her new wounds. These were problems she couldn't even begin to consider solving until she'd taken care of the hundreds of Bullets on the brink of withdrawal.

One problem, however, she could solve immediately.

Without slowing her stride, she popped the flap of Tassos's remote trigger and pressed the code Nettle had discovered. Part of her regretted that she was too far to see the explosion for herself. But she could imagine how it would bloom against the southern seas, vibrant as a bale blossom. Soon, she'd sail out and confirm the destruction, but for now it was enough to know the rig was gone.

"That didn't work," Cepheus said, interrupting her quiet moment of victory.

"What do you mean?" Caledonia snapped the little latch shut, irritation making her sharp. "Tassos lied?"

"Not exactly. There are more bombs on the rig than anyone knows, but the range on that remote is limited." Cepheus glanced over her shoulder toward the Bullets carrying their fallen Fiveson. "He only let people *think* it would work regardless of where he was. Tassos never expected to be far enough to need a strong signal. Thought he'd die on that Net."

Caledonia considered the small black box in her hand. Disappointment perched in the back of her throat, and as much as she wanted Cepheus to be lying, she knew in her gut this was the truth. "Why are you telling me?" she asked.

The sounds of their footsteps against the stone street filled the space between them. A frown flashed across Cepheus's face and she squeezed her lips tight before conceding, "I owe Pisces a debt."

Caledonia thought she caught the hint of affection in the young woman's tone, in the fond way her eyes pinched when she spoke of Pisces.

"How close do I need to be?" Caledonia asked.

"Close." Cepheus shrugged. "A mile and a half."

With a sigh, Caledonia clipped the remote to her waistband. Another problem for later.

Before she could say anything more, the prison appeared at the end of the street. Oran and Sledge were waiting for them outside a building that stretched the length of the *Luminous*. A single pair of heavy doors in the front marked the only way in or out.

Sledge was narrow-eyed, and strain showed in every muscle of his considerable body. "Don't know what you want to do with those already inside," he said.

"Leave them there for now," Caledonia answered quickly. Anyone Lir considered worthy of being locked away was either an immediate ally or someone she had no business freeing. "Any word from the infiltration team?"

A frown tightened Sledge's lips. "Not yet."

Caledonia reached out, slipping her hand into Sledge's and squeezing tightly. She wanted to be sure their people had survived, but the truth was, they'd lost two of those towers. All of their people might have died in that attack, and they had more to deal with before they found out for certain.

Soon, Pisces and half the crew of the *Luminous Wake* appeared on the road, guiding a group of curious Bullets toward the prison doors. They laid Tassos out on a white cloth, the empty gun against his chest, hands down by his sides, then Caledonia and Cepheus stood where every Bullet would have to pass as they were brought to the prison. There would be no doubt that Caledonia had been the one to kill him, that Caledonia was now the one in power.

Caledonia's blood pounded in her ears, and she resisted the

urge to draw her weapon as the first band of Bullets approached. Her own crew had them surrounded, waiting for the moment this went very wrong.

But the moment never came.

The second the Bullets spotted their former Fiveson, something shifted in them. They dimmed, if that was possible, the fight in their faces going momentarily slack as they searched for their new leader. They found their answer in Caledonia's bloodied hand. Some were surprised, others not so much, but one look at Cepheus standing at her side and they all shuffled into the prison without protest.

It went on this way for hours. Every new wave of Bullets that passed bore the same signs of strain. Their eyes were red-rimmed, their expressions wary or too alert. They traveled together, but each one held themselves apart from the others as though the lightest touch might ignite them to violence or destroy them completely. Caledonia had never seen so many Bullets this close to breaking, and the sight was as dispiriting as it was unsettling.

She'd once asked Pine how he came back from being a Bullet. His response threaded her thoughts now as she watched people as young as Nettle and as old as Heron march past her with shades of horror in their eyes.

"We didn't come back from being Bullets," he'd said. *"We just got out of the chamber."*

All at once the day was gone. The clouds turned into pale

smudges against a shadowed sky, and Caledonia felt bruises leaching so far down into her bones she was surprised there was anything left to hold her upright. Pain pierced her ribs with every breath, and her head throbbed in time with her pulse.

The last clip to move was that of the *Deep Cut*. As they marched past one by one, her eyes caught on a familiar face.

"Donnally." Her voice came out in a rough whisper. Only loud enough for Cepheus to hear.

"Tassos thought he might be useful," she explained. "If he decided Lir looked like a better bet than you."

Caledonia couldn't find the energy to be irritated that Tassos had been planning to double-cross her. Her brother was here. She hadn't even had time to consider how she was going to retrieve him from the megaship and now he was here. Her heart stuttered against her chest, relief and sorrow creating an impossible rhythm.

The line moved on, and for a second Donnally's eyes strayed to hers. Her breath quickened and she fought against her traitorous instincts, which continued to demand that she rush forward and throw her arms around his neck. But it lasted for only a second. Without even a glimmer of recognition, Donnally looked away.

The ache in Caledonia's chest sharpened as he disappeared inside the prison. There was no reason for him to be there. Tassos had been denying him Silt long enough to wean him from it. He wasn't a prisoner here. But Caledonia couldn't find the energy to go after him. Tomorrow. She would speak with him tomorrow.

Cepheus was the last to go. She entered the prison with a weary smile, her lips paler than they'd been only a few hours ago. By the time the doors were shut behind her, Caledonia had moved so far into her pain she was sure she'd gone numb. At least, that's what she thought until Pisces guided her back to the wharf and to a room with a bed and probably a few other things she didn't care about at the moment. But before she could collapse, Hime arrived and demanded she sit upright a while longer.

"Ow!" Caledonia cried as Hime pressed against her ribs.

Hime answered by continuing to work her fingers across Caledonia's bruises while Caledonia sat on the edge of her bed in nothing but a thin pair of shorts. Now that she'd stopped moving, her head pounded like a stormy sea and every inch of her seemed to bear some sort of wound. She'd barely made it to her room before she vomited. Her body was exhausted, and every breath drilled small points of pain through her ribs.

"Just tell me they aren't broken," Caledonia said.

She knew they were broken. This pain was both familiar and so much worse than she remembered from past injuries.

One for certain, Hime signed, pointing to the darkest bruising on Caledonia's rib cage. *Several others are fractured, and you have a concussion. I can give you a draught for pain.*

Every part of her wanted to say yes. "But without the pain, how else will I know I'm alive?" she teased.

Now I know you're delirious.

"But I need to stay alert," Caledonia protested, regaining the smallest edge of her composure.

Trust me. There will still be plenty of pain. I can't even begin to treat . . . all of this. Hime nodded, her expression grim as she pulled bandages tight across Caledonia's breasts, flattening them to her body and stabilizing her torso. *Besides, Pisces knows what she's doing. The fleet is secured, and Sledge has established a perimeter around the city. There's nothing for you to do but rest.*

"Fine, fine, I'll take it." She took the small vial Hime offered, knocking it back in one swallow. It tasted both bitter and sweet. It was a truly wretched combination of flavors.

You need more rest than you can take, Hime signed sadly. She was always sad these days, and it pained Caledonia to watch the slow knife of grief carve shallow tracks across Hime's heart. *Just, take as much as you can.*

Caledonia nodded as the girl drifted to the door. "I promise."

But sleep was fleeting. Every time she slipped from consciousness, she jerked awake again with sweating palms and the lingering image of Tassos's face in her mind. She felt like something unfamiliar was taking root in her lungs, sending tendrils to swirl in her belly and dive deep through her guts. Changing her from the inside out.

Giving up on sleep, Caledonia opened her window and leaned out, letting the cool air fill her lungs as she searched for patterns in the stars. It was an old trick to calm her mind, and it might have worked if she'd known as many patterns as Donnally. But she didn't. The few she did know weren't anywhere to be found, so she was stuck with making her own shapes. So far, she'd found a ship, another ship, a gun with a bullet shooting out of its barrel, and the shape of a man who looked exactly like Tassos.

It wasn't helping.

A knock sounded quietly at her door. Not the urgent pounding of an emergency, but the gentle *tap-tap-tap* of concern.

"Come in," she called without moving from her spot.

The door opened and closed softly behind her, only the barest whisper of movement.

"Caledonia."

She turned at the sound of Oran's voice. Too fast. Her ribs screamed at the movement, her head spun, and she gasped.

Concern brought Oran instantly to her side, but he stopped just short of touching her. His hands hovered at her elbows, unsure.

"Oran," she said, voice thin as the pain slowly receded. "What are you— Is something wrong? Is it Donnally?"

His jaw clenched and his lips pulled into a frown at the reminder of the distance that had come between them. At the distance *she* had put there. "I came for you," he said quietly.

"I'm fine. Really." Caledonia grit her teeth and held her arms out wide. Her ribs whined in protest. She forced a smile.

"I don't think you're fine," Oran said. His gaze was so steady, she felt she could lean into it, let it support her for a moment or a turn.

She sighed, pulling away to rest her back against the window-sill, where the night breeze cooled the thin sheen of sweat now coating the back of her neck. "When I tell you I'm fine, your job is to believe me."

"My job."

"Oran," she said, turning his name into both a protest and a request.

"I do believe you," he said, voice low. "And I don't."

It was three words, but with them, he said so much. That he knew she was hurting. That he knew the fight had changed her as much as it had changed everything else. That even now, he wished she'd let him be the one to face Tassos. That he knew how her heart was shifting and twisting in on itself, struggling to keep its shape. But it was a useless battle. Where once her heart only needed to beat for herself and her crew, now it needed to beat for everyone.

"I would do it again," she said. She pressed her lips between her teeth to stop herself from saying more. What more was there to say? She'd killed a man outside of battle, and there was no part of her that regretted the choice. It had been the right one even if it had been a terrible one.

Oran nodded mournfully. "You may have to."

Caledonia had revisited the memory so many times already

that it took very little to summon the image of Tassos kneeling before her, the firm pressure of his throat in her hands. She pressed her eyes closed, willing anything to take its place. Even blackness. But it played out in exquisite strokes. She felt the warm rush of blood over her fingers, saw the slump of his body, tasted the bile on her tongue. And she shuddered.

Oran stepped closer. "It will get easier."

"Easier?" Horror elevated Caledonia's voice. "I don't want it to get easier, Oran, I want it to not be necessary."

"If we do this right, it will be both."

"I don't want killing like that to be something I can do without feeling it!" she said, suddenly panicked. "And I should feel it more than I do, shouldn't I? Have I changed so much that I can slit a man's throat and hold court over his body for—for—"

Her breath came in short, pained gasps and she leaned forward, glad for the moment her hands met Oran's chest and his arms encircled her back. He stroked her lightly, making soothing circles with his palm as the breeze grazed her bare shoulders. Soon her breathing was even and the vise around her throat loosened its hold.

"Oran," she murmured, her forehead still pressed to his chest.

"Yes?" he answered, drawing his hands down to her waist, the pressure of his fingers warm through the thin fabric of her shirt.

"I don't know what happens to us—to *me*—when this is all

over," she said. "But right now, I need you here even if that means I ask you to do terrible things, to watch me do terrible things." She drew her head up to look into his eyes. "Because you've done this. You've compromised parts of yourself in service to others. You've turned yourself into something terrible and vicious. But that's not why I need you. I need you by my side because after you did all of that, you made your way back." She flattened her palms against his chest, feeling the heat radiating off him. "When this is over, I want to be able to come back from all that I've done. I want you to help me do that."

"Hell." Oran frowned, his head bowing slightly, fingers pulling at her waist. "I don't think I came back."

"But you did, I saw you. I know you. And if you hadn't, you couldn't . . . say the things you say."

Oran blew out a breath, staring into her eyes as he wrestled to accept what she was saying. And what she wouldn't say.

In the end, he whispered, "I wish you'd let me take that fight, Cala."

"There are some things no one can do but me."

"I hate that that is true." He sighed sharply, hot breath puffing against her chin, then he nodded. "But I will stand by your side and I won't let you fall. Because I—"

She pressed a hand to his mouth, suddenly desperate not to hear the words she could not, would not repeat back to him, not until after, if she managed to drag herself out of this hell.

But Oran pulled her fingers from his lips and said, "Because I'm yours. To the end."

Caledonia rested her head on his chest as she repeated, "To the end," not really knowing what it would mean for them but feeling certain that the end was much closer than it had ever been before.

CHAPTER THIRTY-SEVEN

Taking over a city was not as straightforward as running a fleet, and the next day passed in a blur of figuring out basic resources like water and food, creating a harbor schedule, and securing the perimeter.

Pine, Tin, Ares, Folly, and Gloriana had all returned from the perimeter, more than a few injuries spread out between them. They'd come early in the day to give their report, telling Caledonia exactly how the attack at the gun towers had initially gone wrong when one of the teams had been spotted on the ground. The resulting fight had delayed their entrance into the towers themselves, leaving Caledonia's fleet to fend for itself. Finally, they'd gained entry, and each team had fought to wrest control of the guns from Lir's Bullets.

"We think Tug's team was losing control," Pine said, voice falling. "They were in the first tower that blew. Tug must have ignited a bomb rather than let Lir keep the tower."

"He died with glory," Gloriana supplied.

The word settled uncomfortably with Caledonia. Tug had

fought for her yet died for an idea she opposed. It was a strange tension of opposites. "He will be remembered," she promised.

The city wasn't as deserted as it had at first appeared, and Sledge, Pine, and Ares had spent the rest of the day dealing with everyone Lir had left behind. There were children who'd been born here, children who'd been conscripted, and their assigned caretakers; there were Hollows and adults who were all too ill or elderly to fight. Every one of them had needs and more than a few of them needed Silt. Figuring out how to contain them as they came through their own necessary withdrawal was a frustrating, delicate process. One Caledonia was grateful to hand over to Ares.

Pisces and Hime worked tirelessly to assess the damage of their crew and every vessel left in the fleet, while Far assigned herself the task of evaluating their food stores, and Gloriana was overseeing the prison itself. And though Oran would have preferred to spend the day at Caledonia's side, she persuaded him to examine Lir's armory for anything they should dismantle or destroy.

In the blink of an eye, the day had passed, and Caledonia was left with an overwhelming sense of having accomplished nothing. She didn't even know her way around the city, and all day she'd been making decisions about what belonged where and how many people to keep on each of their ships at any given time and whether or not they should repair the breakers first or the towers.

Every decision felt momentous. And like a monumental distraction from her true mission. Any minute Lir could come rushing back and steal the Holster from her while she was still trying to decide where everyone should sleep.

She was supposed to be running a war, not a city.

"Pi, come with me," she called when there was a break in the constant stream of administrative business.

Caledonia crossed the office they'd claimed for its proximity to the wharf and pushed through the side door that emptied into a narrow alley lined with orange solar pips. Just beyond the end of the alley, the main thoroughfare buzzed with activity. The rest of the city might have been thinly populated, but with her crews here, the wharf felt very much alive.

Caledonia drew a deep breath and regretted it immediately, bracing a hand lightly at her side and squeezing her eyes shut as pain radiated from everywhere inside her at once.

"I can get another draught of painkiller from Hime," Pisces offered.

"No," Caledonia said, voice pressed thin. "Not yet."

Pisces nodded, waiting for Caledonia to regain control of herself. They hadn't had a moment alone, no time to discuss all that had happened both in the battle and after it, and the air between them was growing thicker with each passing hour.

"I'm going to get Donnally from the prison. I want a room prepared for him when I get back." Caledonia took a shallow breath, gingerly testing her lungs. "Unless you have something to say to me first?"

They'd known each other too long to bother hiding when one of them was upset. Caledonia recognized the purse of Pisces's lips and the way she pushed a breath out through her nose. Pisces wasn't furious with her. This was a simmering kind of distress.

"No," Pisces answered. "Do you want him in the barracks with us?"

"I do. Thank you." Caledonia wanted to press Pisces to clear the air between them, but she'd acknowledged the tension. She had to let Pisces make the next move. "Third floor. Near me."

"Yes, Captain."

Though it wasn't said with cruelty, Caledonia winced at the title as Pisces turned and left her alone in the alley. Caledonia leaned her back against the wall and tipped her head up to study the narrow strip of sky above. Dusk colored wispy clouds in shades of the bruises along Caledonia's body and the first pinprick lights of stars were starting to push through the gloaming. Solitary moments like this were fleeting, and her thoughts were starting to tangle around each other. Pisces wasn't happy with her, and Caledonia didn't have to reach very far to find the reason for it. But she also didn't know what to do about it. She'd made the decision, used the star blossom bombs in a crucial moment that turned the tide of battle. She couldn't undo it.

Pisces was right to be horrified, and with that alone, Caledonia agreed.

She let the cold stone soothe her aching back and then she pulled her knotted emotions back inside and pushed off the wall.

The route from the wharf to the prison was the both new and familiar and she traveled as swiftly as her body allowed. Inside the prison, the air was cool and stale, and the sounds of hundreds of people in the earliest stages of their withdrawal drifted through the building as though the walls themselves groaned. Gloriana admitted Caledonia through multiple layers of locked doors with a weary smile. She'd taken a gunshot to the shoulder during their assault on the towers and her left arm was tightly bound to her chest.

"Checking up on us?" Gloriana asked as two of her staff entered the room with arms full of folded sheets. Their eyes widened at the sight of Caledonia, but at her nod of acknowledgment, they returned to their work.

"I'm here for my bro—I'm here for Donnally," Caledonia answered. "I'm taking him with me."

"Right." Nodding, Gloriana pulled a key from one of many pockets lining her vest. "This way."

Gloriana led her deeper into the prison, where they passed through three more locked doors before entering a long room lined with cells on either side. Donnally stood inside one with arms locked across his chest. His chin tipped downward so his curls cast shadows over his dark eyes.

"Brother." She was prepared this time for the quiet tightening of his mouth at the term. Apart from that, he remained still.

Gloriana took a small step back, giving them as much privacy as she could as the shouts of Bullets echoed down the hall.

"Caledonia." His voice was tired.

"Would you like to come with me?" she asked.

"Do I really have a choice?" he fired back. "What I would like to do is return to Lir. If you're asking."

"Lir is in the wind." She said it before she could stop herself.

A soft laugh fell from Donnally's lips. When he turned his face to hers, the skin around his eyes tightened as though something had suddenly pained him. He said, "You know better than that. Lir is never in the wind. He has a plan, you just haven't seen it yet."

Caledonia swallowed. She might be able to predict Lir's motives, but Donnally *knew* them.

"Let him out," she said.

It only took a second for Gloriana to unlock the door, but it seemed to take an eternity for Donnally to walk through.

"I'm not a prisoner?" he asked.

He should be. She should hold him until this was all over. But of all the things Caledonia was capable of, holding her own brother captive wasn't one of them.

"Come with me," she said.

She led him from the prison and out into the night streets of the Holster. The city glowed softly in lines of orange Caledonia hadn't noticed through her pain last night. Rows of sun pips were placed both in the ground and along the building walls above eye level, ensuring that you could always find your way—or be found.

They walked together in silence, and Caledonia noticed that Donnally seemed at ease here. He wasn't hyperalert or scouring his surroundings for possible escape. He walked with the effortless confidence of someone who knew where he was. Of someone who felt at home.

The realization made Caledonia clench her teeth so hard they ached.

"You should keep me locked up."

"I know," she admitted.

His profile was so painfully familiar. Her breath caught on the way one shoulder rose slightly higher than the other, the involuntary twitch of his lips. She'd seen him make this exact gesture a thousand times or more and she'd forgotten it until this moment. How many other parts of her brother had she forgotten?

There were so many things she wanted to say to him, and now that she had the chance, she didn't know how. She'd never been good at sharing her heart. Not even with Pisces. And she was afraid that if she shared everything in this moment, Donnally would demand to be returned to his prison cell.

"You look like her, you know?" he said, pulling her out of her own thoughts.

"Who?"

One side of his mouth squeezed in an incredulous smile. "Mom."

"Oh." An image of Rhona Styx flashed through her mind. Rhona at the helm, her gap-toothed smile broad and confident; Rhona sitting cross-legged in her bed as she oiled her favorite rifle;

Rhona, feet dangling over the starboard bow, as she taught Caledonia to tie fishing knots. Red hair that roiled in the wind, a laugh as grizzly as the sea itself, resolve as steely as the hull of their ship.

"Oh," she repeated, feeling breathless. "The hair."

"Something more in the eyes. You always have this look, like you can see right through me." Donnally's smile wavered and vanished. "At least, that's what I remember of her eyes; they were discerning."

"Yes," Caledonia agreed, a near-giddy feeling bubbling in her chest. "They were."

This, more than anything, was enough to give Caledonia hope. If Donnally could remember their mother, then perhaps he could remember the boy he'd been before. Perhaps he could still imagine being something other than a Bullet.

He fell silent once more, retreating so far into himself that Caledonia thought maybe she'd imagined that brief feeling of connection. She and Donnally walked down the main thoroughfare, his stride a hair longer than hers and his steps twice as heavy, but they were still, somehow, completely in sync.

When they stopped before the barracks, he paused, a lopsided smile on his pale face.

"What's funny?" she asked.

"You picked the Ready Racks." He laughed softly. "Of course you did. The one place Lir would never have chosen for himself."

Farther into town, they'd found the building that had clearly housed Lir and his officers. It was spacious and comfortable, with easy access to the mess hall and a pool of vehicles that could quickly transport them to the wharf.

"I like to be close to my ships," she explained, leading him into the barracks and up the stairs to the third floor, where Pisces had left a single door ajar for them. This seemed to amuse him even more, though Caledonia couldn't say why.

"You made a good choice." His smile turned self-conscious, fluttering slightly before it disappeared.

"I thought you were dead, too." Caledonia was suddenly desperate to reach him, to win that smile back. "I didn't know you'd survived. If I had . . . Donnally, I would have come for you so much sooner. Do you know that? I used to dream that you'd survived." She paused, tears blooming as she recalled begging her mom to let her take Pisces ashore instead of Donnally. The shame of that moment was always present when she'd dreamed of her brother. "And you did. You survived and I survived."

He turned to face her, and suddenly his hands were in hers, squeezing tight. So tight Caledonia thought her fingers might break.

"I didn't survive, Caledonia. I evolved."

"You did what you had to." Caledonia clutched at his hands. "What matters now is what you do next."

Blinking furiously, Donnally nodded and, after a second,

pulled his hands away. "And what comes next?"

The loss of his touch left her too winded to speak. She swallowed hard. "You make a choice: stay or go."

"You're giving me a choice?" Suspicion clouded his eyes. "Because I'm your brother?"

"No." Caledonia steadied herself before continuing. "Because everyone should have one. Because that's the battle I'm fighting. And because keeping you here by force makes me the same as him. You've come through your sweats, your mind is your own, and you should be allowed to choose what you do next."

Uncertainty and confusion warred on Donnally's face. He backed into his new room, reaching for the door to steady himself, watching her the whole time.

"And if I choose to go?" he asked warily.

"I let you go. I'll even give you a boat."

He continued to watch her as though from a distance, as though she were a mirage he could not—should not—trust.

"When do you need my decision?" he asked.

"I can give you until the morning after next," she answered. "But you should know, if you leave, then this will be the last time we meet as siblings." A weight sat in Caledonia's stomach as she spoke. "If you choose him . . . I'll let you."

Donnally's throat plunged as he understood her meaning. Dropping his eyes to the floor, he took another step into the room, and closed the door.

CHAPTER THIRTY-EIGHT

"Captain." Pisces's urgent whisper woke Caledonia in an instant. She surged out of bed, gasping as the pain in her ribs surged with her.

"Hell," she growled.

"What's wrong?" Oran stirred beside her, already halfway to his feet.

Pisces scooped up Oran's pants and tossed them to his waiting hands. "Ennick's back."

That had Caledonia on her feet, dressing as fast as her wounds would allow. "Has he said anything?"

"He's waiting for you," Pisces answered.

Caledonia nodded as she hurriedly pulled her shirt over her head and was rewarded with bright stabs of pain. She took a deep breath, then stopped rushing. She tucked her shirt into her pants, took her time lacing up her boots, and braided her hair back as she would any morning.

Oran took his cue from her and resumed getting ready at a regular pace. This wasn't a call to battle.

"Right," Caledonia said when she was ready. "Let's go see what he has to say."

They left the barracks as the first hint of dawn strained the darkest edges of night. One benefit of having chosen the Ready Racks, as Donnally had called them, was that they put Caledonia mere steps from the wharf. The command crew gathered in the office that must have once belonged to the harbormaster. Tin was already there when Caledonia arrived, working with Far to set out a loaf of fresh bread along with a nut spread, preserved sour cherries, and a pot of teaco.

Sledge and Pine were the last to appear. They rolled in looking disheveled. Sledge's long hair was out of its braid and floated behind him like a shadow, while Pine's shirt was rumpled and untucked, his eyes still narrow with sleep.

Ennick waited quietly at the far end of the table. His weathered face was streaked with ash and blood and his salt-and-pepper hair was stiff with salt. He'd only been gone for two days, but the man hadn't stopped moving since the battle, and exhaustion showed in the wide press of his eyes.

"Welcome back," Caledonia announced when they'd pulled chairs up to the slender metal table that ran down the center of the room. "Report."

"Captain." Ennick offered a short bow to Caledonia. "I'm afraid that I'm here to report Lir has taken the Net."

Silence descended on the room like a cloud leaving a chill in the air that hadn't been there before.

"Bloat fish," Pine muttered into the dense quiet.

"But he sailed north. To Slipmark." The protest in Pisces's voice was weak.

"At first," Ennick answered with a nod. "But he doubled back and sailed for the Net instead."

"How many ships did it cost him?" Caledonia asked.

If Ennick was surprised at how quickly Caledonia accepted the news, he didn't show it.

"None," he said. "He got on the radio and made the one promise Tassos's Bullets couldn't refuse."

"Silt," Oran said.

"They let him right in," Ennick confirmed.

It wasn't a trick, but it felt like one. Instead of tripling his resources at Slipmark, Lir had gambled on the Net. And he'd won. It didn't matter that they'd left ships behind. It didn't matter that everyone knew Tassos had the Silt Rig peppered with bombs and the trigger to blow them. Lir had called that bluff and won.

"We need to move before he has a chance to shore up his defenses. So, I want options and I want them now." Caledonia cast her gaze around the room.

Why should we move at all? Hime asked. *We have the Holster. We can defend it and anyone who comes here seeking refuge. We don't have to move to resist him.*

Unclipping the black box from her own waistband, Caledonia

placed it on the table. "We should move because right now, we have an advantage."

"The trigger," Pisces said softly as Hime reached for it, turning it over and over before she popped the lid to inspect it.

"The trigger," she confirmed. "That rig is set to blow, but according to Cepheus, this only works in close proximity."

"According to Cepheus?" Pine asked. "How do you know that isn't a trick to get you to return to the Net?"

"Cepheus wouldn't lie," Pisces said hurriedly.

"Wouldn't she?" Pine countered. "You've known her for two minutes, Pi."

"I tried to blow it yesterday morning." Caledonia turned her attention to Ennick. "Was the rig still there when you arrived?"

"We weren't close enough to put eyes on it, but we didn't see anything to suggest it wasn't," he said. "The wind was calm enough that we'd have seen smoke."

"She wasn't lying." Pisces gave Pine a hard look.

"Maybe." He shrugged.

"How close do we need to be?" Sledge asked.

"Cepheus said a mile and a half," Caledonia answered.

"Can we boost the signal?" Sledge turned to Hime for this one.

Hime paused to consider. *Not without rebuilding the trigger. And even then, it's not a guarantee.*

"Then we'll have to be at the Net," Caledonia said.

"Well, someone will have to be at the Net." Sledge leaned forward, forearms crossing the narrow table. "Send us," he said, tipping his head toward Pine. "We can slip in, get close enough to push the button, and get out of there before they know what's what."

"Or just send me," Pine added quickly. "No reason to put more than one of us at risk. Especially on the word of Tassos's second."

Pisces shifted, but didn't rise to the bait.

"We don't have eyes on their defenses. We could be sending you straight into a trap. I don't want to lose you—or our chance to blow the factory," Caledonia said. "Other options."

"We have thirty-eight ships ready to sail, but if we wait a few days, we'll increase that number by ten at least." Pisces tugged at her necklace as she spoke, sliding the charm back and forth. "We estimate Lir got away with a hundred ships. Now that he has the Net, he has a few more than that."

Forty-eight ships against more than a hundred? Hime frowned at the odds.

"Or we stay here." Tin spoke up for the first time. "Defend the Holster like Hime said."

"Without the rig, there's no Silt, and without Silt, Lir has no power." Sledge leaned back in his seat, folding his arms across his mountainous chest. "The rig is how this ends."

"We'll have to move before Lir has a chance to find those bombs," Oran added.

"We won't match them ship for ship, but we don't have to,"

Caledonia said. "We only need to get close enough to blow the rig. Can we put crews on forty-eight ships?" Caledonia asked.

Tin frowned as she considered the numbers. "It would be easier with Tassos's Bullets."

"They won't be ready," Oran answered. "It's too soon to ask them to help us destroy the thing they are suffering for."

Tin nodded. "We'll have to reshuffle the current crews, thin them out to cover all the ships, but . . . we can do it. Barely."

"And how many days do you need to repair those ten extra ships, Pi?" Caledonia asked.

Pisces was quiet for a moment, quickly calculating all the necessary repairs in her head. Finally, she answered, "We can do it in three."

"Good." Caledonia turned to her command crew, letting her eyes travel around the circle. "We sail in three days."

CHAPTER THIRTY-NINE

The following morning, it was Harwell who greeted Caledonia at her bedroom door. His mousy brown hair stood straight up from his head and he held his hands up as if in surrender.

"Ah, sorry, Captain, terribly sorry to interrupt—it's just—well, just that—"

"Harwell," she said, voice calm and encouraging.

"Right, it's just that Lir is on the comm."

Her heart leapt at the name, and her instincts told her to hurry, to run and see what it was Lir had to say to her, but in the next moment, she was calm once more.

"Thank you, Harwell," she said. "I'll be there in a moment."

Behind her, Oran was lacing up his boots. She did the same, taking the time she needed to dress and prepare. When she was done, she strode into the early morning with all the clarity and focus she needed for the day.

The communication tower was no taller than the surrounding buildings, but the roof was covered in broad radio dishes that allowed them to send and receive signals over much larger distances than the receivers on individual ships.

It was strange to be inside the room that for all the turns of her life had collected and disseminated information about the *Mors Navis* and rogue ships like hers. Strange to be in control of a tool that had been used to control and curtail so much of the Bullet Seas. It made her feel like an imposter, like she was about to get caught.

Taking the receiver from a wide-eyed crew member, Caledonia excused those feelings and reached instead for the confidence she felt whenever she stood at the helm of a ship.

"Lir," she said.

"Caledonia." It wasn't the crooning greeting she'd come to expect, but something darker. As if, for the first time, he wasn't pleased to be speaking with her. But it was what he said next that truly startled her: "Where is my brother?"

Caledonia turned wide eyes to Oran, unable to respond as her stomach filled with lead.

"Tassos had him, but I'm here and Donnally's not, which must mean *you* have him." He paused. Silence razored through the static. "I want my brother back."

"He is not your brother." The lead in Caledonia's stomach turned molten, roiling in the deep sea of her belly. If she opened her mouth again, she was sure her breath would be hot enough to sear her lips and melt the receiver in her hand.

"Isn't he?" Lir challenged. "Tell me, then, is he there of his own volition? Or is he a prisoner? Because I know my brother. I know him better than you do, and I would never imprison him as you have."

"He's not a prisoner." A furious wave of anger surged in Caledonia's mind. Lir didn't get to care about her brother. He didn't get to claim him or know him or worry about his well-being. He didn't get to take any part of her family for himself.

"Then I will see him soon," Lir answered, so certain. "And if I don't, I'll be seeing *you* soon."

A hollow wind sang in Caledonia's ears. The receiver was suddenly very heavy in her hand. Static filtered through, and for a long minute all she could do was stare at it. Then, just as suddenly as rage had clouded her mind, it cleared. She dug into her pocket for the garnet from Hesperus, pressing her thumb against its cool surface.

"Open a channel," she snapped at Harwell.

"Yes, Captain." Harwell bobbed his head rapidly. "Open."

Raising the receiver once more to her mouth, Caledonia let all her rage and fear and hope collect her voice. "This is Caledonia Styx. I have taken the Holster from Fiveson Lir. The city, and all its ships, are mine alone, and with them, I promise to end the time of Bullets. I will change the face of these seas, but I cannot do it without your help. If you are listening to this, then I am speaking to you. Now is the time to stand up and join us. Now is the time to fight."

》《

Caledonia went straight from the communication tower to Donnally's room.

If he was more Lir's brother than he was hers, she needed to know it. Not from Lir, but from Donnally himself. She needed her answer.

At his door, she paused, hand raised to knock. If he chose Lir, she had to be ready to harden her heart against him. She had to be ready to face her own brother as an enemy.

She drew in a deep breath, preapring herself for the conversation that would follow, but the door creaked on its hinges, already ajar.

Caledonia's heart thumped swiftly in her chest as she shoved open the door and found an empty room. The bed was neatly made and every trace of Donnally was gone save for a note left on the pillow.

The paper was small, hardly enough to contain more than a few words. Snatching it up, Caledonia unfolded it and read the message:

Caledonia,

> *Please understand, I cannot make the choice you want me to make. Not yet. Not without seeing him again.*

> > *Donnally*

Vividly, violently, she recalled that moment on the deck of the *Titan* when she'd asked him to go with her and he'd refused. He'd called Lir *brother*.

That single word had carved a wound so deep in Caledonia, she wasn't sure she'd ever recover from it. Perhaps that was the moment she'd changed. Perhaps her ability to make terrible decisions, to build and use her own star blossom bombs, to slide a dagger into a man's neck without mercy, all stemmed from the moment her own brother had looked at her and chosen Lir instead. Would she be capable of these things if she had lost less? If she had cared less?

Caledonia shook the thoughts from her head. It didn't matter. All that mattered now was what happened next. Whoever she'd been in the past, she was different now. She was capable of terrible things, even of looking at her own brother and seeing a Bullet. An enemy.

Stuffing the note into a pocket, Caledonia turned her back on Donnally's room and rushed from the Ready Racks. Donnally was gone. He'd chosen Lir a second time. And she had promised to let him.

CHAPTER
FORTY

Nothing distracted from an aching heart like preparing for battle. Caledonia let the work consume every minute of the day and as much of the night as she could bear before collapsing in her bed. The sounds of ship repair in the harbor provided a continuous melody, weaving night into day into night as work teams rotated in overlapping shifts. The entire town stirred and buzzed with an intense kind of focus, never resting.

Oran made himself a shadow at Caledonia's side, but she saw the rest of her command crew in passing. Sledge and Pine on their way to or from the perimeter where they continued their efforts to reconstruct one of the two destroyed towers; Hime and Ares as they did all they could to ease the suffering of the Bullets coming through their sweats; Tin and the Mary sisters locating every available resource the Holster had to offer and figuring out how to use it; and Pisces only when she came to report on the status of their fleet.

Two days into their work, Pisces rushed to Caledonia's

side, her eyes bright and a hint of pink darkening her sunny brown cheeks. "Cala," she said, reaching for her hand and pulling her to a stop. Oran stopped, too, stepping back to give them privacy.

The day was warm, and the sky overhead whirled with gulls and puffy white clouds. All around the harbor was a flurry of sound and action, but it all paled in comparison to how good it felt to hear her sister call her Cala.

"What is it?" she asked.

A smile spread on Pisces's face before she'd even said the word: "Babies."

Caledonia shook her head, laughing. "What do you mean?"

"Two. There were two babies born today." She raised a hand and pointed up the hill, toward the part of town where they'd secured all the children and women bearing them. "The first two born in this Holster. *Your* Holster."

Babies. There were babies here. That wasn't a surprise. She'd known there would be, but as Pisces clasped her hands to her chest and continued to smile that beautiful smile, Caledonia understood exactly why this brought her sister so much joy.

If they succeeded in what came next, those children would never know the devastating pull of Silt. These were the first children of the world they were trying so hard to change.

Caledonia laughed. "That is good news," she said. "Very good news."

"It's good to feel happy about something that isn't a weapon or a fleet or a battle." She shrugged and her smile faded so quickly it was like a cloud moved across the sun. "I'm not mad, Cala," she said. "I know why you used the star blossom bombs when you did. You saved the battle. You saved *us*. I just wish you'd let me help you."

"I didn't want you to have to make that call," Caledonia said.

"Cala." Pisces dipped her chin in exasperation. "I have been by your side from the beginning. My job is to stay by your side, even when our choices get terrible. That's *my* job. Yours is to let me do it so that you can focus on everything else."

She was right. Their choices had been difficult before. Even terrible. But not like this.

"What about when our choices are more than terrible? What about when our choices demand that we become like them in order to win? Because that's what is happening." Caledonia dropped her voice, letting the confession spill from her like a breaking storm. "I'm afraid I can't win this war without becoming like them. Like him. And if that's what it takes, then I'll do it, but I won't take you with me."

Pisces stared at her, her lips parted in horrified surprise, her brow creased with sorrow. "Oh, hell, Cala. You're protecting me?" she whispered, eyes darting to a spot over Caledonia's shoulder. "Is that why you take Oran? You think he's already like Lir?"

But before either of them could speak again, an alarm rose over the town.

"Captain!" Nettle raced toward them, cutting through the crowded wharf like a fish through water. "Captain!"

Behind her, Caledonia spotted Sledge and Pine. All three rushed toward her.

"What is it, Nettle?" Caledonia asked as the girl skidded to a stop.

"The Hands," she breathed. "Of the River."

"Here?!" Pisces's hand darted out to grab Nettle's shoulder. "Are you sure?"

Nettle nodded. "Completely. Spotted them from the towers. There's no mistaking it. Such strange boats! They're on their way into the harbor now."

Sledge and Pine arrived a beat behind her proclamation, both with expressions of hopeful anticipation.

"Thin boats just like you described, Captain," Sledge said. "It's them."

Caledonia's thoughts whirled, and for a second she wasn't sure her feet were planted to the ground. She had so many questions, so many *hopes*, and she didn't know where to begin.

Pisces's fingers threaded through hers, squeezing lightly as she turned to Nettle and said, "Find Hime."

Nettle didn't have to be told twice. They watched her go, their minds churning around the thought none of them was brave enough to vocalize.

When Nettle vanished up the thoroughfare, Caledonia nodded and said, "Let's go greet our guests."

Two narrow boats entered the harbor, weaving between the breakers like the current itself. They were similar to the boats Caledonia had seen on her one visit to the rivers, but these were larger, each carrying six people. Caledonia and her team waited at the end of an open berth as the Hands cut across the harbor, their shallow hulls barely leaving any tracks in their wake.

Caledonia held her breath as they drew up to the dock and tied on; she clenched her fists as the crew began to disembark. And as the sight of a familiar face appeared before her, she could not have held herself back if she'd tried.

"Amina!" Caledonia rushed forward. The girl had barely set her feet on the dock before Caledonia wrapped her in a hug. Pisces was there, too, her arms adding another strong layer to their embrace.

"We thought we'd lost you," Pisces said, her voice muffled by someone's arm or cheek or hair.

"Spirits, girls, if you hold me any tighter, you still may." Amina laughed as they reluctantly let her go. "It is good to see you, too."

"It's more than good," Caledonia said, aware that her eyes were brimming with tears and her voice was strangled with the same. Her friend was here, she was alive and smiling, and she looked whole and healthy. "What happened? How did you survive?"

"I got pinned down right after the first explosions. I couldn't get to you, so I decided to give you as much time as possible, but

I was hit," she said with a shrug, gesturing to a spot high on her left shoulder. "By the time I made my way to the northern canals, nearly everyone was gone, but I found a boat—fixed it—and made for the Hands. I wasn't sure where you'd be by then and I needed medtech. Seemed like the best plan."

"It was the best plan," Caledonia agreed. "It is so good to see you," she repeated.

"And it's about to be better." Amina stepped back and for the first time, Caledonia realized there was a second familiar face in the group.

"Osias of Kyrasi Water," Caledonia said, raising her hands in greeting. It had been a full moon since their last encounter at the mouth of the Braids, but she would know his face anywhere. "Welcome to the Holster."

Osias raised his hands, mirroring her gesture. "We have come to aid in your battle, Caledonia Styx."

At Caledonia's confused silence, Amina explained, "Sister came for the Hands. After word of your alliance with Tassos reached her, she saw an opportunity to expand her reach beyond Slipmark. I'm certain she regretted the decision."

"If Amina had not come to us when she did, we would not have understood the scope of the danger," Osias said, turning a reserved smile on Amina. "We did not come into this fight willingly, but we would like to help you end it."

"Osias has brought forty-two of his fleet," Amina said. "All smaller craft as you see, but they pack a much larger punch than you might expect."

"We welcome your aid," Caledonia said, still too bewildered to do anything but accept this completely unexpected gift. No matter their size, she would put these vessels to good use. "Please, bring your ships into the harbor. Your people will be given quarters while we bring you up to speed, but we sail the morning after next. Your timing couldn't be better."

Osias nodded, returning to his delegation to make arrangements. Amina didn't follow. Her eyes landed on a point over Caledonia's shoulder and suddenly, she wasn't a part of their conversation any longer. With a small gasp, Amina moved as though pulled by an unseen force, her steps measured and strong as she passed Caledonia and crossed the dock until she stood mere inches from Hime.

The smaller girl breathed hard, as though she'd raced across the entire city to get here. Her hair had come loose from its short braid and her eyes were wide and unbelieving as she tipped her head back to stare into Amina's face.

Then, taking Hime's face in her hands, Amina pressed a deep kiss to Hime's lips.

After a second, Hime pushed up on the tips of her toes, wrapping her arms around Amina's neck and blocking their kisses from view.

"They're going to make me blush." Pine pulled his eyes away from the couple with a small smile.

"I thought that was Sledge's job," Pisces teased.

"Sometimes," Pine answered, turning his dark gaze firmly on Pisces. "But we're not exclusive, if that's what you're asking."

Caledonia was certain she'd never seen her sister blush so hard or so fast. Her light brown cheeks, already rosy from all the excitement, flushed a deeper pink that spread down her neck. Her eyes skated down Pine's torso, where sweat held his shirt tight across his densely muscled chest and stomach, and then darted away to Caledonia's face.

"I should go make arrangements for their people, right?" Pisces asked a little too forcefully. "I think I should, so I'm going to go do that."

Caledonia couldn't contain the laugh that fell from her lips. Pisces had never been shy, but she preferred discretion when it came to her entanglements, as she called them. Flirting openly was a sure way to drive her usually levelheaded nature deep underground. A strategy Redtooth had frequently employed to avoid her least favorite duties on the *Mors Navis*.

The dock cleared and news traveled swiftly through the town. By that evening, Far had prepared a feast, and pockets of revelry cropped up along the wharf.

It was the celebration they hadn't had an opportunity to take and it was long overdue. In another day, they would sail to fight again. Caledonia might even find herself facing her own brother, but right now, they could enjoy this moment of alliance and the return of their lost friend.

"You're coming with me tonight," Pisces said as Caledonia returned an empty plate to the kitchens.

"I shouldn't," she protested.

But Pisces wasn't having any of it. "You should," she said, dragging her down to the wharf, where a racous fire was ringed with dancing figures.

Strains of fiddle and flute raced above the throaty beat of a single drum, and bottles winking dark red in the firelight traveled from hand to hand. Among the revelers were Amina and Hime, their hair loosed and flying around them as they spun to the rhythm of the song. Just behind them came Tin and Nettle, their cheeks rounded with smiles.

"We should dance," Pisces said into Caledonia's ear.

"I don't think I do that." In fact, Caledonia was sure her body didn't move that way, especially with her ribs still aching. The thought of tossing her arms to the sky without worrying what was behind her or beside her or ready to drive a dagger into her belly left her physically uncomfortable.

Pisces laughed, tugging Caledonia forward a little at a time. "I'll be right beside you," she said. "I'll protect you."

"I don't need protection." They were near enough now that the fire warmed her skin, and the sounds of her girls laughing together were tempting.

"You do," Pisces said. "But mostly from yourself."

Caledonia hadn't joined them the night of their victory at

Cloudbreak seven moons ago. The battle had left a heavy burden on her shoulders, and the thought of dancing when so many deaths lay at her feet had been untenable. But this moment was different. They were once more on the brink of the unknown, and in another day she would have to bear the weight of every life she intended to risk, but tonight . . . perhaps she could take a moment that was just for her.

She let a smile stretch her lips as she nodded to Pisces, who whisked them into the dance with a small yelp of joy. The fire was hot, and the ground warm beneath their feet as they traveled in a ring. Caledonia followed her sister's lead, raising her arms to twirl in tight circles, sipping from the bottles of cherry wine that landed in her hands. When she tipped her head back, the stars winked, catching up the sparks of the fire in the dark spaces between.

All that surrounded her were the threads of that reel, the untethered laughter of her sisters, the searing kiss of that fire, and the cool promise of the night. Her head spun just enough to be pleasant, and sweat slipped from her temples to her chin, making her shiver.

Amina moved with grace, her braids swirling around her shoulders. Her dark skin shone, and her laughter was a low, rumbling sound. Hime was like a seedling spinning through the air, quick and frenzied, her pale skin slashed with shadows. Tin's lithe figure seemed to slip in and out of the light, flashing here and there. Nettle was like a firefly, popping in and out, punctuating the space between her sisters with her smile. And Pisces was the sun, her arms flung wide and her dark eyes bright and uncompromising. These were her sisters, her warriors, and they were glorious in their joy.

Soon, the moon had climbed high in the sky and Caledonia stepped out of the circle, giving herself a moment to catch her breath and watch them revolve around the fire in an endless ring. The faces had changed, but the energy that wove between the dancers was just as perfect and powerful. There was Oran and Pine and Sledge. Even Harwell had joined the dance.

With a contented sigh, Caledonia turned away from the fire, aiming for her quarters. Before she'd gone more than a few steps, however, someone called her name. She turned to see four girls trailing one after the other with hurried paces.

The Mary sisters. Tin was in the lead and behind her, Shoravin, Abrasin, and Erin carried a bundle between them, their arms curled protectively around a mass of dark fabric. There was still a breath of a second when Caledonia searched for Lurin before remembering, and sorrow sank sharp teeth into her heart.

"Captain," Tin said in greeting, an unusual smile on her face. "We thought now was an appropriate time to share something with you."

Caledonia's gaze flicked to the bundle, but the girls made no move to reveal it. "What is it, Tin?"

"When we first joined you, we were looking for a place where we could be angry and safe. We wanted to fight, and we wanted to hide, and that's exactly what you promised us on the *Mors Navis*. Hit hard; hide fast." Tin paused, and Caledonia nodded at the familiar words. "But that's not the case anymore. It hasn't been for some time.

"We aren't hiding anymore. *You* definitely aren't hiding anymore, and we think it's time we made ourselves even more visible." Tin gave her sisters a nod and they began to unfurl the fabric. "Tomorrow, you're going to lead a fleet that's entirely your own. We thought it was time we made that fleet official."

The fabric opened and the girls raised their arms to reveal the design. At first, it was nothing but a black flag, then small solar cells stitched into the center began to glow, revealing a pattern little by little until Caledonia's family sigil glimmered in blue and white. Soon, the glimmer transformed into a brilliant glow. Here on the wharf, it was overwhelming, but hoisted high over a ship, it would be a beacon.

"We found a stash of clothtech," Tin explained.

"And a whole bunch of unused solar cells," added Abrasin, her chin resting in the black fabric with hands on either side. "Erin had an idea how to weave them into the cloth so that they made a pattern."

Erin, standing between Abrasin and Shoravin, ducked her head at the admiring tone in her sister's voice. She'd been painfully shy all the turns Caledonia had known her, and she was rarely seen without at least one of her sisters.

"We wanted to make sure there was no doubt which ships were yours," Shoravin said, fluttering the fabric so the sigil shimmered. "So anyone else who's angry can find you like we did."

Caledonia didn't know how a single flag was going to do that, but before she could raise the question Tin spoke again. "We've made thirty-five. Not enough for the fleet, but most of it."

"Thirty-five?" Caledonia moved forward to lift a corner of the flag, and ran a hand over the solar scales.

To make that number in the time they'd had, they must have been stitching through the night; the four of them seated in a circle around the blue-and-white glow of solar scales, singing softly and missing the airy harmony of their sister Lurin.

"They're perfect," Caledonia said, smiling. All the time she'd spent trying to hold her army together and her crew was working on the same problem from a different angle. It was time to stop thinking of herself as a baseless rebel and time to start thinking of herself as a powerful resistance. It was time to make an indelible mark on the Bullet Seas.

"Sisters," she said, "I think it's time we hoist our colors."

CHAPTER
FORTY-ONE

Before the sun set on the following evening, the fleet had become a constellation. The Mary sisters had distributed every one of their flags, turning the harbor into a beacon. Caledonia's family sigil flew from the three gun towers like a crown marking the Holster as a place where others were welcome.

She'd spent hours last night with her command crew making final preparations for the fight ahead. Even so, she'd risen well before dawn, unable to compel her mind to sleep any longer. Oran hadn't stirred, so she tucked the blanket around him and dressed quietly.

Her steps carried her along the wharf, then down a long broad dock that offered a view of the harbor. At the end of that dock stood a mountain.

"Mind if I join you?" Caledonia asked as she drew up level with Sledge.

"My final crews are boarding now," he answered. "It's an impressive sight."

Even against the brightening sky, the flags shimmered like stars. Somehow, it made the fleet look more expansive and powerful. This was a fleet that had recovered from loss and was ready to sail boldly once more.

"I let Donnally go." The admission surprised her. She'd told her command crew about Donnally's departure days ago. At the time, all she'd been able to say was that he left. He didn't know enough to be dangerous and he left. But there was more to it than that. "I . . . I thought he might choose to stay."

Sledge turned to face her, eyes filled with sympathy both for her and for Donnally. "You've given him something he hasn't had in a long while, Caledonia. Sometimes it just takes a while for the impact to reveal itself." He sighed. "And, in the end, you did what you could. He has to do the rest. Whatever that may be."

She knew it was true, just as she knew there was every chance Donnally would not survive what came next.

Seeing her frustration, Sledge sighed and added, "This part of the fight was always going to be slow."

"I know." Slow had never been her speed, and she was afraid it was going to get Donnally killed. Swallowing hard, she changed the subject. "Are you clear on everything?"

The plan was two-pronged. Sledge was in charge of stage one. He and half the fleet would leave first, sailing due west until they reached the Bone Mouth. From there, they would turn around and approach the Net. They were the distraction.

Caledonia was in charge of stage two. While Lir's fleet sailed out to meet Sledge, she would sweep in from the east, getting close enough to blow the rig while Lir was too far away to stop her.

"We'll draw them out," Sledge said with confidence. "Those flags all but guarantee it. Lir won't be able to resist them. And we'll distract him long enough for you to get in position and trigger the bombs on the rig, saving the Bullet Seas."

As far as plans went, this was as simple as it got: get in, destroy the rig, get out. And let Lir's army turn on itself when the Silt ran out. Easy.

As far as hopes went, they didn't get higher. If they did this right, no one would be able to produce so much Silt for a long time. Maybe even ever again.

"Whatever happens after this, I want to say that I'm thankful for everything you've done." A frown bent Sledge's lips as he spoke. "You encouraged us to move and fight when I would have let us hide until it got us killed. You gave us everything we needed to help bring Bullets back, and that has meant a great deal to me."

It was so rare for Sledge to open up like this. Caledonia was afraid that if she spoke, she would destroy the moment.

"There was a time after we pulled you out of the ocean

when I regretted doing it." His frown deepened and his shoulders shifted uncomfortably. "When the bombs fell and everything I'd worked so hard to create was destroyed in the space of a few moments. I blamed you." He pushed out a puff of air. "I almost sent you packing. But I knew that you'd lost as much as any of us, and if you could still find it in you to fight, then I could, too. I'll never regret that choice. I don't think any of us will."

Tears warmed in Caledonia's eyes and she blinked furiously to hold them at bay. Sledge did the same, but with less success. Two large tears slid down his tan cheeks.

"It has been an honor, Captain," he said, raising his hands, palms out.

Caledonia raised her hands to his, letting the pads of her fingers press into his skin. "May the seas be your ally," she said.

"And yours," Sledge answered.

His fingertips were warm against hers, and heat pooled between the palms of their hands as they stood. There were no guarantees in this fight. The only thing either of them knew for sure was it had the potential to change everything. And there was no telling who would live and who would die.

"Thank you for saving my life," Caledonia said, not sure if she'd ever said it. She smiled even as her lungs swelled with something like sorrow. It was so easy to let the terrible moments in her past dictate who she was now, but there were just as many good moments. It wasn't only Lir or Donnally who had made her who she was, it was Sledge and Pisces and Nettle. It was Redtooth and Lace and Triple and Hesperus. Oran. "Thank you for fighting with me."

With one final smile, Sledge answered, "Thank you for showing me there was more than one way to win a war."

CHAPTER
FORTY-TWO

Sledge's fleet sailed away from the Holster, each flying flags bearing Caledonia's sigil, which glittered against the dawn sky. For a long while, those still waiting to shove off could track them. They watched as the lights traveled steadily away until the sea and the sky swallowed the ships whole.

In her mind, Caledonia tracked them still. She let the sea unfurl in her mind, and on it she placed Sledge and those who had sailed with him—Harwell, Ares, Pine, and so many others she cared for and trusted. They would reach the Bone Mouth by dawn tomorrow and with any luck, they'd lure Lir's fleet out.

As soon as Sledge's fleet was out of sight, it was time to ready her own ships. She found Pisces waiting for her at the northern end of the docks, and together they approached the *Luminous Wake*.

Her crew ringed the deck, each one of them steel-hearted and ready to go. Caledonia stopped to take it all in, letting her eyes trace every line and every face. Among them she spotted Cepheus, her skin still blanched and her cheeks burning pink. Caledonia paused to give her sister an expectant look.

"She wanted to come." Pisces answered the unspoken question. "I think she deserves to be here."

"You're sure she's ready?" Caledonia asked.

"I'm sure." Pisces took Caledonia's hand in her own, squeezing lightly. "Your crew is ready, Captain."

"One last time," Caledonia said softly, squeezing back.

The instant she left the gangway, Tin's voice shouted, "Captain on deck!" and as one the crew stomped their feet, creating a thunderous clap.

The force of it rumbled through Caledonia's body. She paused, Pisces at her side and Oran close behind, and looked over each of their faces. They'd all changed in the past ten-moon. The midmorning sun washed them in glorious shades of gold and pink, making them stand out against the vibrant blue sky. They watched Caledonia intently and with a kind of confidence that surprised her.

"We have never fought a fight like this one," Caledonia said, letting her steps carry her to the middle of the main deck. "But there has never been a crew like ours."

As she spoke, she felt the bone-deep truth of her words. This crew might have come together because they feared the same things, but they'd stayed together because they trusted one another. And that was something Lir could not destroy.

"The *Mors Navis* was once our home," she called. "She protected us and served us well, and if we have the opportunity to win her back, we'll take it."

Watching the *Mors Navis* sail from this very harbor only days before had been salt in an old wound. Knowing that they might see her again in the coming fight was something they needed to be ready for.

"But if she is used against us, I expect no hesitation! Fire on her as you would any Bullet ship and give her the kind of end she deserves!"

Her crew roared, angry and determined.

"We fight together!" she shouted, and the response was instantaneous and fearlessly loud.

"Or not at all!"

Caledonia let their voices fill her as she raced up the companionway ladder to the bridge. "Nettle, take us out."

"Yes, Captain!"

The *Luminous Wake* led the way. Leaving seven ships and four functional gun towers behind to guard the town. Sledge had sailed with forty-six, leaving Caledonia with thirty-seven. They were a mix of large vessels and the smaller, sleeker vessels of the Hands of the River, still not enough to match Lir's forces, but they were what she had. If everything went according to plan, she wouldn't need any more than this.

They sailed through the day and drove into the night. As

soon as the sun vanished beneath the horizon, they extinguished the lights. Up and down the fleet, solar flags and sun pips winked out until they were nothing but shadows. Nothing but ghosts.

Caledonia stood on the command deck with her eyes on the black waters ahead, and without meaning to, she thought of her mother.

Caledonia had spent most of her life wishing she could be more like Rhona Styx. Rhona had been brave and bold and careful. She'd commanded her own ship and kept all the families aboard safe for turns by following a set of rules. Caledonia had tried to follow in Rhona's footsteps but had been unable to avoid the part of her that wanted to fight. That same part of her had always feared that her mother would disapprove. Fighting back made you vulnerable, made you a target, and when you made yourself a target, everyone around you became one, too.

But as she sailed steadily toward the most important fight of her life, she knew without a whisper of doubt that Rhona would be proud of her. This wasn't a fight over a single barge or a city, it wasn't a fight for revenge. This fight was for the rig, and destroying it could change the Bullet Seas forever.

The crew took their rest in smaller shifts than usual, but there was little sleep to go around and most didn't even try. They stayed on deck with their eyes glued to the dark, invisible horizon.

They sailed through the night, turning westward and keeping a careful distance from the Net as the faintest edge of dawn grazed the face of the sea. The crew was already in their battle stations when a sharp whistle came from the lookout and Amina announced, "Ten miles out!"

Caledonia's heart leapt. The journey that had seemed so long suddenly felt perilously short. Everything rested on what happened next. Everything. She had to get this right.

She turned the remote trigger over and over in her hand, waiting for the moment they were close enough to enter the code.

"Five miles, Captain," Pisces said, coming up behind her.

Caledonia spun toward the sound, letting the wind propel her steps a little faster. "Are we ready?"

Pisces licked her lips and nodded. "We've never been more ready in all our lives."

They reached for each other in the same moment, their hands knotting between them. Their skin was hot and their eyes bright. They looked into each other's eyes, each understanding what the other had not said aloud. Neither of them had ever dared to imagine they'd come so far. Now that they were here, it felt inevitable. They were going to finish what had started so many turns ago on that beach, and they were going to do it together.

Behind them, rogue ships, Bullet ships, and the Hands of the River sailed as one. All with a single goal in mind: to blow the rig.

Ahead, the first explosive sounds of a battle raged in the distance. Sledge was drawing fire.

"Nettle, take us in!"

Caledonia's cry was met with immediate action. The engines roared and the crew roared right along with them. The *Luminous Wake* surged forward with so much power Caledonia felt it in her gut.

Caledonia focused on breathing. There was no way to know exactly what they would find. She hoped Sledge had been successful in luring Lir's ships far enough away that they wouldn't have time to intercept her, but she had to prepare herself for every possibility.

"Guns ready!" Tin shouted from the deck, where a line of crew raised shields and prepared to fire. Hime was among them, her hair bound back in a tight braid, a short sword ready at her hip.

Suddenly, the battle appeared on the water. Caledonia had an instant to take in the scene. The Net was stretched out before her, a steely line against the horizon, every stable ship exactly as it had been the last time she'd seen it. And less than two miles to the west, that strange megaship crouched at one end like a beast, watching the battle unfold through those dark tunnel eyes.

And just as she'd hoped—planned—Sledge had successfully lured Lir's fleet beyond the megaship, into the western waters. The only thing standing between Caledonia and the rig was the Net. As her crew gave a triumphant cheer, it was hard not to cheer with them.

"Stay steely!" Caledonia cried. "Nettle, take us right up to the megaship."

"Yes, Captain," she responded with a grin.

They roared ahead as high on the stationary ship decks, dozens of cannons targeted Caledonia's fleet, waiting for the moment they sailed within firing range. Nettle charted a swift course parallel to the Net, keeping them away from those cannons until there was nothing left to do but turn directly toward the megaship.

Caledonia waited with her fingers poised over the keypad as the megaship fired.

"Incoming!" Amina cried.

Still Caledonia waited. They hadn't come this far for her to jump the gun. They needed line of sight.

Gunfire shattered against the hull and her own crew returned fire as they swiftly closed the distance to the megaship. Finally, Amina called, "Rig! Go on the rig!"

With shaking fingers, Caledonia hit the numbers, and the world around her exploded.

CHAPTER
FORTY-THREE

Water and fire rose on all sides as the sea itself exploded. It tore screams from her crew and the crews of the nearest ships, punching holes in their bellies from below.

Through the mist and smoke, Caledonia could see that the bombs had been spread out across a short distance here in the open ocean. The explosion had damaged a handful of her ships, but several vessels of the Hands were shredded.

In a flash, she understood what had happened. The trigger had worked, but Lir had found the bombs and planted them here. He'd planted them for her.

"Captain?" Nettle shouted to get her attention. "Your orders?"

In the west, Lir's fleet was peeling away from Sledge's attack and turning toward her. In another minute, they would be on her and she would be locked in the ship-to-ship battle she'd hoped to avoid.

"Back us off from the Net," she said, stomach plummeting. "Regroup and get ready for incoming."

The *Luminous Wake* turned instantly, its thrusters churning hard to complete the tight turn Nettle demanded of it. Caledonia hurried outside the bridge, calling her command crew to join her. The wind buffeted them from all sides as they put their heads together.

"Options," she said.

"What if we use mag bombs?" Amina said, her soft voice still so unexpected, and so very welcome. "There are several in the locker. Three or four well-placed bombs can destroy the hull of any ship. If we plant that many or more on the rig, we can take it down, but we will still need to get through the Net."

"Good, but how do we that?" Caledonia said.

"Can we sail between the stationary ships?" Pisces asked. "We've seen the razor wire. One good shot will clear the way."

"The rest of the Net's defenses are still intact," Oran said. "Trust me, those cannons will demolish the *Luminous* before you've made it to them, but they don't swivel well. A smaller ship would have a chance if it's quick and agile."

"Too risky," Caledonia said.

The tunnels, Hime signed with excitement. *The channels they use to transport baleflowers. We can get someone through there.*

"That could work," Caledonia said. "One person to the rig."

"We'll have to cover them the whole way to the megaship," Pisces said, turning to study their wake. Bullet ships would soon clutter the distance between them and the megaship.

"The Hands can help with that," Amina said confidently.

Caledonia studied the battle reshaping itself before her. Lir's fleet was spreading out, half pushing toward her, half continuing to engage Sledge. Her own fleet was spread thin, already struggling to manage a fight on two fronts. They were outnumbered, outgunned, and they weren't going to be able to hold here for long. It just had to be long enough.

"I'll go," Pisces said. "I'm the best with the tow. I can do it."

Sharks, Hime signed. *The tow is too dangerous. Has to be a boat.*

Caledonia's lips felt numb. Her eyes landed on a dark spot just beyond the Net. The Silt Rig was the final piece of this long fight. None of this had ended with Aric and it wouldn't end with Lir; it had to be the rig. And whoever went to destroy it was very likely not coming back.

In Caledonia's mind, that left one option: her.

"Incoming!" Tin shouted an instant before the *Luminous Wake* bucked and lurched heavily to port.

The battle was coiling around her, Lir's ships, Sledge's ships, they were all pulling together into a dense cluster. If she didn't get out soon, she never would. And to get out, she needed her fleet to protect her, to form up around her while she aimed for the tunnels. It would make them even more vulnerable than they were now; they were too few in number.

In order to win the war, she was going to have to lose the battle.

No sooner had she had the thought than another shout came from high on the lookout. "Tails! Tails! Tails!"

Following the line of the lookout's hand, Caledonia's heart stumbled before it squeezed.

There, along the northern horizon, dozens of ships roared toward them, pushing tall plumes of water into the sky. As they drew closer, she recognized them: there were colonists and Slaggers and rogue ships. Everyone who had ever sought to elude Aric and Lir was here now, joining the fight at her side.

The sight of them sent a spur of energy through the entire fleet. They roared, cheered, and dove back into the fray knowing that reinforcements were on their way.

This was exactly what they needed to turn the tide in their favor. And it was exactly what would allow Caledonia to leave it altogether.

"Pi," she said, reaching for her sister. "Pi. It has to be me. I have to go to the rig."

"No." Pisces shook her head. "It's too dangerous. We need you out here, commanding this fight. I can't do that. I should go."

"You can," Caledonia said, settling into her decision more fully. "You've always been able to command, Pi. I've seen you do it. You just have to trust yourself."

"But you—"

"Pi."

Pisces stopped, squeezing her eyes shut and drawing in a deep breath. "All right. You're right. We'll keep them distracted while you set the charges. Amina, get on the comm and tell the Hands to be ready. She'll need cover until she's through. And tell Nettle to bring us around; we need to get her as close to the megaship as we can."

"Understood." Amina turned on her heel and sprinted for the bridge.

"Hime, ready the mag bombs." The girl nodded once and disappeared. "Ready a boat!" Pisces shouted. "The captain's going in the water!"

Right before her eyes, Pisces was transforming, from the supportive second-in-command she'd always been into a leader. They hurried down the ladder and across the deck, ducking below the aft port rail as bullets rained against the hull.

"Pi," Caledonia said, reaching for her hand.

"I know why you have to do this," Pisces said as though reading Caledonia's mind. "You can end it."

Two missiles exploded in the sky above. Ash drifted down around them, dusting their heads and shoulders in pale gray. The world around them was on fire, yet they were alone. It was just Caledonia and Pisces deciding what came next. And they were making the decision together.

With a sudden surge of love, Caledonia pulled her sister against her, hugging her tightly. "Thank you," she whispered before pulling away again.

Amina raced across the deck as the *Luminous Wake* hurtled back toward the megaship and half of Lir's fleet. "The Hands are ready," she announced. "And Sledge says the *Blade* will cover you as well."

"Boat's in the water!" Folly's voice rang out clear as a bell.

Hime arrived then with a backpack clutched in her hands and a helmet tucked beneath one arm. Her face was streaked with gun oil and sweat, her jaw clenched tight as she handed the items over. Caledonia accepted the pack with a nod of thanks and quickly slipped the straps over her shoulders. The helmet was made of matte black metal with a visor of self-repairing glass. Caledonia pulled it on at once, tightening the strap beneath her chin.

"There's a flare in here as well," Oran said, securing a strap on the side of the bag. "Give us a sign if you need help."

"If I need help, it'll be too late," Caledonia said, voice grim.

Oran didn't answer. They both knew it was true. Once Caledonia hit the water, she was on her own.

"Incoming!"

The ship rumbled. Fire sprayed across the deck and the girls scrambled to put it out. Then the moment they'd all been waiting for: the *Mors Navis* turned her sleek bow toward them and moved to engage. Caledonia jumped to her feet. Lir was on that ship. Maybe Donnally, too, and every instinct urged her to stay with her crew and fight, but Hime stood in her way.

End this.

Caledonia's eyes strayed back to the deck of her ship, where her crew was moving together so seamlessly it might have been choreographed. They needed her, but they also didn't, and that gave her all the confidence she needed to redirect her thoughts and her mission. Theirs was to finish this battle. Hers was to end the war. And as much as her heart still longed for vengeance, Lir wasn't the war.

"I will," she promised. "Pisces! You're in command!"

"I have command!" Pisces shouted for all to hear.

Smoke now stretched across the deck, and Caledonia's crew turned to her as she draped one leg over the rail of the ship. They were all there. Ready to hold the line for her, ready to finish this together.

Even Oran. He stood in their midst with a gun in his hand, and though he looked as if it took every bit of his will not to race to her side and haul her into his arms, he didn't.

"See you after, Captain," he said.

The unspoken promise lingered just beneath the surface of those words. Caledonia intended to come back for them.

"Stay steely, girls!" she shouted, and then she dropped over the edge.

CHAPTER
FORTY-FOUR

Her boots hit the shallow hull as a spray of gunfire peppered the *Luminous Wake* just above her head; a missile drove beneath the waves and exploded nearby; and all around the ocean was furious with vigorous, slapping waves that rocked her small boat.

She dropped her pack, revved her engine, and ducked low behind the wheel, aiming for the megaship. The second she pulled away from the *Luminous Wake*, three ships drove up on either side of her. Narrow noses sheared through the waves like needles, sliding alongside her with ease. Each bore a single pilot, their bodies bent low so that they were nearly prone against the boat. From their slender hulls, webs of electricity arched in a dome, cocooning them in a shield that dispelled gunfire as if it were nothing more than rain.

The two nearest edged in until they were close enough that Caledonia felt the hum of electricity against her skin. Then, with a snap and a vibrant shock, the two shields merged into one with Caledonia safely in the center.

They drove hard, skimming along the waves as they angled

around and between larger ships. Inches above Caledonia's head, gunfire snapped against the shield in a constant refrain. Ahead, the megaship loomed large against the blue sky, while just beneath, two dark holes like eyes marked the channels that would carry her through to the other side. She aimed for one, bracing her feet on either side of the narrow hull.

As she drew closer to her target, the battle shifted suddenly. It was as if all at once, the Bullets understood her goal and together turned their sights away from her fleet and onto her. They approached from all sides, firing relentlessly. The shield sparked and snapped. Fire flashed across the nose of her ship and for a second the mouth of the tunnel was lost behind a wall of smoke.

When it cleared, what she saw made her stomach drop.

A crusher was aimed right at her. And Caledonia suspected that no matter what kind of tech the Hands of the River had on their small boats, it wouldn't matter when that prow hit them dead-on.

The slender wheel vibrated against her slick palms. She wasn't going to make it. Either she changed course now or she would feel the full, punishing effect of that ship's substantial prow.

But before she could do anything, another ship surged into her peripheral vision. Caledonia recognized it as the *Blade*. Sledge's command. And all at once she knew exactly what he was going to do.

The *Blade* swept in, gaining speed as they arched like an

arrow flying through the air. Ice gripped Caledonia's lungs. The *Blade* soared ahead of her just in time to slam into the crusher.

The air fractured around the sound of impact. The nose of Sledge's ship vanished inside the crusher and plumes of angry fire jumped into the sky. Explosions chewed along the hulls of both ships, ripping into steel with ferocious teeth.

Smoke and debris flew across Caledonia's vision even as the way ahead cleared.

But the *Blade* burned.

She could not stop now, though for a moment she thought her heart might. The screams were blistering, and the last thing she saw before she ducked her head low, aimed for the tunnel, was Sledge's crew leaping from the aft deck of the *Blade*, their bodies bright with flame.

There was nothing she could do. She heard the electric snap as the Hands of the River disengaged their shield and peeled away, and then darkness enveloped her.

She recognized the dank smell, the strange wet coolness of the air as she zipped down the corridor. Within seconds, she'd spotted the bright end of the tunnel, and soon she was through the Net.

The other side of the megaship was strangely quiet. With one hand on the wheel, Caledonia turned to search for signs of pursuit or anyone ready to fire on her from above, but there was no one here. They were all focused on the battle raging on the other side.

The fins of a dozen sharks dragged lazy trails around her small boat as she cut across an empty mile of sea toward the rig. The closer she got, the more the air smelled of that Silt-sweet perfume. Lofted high on a dozen sturdy legs, a platform supported the heart of the factory. The only way to reach it was to climb.

The sea remained empty as she closed in and tucked her boat beneath the rig. Caledonia tied on to the floating dock beneath the tent of its legs and hoisted her pack onto her shoulders. She stepped tentatively onto the dock and began to climb, pausing to listen for danger every so often. But the rig was silent. The only sounds were of the battle raging far in the distance and the pounding of her own heart inside her head.

She climbed, hand over hand. The mag bombs at her back weighed her down and lifted her up at the same time. She was so close to breaking the cycle. All she had to do was get to the top and set the charges. This was it.

The ladder ended on a shallow platform beneath the main level. Caledonia had a moment to note how this sublevel was open to the air on all sides, and she was beginning to consider where to place the first bomb when a fist cracked against her cheek.

Stars burst behind her eyes. Before she could open them, a kick to the back of her thighs knocked her off balance. She landed hard on her hands and knees, the weight of the mag bombs pushing her even lower.

Blood coated the inside of her mouth and she reached for the gun strapped against her leg, but a hand snaked out and caught her wrist.

"Caledonia." Lir said her name like a caress. "I knew you would come."

Before she could answer, his fist came down again and all went dark.

CHAPTER
FORTY-FIVE

Pain and light returned in the same instant. The sun was too warm on her right cheek, the ground too hard against her left. She was lying on her side on a platform high above the ocean with hands bound behind her back. The sun beating down on her told her she was still outside, and quiet voices nearby told her she was not alone.

Caledonia blinked, willing the fog to clear from her vision. When it did, she almost wished it hadn't.

She was on the main level of the rig, the wide platform stretching out like the deck of a ship. On one side of the platform a line of cranes curled over the edge from which crates of baleflowers or Silt could be loaded and unloaded from ships far below. On the other side of the platform the factory itself seemed to grow up from the floor, smooth walls extending into snaking pipes that coiled and twisted through the air.

Only a few feet away, two young men stood side by side,

their heads tipped together as though in deep discussion. Lir. And Donnally.

Lir held a knife loosely between his fingers, spinning the blade against the tip of his index finger, listening with a distant expression on his cold features, while Donnally stood with his arms folded across his chest, emphasizing whatever he said with tight bobs of his head. Between them sat her pack of mag bombs and a small collection of weapons they'd removed from her body.

Nausea swirled in her belly. They weren't supposed to be here. Lir was supposed to be on the *Mors Navis* in the thick of battle. And Donnally— She had hoped this moment would never come. He'd made his choice and now she had to consider him a Bullet instead of a brother.

Spitting the blood from her mouth, Caledonia struggled to sit up and climb to her feet. Lir watched her as if her presence relaxed him. As if the sight of her *delighted* him.

"We're so glad you could join us." A smile touched Lir's star-pale eyes as he savored those words.

A spear of ice shot down Caledonia's spine and she searched Donnally's expression for any sign that Lir was lying. Muscles flashed in Donnally's jaw and he kept his eyes resolutely away from hers, letting Caledonia's worst fears take root. This was a trap. One laid by both Lir and her own brother. Lir always knew how best to take advantage of her weaknesses. Her *mercy*.

They'd anticipated her perfectly.

"This started all those turns ago with the two of us on an island," Lir continued. "It was always going to end the same way. You and me."

"It won't end the same way." Caledonia struggled against her bindings.

"Have you come to surrender to me?" Gunfire sounded relentlessly in the distance and Lir shook his head. "That doesn't sound like surrender."

"It will soon," she promised.

Lir's eyes narrowed in sharp amusement. "Donnally," he said, taunting and cruel. "I'd like a moment alone with Caledonia. Take her mag bombs and sink them."

"No, Donnally," she said, fighting to keep her voice from betraying her terror as Donnally stooped to collect the bag and swing it over his shoulder. "Donnally, don't do this. *Use* those bombs instead! I know you think he's your brother and maybe—maybe he is, but if that's true, he'll be your brother even if you destroy this place."

Donnally paused just long enough to raise his eyes to hers. They were a deep brown, just like hers, but where she expected regret and submission, she thought she saw something more defiant.

"From Silt comes strength," Lir said. "My brother knows that as well as anyone."

"You were strong before," she said, pleading with her brother to remember.

Only a few days ago, they'd walked the streets of the Holster. They'd shared a memory of their mother and Caledonia had dared to think that for a moment, Donnally might come back to her. Now, as he tugged the pack onto his own shoulders, she didn't know what to believe.

"Hoist your eyes, Nia," Donnally said. "I know who I am."

Nia. She hadn't heard that name in so long.

"Go," Lir commanded.

Panic spiked in Caledonia's blood. Donnally turned to give her one last look, then he was gone, and Caledonia was alone with Lir.

Sweat made quick tracks down Caledonia's back. It slicked her palms and made the ropes around her wrists bite into her skin. She adjusted her stance watching the way Lir spun that knife around and around, but to her surprise, he put it away, tucking the blade into his waistband.

For a moment, he stood across from her without saying a word. His eyes traveled from her hair to her lips to either side of her hips where her guns should have been. He took his time consuming the sight of her and then he took three slow steps forward.

It took every bit of willpower she possessed to stand as if planted in place. Her mind rang with the memory of Donnally calling her Nia. It was his name for her. Not even their parents had used the nickname. It had only ever existed between a brother and a sister and Caledonia couldn't shake the terrifying hope that it had been a message: *Sister, I am with you.*

Maybe, just maybe, he wasn't dropping her bombs in the ocean, but planting them as she'd meant to.

Doubt coated the thought. It could be another trap. Just a ruse to toy with her heart. But hope was all she had left.

"It took me a long time to understand that I needed you," Lir said, as if they'd been in the middle of a conversation. "You are the reason I survived to take the Bullet Seas for myself. And you are the reason I'll keep them now."

The distant sounds of battle rushed to fill his silence. His confidence was a performance, or it was delusion. But most of all it was a sign that he believed Donnally would never betray him.

"I know because that is your purpose. You resist me, you stand against me, and every time you do, I gain a little bit more. Do you know what that makes us?"

Caledonia only glared in response.

Lir's smile softened. It was amazing how much it changed his face. He could move from dangerous to innocent in the blink of an eye. Caledonia recalled viscerally how she'd dropped her own guard for that glimmer of vulnerability. It was no more real now than it had been the first night she'd seen it. This time, though, she knew it for what it was.

"It makes us polar opposites. We are the cardinal directions that give this world meaning. You are the rebellion. You've made yourself the solitary symbol of hope and resistance." His smile sharpened and a breeze stirred the shattered crown of his blond hair. "And when I kill you, all that hope will vanish. I will be all that's left. What will that even look like, Caledonia? I can't imagine what comes after this." He shook his head eagerly, as if not knowing excited him.

Then he moved forward again. This time he was close enough to touch her. He raised a hand, but instead of caressing her cheek, he let it hover an inch from her skin. The heat of it skimmed along her jaw, but she remained still, kept her eyes hard as behind her back she tugged at her bindings.

"You're not afraid." Wonder made his words soft. "Of course, you're not afraid."

"I haven't been afraid of you for a long time," Caledonia said.

At this, a low laugh tumbled from Lir's lips. Without warning, his hand darted forward, gripping the back of her head and tugging her against him. Caledonia clenched her jaw against the pain as Lir bent over her.

"There is another option for us," he said. His breath was hot against her mouth. "If you choose me."

She forced herself to look into his star-pale eyes. They had haunted her dreams and more of her waking moments than she should have allowed. She'd only seen them four times in her life, but she could have described them in exquisite detail. The threads of ice that spidered through them. The way the inner rings shattered around the black center of the pupil. It was as if a bomb had exploded in the center of those eyes. As if a bomb had been exploding inside Lir all his life.

Choose him? Choose him.

He was offering her the chance to sit at his side, to save the lives of everyone who fought against him. If she agreed, her submission would crush the spirit of the rebellion she and so many others had fought and bled to build. He wanted her power. He wanted all the Bullet Seas.

But he was also asking her. He *wanted* her to choose him over everything else because no one ever had. All the choices he'd ever made had been demanded. All the trust he'd ever received, he'd also demanded. And that wasn't trust. That wasn't choice. It was power without consent.

Sympathy raced through Caledonia, unexpected and unwelcome. Part of Lir was still a little boy, wondering why no one loved him. He had been created by a violent force, and that was worth her sympathy. But he'd done everything he could to gain power over others, and that wasn't.

"I can't," she said plainly. "No one can choose you. No one ever has."

Lir's grip in her hair loosed in shock. His eyes widened and in them Caledonia saw fear and anger twist together like smothering vines.

"Donnally chose me." His teeth bit off the end of the last word. Before Caledonia could respond, he threw her to the ground, pressing her onto her back. He crouched over her. The knife was in his hand once more. Her knife, she realized with a jolt. The same black blade he'd used to stab her so long ago, that she had carried with her ever since. He'd taken it from her and now he threatened her with it. She could do nothing as he leaned in once more and repeated, "Donnally chose me."

"He didn't," Caledonia challenged. "The only choice he made was to stay alive. He was no more your brother than Aric was your father. He didn't choose you then and he hasn't chosen you now."

"That's a lie." Calm washed down Lir's face and his body relaxed. He shook his head and brought the dagger to her throat, pressing the blade into her skin. "I gave you a choice, Caledonia."

"You gave me *nothing*," she answered. She had to keep stalling.

"I hope you'll believe me when I say I wish you'd made the other choice." The blade bit into her skin, lightly at first. Caledonia shifted her weight to the balls of her feet, preparing to use her body against him.

But before she could do anything, the sky exploded.

CHAPTER FORTY-SIX

Silence. Light. Orange. Smoke.

Caledonia blinked. The sky was gone. It was lost behind a haze of orange. And it was so quiet. It was as if sound had been sucked from the air and all that was left was this muffled ringing.

Caledonia blinked again. The ringing grew louder, and she realized that she was lying on her back, hands twisted painfully beneath her. She climbed awkwardly to her knees and paused as her head spun so violently it threatened to send her right back to the ground.

Orange smoke hung thick in the air. No, not smoke. It smelled sweet. Too sweet. And she could taste it on her tongue. It was like honey and it coated the inside of her mouth and her nose. This delightful sweetness consumed her senses. She wanted more.

No. Wait.

Caledonia spat on the ground. Bloody saliva landed at her feet and she spat again, but there was no escaping it. This wasn't smoke, it was Silt, powdered and hanging in the air around her, flooding her lungs with every breath, sneaking into her body with every swallow. But why?

The factory. The answer hit her as soon as the question. Donnally! He'd done it. He'd taken her charges and destroyed the factory. Squinting through the haze, she confirmed her suspicions. The factory was demolished. Fire tore through the roof, sending plumes of muddy smoke into the air while all around its base, Silt created a dense ring.

Lir. Lir had been so close. Holding a dagger—

Caledonia spun. There was a heat at her wrists as if her bindings burned there, and her head was starting to float or grow or bloom like a flower. It was a nice feeling. An exciting feeling. Her pain was there but muffled, and as the ringing in her ears slowly receded, she felt sharper, stronger.

Something barreled into her side, knocking her off balance and driving her shoulder into the ground. There was a growl in her ear and then her head snapped back.

Blood spilled down her chin. She felt the warmth of it more than the pain, and for a second she was struck with wonder. Then Lir hit her again and she rolled backward, skidding up onto her feet.

She crouched low. Lir mirrored her position just a few feet away. All trace of his strange sorrow had been erased from his features. All that was left was pain. He was hurt, Caledonia realized. Not by her, but by Donnally.

Betrayal had dragged its steely fingers across Lir's heart, what little of it there was. He was wounded and he was angry.

Through the sharpened lens of her Silt-soaked mind, Caledonia understood that this was not the same Lir who had asked her to choose him just a moment before. This was a Lir rejected by the one person he thought loved him. And now that Donnally's allegiance had been stripped away, Lir would take out every drop of his brutal hurt on her.

"Ask me for mercy," Lir said, voice a growl.

The words made Caledonia's gut churn. *Ask me for mercy*. He had asked for her mercy the night they met on that beach. She'd given it and he'd taken everything from her. Now he wanted her to do the same. Not because he intended to give it. But because he planned to withhold it.

Asking for mercy from someone with a knife in your gut was to acknowledge their power. And Caledonia was done acknowledging Lir's power.

"You don't have any to give," she spat.

With a snarl, Lir dove for her. Caledonia dodged, rolling swiftly out of reach. She tugged at her bindings, hoping whatever spark had landed there had weakened the rope. Wet warmth spilled down her hands and she tugged harder.

Lir renewed his attack. This time he went high, forcing her to dodge. She spun and danced out of his way, but with every movement, her head spun a little more than the rest of her. She'd never tasted Silt in her life and suddenly she was inhaling it with every breath.

Where Lir seemed to thrive on the additional dose, Caledonia struggled to know where her body ended and the air began. She couldn't sustain this for long. And she definitely couldn't win in this condition. She needed help.

Donnally. Where was Donnally? Had he survived the explosion?

Again, she tugged at her wrists. This time, she felt a hint of movement.

Time passed in a blur. Caledonia evaded Lir's attacks but each time her feet felt slower, her lungs tighter. Her hands grew hot and wet as she fought to pull them apart with no luck. Lir lashed out, dragging the blade across her chest. A curtain of blood dripped down her front. She felt the pressure of it, but not the sting. Lir laughed, low and confident. As if he were toying with her.

It took her a second to realize that was exactly what he was doing. He was wearing her down. He would enjoy cutting her apart a little at a time over killing her with a single blow. And that was something she could use to her advantage.

Dodging again, Caledonia let her breath come a little harder, and she fell briefly to one knee.

Lir slowed his own steps in response, giving her a moment to recover. Or perhaps he was savoring her struggle. Blood shone on the edge of his knife as he stood with the sun on his face. "Bale

Blossom," he said, teasing her with the name. "Your final gift to me is your life."

He struck, darting forward with incredible speed. Caledonia tugged at her wrists and felt the snap of the ropes. Her hands came free just in time to deflect Lir's attack.

Surprise painted his face as Caledonia used his own momentum against him, twisting his wrist and driving him into the ground in one smooth motion.

He dropped her dagger and before he could recover, Caledonia scooped it up and drove it into his gut.

Lir's eyes widened in surprise. His mouth gaped. Blood bloomed over Caledonia's hand and she barely stopped herself from driving it all the way through him.

She could kill him now. Easily. His life was in her hands. Most of her wanted to take it. To kill him as she had Tassos. The world would be so much better without him lurking in the shadows.

A wind ghosted across her cheeks, bringing with it the voices of her mother and Pisces, "We can fight them as long as we don't become them."

For a shuddering breath, Caledonia believed that it was too late. She was too much like Lir and there was no coming back. Someone needed to end this, and why shouldn't it be her? All of her terrible choices had prepared her for this moment. She could make one more.

But she didn't need to.

With a shaking hand, she pulled the dagger free and stepped away.

"You said I gave you power. My resistance made you stronger, but you were wrong," Caledonia said as Lir panted on the ground, one hand pressed to the wound in his gut. "The only thing I've ever given you is mercy."

Laughter bubbled through Lir's lips. "Mercy is weakness."

Caledonia considered that. She'd shown him mercy and lost her family instead. She'd offered mercy to any who asked for it and lost all of Cloudbreak. If she wanted to believe mercy was a weakness, she had every reason in the world. But mercy was something else. Mercy was trust. And the only way to make this world something other than what it was now was to trust that other people wanted the same thing. Trust was the opposite of violence. And that was something Lir would never understand.

She smiled at Lir and was surprised to find some of her own anger was unraveling at the edges. "Mercy," she said, "is more powerful than a bullet."

CHAPTER
FORTY-SEVEN

Caledonia woke in her bed aboard the *Luminous Wake* late the next morning. Her head was heavy, and her body felt slow. Hime had warned her that the after-effects of such a high dose of Silt would linger for some time. Caledonia had been glad of the drug as Hime stitched the long gash across her chest. She'd been less glad of it when it started to wear off and her first thought was how to find more. One shot of that drug and already it had laid some claim to her mind. She'd never doubted its power, but feeling it work inside her own body and her own mind was truly terrifying.

Now that the factory had been destroyed and Lir deposed, the number of people who would crave the drug more furiously than Caledonia was staggering. And without Sledge to help transform their lives after, the work was going to be much more challenging.

Without Sledge.

He'd driven the ship into the crusher, steering with his own hands, never straying, planting himself like a mountain at her flank. Pisces had shared the story through a steady stream of tears. Sledge had seen what needed to happen and his crew had agreed. His last call had been to Pine aboard the *Triple*.

Sorrow pulled at Caledonia, a too-heavy stone in her pocket. There was so much more of it to come. Sledge had sacrificed himself to get her through the megaship and he wasn't the only one. The battle was theirs, but the cost had been great.

The fight had not lasted long once Donnally blew the factory. By the time Caledonia had bound Lir and found her brother, tossed free of the explosion but unconscious, her crew was on their way to her.

Before she knew it, she was aboard her ship, separated from her brother once more. Part of her had been desperate to go to him, but Hime insisted that she rest and give the Silt time to work its way out of her system. They were taking care of the fallout. Pisces remained in command and everything would survive if she closed her eyes. Didn't she want to see her brother again with a clear head? She did. And last night, it had been enough to know he was safe. Now, however, she couldn't tell if the tremble in her blood was exhaustion or the prospect of seeing Donnally.

Careful of her stitches, Caledonia rolled out of bed and braced her hands against the sink. The ship rocked as much as her head and it took a moment to find her balance. She splashed some water on her face and wrestled her hair into a braid, doing her best to pick out the knots masquerading as curls. Sluggish or not, she had work to do.

As she slipped a fresh shirt over her head, the skin pulled painfully around her stitches and she wondered if there'd been enough Silt in her blood to paint the scar orange when it formed. Some part of her hoped it would. That there would be some outward sign of all the turmoil she would carry with her.

The air in the hallway tasted cold as she headed topside, where familiar sounds layered over one another—the clink of metal against metal, the bright calls of her crew, the constant churn of the desal tanks down on level three. Everything had returned to a less frenzied pace.

The minute she appeared in the hatchway, her presence was announced by a call of "Captain on deck!"

As one, her crew paused to acknowledge her. They'd been working around the clock and exhaustion showed in their eyes, but there was also a new kind of energy, a vibrance and sense of wonder at having defeated the sprawling beast that had hunted them for so long. What did that mean for tomorrow? None of them knew.

"As you were," Caledonia said, releasing them back to their duties and turning her own steps toward the lookout atop the bridge.

It was well past dawn as Caledonia began to climb. She moved slowly at first, trying to find the movements that didn't pull at her stitches, then she rushed upward. Hand over hand, she pulled herself up and up, relishing the moment sweat kissed her skin and the burn of the sun at her back. When she reached the high platform, she planted her feet wide and turned to survey the fleet.

There were more ships than she could count, stitching the *Luminous Wake* into the center of a glittering tapestry that pooled against the Net. Later, it would be dismantled, carefully and systematically, but for now, it was enough to contain it.

At first glance, the press of ships was overwhelming, but the longer she let her eyes play over their shapes, the more evidence she found of order. Her own fleet was organized in long rows extending out from the Net like blades of grass. In between those blades were Bullet ships in various states of disrepair. Crowning the whole system were the slender ships of the Hands of the River, and beyond those were the bale barges Lir had managed to slip out of the Holster.

They'd been harnessed together into a kind of island and were covered in thousands of baleflowers. Their orange petals thrived in the sun, each one burning against the sea like a tiny spark of fire. The sight of them left Caledonia uneasy. They were lovely and dangerous and the urge to eradicate them was a constant thrumming in her blood, but destroying them wasn't the answer. In that way, they were a little like Bullets. The next part of this fight wasn't going to be about blood and guns, it was going to be about hearts and minds. She had to let both exist if she wanted them to change.

These were the new Bullet Seas. They would need a new name. One that promised something other than violence and fear. Sledge had taught her the power of names. The sooner they stopped calling people Bullets, the sooner they'd stop acting like them.

There was still so much to do before they disbanded the fleet. And after that, there would be even more. Removing Lir from power was a start, but they would have to put something in his place. Maybe several somethings. And they had to do it quickly or the likelihood of finding themselves right back where they started was high. Sister was still out there, and others eager to siphon power for themselves.

But before all of that, they needed to release some of this tension. They needed to eat and laugh and take a moment to revel in what they'd accomplished together.

Caledonia let her eyes travel slowly across the seas, settling on the exploded husk of the rig. A symbol of conflict and war. What she needed was a symbol of change. She turned her eyes back to the baleflowers. Their blooms were so vivid and so dangerous still. And exactly what she needed.

>«

The night sky was open and clear, and moonlight pooled in the center of a thousand baleflowers drifting out to sea. As people stepped onto the island of bale barges, they cut a flower and dropped it into the water. Together, they would clear the soils and create room for a new future.

Caledonia stood at the edge of the barge with a blossom cupped in her hands. They were surprisingly firm, yet soft, and deep inside the cave of its mouth the petals sank into a brilliant blue. Just as Lir had depicted them on the wall of his quarters. They really were like small flames. Capable of burning you from the inside out.

"They're like stars." The voice startled Caledonia. She hadn't expected her brother to attend, but she turned to find him standing close behind her. In his hand, he also held a single blossom.

"How so?" Caledonia asked.

"They burn too hot." His thumb pressed into the center of the flower, forcing its petals open in a perfect circle. He tossed it into the water and raised his thumb for Caledonia to see the slick of orange nectar left behind. He stared at it for a long moment before wiping it along his pants leg. "It's hard to look away."

"I should have taken you with me." Caledonia surprised herself with the words. She'd thought of a hundred things she might say to her brother when they were finally together again. This was not among them. "That night when Mom wanted to send you, and I told her to send Pi with me instead."

The frown that appeared on Donnally's face was the same one she'd seen that night on the *Ghost*. Equal parts fear and frustration. "It isn't your fault," he said in a hoarse whisper. "I didn't want to go."

She nodded, knowing it was true, but also knowing that she'd regretted leaving him behind since the moment it happened. "I'm sorry," she said. "I'm so sorry."

"Nia," Donnally said with a sigh. "Don't do that."

"Do what?"

"Apologize." He ducked his head to look straight into her eyes. His own were rimmed in red. "I guarantee I have more to apologize for than you. *You* are the only reason we get to have this conversation at all. *You.*"

Her stomach clenched at the thought of all the things Donnally might have to apologize for. "You can tell me anything," she said, giving him a steely look.

A rueful smile bent his lips. "Maybe."

Her hand warmed around the blossom, and she was glad to have something to hold onto as she considered the one question she truly wanted the answer to. "What made you choose me?"

In the silence that followed, the sounds of the celebration swelled between them. The moon above was full and blue light ringed the barges like pools of starlight. All around, the ocean was covered in orange petals. Every last one had been plucked and delivered to the sea. Except the one Caledonia held as she waited for her brother's answer.

Donnally raised his eyes to the stars, then slowly brought them back to Caledonia. When he spoke, the words were careful, measured, as if each one had been weighed out precisely.

"I think it's more accurate to say I'm still working on it. But I'd never been given a choice before. Not like that. Lir saved my life, and I guess I wanted a chance to do the same for him. Save his life."

The idea that Lir had ever done anything to save her brother's life was infuriating. It was all Caledonia could do to concentrate on not crushing the blossom in her hand. If she could keep from doing that, she could keep from lashing out.

"He's . . . he's my brother." Donnally said it as kindly as he could, but without apology. Whatever had happened in his life, he'd ended up with the person she despised most in the world and they'd become family.

Caledonia caught herself midway through a snarl. Fury burned in her cheeks and she tossed the blossom into the water. "You still think that? Even after standing against him? He took *everything* from you."

"I do," Donnally answered quickly, then paused, licking his lips before saying anything more. "Do you— Are you going to execute him?"

The question surprised her. But not nearly so much as the realization that it mattered to Donnally if Lir lived or died.

"I—we haven't decided." She gave the most honest answer she could.

Donnally nodded and seemed to struggle with what he wanted to say next. "Whatever you decide to do, I won't stand in your way, but if you do decide to execute him, I'd like to make a request."

"What?"

"I'd like to see him before he dies. Just . . . I'd like to say goodbye."

Caledonia's head felt light and her stomach churned. She wanted to deny him. She wanted to deny *Lir* the privilege of seeing her brother one last time.

But hurting Lir at the expense of her brother wasn't worth it.

She blew out a breath as she nodded. "I'll make sure you have the opportunity."

"Thank you." He relaxed visibly after that. It made Caledonia feel marginally better to know that asking the question hadn't been easy for him.

"You're welcome," she said, voice softer now.

For a moment they stood quietly side by side. While she watched the revelry spinning across their island of boats, Donnally tipped his head to the sky. He was so familiar to Caledonia and so foreign at the same time. The distance between them was much greater than the few inches between their bodies. It left Caledonia feeling impatient and unsettled in her own skin until finally she broke.

"Donnally." Before he could answer, she threw her arms around his neck, pulling him into an embrace. He tensed. She tensed. And then they laughed together. He was taller than he'd been, Caledonia had to stand on her toes to avoid smushing her face into his chest. His arms circled her waist and he lifted her easily from the ground.

They parted wearing the same awkward smile, and Caledonia knew that while their way forward was still choppy and full of rocks hidden just beneath the surface, they would navigate the way together.

CHAPTER
FORTY-EIGHT

The streets of South Haven were busy in the evenings. Sailors rushed up from the harbor while farmers spilled down from the fields, and children raced along in small groups, hurrying toward the mess halls for the evening meal.

South Haven, or the Holster, as it was once known, had changed shape overnight, it seemed. In the weeks since the Battle of the Bale Blossom, people had flocked to its harbor. At first, it was because they were hungry, but then, as people found the place changed, they came to stay. They came to make the city their own. There were signs of change everywhere, from the ships free of desiccated bodies displayed on spikes to the covering of bandolier scars. South Haven was a place where people went to change.

The gun towers still flew the banner of Caledonia's fleet, shining boldly through the night. The fleet itself still existed. Fifty ships had been sent in all directions, offering aid to anyone who needed it and resistance to anyone seeking to continue the traditions of the Bullet Seas.

Caledonia spent more of her time thinking about the ocean than actually seeing it. Every decision fell to her, and while she no longer felt the immense pressure of every single one, she also wondered if the only reason she was still the one making them was because she was the one everyone feared now.

Respect. That's what Pisces said. Not fear. She might have been right, but when people saw her for the first time, it was hard to read their wide-eyed expressions as anything but fear. She'd turned herself into something ferocious on purpose. She'd needed to be in order to have any chance at winning that fight. And there was no coming back from it. Not in the eyes of others. She'd known that. She'd made the choice with her eyes open, and now she was feeling the full press of the consequences.

Caledonia tucked her chin as she hurried around a corner that brought her out of a sheltered alley and into a main thoroughfare. It didn't matter what she did to avoid notice, people found her red curls whether she'd wrapped them in a scarf or bound them in a tight braid. In spite of the sticky evening humidity, she'd donned a hooded jacket, but even that wasn't enough. She heard the gasp of the first person to notice her—a child with big brown eyes and pale brown skin—and did her best to appear unthreatening.

It never worked. People watched her pass, some of them even bowed slightly, and she was reminded all over again of the things she'd done to earn that response from strangers.

Pisces would tell her to think of all she'd done to ensure those same strangers got to choose who they followed and who they didn't. It was comforting, but only just.

As Caledonia's steps brought her near the city center, she strode past a row of colorful murals now splashed across tall walls. They'd grown little by little as stories and dreams took root in the city. The first depicted ships like stars streaming into the night, the second fields of bushy green crops growing in neat rows from earth so brown it was almost black. The most recent was a crew of girls on the bow of a ship with their eyes hard and bright and fixed on some point in the distance. In the center stood a girl with streaming red curls that dripped into the waves, tangling there as though she were part of the sea.

When it had appeared, Pisces pulled Caledonia from her bed late at night, knowing she wouldn't want to see it when there were witnesses. Hand in hand, they had hurried through the dark until they stood in front of the painting.

"They love you," Pisces said, as if this should be proof that what Caledonia interpreted as fear was in fact love and respect. "You're a legend."

Caledonia couldn't speak immediately. The image of herself was stunning, but the other girls were what caught her attention. Tin and all four of her sisters held a flag between them, their grip firm as the wind rippled through the fabric. Amina stood on the rail with her long braids bending at her back like a sail, and she pointed north, toward the Hands of the River. At her side stood

Hime, calm and poised; she wore a hood to symbolize her work as a healer. On either side of Caledonia were Nettle and Pisces. The smaller girl was tucked beneath Caledonia's arm and unlike the others, she smiled broadly and boldly into the sky. Pisces was on Caledonia's other side, her shoulders bare, her own family sigil drawn on her temple, and her fingers entwined with Caledonia's, a bit of lace caught between them.

Behind them all, two figures stood in the background. Red-tooth, tall and strong with the tips of her blonde braids coated in red clay. And Lace, a rolled map clutched in her hands.

When Caledonia found her voice again, she turned to Pisces and said, "We."

"What?"

"We are a legend." She corrected Pisces's earlier statement.

Pisces smirked, but conceded the point.

Beyond the row of murals, the city coiled around a central square. When this had been the Holster, it had been a place for Aric's terrible theater. Now it was transforming into a market that reminded Caledonia of Cloudbreak. She wove through dozens of stalls, all closing up shop for the evening, until she found herself on the other side, where the streets soon emptied and turned quiet.

The northeastern quarter was a place few people had reason to go. The vast majority of the quarter was devoted to helping former Bullets through their addiction. They stayed behind closed doors, venturing out only at specified times and only on specified routes through town. It was a massive undertaking, and one Cepheus had offered to take on. Ares was helping, and to everyone's surprise Pine was not.

Guards stood at each door along the barracks, where windows glowed with warm light. It wasn't a prison, but it was close. Anyone who had once called themselves a Bullet had a lot of work to do before they earned the city's trust. But Caledonia had made it clear that violence toward former Bullets would not be tolerated in South Haven. It was hard enough containing their violence toward each other, and they'd lost hundreds of lives in the fight.

Even walking through town, she had to confront the two sides of Caledonia Styx. There was the side that people adored, the part that was being spun into legend and splashed across walls, and then there was the side people feared. The part that made people stop when they saw her on the street. Neither side felt true, but she wasn't sure she knew what was true anymore. It was that feeling that drove her past the barracks toward the low bank of the prison.

At Caledonia's approach, the guards opened the door with brisk nods. She met the bailiff inside and without asking, the woman handed Caledonia the keys she'd come for, then led her through the fortified interior doors.

Caledonia had struggled with this decision for weeks, but Oran had been encouraging. She had nothing to fear, after all. Not anymore.

The prison was a labyrinth of narrow corridors that reminded Caledonia of a ship except these were built of stone, and they pinched together at several points so that only one person might pass through them at a time. She'd only been here once, but the way to Lir's cell was seared in her memory.

Lir was alive and he would live here until something other than Caledonia's blade or her order took his life. The decision hadn't been an easy one. Caledonia herself had argued for his death at first, but after several days of discussion, the command crew had decided Lir would live. Killing him would be to align themselves with his own tactics. It was better to let him live. Even if he was imprisoned.

For days, Caledonia had tried and failed to quiet the drumbeat at the back of her mind: *Lir. Lir. Lir.* She'd won, but there was a part of her that needed to know she hadn't simply become the thing she hated. She needed to look into his eyes and know that they were not the same. Then she would finally be able to close the door and walk away.

The air was cool and a little damp this far inside the building. There were no more windows to give a sense of direction or to offer the rhythm of day and night. Here, the world was nothing but stone and solitude.

She'd practiced what she might say to him. The temptation to reflect his own cruelty was strong. That was part of the reason she'd come. She needed to see what she would do, who she would be now that they'd traded places. She was in power and he was not. It had changed them both, though she wasn't sure what she would find in him. Would he cling to his arrogance? Beg for death? Would he show her fear? And how would she respond?

Lir's cell was at the end of a short, narrow hallway. There was a window at eye level with a hatch that could only be opened from the outside. Just inside, Lir likely lay on his cot. While his wound had nearly healed, his recovery had been complicated by his withdrawal. The healers reported that he would remain weak for many moons to come.

Without meaning to, Caledonia reached for the old scar on her belly. Her fingers curled into the fabric of her shirt and for a moment she imagined that Lir had been right all along. Their lives had been connected from the moment they'd met on that beach. Without her, he'd never have risen to power. Without him, she'd never have had to take it.

That wasn't right. But that plaguing thought was exactly the reason she'd come.

Caledonia reached to unlatch the window, then stopped. What good would it do to announce her presence? She should just go inside. She raised the key.

Her breath came more quickly. Not from fear, but from anticipation. What part of herself would she find in his star-pale eyes? Who would she be when she entered that room?

Who would she be after?

The key slid into the lock with a soft metallic kiss. In the back of her mind, the question spun, sending invasive winds through her thoughts.

You are a reflection of him, they hissed.

She closed her eyes and paused with the key in the door. A fine sweat coated her palm. She felt as she always did on the brink of battle, when her senses were as vast as the ocean itself. Only now she had no one to fight.

You are the person he made you, the winds moaned.

But that wasn't right. That had never been right. Caledonia was the person she'd become because of herself, because of Pisces, because of every girl who'd ever joined the crew of the *Mors Navis,* because of Oran and Sledge and the rest of the Blades. She was the person she was in *spite* of Lir. He'd stolen pieces of her against her will. She had nothing to gain from him. She never had. But if she walked through this door, she'd give him one final victory.

Caledonia pulled the key from the lock, then she turned and left the prison.

Lir had been the focus of her story for too long. His door was shut. And Caledonia had so many more to open.

CHAPTER FORTY-NINE

The *Mors Navis* had never been so beautiful. After the battle, she'd been reclaimed, repaired, and more. The sails were crisp and white, the solar sail inky black in contrast, and all around the railing hung garlands of fragrant green leaves woven through with sprigs of lavender and tiny white flowers. Swaths of deep green fabric wrapped the bannisters of the companionway ladder and bells were strung from every available perch so that whenever the wind blew, the air stirred the ship into song.

Caledonia stood on the balcony overlooking the main deck from the narrow platform behind the bridge. She'd stood here so many times before. Always to rally her girls or deliver bad news. This time, however, she was wedding two of her dearest friends.

Hime was radiant in a blouse of deep blue and brown pants with lengths of pale blue satin stitched down either side. Nettle had insisted on doing the needlework herself. Hime's hair was bound in a simple braid and she wore a crown of the same tiny white flowers that ringed the ship. Standing opposite her was

Amina. She wore a dark blue shawl, wrapped around her shoulders to spill down her back. Beneath it, her shirt and pants were the paler compliments to Hime's blue and brown. Her long braids were coiled atop her head and woven with spears of lavender.

Each stared warmly, calmly into the other's eyes. At Caledonia's prompting they gave the sign of consent and then it was Hime who leaned forward and cupped Amina's cheeks between her hands, drawing her forward into a kiss.

"Before our eyes and our hearts, you consent to love one another from now until the stars fade from the night sky," Caledonia said.

A cheer rose from the main deck and the air filled with flowers and lavender, all tossed into the sky before they landed again where they would be crushed into a fragrant carpet beneath dancing feet. Caledonia let tears warm her eyes and backed away to give the couple their privacy. Or, as much privacy as they could have in the midst of a hundred people.

The sun was hanging low enough to tease the horizon, and the sky was painted in brilliant pinks and oranges, the clouds catching color along their bellies before sweeping into deep pockets of silver and gray. The breeze was light and warm, and the waves lapped at the hull of the ship. Dotted along the water around them were several smaller ships, all waiting at anchor, their crews here on the *Mors Navis* to witness the occasion.

Hime and Amina were drawn down the stairway to the deck

by the commanding rhythm of a reel. Soon, the floor was lost beneath dancing feet, and the musicians struggled to be heard above joyful laughter. Caledonia followed more slowly, enjoying the sight of her crew dancing on the back of the sea without fear that someone might hear them and take advantage of their distraction.

"Couldn't leave the gun behind." The voice was amused and dark in a way Caledonia associated with only one person. "Though it's nicely hidden, I'll give you that."

Caledonia's hand strayed to the pistol secured at the small of her back. She'd tried to leave it behind but at the last minute, she'd tucked it into her waistband. It was a comfort to have it near. Not having it there . . . well, it was a step she wasn't ready for.

"I'm certain you've got at least two on you, Pine."

They were hovering on the aft deck, stained in sunset colors. Pine was dressed not for celebration but for travel. His hair was slicked into a tight ponytail at the nape of his neck and there was a gun strapped across his back. He smiled, but sadly.

"I can't stay here," he said.

"You can," Caledonia answered, but without any urging. "Where are you going?"

His eyes turned south. "To see what's out there. Beyond the Net."

The Net didn't exist anymore, but it was going to be a long time before people stopped referring to the place where it had been by that name. The line of ships was a part of their imagined world. It would take time to change that.

"Who's going with you?" Caledonia asked.

"No room for anyone else on my boat with me and all my demons." Pine's answer was as playful as it was serious. "And all my ghosts." He added the last softly.

Caledonia didn't like the thought of him sailing off into the unknown without anyone to watch his back, but it was an argument she wouldn't win. They'd held a memorial for everyone who'd given their lives in the great battle. The names had been recorded with as much accuracy as they could manage, and then they'd put out every light in South Haven and flooded the harbor with floating lanterns. There had been more than one lit for Sledge, but not by Pine. Caledonia knew he'd watched the ceremony from a distance. Pine wasn't the sort to release his ghosts so quickly.

"Will you come back?" she asked.

"If I don't get killed." He laughed at himself, then stepped forward and pulled Caledonia into a crushing embrace. He tucked his head low and spoke in her ear. "If you're going to stay with him, at least promise me you won't let his demons become yours."

"Who?" she asked, realizing too late he could only mean Oran.

She felt the rumble of laughter in his chest. "Exactly."

"Pine," she warned, pulling back with more of her senses intact. "You know I can take care of myself."

"With a gun and on a ship, I have no doubt. But with him?

I doubt everything he does because I also doubt myself." He shrugged. "At least I'm doing the responsible thing and leaving."

Irritation strummed a single chord in Caledonia's mind, but it wasn't about Pine. "Just remember that you have friends here. And you—and all your demons—are always welcome."

With a distant smile, Pine spun on his heel and aimed for the ladder on the aft deck. On the water below, a tender boat waited to ferry him to his small ship. Caledonia breathed deeply for a moment, knowing it was likely the last she'd ever see of her hard-won friend. Knowing that it was the best thing for him right now. He gave a little wave and then he was gone, gliding over the water toward his next journey.

It took Caledonia a moment to swallow the sorrow that perched in the back of her throat and return her attention to the celebration. When she did, Amina and Hime spun past her in a blur, their hair shedding flowers as they twirled and laughed together. They didn't know it yet, but Caledonia and Pisces had agreed that the *Mors Navis* would be theirs now. Most of the crew wanted to be out on the seas, helping to keep the peace, and there was no better team than Hime and Amina to stand at the helm.

Caledonia found Pisces and Cepheus tucked against one of the mast blocks, their lips tracing delicate patterns across cheeks and eyes, throats and mouths. They'd been together more and more often, but to see Pisces inhabit her passions so openly was akin to her shouting for everyone to hear that she adored Cepheus.

Nettle had assumed a spot on the bridge balcony, where she was encouraging Abrasin Mary to toss flowers over the heads of the dancers. Far appeared a moment later, with Folly close beside her, bearing baskets of small cakes. Far's mind still struggled with crowds, and she much preferred the quiet dark of a pantry, but every once in a while, they coaxed her topside and reminded her that the world didn't have to be cruel and that her family loved her. Caledonia was glad to see this was one of those moments. The woman had even added a flower to her unruly black curls. Ares was here, too, and for the first time, he didn't look like he thought the sky might explode at any second.

Donnally was the only one missing. Caledonia had asked him to come, but he'd only smiled and reminded her that he didn't belong there. Not yet.

Despite that, everything felt *good*. Recovering from all they'd been through was going to take time and Caledonia wasn't sure exactly how she fit into this picture any longer, but this moment was good.

"You're glaring," Oran said from just behind her. "It's starting to make people nervous. See how they've carved a path around you?"

Caledonia smiled. "I didn't ask for your opinion."

Oran slipped his fingers through hers and tugged her close. "Did you want me to lie?"

"Never." She wanted to press her lips against his, but there was still a question between them that hadn't been answered. "I only want your truths."

As the sun burned into the horizon it cast a shimmer of gold across Oran's features. The light caught in his lashes and plunged into the endless brown rings of his eyes. He tipped his head toward hers, just enough that his hair brushed her forehead.

"Are you sure?"

"I'm sure." Caledonia stood rooted in place, every bit of her body aware of his.

"All right," he said, his smile becoming serious. "Then I promise to be true."

Oran had worn many faces in the time they'd known one another. He'd been the hopeful prisoner, the steely Fiveson, the shadowed Steelhand. But here he was someone new. He was warm and vulnerable and confident. He was changing and he wasn't afraid.

Caledonia leaned forward and pressed her lips to his. She didn't care that the eyes of her entire crew were on them, she only cared that Oran's arms were around her and hers around him and they would have a tomorrow. It didn't have to be forever. Neither of them could make that promise, but they could promise to figure that out together.

Caledonia kissed him again, tasting his tongue against hers and breathing in the sea-kissing salt of his skin. Only when the cheering started did she pull away, breathless and smiling.

"I love you," she said.

Oran nodded as if they were both the most obvious words and the sweetest he'd ever heard. Then, laughing, he pulled her toward her crew and they danced as night fell and stitched them into the black sea.

EPILOGUE

The waters of the Bone Mouth were alive with sunlight. Layers of vibrant blue rocks and sediment ribboned beneath the surface as Caledonia and Pisces dipped their oars in a steady rhythm. Behind them, the Gem rolled out of the sea like the humped back of a turtle with emerald green smeared unevenly down the middle. They drove their small boat into a bank of reeds and pulled it out of the clutches of the tide so they could empty its contents on shore.

They'd made this trip three times already and each time they brought a few more supplies. Solar plates, bolts of canvas, and tools for building had come first, followed by a full crate of seedbrick, soiltech, and a few seedling plants that would someday produce juicy tomatoes and peppers. For now, it was enough to sustain a person for several moons. The rest would come later with Oran.

When they'd unloaded the remaining supplies, they walked down the narrow strip of beach between the ocean and the forest. Waves rolled in and out, sighing against the shore and turning the sand into a glassy plane. The island supported fruit trees and small animals, both of which would supplement the food Caledonia had brought with her. Beyond that, it was quiet and empty.

"Are you sure?" Pisces asked.

A warm breeze pushed at their backs, throwing Caledonia's curls against her cheeks. She'd chosen the Gem because it had been an open wound for so long. Returning to it seemed like the only way to make peace.

"I'm sure," Caledonia said.

The city was in good hands, Pisces's hands, and there were too many stories about Caledonia and her exquisite vengeance to make her an effective leader. It was too hard to believe she was anything more than someone who'd done terrible things in pursuit of something better. She needed room to find her way back to the person she wanted to be, not the person she'd needed to become. And she couldn't do that under the eyes of people who only knew the story of Caledonia Styx. The Gem had been a part of her story from the beginning, so it had felt like a natural choice. Already her chest felt lighter.

"I need some time to—" Caledonia paused. Pine had called them demons and that had felt familiar to her. All the terrible decisions she'd made were still with her. They snarled in her dreams, made messy nests in her heart, and slipped into her thoughts when she least expected it. They were always there, and she was beginning to think maybe they always would be. She shook her head. "I need time to heal. And I need to give everyone else time, too. They can't heal if I'm always there to keep the fight alive. I'm surrounded by ghosts and I'm beginning to think maybe I am one, too."

"I understand what you're saying, Cala, and I want you to take your time." As always, Pisces was gentle and firm, guiding Caledonia toward smoother emotional waters. "There are ghosts everywhere these days."

"I just want them to go away." It was petulant and Caledonia knew it, but it was how she felt. Pisces laughed and Caledonia sighed hard. "Only you would find that funny."

"You don't banish ghosts, you turn them into warships, or whatever you need them to be." Pisces fixed Caledonia with a pointed look, conjuring the ship Caledonia's mother had named and they had rebuilt. "After that you have to *let* them go."

"I don't know how to do that," Caledonia admitted.

The thought of letting go sat uncomfortably. She'd spent so much of her life holding on, clinging to everything she had and fighting to keep it. Even her anger. She clung to her anger because it kept her alive. She clung to her hurt because it kept her resistant. She clung to her ghosts, she realized, because they were her family.

Pisces stepped in front of Caledonia, stopping them both in their tracks. Her eyes narrowed slightly, and she cocked her head to the side as if Caledonia were a question in need of answering. Then she reached forward, and her fingers closed around the hilt of the black blade tucked snugly into Caledonia's waistband. She tugged and the blade pulled free.

"I think I know where to start," Pisces said.

Caledonia's eyes fell immediately to the push dagger. It sat in Pisces's palm, no longer than the length of her hand, its worn wooden handle narrow enough to fit between two fingers, allowing the dagger to protrude like a third, deadly one. She didn't need it anymore, but it had become a part of her. Against her will at first and then because she'd grown used to the sensation of it at her hip, like a bullet lodged into the trunk of a tree.

Together, they unlaced their boots and waded into the surf. Waves pushed and pulled at their legs as they moved out beyond the break. The water was warm and welcoming, the sand soft beneath their toes, and before them the islands of the Bone Mouth tumbled across the horizon like scattered stones.

Pisces held the dagger out for Caledonia to take. She closed cold fingers over the blade and held it to her chest. For so long, the dagger had been a strange kind of comfort. It had connected her to her past and her future. Now it was only a relic. It had nothing more to give her, so why was letting go of it so hard?

She looked to Pisces, unable to speak. It was as if the ocean were filling her up, swelling inside her and roaring in the back of her throat. She was crying. And her fingers trembled.

Pisces nodded. "It's time, Cala."

With a scream that had been building in her chest for turns,

Caledonia threw the dagger into the sky. It soared long and far before it fell against the sea and vanished beneath the waves.

It felt good. And terrible. And absolutely right.

"What comes next, Pi?" Caledonia asked.

And with a smile, her friend answered, "Whatever it is, we get to choose."

ACKNOWLEDGMENTS

At the beginning of this trilogy, I was writing a vicious and joyful response to *Mad Max: Fury Road*. That movie was an answer to a question I'd been nurturing for a very long time. As a young reader, I adored fantastical stories with epic quests and the highest of stakes, but I struggled to feel like I had a place in those stories. *Mad Max: Fury Road* changed that. It was an invitation not only to join the adventure, but to demand a role in it. While this story may have started as a love letter to that movie, it became one to the reader I was as a young adult, and I am grateful to all the people who helped me write it.

My wife, Tessa Gratton, deserves first and last thanks for always asking the one question that unlocks crucial pieces of the story. Even if I don't like the question at the time.

Throughout this entire trilogy, my father has answered every nautical question I threw at him, frequently with so much more detail than I could possibly include here. I'm still sorry I couldn't work in that detail about the captain's chair being ziplined from one ship to another!

To Lydia Ash, Dot Hutchison, Adib Khorram, Amanda Sellet, and La Prima Tazza, I am thankful for weekly meetups and lunches. (Fingers crossed we get to do that ever again.) And I will never have enough thanks for the friends who listened to me attempt to excavate parts of this story with semi-wild ravings: Becca Coffindaffer, Zoraida Córdova, Julie Murphy, and Sierra Simone.

My editor, Chris Hernandez, who helped raise the stakes and close this trilogy in the best way possible. To all the unsung heroes at Razorbill and PYR who work behind the scenes to design, copyedit, proof, produce, and sell my work, thank you.

This trilogy wouldn't exist at all without team Alloy. Lanie Davis, who has helped me identify who I am as an author, and Josh Bank, who is a lot nicer than he wants you to think, I couldn't do this without you both.

My agent, Lara Perkins, for being a mentor, friend, and steady hand in rough seas.

To all of the booksellers, librarians, and teachers who have championed this series, especially the team at the Raven Book Store.

And to my readers, for sailing with Caledonia and her crew from the very beginning. Thank you.